'We're big fans of Diane Chamberlain here at *Bella* and her latest novel doesn't disappoint'   *Bella*

'Powerful and thrilling ... This tautly paced and emotionally driven novel will engross Chamberlain's many fans'   *Booklist*

'A page-turner to the very end. A must for all mystery lovers and those who like reading about family struggles'
                    Library Journal

'Chamberlain has written an excellent novel with well-thought-out plotlines that never lose the suspense lover's interest for one solitary second'   *Suspense Magazine*

'Diane Chamberlain is a marvellously gifted author! Every book she writes is a real gem'   *Literary Times*

'An excellent read that will be loved by her fans and anyone who enjoys reading'   Jodi Picoult

'A⸱   redibly moving story, very sensitively told, that is ric   ⸱ character and atmosphere. I truly couldn't put it do⸱ ⸱   Susan Lewis

'I   e Diane's writing . . . so powerful and beautifully   ⸱n'   Cathy Kelly

⸱pletely LOVED this book'   Jane Green

e Chamberlain's characters are so realistic that you ou know them in person, and when you get to the f the book, you miss them'   Tatiana de Rosnay

nberlain takes the reader on a taut journey filled secrets, heartbreak and the power of hope. Im-le to put down, *The Midwife's Confession* will break eart and then mend it tenderly back together'
                    Heather Gudenkauf

ıberlain puts so much grit, emotion and drama er books that it's impossible to stop thinking about ⸱t'   *Heat*

'An excellent read'   *Sun*

Fire and Rain

DIANE CHAMBERLAIN is a bestselling author
of numerous novels. Her storylines are often a
combination of romance, family drama, intrigue
and suspense. She lives in North Carolina with
her partner, photographer John Pagliuca, and
her shelties, Keeper and Cole.

Visit dianechamberlain.com

By Diane Chamberlain

Fire and Rain

Diane Chamberlain

PAN BOOKS

First published 1993 by HarperCollins

First published in paperback 2016 by Pan Books
an imprint of Pan Macmillan
20 New Wharf Road, London N1 9RR
Associated companies throughout the world
www.panmacmillan.com

ISBN 978-1-4472-5660-1

1 3 5 7 9 8 6 4 2

A CIP catalogue record for this book is available from the British Library.

Typeset by Ellipsis Digital Limited, Glasgow
Printed and bound by CPI Group (UK) Ltd, Croydon, CR0 4YY

Visit **www.panmacmillan.com** to read more about all our books
and to buy them. You will also find features, author interviews and
news of any author events, and you can sign up for e-newsletters
so that you're always first to hear about our new releases.

"To the unsung heroines in my life—
my women friends—who are,
quite simply, always there."

1.

The house glowed in the darkness. Thick smoke billowed from broken windows and jagged holes in the roof, forming black smudges against the eerie, orange-tinged sky. Carmen stepped out of the News Nine van, wincing from the sting of soot in the air and the blare of sirens. A weariness settled over her, an exhaustion more emotional than physical that she couldn't allow to show in her face. In the past few days she had watched twelve houses burn. It had been exciting at first. Something for her to report. Something for her to do. But now she'd had enough.

Over breakfast that morning, she'd noticed that the scent of smoke still clung to her hair despite her shower. Her ears still rang from the nighttime howling of coyotes driven from the canyon by the fires, and outside her kitchen window, the sun beat hot and yellow on the sparse vegetation in her yard. The sun had become an enemy, a relentless killer of everything that had once been beautiful in Valle Rosa.

This house, like the others burned in the past few days, was set on the rim of Cinnamon Canyon, a beautiful pristine chasm that carved a wide, deep path through the sprawling reaches of Valle Rosa. The canyon was thick with crackling dry chaparral, so thick that in the shadows of dusk and dawn it looked as though someone had dropped a soft, nubby quilt over the earth. But Cinnamon Canyon was no longer beautiful, no longer unspoiled. These days the residents of Valle Rosa awakened with damp palms and racing hearts. They looked out their windows to see how the fires had changed the canyons overnight, to see how much of the earth had been blackened, how close the plume of smoke was to them now.

Carmen held Craig Morrow's dampened handkerchief over her nose as she stood in front of the burning house. The camera crew was setting up, and Craig scrambled around, talking to fire fighters, ambulance drivers, gathering information for her. The ranch-style house, barely larger than a trailer, didn't look well cared for, but that was hard to determine after what it had suffered tonight. It perched on a small plateau jutting up above the canyon. The side yard was barely large enough to hold a swing set and a sliding board, which looked like a strip of molten steel as it reflected the glow from the fire. A tricycle lay on its side near the swings, and toys were scattered across the narrow thread of dirt that served as a front yard. A few bulging black garbage bags lay in the middle of the short driveway. Behind the house, Cinnamon Canyon was an enormous bowl of fire. Carmen took a few steps toward the canyon, mesmerized, shuddering. If hell existed, it could be no worse than this.

A small plane buzzed above the conflagration, spewing its cargo of chemicals, and behind her, the fire fighters sprayed their precious water on the few other houses that rimmed this part of the canyon, struggling to hold off the flames. How small they seemed—the fire fighters, the planes. How insignificant.

Craig was suddenly beside her, rattling off the address of the house, the time the fire started, the gloomy prognosis for the surrounding homes. His thinning dark hair stood away from his scalp in crazy tufts and he was wild-eyed. *He loves this,* she thought as she jotted down the information on her pad.

"The dead kids were two, four, and five," Craig said.

"Dead kids?" she asked, startled. Houses had been lost, true, but so far no one had died.

"Yeah." Craig motioned toward the bags in the driveway, and Carmen realized with a jolt they were not garbage bags at all, but small body bags. Her knees turned to rubber, and she pressed the handkerchief to her face again.

"Hey!" Craig called out to the *News Nine* crew. "What's the names on the three kids?"

Someone yelled back at him, "Joseph, Edward, and Hazel," and Craig shook his head, actually chuckling to himself.

"Hazel," he said. "Can you imagine naming a kid Hazel?" His voice seemed to come from very far away.

Carmen wrote down the names, the pad and her hands glowing like hot coals. She was trapped, by the fire, by Craig, by the smoky golden air. By what was expected of her in the next few minutes. Her mouth was dry, the air a hot poker in her throat. She glanced toward the camera crew. They were nearly ready for her.

"We'll put you right about here, in front of the house," Craig pointed with his pencil to a spot a few feet from where she stood. "We'll cut to the dead kids there." He whisked his pencil toward the driveway, where the orange light from the canyon licked at the smooth black vinyl of the bags, making Carmen think of Halloween, of children in costume, of candy corn. "Then you can have a word with the mother."

Carmen followed Craig's pencil as he pointed toward the ambulance. The broad rear doors were open and someone was wrapping gauze around the hand of a dazed-looking woman. A little girl—a delicate, dark-eyed cherub—clung to the woman's leg, pressing her free hand against her ear as another fire truck, siren blasting, pulled into the cul-de-sac.

"You going to be able to talk over all this?" Craig asked.

"No problem." She was perspiring. Her face, no doubt, glistened. She hoped Craig would think it was from the heat of the fire pit behind her, nothing more. She lifted her heavy dark hair and coiled it loosely at the back of her neck, securing it with a clip from the pocket of her skirt.

"Mother's name is Janice Reisko." Craig held out his own pad for her to copy. "You okay?" he asked as she wrote. "I mean, do you think you can handle this?"

"Why wouldn't I be able to?" Had they told him to keep an eye on her? She didn't look up at him. She wouldn't let her eyes betray her. Surely he knew that in her two shaky months back at *News Nine*, nothing of this magnitude had happened.

She looked again at the mother, whose sooty pale face was streaked with tears, at the little girl who now had her thumb rooted firmly in her mouth, and she turned her eyes away, toward the sickly glowing sky above the canyon. Five years ago she would have hungered to know the story of this woman and her children, hungered to take the facts and embellish them, to feed them, inflated and sizzling, to her audience. She couldn't let on to Craig that she had any doubts about her ability to get through this. One weak moment. That was all they'd need to get rid of her.

"Ready?" Craig held the microphone out to her.

She took the mike from his hand and stepped in front of the camera, remembering too late that her hair was still up. *Damn*. Between that and the ever-widening streak of silver on her crown, she would look like an old woman. Washed up.

The red light appeared on the camera. "This is Carmen Perez," she said. "I'm in Valle Rosa, at the edge of Cinnamon Canyon, where the drought-spawned fires that have burned out of control all week tonight claimed their first young victims." She glanced down at her notepad. "Fire fighters were able to rescue three-year-old Jennifer Reisko and her mother, Janice, from the flames that quickly engulfed their home, but they were unable to reach five-year-old Edward, four-year-old Joseph and two-year-old Hazel."

The camera panned to the three small body bags in the

driveway, then slipped to the open rear of the ambulance as Carmen approached Janice Reisko, too quickly, as though she could make this less painful by rushing through it. "Mrs. Reisko, can you tell us what happened here tonight?"

The off-camera flames from the canyon cast a yellow sheen on Janice Reisko's damp skin. Her thin brown hair was unattractively cut to fall just below her ears, and her bangs were short and stubby.

"My babies," she rasped into Carmen's microphone. She turned her head slowly from side to side, her eyes dark and blank. "My *babies.*"

Carmen saw Craig out of camera range, signaling her wildly with his hands to ask the woman another question, but she pretended not to see him. She managed to make some insignificant closing statement into the microphone before lowering it to her side and stepping away from Janice Reisko and her one surviving child.

Once off camera, she slipped quietly into the empty van, taking a seat near the front to wait for the others. Craig was first to climb in after her.

"Why didn't you ask the kid anything?" he asked as he sat down. "You know, 'Were you scared?' Shit like that."

"Didn't occur to me," she said. The rest of the crew, three men and two women, squeezed into the van and quickly drew Craig into their conversation. They had little to say to her. Except for Craig, they were all younger than she, by a decade or more. They opened cans of soda and began passing a bag of popcorn between them, its buttery scent suffocating in the close air of the van. Carmen leaned her head against the back of the seat, trying to shut out their voices and the nearly rancid smell of the popcorn. She knew she was going to be sick.

"Hazel," Craig said. "Can you picture it? Ten-to-one they're on welfare, churning those kids out one after the other. Ran out of decent names."

Carmen leaned forward and clutched the driver's shoulder. "Stop for a second, Pete," she said. "I thought I saw something on the road back there."

Pete jerked the van over to the side of the road, and Carmen slid the door open.

"Where the hell are you going?" Craig asked her.

She didn't answer. Her stomach churned. She stepped out of the van and walked as far behind it as she could before kneeling down by the shoulder to get sick. How clearly could they see her? Could they hear her? It was so quiet here above this dark, cool sweep of Cinnamon Canyon, this section as yet untouched by the fires.

"Hey, Carmen," Craig called. "What is it?"

"Just my imagination," she called back, fumbling in her purse for a mint. When she got to her feet, the muscles in her legs seemed barely able to hold her upright. She slipped off her heels for the walk back to the van.

"Call came while you were out there," Craig said when she had taken her seat again. "Fire's hit the north ridge of the canyon and is nipping at the rafters of guess whose house?"

"Whose?" she asked, not following.

"Your favorite ex-pitcher. You know, the one who has

now brought his staggering credentials to Valle Rosa's political quagmire." There was some chuckling from the back of the van.

"Chris?" she asked stupidly. "Chris's house is on fire? Is he okay?"

"Apparently Mr. Mayor is not at home."

She leaned forward to pick up the cellular phone. "He's probably still at his office," she said. She had to call information for the number, and although it was after nine, she wasn't surprised when he answered.

"The Cinnamon Canyon fire's reached your house," she said. "We're headed over there now."

There was a short silence on Chris's end of the phone. The two female members of the crew broke into a poorly harmonized rendition of the Doors' "Light My Fire," and Carmen covered her ear with her hand to block them out.

"You'll be there?" Chris asked. "You mean, with *News Nine*?"

"Yes."

Another beat of silence. "Okay," he said, "I'm on my way."

Ordinarily the drive from his office in the so-called heart of Valle Rosa to his home on the rim of Cinnamon Canyon took Chris fifteen minutes, but tonight he would make it in ten. He knew the hairpin curves and the way the road pitched and curled and clung to the side of the cliff. He'd learned to drive on this road, twenty-five years earlier, his father a patient teacher. Chris could drive it without taking his eyes off the orange glow in the distance.

He had heard about the children. Don Eldrich had called him an hour earlier. Don worked for the fire department and sat on Valle Rosa's board of supervisors. He'd been responsible for getting the rest of the board to shift Chris into the mayoral spot after George Heath's death had left the position vacant. Chris had taken the job with great reluctance, acknowledging that, as a high-school teacher with the summer off, he could take a leave from his work more easily than anyone else on the board. But Heath had left a mess behind him, and the mess was growing rapidly. It was out of control, and Chris had no idea what to do about it, which was becoming increasingly apparent to the people of Valle Rosa as their avocado and orange crops withered in the ceaseless drought. He had no idea how to take control of the thirsty monster that had sucked most of the life from Valle Rosa and now seemed poised to burn what little was left.

But it wasn't Valle Rosa that absorbed him as he drove home. He thought only of Dustin. Dusty wasn't there—he had never been to the house—but there were pictures. Photograph albums. Chris hadn't realized how desperately he needed them until that moment. Even his guitar and his trophies seemed immaterial by comparison. He didn't want to lose the only pictures he had of his son.

Camino Linda was so clotted with police cars and fire trucks and ambulances that he had to leave his car and run the last quarter-mile to his house.

At first he thought the fire had spared him, but he was only seeing the hulk of the *News Nine* van in front of the house. Behind it, flames shot out of the roof—the new roof he had put on himself in the spring. He stood in the street, trying to size up the situation, trying to keep his mind lucid. Right now the fire seemed contained in the southern half of the rambling house. The small family room, where his photograph albums, guitar and trophies were kept, was as yet unscathed. Could he slip in the French doors on the veranda?

Carmen suddenly appeared at his side. It had been a while since he'd seen her, although he had watched her news reports these past two months since she'd been back on *News Nine*'s evening broadcast. They'd given her a few brief minutes of North County news, three times a week, something he was sure felt like a slap in the face to her given what she'd meant to them in the past.

"I'm so sorry, Chris," she said, keeping her eyes on his house.

"Do you think I could get into the family room?" he asked, as though she might somehow have the answer. "Take a few things out?"

She frowned at him. "Of course not. Look at it." She nodded toward the smoking, crackling house. "Your trophies aren't worth risking your life for."

"It's not the trophies," he said, quietly. "It's the pictures of Dustin."

She turned away abruptly, and when one of her crew called to her, she left Chris's side without another word.

Chris watched as she took the microphone from some guy's hand and stepped in front of the camera. The throbbing whir of a helicopter above the canyon and the shouts of the fire fighters prevented him from hearing what she said, although he could imagine: "Fire tonight reached the home of Valle Rosa's acting mayor, Christopher Garrett."

After a moment, the red light on the camera went off and Chris heard the sharp tones of an argument between Carmen and a male member of the crew. She was shaking her head. "*No*," she said. "Please." They glanced toward Chris, and he suddenly understood what was happening. They wanted her to interview him, to shove that microphone in front of his face and tape his grief for all of southern California to witness. Carmen didn't want to do it. That much was obvious, and he was grateful. Yet he knew she couldn't win the debate. They would insist, and she would comply. She had to earn back the trust she'd lost these past few years. She had to earn back her reputation as the hard-nosed, tough, and confrontational reporter she had been before her four-year leave of absence. She had to show them she was still strong, still had what it took to do her job.

And so he would spare her, spare both of them. He turned away from his smoldering house and lost himself in the crowd that had gathered. He found a safe spot some distance away, and from there he watched Carmen search the crowd for him. He could almost see the relief in her eyes at not being able to find him. She shrugged and said something to the man at her side. Then she turned back to the house just as the roof caved in above the family room. Chris wondered if she thought about what he'd said, about Dustin's pictures being in there. Did she care? Did it make any difference to her at all?

Carmen looked back at the crowd. Her eyes moved in his direction, and he knew she could see him now. Maybe she'd been able to see him all along. He allowed himself to stare back at her, allowed their gazes to lock. If anyone should understand how he felt to lose Dustin's pictures, it would be Carmen. After all, she was Dustin's mother.

2.

Damage.

Mia typed the word, black and sharp, at the top of the page. Chris had asked her if she minded typing this list, this recitation of what had been done to his home, what he had lost, and she, of course, had agreed. But no matter what she typed below it, the word at the top of the page taunted her.

She was a halting, two-fingered typist, although she had improved greatly during her month and a half as Chris's office manager. He didn't complain, but then, he could hardly fault her; she'd been completely honest with him about her lack of secretarial skills. She'd told him she was twenty-eight years old and an artist, and that the only other skills she possessed were those she'd picked up over the years of caring for her invalid mother.

He'd hired her as easily as if she'd said she'd graduated at the top of her class in secretarial school. Mia learned quickly that he did most things that way—easily, unhurried. Not much seemed to shake him, as though he expected little out of life, as though when she'd shown up to apply for the job, he'd fully expected her to be unqualified.

She had been the one to find the file. While cleaning out the previous mayor's rickety oak file cabinet, her fingers caught on a folder tucked beneath the rest. It was unmarked, and something about it—the way it had been hidden, perhaps, or the way it was held closed by three paper clips along its open end—made her take it to Chris without looking at it herself.

Chris sat on the corner of his desk, plucking the clips from the file and laying it open on his knee, and she remembered seeing the color drain from his face as he read its contents.

"Jesus." He looked up at her, a flash of uncharacteristic anger in his pale-blue eyes. "Heath sold our water," he said. "He sold our water to a development on the other side of Cinnamon Canyon. Do you believe it? We're in the middle of a drought! Everybody's got plastic dams in their toilet tanks to save a couple of gallons a day, and he sells our water to a bunch of money-hungry vultures. No wonder the reservoir's nearly dry."

Mia knew Chris had grown up here, during a time when Valle Rosa was even smaller and sleepier, and that he took every infraction against the town as a personal affront. He had wondered aloud to her how George Heath had afforded his Mercedes, his sailboat. Or the private plane he'd chartered to fly him to Sacramento, where he was supposed to have met with other government officials to discuss the drought. Ironic that he'd used the profits from his water deal on the plane that had taken him to his death.

Mia was typing the last item on Chris's inventory of

his damaged possessions when the outside door opened. A man stepped into the office, a stranger, accompanied by a gust of hot, dry, Santa Ana wind that rustled the papers on her desk. One paper rose from the blotter, floating in the air for a second before slipping to the floor, and the stranger bent to pick it up.

"Sorry." He placed the paper on her desk. He didn't quite smile. He wore a brown-and-red Hawaiian print shirt, tan chinos. Tennis shoes without socks. He looked freshly showered, scrubbed clean. She could smell soap.

His eyes ran over the cheap walnut-colored paneling, the worn brown carpet. "Is this Chris Garrett's office?" He looked down at her—*through* her—and she was struck by the symmetry in his face, by the angles of his jaw, his nose, his cheekbones. His eyes were a dark, opaque blue, but there was a light in them— something burning there.

"Yes," she said.

"Is it possible for me to see him?" The near-smile again. He had to work at producing it. He was holding a map in his hand, and he waved it in the direction of Chris's office. "My name is Jeff Cabrio. He doesn't know me."

She was staring, imagining how the angles of his face would transfer to her clay, and she dropped her gaze to the intercom on her desk. Punching the button, she called Chris. He sounded surprised to hear there was someone to see him. Since she'd been working for him, only a few people had come to the office—including a few of the kids Chris had coached in baseball who tried to convince him to "chuck this lame job and come back to Valle Rosa High

School." Chris had said there was nothing he would like better, but that right now his first responsibility was to all of Valle Rosa, not only the high school's fledgling baseball team.

Mia hung up the phone and told Jeff Cabrio to have a seat, that Chris would be out shortly. He sat down, spreading the map open on his knees. As he traced routes with the tip of his finger, Mia slipped a piece of typing paper onto her desk top and began sketching him. Surreptitiously. Looking up, down. Growing more brazen as she realized he was absorbed in his map and unaware of her.

He was what Glen would have called an artist's lure— someone an artist couldn't resist, someone born to be painted, photographed, sculpted. Mia had been Glen's student long before she was his lover, and he had taught her how to pick a lure from a crowd. "Not a classic beauty, necessarily," he had said in his clipped London accent, "but someone whose features will transfer to the clay with an element of drama."

Mia wished Glen could see Jeff Cabrio. Glen would have to exercise enormous self-control not to approach him, not to ask him if the planes of his face and arms and hands were reflected in the rest of his body. He would be too well-mannered to do that, of course, but not too polite to stare. Blatantly. More than once Glen had been propositioned by other men who had caught him staring unabashedly at their biceps, thighs, or buttocks.

Glen had told Mia she had the body of a lure, but not the face. "Your cheeks are too full," he had said. "Your lips are too pouty." At the time, she had been so convinced of his love for her that she hadn't thought to take his words as an insult. "But your body, Sunny. Your body is a lure, pure and simple."

She'd been twenty-four then, a born and bred southern California girl who didn't fit the mold. She wasn't tan. Her dishwater blond hair bore no sun streaks. She was slender, so slender in fact that every muscle, every tendon, was visible beneath her skin. The muscles hadn't come from surfing or skating or a health club. They'd been earned over the years from lifting her mother, turning her, helping her into the bathtub.

It was the way her calf muscle shifted just below the skin that had intrigued Glen, the way her long, delicate fingers slipped over the clay that had made her a lure in his eyes. He had asked her into his office early that school year, where he told her that she was extraordinarily talented—"It's frightening, really," he'd said—and that when he watched her, when he saw the smile grow on her face as she lost herself in her work, he felt something "very deep" inside himself.

But Glen was ten years her senior and ever the gentleman. He would never have wanted to suggest impropriety. "You're my student," he had said, disappointing her, "and as long as you are, I won't act on my feelings."

After her graduation ceremony, he approached her, took her hands, leaned down to whisper in her ear. "I want to take you someplace wonderful for dinner," he said. "I want to sculpt you. And I want to make love to you."

"In that order?" she asked.

"In that order."

She was only mildly taken aback by his desire to sculpt her, although she knew that he meant to sculpt her in the nude. She was accustomed to working with nude models in the classroom.

She had never, however, thought of being on the other side of the clay.

She undressed for him beneath the wash of sun pouring through the skylights of his studio. Although she had never before undressed in front of a man, she so completely trusted his integrity that her fingers hadn't trembled, and she didn't once lose her smile. Sunny, he'd called her, because her smile was constant, her cheeriness unflappable, despite all she was dealing with at home. He'd walked around her while she unbuttoned her blouse, while she unwrapped her long skirt from her hips and let it fall into the pool of light on the floor. She'd removed her underwear, her watch, the silver chain that had belonged to her grandmother, and her body glowed lean and hard as the sunlight shifted and swam in the air around her. She'd felt very brave.

"You're exactly as I imagined," Glen had said, circling her, the sun glittering on his own pale gold hair. "Exactly as I'd hoped. You know what I mean, don't you?"

She nodded. He had trained her well.

"So sensuous, in an innocent sort of way. Ingenuous. You're quite perfect, Mia."

He paid her, and although she was uncomfortable with that part of the arrangement, she took the money. She needed it too desperately to refuse. For nearly two weeks, she sat amidst a pile of pillows on the dumpy sofa in his studio, wearing the wide-brimmed felt hat he'd perched on her head and the long narrow scarf he'd draped around her neck. She sat at an angle among the pillows, one knee drawn up, one end of the scarf held in her hand, the other falling between her breasts.

The resulting pose was cocky, coquettish. She shuddered now to think of how easily she had taken her body for granted. She'd had a couple of cocky years. There would never be another period in her life like it.

Not the first day of her posing, or the second, but perhaps by the third, she'd felt a change in herself as she sat there on the sofa. A warmth in her groin, a feeling so alien and inappropriate to the moment that she was annoyed with herself. *You're an artist; he's an artist.* When he touched her, when he shifted the pillows—slipping one beneath her knee, pressing her shoulder against another—she cursed herself for the traitorous tightening of her nipples.

By the end of the first week, she was deliberately mispositioning herself so that he would have to approach her, have to touch her with his warm and practiced hands.

Despite her slender build, leaning on her side made her belly droop just a little. She would self-consciously pull it in, and he'd scold her, laughing.

"No, no, Sunny. It's perfect. Your body looks so strong, that little bit of softness there gives you just the tenderness you need. Can't you see it? I'm trying to express those different parts of you—the strength, the sensuality, the joy, the gentleness."

And he'd touch her there—"Hold it in. Look at it. See? Quite unnatural. Now let it out. There that's right. Oh, that's splendid." He'd stroke his fingers over her belly as though it were the clay he was touching, and she would feel the quick involuntary warming between her legs.

In the end, he made the nipples of her small, firm breasts slightly raised, just enough to "suggest alertness." The sculpture was fifteen inches high, made in terra cotta, later to be cast in bronze. Eventually, it won Glen three awards.

She had always been a dreamer, always lived her life partly in fantasy. So it was no surprise to her that, during the two weeks of her posing, she had thought constantly of Glen, of his touch, of what might happen between them.

She began to wonder though, if after coming to know her body so intimately from his professional stance, he no longer felt the urge to possess her in any other way. He hadn't touched her other than to shape her for the clay. He had never kissed her. He had given her no indication at all that he was drawn to her, as he had claimed weeks earlier. She felt of no more personal importance to him than the paid models in class.

When she was dressing in his studio for the last time, he said, "I think you've understood, Sunny, that I wanted what goes on here, at the studio, and what goes on in here"—he rested his hand on his chest, over his heart— "to be completely separate. But now that the sculpture is finished, I can finally ask you to come home with me tonight."

She let out her breath in grateful relief. "I want to, Glen," she said, "but I can't tonight. My mother."

He scowled. "You're bloody chained to her."

"Come home with me," she suggested. "She wants to meet you, and I'll make you dinner. Then you can spend the night." She hesitated, guiltily. "She won't have to know."

He helped her cook in the small, cozy kitchen of the house in which she'd grown up, and she found herself talking non-stop. She'd had so few people to talk with over the past few years. She had to slow herself down, not wanting to overwhelm him.

She told him about her father's death in Vietnam when she was five, about the few foggy memories she had of him. She told him about Laura, how beautiful she was, how she had already started college when their mother was first struck by cancer, how it had made more sense for Mia to take care of her than for Laura to come home. ("So where is she now?" Glen had asked, with the first hint of anger she had ever seen in him. "Where's the beautiful sister while you're stuck at home year after year?") She brushed aside his questions, having long ago adjusted to life's inequities.

They had dinner with her mother, who managed to sit at the table with them for a good hour before returning to the sofa with a fresh fit of coughing that obviously alarmed Glen. But he was drawn to her mother, the way most men were, despite the fact that Liz Tanner had grown reed thin and frail, that her once beautiful blond hair had been replaced by a blue paisley turban. Still, her smile was animated. She regaled them with several stories from her years as an elementary school teacher, and Mia was delighted to see Glen laugh.

He did the dishes while Mia got her mother into bed. Liz Tanner squeezed her hand. "He's wonderful," she said. "And you're a grown woman. Don't make him go home if you don't want him to." So Mia, astounded by her mother's invitation, took Glen openly and guiltlessly into her bedroom, but not before she had told him she was a virgin. It seemed to be something he should know, something she doubted he would guess of a twenty-four-year-old woman. But he wasn't surprised.

"I quite expected that, Sunny," he said. "When have you had the freedom to be anything but?"

He undressed her as though he wasn't already intimate with her body, as though every inch of her skin was a new discovery. She was so hungry for him, so eager, that he asked her, "Are you certain you're a virgin? You have absolutely no inhibitions whatsoever." Glen's lovemaking was so exquisite that she thought, *this is it, this is forever, this is all I'll ever need.* Only somehow, it hadn't been enough for Glen. Not enough to let him overlook the damage.

Damage. Mia cast a glance at the word on the piece of paper in her typewriter, then at the drawing she had made of Jeff Cabrio. She had sketched as much of him as she could manage without asking him to turn his head, lift his chin. She had done a good job, but it wouldn't be good enough. Maybe she would get another chance.

"Do you live around here?" she asked.

He looked up from his map, blankly at first, then shook his head just as Chris appeared at the door to the reception area.

Chris looked a little beaten this morning. Mia knew he'd spent the night on the couch in his office. He had on the same blue shirt and faded jeans he'd worn the day before, and as usual, his Birkenstock sandals.

He held out his hand. "Mr. Cabrio, is it?"

The stranger stood up, his smile finally breaking free. "*The* Christopher Garrett," he said, and it took Mia a second to realize he was referring to Chris's defunct baseball career. "It's an honor to shake your hand. May I have a word with you?"

Mia watched the two men walk back to Chris's office, realizing only then that the air had been charged with Jeff Cabrio in it and now seemed flat and still. She looked down at her drawing and immediately saw it—the damage. It was there in his downcast eyes, in the taut line of his jaw. She wondered what he had seen, what he had done, to put that pain and fear in his face.

Jeff Cabrio was unquestionably good-looking, the kind of man who always made Chris feel disheveled, short, and paunchy, although he was none of those things. He cleared a pile of folders from his office couch and offered a seat to his visitor, asking, "What can I do for you?"

"I saw the news last night," Jeff answered as he sat

down. "I was sorry to hear about your house. I didn't know about all this"—his gaze swept the cluttered office—"about you being in politics. Though I knew a lot about you back when you were pitching. You were incredible."

"Thanks. You're a Padres fan?"

"Well, no. Not really. I've always had a soft spot for the Phillies. But it doesn't matter when it comes to admiring a pitcher. Must have been hard to walk away from it."

"Well, I didn't exactly walk away. I was pushed, if you'll remember." Chris smiled, though a splinter of pain lodged in his chest. "As for the politics, I'm here by accident, really. Just trying to hold down the fort until the election in November when we can get someone in here who knows what they're doing." He grimaced, annoyed with himself for his self-deprecation. "Valle Rosa has some frightening problems."

"The drought seems worse here," Jeff agreed.

Chris was tempted to go into the reasons why that was true, but held his tongue.

Jeff continued, a hint of an apology in his voice. "That's why I'm here," he said, "and I know this is going to sound bizarre, but please hear me out."

Chris waited.

"I'm just passing through the area. I'm in a hotel in San Diego right now, where the water pressure's so low you can barely get the shampoo out of your hair. I knew you folks were in the middle of a drought, but I never guessed how bad it was. Anyhow, last night I was packing so I could get an early start out of town this morning when I saw the news coverage of that canyon fire, and your house, and those kids who died." He shuddered. "I wish I hadn't seen it, but I did, and I can't ignore it. I couldn't sleep afterward. I kept seeing those body bags. And the face of that terrified little girl hanging onto her mother's leg, while that bitch of a reporter stuck the microphone in the woman's face."

Chris held up his hand, smiling. "That 'bitch' is my ex-wife."

Jeff sat back in his chair, a look of surprise on his face. "Oh," he said. "Sorry."

Chris thought briefly of defending Carmen, but it would take so many words, so much explaining, and the man was a stranger. "No problem," he said.

"Anyway, I'm certain I can help you. Help Valle Rosa. Like I said, I'm only passing through, but I can't walk away from a situation when I know I can make a difference."

Chris looked at him skeptically. "What can you possibly do?"

An instant of silence passed before Jeff answered. "I can make rain fall over Valle Rosa."

Chris felt the flame of hope the stranger had ignited in him disintegrate. "Right," he said. "And someday I'll pitch another no-hitter."

"My background's in environmental engineering, and I consult for a number of companies," Jeff said. "They tell me their problems, and I come up with solutions. I've been working on a way to modify weather patterns, and I think I've finally perfected it. But I haven't had a chance yet to try it out in the field. My work was interrupted." He looked down at his hands for a full thirty seconds, long enough to raise the hair on the back of Chris's neck, then lifted his gaze once more. "The children," he said, referring again to the victims of the fire, or maybe to those children the fire would take today or tomorrow, and something rolled over in the pit of Chris's stomach. "You'd be doing me a favor," Jeff continued, "letting me help. All I ask for is a place to stay and grocery money, and the cost of the equipment I'll need."

Chris cleared his throat. "Are you talking about cloud seeding?"

The stranger shook his head. He began describing the technology he would use—something about altering sound waves to change the atmospheric pressure—and Chris was quickly lost, although he continued to listen with a skeptical smile. The man was a charlatan, no doubt, and yet something about him was convincing. The intensity of his eyes, the sincerity in his voice. He didn't seem crazy. He didn't seem delusional.

"How about some references?" Chris asked.

Jeff shook his head. "Can't help you with that. There are certainly plenty of folks who could tell you how good my work is, but I'm afraid I'm in a position where I can't contact them right now."

"Are you in some kind of trouble?"

He didn't answer. Instead, he stood up and leaned over Chris's desk, writing his name and the name of his hotel on a notepad. "I can help you," he said, straightening up again. "I don't blame you for your doubts. I don't want to be here. I don't want to stay in this area any longer than I have to. But when I see something like that fire . . ." He shook his head. "So, I've made my offer. I'll be around another day or so. That's it."

Chris stood up as well and walked him to the door of his office. "Thanks for stopping in," he said. "I'll give it some thought."

He watched Jeff walk down the hall toward the front door. Clearly, this was a man in trouble. With the law perhaps. Definitely with his own demons.

Jeff nodded at Mia as he walked past her desk, and Chris was surprised by the flush in Mia's cheeks, by the way she followed the stranger with her eyes. He had come to think of Mia as quiet, bookish, sexless. Instantly, though, he knew he'd been wrong. Her response to Jeff Cabrio seemed nothing less than visceral.

"Oh," she said, noticing Chris in the doorway. "Carmen Perez called while you were meeting with Mr. Cabrio."

"Thanks," he said, surprised.

He returned Carmen's call from his office phone.

"I was thinking, Chris," she said. "Two of the cottages are vacant. You're welcome to stay in one of them while your house is unlivable."

He thought of Sugarbush, Carmen's sprawling eight acres that had once belonged to both of them. Eight acres surrounded on three sides by Cinnamon Canyon. He had loved that property from afar as a child and had proudly bought it with cash as an adult. He pictured the shaded patio where he and Carmen had relaxed in the evenings. He thought of the hot tub on the raised deck where they'd soak late at night, naked in the darkness, just the two of them and the stars and the distant howling of the coyotes.

Carmen now lived alone in the huge, 130-year-old adobe at the heart of the property. She had turned the three small outbuildings which rested along the edge of the canyon into rental cottages, and he knew she was renting one of them to Mia.

He hadn't thought through where he would live, what he would do until his house was raised from its ruins. He supposed he'd been thinking in the back of his mind that he would stay here, as he had last night, spending his nights cramped on the couch. One night on the couch, though, had changed his mind about that. But Sugarbush? No matter how thoroughly those three outbuildings had been renovated, no matter how charming and comfortable they had become, he would never be able to think of them as anything other than shacks, suitable for little more than storage.

"I can find someplace else," he said. "I mean, it could be quite a while before the house is ready. Wouldn't it be hard for you, having me in your back yard?"

"I'll survive."

"Well, I'd pay rent of course."

"Don't insult me, Chris, all right?" She hesitated for a moment. "It's true that money's tight right now, but I don't want yours. And there's plenty of land between the cottage and the adobe. We'll never even have to see each other."

Money was tight? His alimony hadn't amounted to

much after his retirement, but he certainly didn't think she had financial problems.

He told her he would think about it. Then he went home—to what was left of his home—with the list of losses Mia had typed up for him. The insurance representative was due to meet him there at two, but Chris wanted a chance to go through the rubble himself. He found some clothes he would need to have treated for smoke, but at least they were still in one piece. In the family room he collected his soot-covered trophies, his Martin guitar, nearly clean in its case, and the photograph albums, which had been somewhat protected by being in the hutch. He piled the things in the trunk of his Oldsmobile and then returned to the house.

After meeting with the insurance agent, he spent the rest of the afternoon driving around Valle Rosa, assessing the fire damage. Despite its small population, Valle Rosa covered a great deal of land dissected by hills and canyons and avocado groves. Isolated neighborhoods sprang from the hillsides, some of the homes old and ramshackle, others new and imposing, all of them at risk. The fire showed no favoritism.

At the relief center set up in the high school by the Red Cross, Chris visited some of the families who had lost their homes. Until last night, they'd been objects of his sympathy. Now, suddenly, these people were his fellow victims. Some of them were defeated and numb; others were angry, and they directed their anger at Chris for want of a better target. The woman who had lost three of her children had been hospitalized in a psychiatric unit, and he sat with her for half an hour while she stared past him. He wasn't even certain she knew he was there, and it gave him time to think, time to feel his impotence, his helplessness over what was happening to Valle Rosa. He had never felt so alone. When Jeff Cabrio's offer sifted back to him, it came in a new light.

It was ridiculous, of course. If it were possible to alleviate the drought by making rain, someone would have done it long before now. But there was something about Jeff, something Chris couldn't put his finger on. He trusted the stranger. It made no sense, yet the feeling was as strong and deep as anything he had ever felt before, and he knew he was going to ask Jeff Cabrio to help him shoulder the burden of Valle Rosa.

3.

Chris slept that night on borrowed linens in one of the small cottages at Carmen's sprawling Sugarbush. It was long after sundown when he arrived, and the three cottages, including Mia's, were dark. He was glad of the darkness, glad he couldn't see Sugarbush in its sunlit beauty, glad he couldn't see Carmen's spectacular, award-winning rose garden, or the way the manzanita trees clung to the edge of the canyon. But he could smell Sugarbush, and that was nearly as bad. The musky scent of the ornamental eucalyptus enveloped him as he watched Carmen unlock the door to the easternmost cottage. There was nearly half an acre between Mia's dark cottage and his, and the remaining cottage stood between them. Behind the cottages, the canyon was a dark abyss.

Carmen switched on the lamp in the living room. "What do you think of the new color?" she asked, dropping a pile of sheets and towels onto the sofa.

Chris looked at the walls. She'd painted them a soft mauve shade, a color he had long associated with her. "Very nice," he said. "Did you do all three in the same color?"

"Mia's is yellow, the middle one's blue."

"How's Mia working out as a tenant?"

Carmen shrugged and sat down on the arm of the sofa. "I rarely see her," she said. "She's quiet. Comes home alone every night and locks herself in her cottage."

Carmen had been the one to suggest that Mia talk to him about a job. He'd hired Mia for many reasons, none of which made good business sense. He'd liked the idea that Mia would be living at Sugarbush, as if that would somehow keep him closer to Carmen. And there'd been something about Mia, some desperate quirk in her smile, the way she bit her lip after telling him she had absolutely no experience doing any of the things required of the position. *Well, so what,* he'd thought. *He was green, she was green. A perfect match.*

Chris raised the window shade to look out at the canyon. He could see no lights other than the stars. "There's someone I might hire," he said, testing the words. "Someone to help out with the water problem. If I do, would you consider renting the third cottage to him?" He turned to see Carmen's frown.

"What are you talking about?" she asked.

He had invited Jeff Cabrio to meet the following day with Rick Smythe, one of the engineers working in Valle Rosa's water conservation program. "A guy came to see me today. I'm going to meet with him again tomorrow and make a decision about hiring him."

"Hiring him to do what?"

"Make it rain."

There was a moment's silence before she laughed. "I hope you're kidding."

He smiled. "Actually I'm not."

"Remember that movie with Burt Lancaster? *The Rainmaker*? You'd better rent it, Chris. You can borrow my VCR. The guy was a con artist."

"I think this one's for real."

Carmen gave him that look of disdain only she could achieve. "Chris. The media's going to eat you alive."

"You included?"

"Me first and foremost. I think you've lost your marbles."

"Maybe," he said. "I've lost everything else." He was referring to his house, his possessions, but as soon as he spoke, he knew Carmen thought he was referring to her. She stood up and walked into the kitchen, where he could hear her opening and closing the cupboards.

"I'd apologize for the mouse droppings," she said, "but they're everywhere, even in the adobe. The drought's really driven the mice out of the canyon."

"I know." He walked to the doorway of the kitchen. "I've had them, too."

"If this guy's sane, he can rent the cottage," she said. "Otherwise, spare me, all right?"

"Fine." He leaned against the door jamb. "By the way, I wanted to thank you for not interviewing me last night at the fire."

"I would have if you hadn't disappeared."

"It was good to see you working again. It must have been hard though, with all that was going on."

She let out an exaggerated sigh. "Not you too," she said. "The work's a piece of cake, Chris, just as it always has been. But the way everyone's treating me is pissing me off."

"What do you mean?"

"Like I'm the new kid on the block. I've got to jump through all their goddamned hoops all over again."

"I'm sorry, Carmen," he said, as though he were to blame. In a way, he was. This close, he could see new lines across her forehead and at the corners of her mouth. She wore jeans and a long-sleeved blue silk blouse. Someone had told him she always wore long sleeves now, that the scars were too noticeable. Her hair was still thick and shimmering, but the trademark swath of gray had widened over the past few years. "You're still very beautiful," he said.

She waved the compliment away. "The make-up guy spends about an hour on my face before I go on for my puny little *North County Report*. Thank God for the fires. At least this week I've gotten a little more air time." Her face darkened. "I'm sorry. I didn't mean that the way it sounded."

Chris shrugged away the apology. "My Martin survived. And the photograph albums."

"Always were sentimental to a fault, weren't you?" She closed a cupboard door and peered inside the oven.

He suddenly remembered all the anniversaries they'd spent at the seedy bar where they'd first met. She would insist they go there and sit in the same booth, eat the same greasy burgers they'd eaten that night many years earlier. If anything, she had been more sentimental than he was. The hardness she was projecting tonight was an act. In the past, though, it had been an act for the rest of the world, not for him.

She shut the oven door and leaned back against it.

"They treat me as though I'm going to fall apart any minute at work," she said. "I'm absolutely fine, and they tiptoe around me like I'm some pathetic little porcelain doll. Have you seen the woman who took over *San Diego Sunrise*? If I can call her a woman. I swear, she must be no older than nineteen."

He nodded. Of course he had. For a year or so after Carmen's breakdown, *Sunrise*, the early morning show she had created and anchored, flew through a series of hosts, none of whom could begin to match Carmen's combination of brains, brass and beauty. But then they hit on Terrell Gates and quickly knew they had a winner. Terrell's style was much different than Carmen's. Her scrubbed, girl-next-door looks made her sudden eruptions of bite and sass disarming to her guests and titillating to her audience.

"Do you think she's any good?" Carmen asked him.

"She's very young," he answered carefully, "but I think she's finding her niche."

He saw the sheen of tears in her eyes as she turned away from him, and he wished he had found another way to answer. He wanted to touch her. He hadn't touched her in so long.

She walked past him quickly, avoiding his eyes. "Mia

didn't want a phone," she said, "but I suppose you will, so go ahead and arrange it."

He opened the door for her, and she stepped out onto the small wooden porch. "Carmen," he said, "if you ever want to talk . . . You know, sometimes when you used to get upset at work, when you had to do something like interview that mother last night or whatever, and you'd come home and want to talk about it . . ."

She cocked her head. "Look, Chris, I invited you to move in here because I felt sorry for you. I'd feel sorry for anyone who'd lost his home, okay? You need a place to live, and I've got a place you can have. That's all there is to it. I am really sick of people treating me like I'm made of glass."

"Don't do that," he said.

"What?"

"This is *me*, Carmen. You don't have to try so hard to act tough with me."

"I don't know what you're talking about." She stepped off the porch, and didn't bother to face him when she spoke again. "Let me know if there's anything else you need, all right?"

He watched her walk across Sugarbush until she melted into the darkness. Behind him, the small, mouse-infested cottage waited. He was going from bad to worse, he thought, the continuing saga of his life the past five years.

The double bed took up nearly every inch of space in the cottage's one bedroom, and a soft breeze blew in through the open window as he made the bed. He had nearly drifted off to sleep when the coyotes started their eerie howling. It sounded like a dozen or more of them, but he knew two or three could easily make that much noise. They sounded very near. He lay there, listening. He'd forgotten how close Sugarbush was to nowhere.

After a sleepless hour, he got up to bring the photograph albums back to the bed. He looked through the first one, the one he and Carmen had started more than a decade ago, with pictures of their two weddings. The first wedding had been held in San Diego, with all the hoopla and media attention. Augie was there, his broad, beaming smile focused in every picture on his son and new daughter-in-law. Chris's other relatives had flown in from Arizona, but Carmen's family was noticeably absent. The aunt and uncle who had raised her and the cousins she'd grown up with were no longer speaking to her by that time. Women were not supposed to flaunt themselves on television, they said, and she was so unfeminine on TV. So pushy. Cold. The qualities for which Carmen was rewarded professionally made her the object of disdain in her Latino family. He didn't think she had ever quite recovered from the pain of their rejection.

The two women Carmen had considered her closest friends appeared in many of the pictures. Chris had heard separately from each of them in the last year. Carmen wouldn't see them, they complained. They wanted to help, wanted to do whatever they could to get her on her feet again, but she ignored their phone calls and their invitations. Their children missed her, they said. Indeed, Carmen had always had a special relationship with any child who crossed her path. Chris tried to explain to her old friends as best he could his interpretation of the problem: Carmen couldn't bear to see them or their children. She couldn't bear to be reminded of what she'd longed for and what had been taken from her.

Chris turned the page of the album, and the setting of the photographs switched from San Diego to Mexico City, where the second wedding, an intimate affair in a small chapel, had been held for the benefit of Carmen's elderly parents. Her parents, who had worked all their lives as migrant farmers, had sent Carmen north of the border when she was five years old to give her a better chance for a decent education. That she had received, but her excellent performance was rarely rewarded by her aunt and uncle, who had tried to groom her to be a good wife and mother and little more.

It had been a long time since he'd looked at those pictures. Carmen was so beautiful, so happy. She was twenty-seven and he was twenty-eight. They had met while she was working for *News Nine*, covering a baseball scandal in which he, thankfully, had no involvement. They began dating and made an attractive, high-visibility couple, both of them having solid reputations in San Diego and rising rapidly to the top of their respective careers. There was a good deal of speculation as to whether or not Chris Garrett would be able to settle down. He was known for a wild streak that seemed incompatible with marriage, but he surprised everyone, including himself, at his ability to give up the other women and the excessive drinking and the escapades. Only Carmen had believed him capable of being a good husband, and in her he discovered the joy of having a real friend. Before that, his friendships had been limited to those men with whom he played ball. Friendships which were intense and engrossing and playful, but in the final analysis, superficial. These days, though, he didn't have even that. He'd lost his teammates the same time he'd lost his wife. Despite the few friends he'd made at the high school where he taught, it had been a very lonely five years.

Trying to shake off the melancholy that had suddenly settled over him, Chris turned another page in the album. And there was Sugarbush. He and Carmen had bought Sugarbush shortly after they were married, then had set about remodeling the beautiful old adobe for their home. It wasn't long afterward that Carmen was given her own show, *San Diego Sunrise*, a half hour every morning during which she'd interview politicians, movie stars, whomever she chose. Her guests were always apprehensive, never knowing how kind Carmen Perez was feeling that day. She bent the rules of journalistic etiquette, but the staff of *News Nine* gave her free rein despite any fear they might have had of legal reprisal. Her ratings were simply too good. Carmen wasn't yet thirty and had everything she'd wanted. Everything except a child.

Chris opened the second album. These pictures were far more familiar to him. He looked at them often. The first was a shot of the scoreboard taken during the Padres–Pirates game, the announcement reading, "It's a Boy!!! Dustin Garrett, 6 pounds, 3 ounces!! Congratulations Chris and Carmen!!" Then followed a series of pictures of Dustin in the hospital, snuggling cheek to cheek with a radiant Carmen, his already thick, dark hair so much like hers. Chris remembered sleeping poorly after they brought Dustin home from the hospital, not so much because of Dustin's own wakefulness, but because he couldn't still his thoughts. He imagined teaching his son to ride a bike, coaching him in little league, all the things Augie had so enthusiastically done with him.

Once they brought Dustin home, Chris took so many pictures of him that the camera broke. ("You wore it out, man," said the young clerk in the camera store.) And then the setting of the pictures switched back to the hospital again. He'd had to force himself to take those pictures. Dustin looked so small and gray, a painful array of tubes and needles invading his doll-like body. They'd told him Dustin was going to die, and he'd thought these pictures would be all he would have of his son. But the little boy hadn't died. He'd surprised his doctors. Disappointed them, too, Chris had thought at the time. In their kind hearts, they had wanted this particular child to die. He was certainly blind, they told him, definitely deaf. The brain damage was severe. *Profound* was the word they used. *Irreversible.* He could still remember Carmen's screams when they told her.

In the morning light, Chris was stunned by what had become of Sugarbush. Nothing short of the fires could have provided such graphic evidence of the changes wrought by the drought. He had seen his own yard and the dry chaparral of Cinnamon Canyon daily, and so he had barely noticed the slow and insidious changes there. But it had been several years since he'd gotten a good look at Sugarbush, and what he saw sent a chill through him. Every growing thing seemed to be withering, dying. Carmen's once dazzling rose garden was nearly dead. There were only a few bushes near the middle of the garden that appeared to be hanging on, as though she had given up on it slowly, focusing her time and water on the center as the edges died away.

How had she tolerated it, watching the one thing she still treasured, the one thing in which she could still take pride, fade away? "Gardening's excellent therapy for her," one of the shrinks had told him. "Gives her a chance to nurture something."

He walked over to the cottage Mia was renting and knocked on the door. She opened it and gasped her surprise at seeing him there. She was barefoot, wearing blue shorts and a baggy white T-shirt.

"Morning, Mia," he said, and with a gesture toward his cottage, added, "I'm going to be staying out here while my house is being rebuilt." He was certain she knew that he and Carmen had once been married. What she would make of him living in an outbuilding on Carmen's property, he had no idea.

He peered past her into the living room. The walls were bare, and he could see no furniture whatsoever from where he stood. But there was sheet plastic on the floor.

"Wasn't the cottage furnished when you moved in?" he asked.

She glanced behind her to see what he was seeing.

"Oh, yes. I moved most of the furniture into the dining room so I could have a big space to work in."

"Work?"

"Clay," she said, shrugging, as though he should have known. "It gets messy."

He was curious, but he had too much to do today to question her further. Obviously there was more to Mia than he had thought.

"I'm going to be in late today," he said. "I have to buy some clothes and a few other things. Then I have a meeting with the guy who stopped by yesterday."

Mia colored, and he knew he had mentioned Jeff only to see the reaction in her face.

"At the office?" she asked.

He smiled. "No, at a restaurant. Would you rather I invited him back to the office?"

She jutted her chin at him indignantly. "You're misinterpreting my interest," she said. "He has extraordinary bone structure in his face."

"Right, Mia," he said with a wink, then turned to step off her porch. "I'll probably be in around two or so."

4.

"It's like this," Jeff Cabrio said, drawing invisible lines with the tip of his finger on the red Formica tabletop. "If you put the trans-hydrator here"—he lifted the salt shaker and set it on the edge of the table—"the rain will fall within these boundaries." He moved his empty glass and the pepper shaker to form a triangle. "That's on a small scale. For all of Valle Rosa, of course, we'd need something much grander. First thing we'd have to do is figure out how much land we want to cover."

Chris was leaning back in his chair, arms folded across his chest as he watched Jeff explain his rainmaking technology to Rick Smythe, whose green eyes were wide, incredulous. Chris wasn't quite sure about Rick. He was twenty-seven, nearly a decade younger than Jeff, but he looked closer to twenty. His hair was sun-bleached and long enough to cover the back of his shirt collar. He'd eaten an avocado-and-alfalfa-sprout sandwich for lunch, while Chris and Jeff dined on the catfish that had earned this restaurant—one of three in Valle Rosa—a little fame over the years.

Rick told them he'd surfed before going into work that

morning, that it was a necessary prerequisite to the start of his day. He had the look of a college kid who spent his afternoons on the beach and his evenings partying. There was a density about him, a doltishness that worried Chris. He'd been told, though, that Rick was brighter than he seemed and the best engineer in Valle Rosa's ineffectual water conservation program. But perhaps that wasn't saying much.

Nevertheless, in the last hour Chris had watched the younger engineer's amused skepticism turn to intrigue as he slipped under Jeff Cabrio's spell. Chris himself had tried to resist it today, tried to keep his thinking clear, but in the small window of time between placing their order and receiving their food, Jeff had cured Rick's hiccups by guiding him through an intricate set of finger exercises, had helped their gangly young waitress pick up pieces of broken glass with a slice of bread, and had the other diners in the cramped restaurant generally staring at him with open curiosity. Chris had simply given in. Given up. *Let him help you,* he thought to himself. *What can it hurt?*

Rick lifted his third glass of orange juice to his lips while studying the triangle Jeff had formed on the table. "How exact can you be with the rainfall?" he asked.

"With the right equipment, very," Jeff said. "If I do it at all, I'll do it with precision."

Rick seemed unable to shift his gaze from Jeff's, and Chris knew how he felt. Jeff had a way of holding you to him with his eyes, of not letting you go until he was ready.

Rick finally broke the stare, letting out his breath in a

laugh. "This is ridiculous," he said. "I feel like we're having a conversation about Santa Claus, you know? Like, what he eats for dinner, how he works out his delivery schedule, how we could build chimneys to make it easier on the old dude." He looked at Chris with a plea in his eyes. *Save me*, he said. *Tell me this is all a joke before I make a fool out of myself believing this guy.*

Chris leaned forward. "So, tell me, Rick. With your background and your training, does what he's saying make sense?"

Rick's tan took on a grayish hue. "Don't base your decision on me, man," he said, a shiver in his voice. "I mean, yes, in theory it makes sense, at least the way he's explaining it. But in practice? Why wouldn't anyone have thought of it before?" He looked back at Jeff, who shrugged, not stating the obvious: *Because no one is as smart as I am.*

"It just sounds too damn simple," Rick said.

Jeff offered his shadowy half-smile. "I could make it sound more complicated if you like."

Chris knew there were questions he should ask, but he no longer cared about the answers. Six more houses had burned last night, a two-year-old child was missing, and across from him sat a stranger who promised relief. Still, he didn't want Rick to think he was a complete fool. He'd already told him that Jeff could offer nothing in the way of references.

He pressed his hands flat on the tabletop and looked at Jeff. "If I could speak to your previous employers, what would they tell me?" he asked.

Jeff stared at him for a few painfully long seconds and Chris felt his face go hot.

"Give me two months," he said finally. "If I don't produce rain by then, I'll leave. And I'll find some way to pay you back for the equipment and whatever else you've shelled out for my expenses."

Chris lowered his hands to his thighs. His palms were damp. "We don't have the money for this. Rainmaking isn't in the budget. I'll have to shift things around." This would be tough; there was little slack in the city coffers. "I'd like to have Rick work with you, all right?"

Rick froze, his juice glass halfway to his lips as he waited out Jeff Cabrio's verdict.

"Fine," Jeff said.

"Is that all right with you, Rick? I'll arrange to move you over."

"Great." Rick grinned. "There's not much to do at the reservoir these days except panic."

The young, dark-haired waitress cleared their plates away, her eyes on Jeff the whole time. He had won her over when he'd helped her clean up the glass she'd dropped and when he'd shot a curdling look at the older waitress who chastised her for her clumsiness. But he paid no attention to her now, and as she walked away from the table, he leaned toward Rick and Chris. "There's something I have to get straight with both of you, or the deal's off."

He was speaking very quietly. Chris had to pull his chair closer to the table to hear him.

"I don't want to be asked questions about myself,"

Jeff said. "My private business will remain my private business."

Chris felt Rick's eyes on him. "All right," he said.

"All right," Rick echoed.

"I have no intention of socializing or of being part of the community or of making friends. I'd rather not talk to anyone except the two of you. I'll give you one hundred percent of my waking hours. The sooner I'm done, the sooner I can leave."

An ultimatum. Jeff Cabrio was going to call the shots, that was clear.

"Agreed," Chris said. He turned to Rick.

"Hey," Rick said, grinning again, "whatever. I'll be happy just to—"

A shriek from the kitchen interrupted him. Their waitress backed out of the open kitchen door, crashing into their table, knocking over the one empty chair.

"Oh, God, I'm sorry." She glanced down at them, then back to the kitchen. Every eye in the restaurant was on her, and she hugged her large round tray to her chest like a shield. She pointed toward the kitchen. "There's a mouse in there."

The burly older waitress appeared at the door, hands on her hips, scowling. "Why don't you announce it to the entire county?" she asked. "Get back in here. You've got a job to do."

The younger waitress shook her head. "I'm terrified of mice. I know it's ridiculous, but . . ."

Jeff Cabrio stood up. He touched her shoulder. "Do you have an umbrella?" he asked.

She looked too stunned by the question to answer him, and the older waitress snorted. "An umbrella? It hasn't rained here in five years, mister."

"I think I have one in the trunk of my car," Chris said.

"What color is it?" Jeff asked.

The other diners were staring at them, forkfuls of catfish hanging forgotten in the air.

"Black," Chris said.

"Perfect."

Chris walked out to the parking lot. Out of a habit formed over the last few days, he looked in the direction of Cinnamon Canyon and saw the all-too-familiar plume of smoke against the hazy sky. It was farther east now, headed toward the homes on the eastern ridge of the canyon.

He opened the trunk of his car and dug through baseball mitts and bats and smoke-damaged clothes until he found the old umbrella. Feeling foolish, he carried it back into the restaurant.

Jeff took the umbrella from him and walked into the kitchen, while Chris, Rick, the two waitresses and the chef watched from the doorway, and the hushed diners held their breath.

"It's over there." The young waitress pointed toward the floor near the broad refrigerator.

A small gray mouse scurried a couple of feet along the baseboard, then stopped. Jeff took a step toward it, then slowly opened the umbrella and held it on the floor; curved edge toward the mouse. "Chase it into the umbrella, Rick," he said.

"What? How the hell am I supposed to do that?" Rick asked, but before he had even finished his sentence, the mouse darted of its own accord into the umbrella, which Jeff snapped shut.

"Done," he said, handing the umbrella to Chris.

Chris took the umbrella from him, dumbfounded. Some of the diners broke into applause, which he encouraged by raising the umbrella in the air like a trophy.

Jeff, though, wasn't smiling. "I'm getting out of here," he said quietly. Heads turned to follow him as, with a few long strides, he walked out of the restaurant.

Chris watched him go. Jeff was crazy to think he could keep a low profile in Valle Rosa. The town was far too small to absorb him unnoticed. The people in this restaurant would be talking about him over dinner tonight.

He left enough money with Rick to cover their bill and then went out to the parking lot. Jeff was still there, sitting in his black Saab. Chris walked over and set a hand on the open window.

"You're on, Jeff," he said. "But this is a very close community. I'm not sure how long you'll be able to remain anonymous."

Jeff squinted in the direction of the smoke. "Have they found that kid yet?" he asked. "The one who was missing after the fire last night?"

"Not that I've heard."

Jeff glanced down at the umbrella. Chris was leaning on it like a cane. "Mice are attracted to black," he said.

"What?" Chris looked down at the umbrella himself. "Oh."

"You can free him over there." Jeff pointed to the chaparral at the side of the parking lot. "And then you'd better wash out the umbrella. It'll have mouse excrement in it."

Chris shrugged. "It's not worth the bother. I never use it."

Jeff turned the key in the ignition, then smiled up at him, a full-blown smile. "You will," he said. "You will."

5.

The scent of fire was always in the air. Even in the little Valle Rosa market that Mia frequented after work, the acrid smell hung above the produce and nothing looked very appealing. She selected broccoli, a handful of snow peas, mushrooms and a bag of carrots, all the while hearing Dr. Bella's words as clearly as if he stood behind her: "The best thing you can do is cut back on fat. Even so, your genes will have the final say."

This was a form of mental illness, she thought, a compulsion of sorts, that she could no longer shop without hearing his voice. She'd thought it would be hard to give up the burgers, ice cream, and tortilla chips, but it hadn't been difficult at all. She had simply lost interest in food. When she'd awaken in the mornings, her hip bones formed little hills beneath the sheet. At first, she'd studied the hollows in her cheeks in the bathroom mirror with fascination, but on the one occasion when she'd closed her eyes and run her fingers over her skin, she'd jerked her hands away, horrified to realize her cheeks felt like her mother's in that year before she'd died. The body that Glen had called an artist's lure no longer existed.

The drive from the market to Sugarbush along the winding narrow road hadn't yet lost its enchantment for her, even though sections of the chaparral and the earth beneath it had been blackened, even though the plume of smoke still rose in the distance, and cottony-gray ashes fell like snowflakes on her windshield. The road reached a dizzying height above Cinnamon Canyon, and the enormous granite boulders scattered below took on a neon-yellow glow from the falling sun. Just before the final twist in the road, the Valle Rosa Reservoir came into view, a crater cut deeply into the earth with a shallow pool of vivid blue at its core. Once she'd seen two coyotes drinking at it, and she'd nearly flown off the road and out into space as they stole her attention from her driving.

It was that natural, almost primitive feeling of Valle Rosa she loved best. She'd selected the town from a map. The tiny, black, inviting pinprick appeared to be little more than an hour from San Diego and the medical community on which she was still dependent, but worlds away in terms of peace and isolation. And she had been right in her assessment.

She arrived at Sugarbush as she always did, close to seven, when the sun was quickening its decline in the sky, and the sparse vegetation—the stubby, leathery chaparral, the red-barked manzanita trees and the dry and dying scrub oaks—sent crisp black shadows across the warm earth. A black Saab with Ohio plates was parked where she usually parked, at the edge of the packed dirt by Carmen's adobe. Jeff Cabrio's car, no doubt. He would be in the middle cottage, Chris had told her, the cottage between hers and his. She wasn't to disturb him. "Leave him and his bone structure alone, Mia," Chris had said, with that glint in his eye that let her know he was, at least in part, teasing. "He's an eccentric," he'd added. "We're going to have to play by his rules."

The cottage she had chosen for herself was the farthest from the adobe. She'd intentionally sought the seclusion it offered, the sense of having all eight of Sugarbush's dusty acres practically to herself, although at first the nights had been difficult. The relentless darkness surrounding her cottage had unnerved her, and the late-night howling of the coyotes had sent her flying, breathless, from her bed. Now, though, she welcomed the darkness. The coyotes still awakened her, but she could lie in bed, listening to them until the howling faded away.

She had to walk past the other two cottages to get to her own. Chris's was empty, as she knew it would be. She'd left him on the phone, a stack of paperwork on the desk in front of him.

She gave the second cottage wide berth, but as she rounded its far corner, she saw Jeff standing by the back steps above the canyon. He was staring at something on the ground, a black glove perhaps, or a rag. He called her over with a wave of his hand.

Clutching the bag of groceries to her chest, she walked toward him, realizing as she did so that the thing on the ground wasn't a glove at all but a tarantula. She stopped in her tracks.

"Good," he said. "By your reaction I assume this isn't an everyday occurrence."

She shook her head. "The first I've seen out here."

Jeff looked back at the enormous furred black spider. "I know they're not dangerous, but I still wouldn't want to share my house with a family of them."

"No."

He raised his eyebrows toward her. The slant of the sun turned his face into a vivid array of light and shadow, the angles sharp and clear. "Mia, right?" he asked.

She nodded. "And you're Jeff." She stared at him a moment longer, trying to commit the play of light on his face to memory. Then she lowered her gaze into the bag she was holding as though it might offer her a clue as to what to say next. "I've been ordered not to talk to you," she said, returning her eyes to his, "other than 'Hello, have a nice day.'"

"Ah." He stood up straighter, slipping his hands into the pockets of his jeans. "That's probably wise."

"Chris said you'd want to know they found the little boy."

"And . . . ?"

"And he's fine. Apparently he was in his yard when he saw the fire coming, and he got scared and ran off into the canyon. One of the dogs found him, safe and sound."

He nearly smiled. "That's good. That's really good. It's been bothering me."

She shifted her bag of groceries to her other hip, glanced inside it again at the broccoli. "Well, Jeff." She shrugged. "Have a nice day."

"You do the same, Mia."

Like the other cottages, hers stood on the edge of the

canyon, nestled between two boulders nearly as large as the structure itself. Once inside, she dropped the bag on the kitchen counter and grabbed her pad and charcoal to quickly sketch Jeff's face as it had looked moments earlier. She rested the rough drawing against the backsplash, glancing at it from time to time as she cut the vegetables and put them on to steam.

She was scooping cooked rice into a bowl when she looked out the kitchen window to see her new neighbor crouching in the dust, watching the tarantula walk off into the scrubby growth behind his cottage. Then he stood again to study the dying leaves of the sugarbush tree at the rim of the canyon.

By the time Mia returned her attention to the stove, the green of the broccoli had faded and the slices of carrots broke apart when she pierced them with a fork. She spooned them onto the rice, then looked outside again to see that Jeff had disappeared.

She carried her bowl of rice and vegetables into the small living room where she sat on the sofa. It, and the coffee table on which she kept her clay and supplies, were the only pieces of furniture she hadn't moved into the dining room, already cramped with its old wicker table and chairs, in order to give her more work space in the living room. The aging color television that had come with the cottage rested in the corner of the room. Mia liked to watch the news while she ate, before settling down with her clay for the evening. It was Wednesday, and Carmen would be on with her *North County Report*.

Carmen was wonderful to look at, and each time Mia

saw her she thought of how challenging it would be to sculpt her, to capture the exact blend of strength and softness that marked her features. Carmen intimidated her, though. Mia felt young around her. Young and plain and unsophisticated. She could never ask her to pose.

The day that Mia had come to look at the cottage, she'd asked Carmen if they had met before; the older woman looked very familiar, but Mia couldn't place her. Carmen told her about *San Diego Sunrise,* and Mia immediately remembered her as the acerbic host of that early-morning show. She had often wondered why people agreed to appear on *Sunrise.* Carmen had been a woman in total control, like a champion prizefighter taking on challenger after challenger and thrashing each of them in turn. Her guests never stood a chance.

Carmen seemed like a different woman that day, though, as she showed Mia the cottage and the grounds. The snappy, daring, feisty side of her didn't exist, and she seemed intent on Mia's comfort. She told her about the rules governing their water usage, and about covering her food to protect it from the mice. She told her about the illegal aliens—'undocumented workers,' she called them—who lived in makeshift camps in the canyon. "You'll see them on the streets of town in the morning, looking for work, but in the evening they disappear back into the canyons. You should know that they're there, but they won't bother you."

Mia had asked many questions to keep her talking about Sugarbush or Valle Rosa or the drought, not wanting to give her new landlady a chance to ask her anything about herself.

When Carmen appeared on the television screen, Mia turned up the volume. Carmen sat next to the anchor, Bill Jackson, whose hair always looked as if it had been painted onto his scalp with black shoe polish. Once Carmen was on, though, the camera was hers, and Mia couldn't help breaking into a smile of admiration at seeing that confident, almost regal, bearing. Behind Carmen, footage of the Cinnamon Canyon fire ran while she spoke.

"Today," Carmen said, "Valle Rosa's acting mayor, former Padre pitching ace, Christopher Garrett, who has spent his first two months in office battling Valle Rosa's serious water problems, announced he is hiring an environmental engineer, Jeff Cabrio. Cabrio claims he can make rain fall over Valle Rosa." Carmen's voice, marked by a delicate, almost imperceptible, Spanish accent, had taken on a slight cynical edge. A smile played at the corners of her lips, an almost conspiratorial smile, as though she wanted her viewers to know she thought Chris was as crazy as they did.

"In response to questions as to how he intends to pay for Cabrio's service, Mayor Garrett said he would be shifting funds earmarked for road improvement into the fund for water resources, saying that 'water is a more pressing issue right now.' There's been no word as of yet on how the transportation board in Valle Rosa is reacting to this news. On Monday, Mayor Garrett lost his own home to the Cinnamon Canyon fire."

The camera pulled back from Carmen to add Bill

Jackson and his patent-leather hair to the picture. "Sounds like that's not all he lost," Jackson said with a chuckle, and Mia winced at the implication. Until this moment it hadn't struck her as unreasonable that Chris would hire Jeff Cabrio to make it rain. Like a true charismatic, Jeff had walked into the office and had them believing. Listening to the turn of events from Carmen's mouth, though, Chris's decision seemed ludicrous. Mia glanced out the window toward Jeff's cottage, wondering if he was watching the news himself.

When she had finished eating, she turned off the television, changed into shorts and a baggy T-shirt, and settled down on the floor in front of the piece on which she was working. It was the head of a man, and it rested on an old orange crate. Leaning against the coffee table was a large bulletin board covered with photographs, mostly five-by-sevens, of a smiling but bedraggled middle-aged man. As she carefully unwrapped the plastic from the bust, she glanced back and forth between it and the pictures, her smile growing. Henry was perfect. Nearly finished. She was taking a ridiculous length of time with this piece, and she couldn't have said why. She'd destroyed and rebuilt his perfectly fine left ear a half dozen times.

She'd been walking in downtown San Diego with Glen, both of them ready for their next project, both of them searching for a lure. They'd spotted Henry at the same moment, plucking him from the crowd with their eyes, catching their breath in the recognition that he was perfect.

"He's mine!" Mia called it first. Glen relented after a few hostile minutes there on the sidewalk, while Mia kept her eye on their scruffy find to make sure he didn't disappear. They were often drawn to the same subjects. "The price I pay for having taught you all I know," Glen had said, more than once.

She knew Glen saw exactly what she saw when she looked at Henry Jared Cash—the bounty of spheres that formed his face. The high round cheeks, the bulb of a nose, the ruddy orb of his chin. His face was a study in circles, the way Jeff Cabrio's was a study in planes. His hair was straggly, wispy, the color a graying blond. His eyebrows were wondrously thick and fair. He was perhaps fifty, and even standing alone and still on the corner, he wore a small smile on his face. It was impossible to imagine him frowning, or weeping. Mia knew that Glen felt the same hunger that she felt, that his hands nearly ached to transfer what he was seeing here, on Broadway, to his clay.

She was certain the man was homeless. He carried a ratty-looking bedroll, and she could see the shape of a flask in the pocket of his light, army green jacket.

"I want him clothed," she whispered to Glen as they approached him. "I want the bedroll in it."

Glen nodded, and she knew without telling him any more that he understood. She wanted the contrast between his sad and shabby packaging and the immutable joy in his face.

"Excuse me, sir," she began, resting her hand on his arm. "I'm an artist and I'd like to take some pictures of you that I can use as a model for sculpting. It would take about an hour, and I'll pay you."

Henry laughed, a tinkling laugh, the sort you'd expect to hear from Santa Claus, and she realized that was who he reminded her of. A robust, cherry-cheeked, streetwise California Santa.

She and Glen walked with Henry over to Horton Plaza, where they posed him in the sunlight, as Mia circled around him, snapping pictures, zooming in on the shape of his ear with its fat round lobe, and the stubble of blond whiskers on his chin.

In addition to the thirty dollars she paid him, they bought him lunch. He told them he had lived in Paris and Athens and Istanbul. He had taught philosophy in Boston, he said, and trained race horses in Kentucky. Mia listened, fascinated, and it wasn't until that night, after she and Glen had made love, that she could entertain the notion that Henry's tales had been mere fabrication. "You are so gullible, Sunny," Glen had said, "so thoroughly guileless."

It was one week to the day after she'd taken those pictures that her doctor called with the news. She had just bought the clay to begin working on her sculpture of Henry, and she deliberately unwrapped it and ignored it, letting it harden to a dry, wasted brick on her work table. She had done nothing with Henry's pictures, nothing with her clay at all, until moving to Valle Rosa. All her energy had gone into simple survival during those months between that phone call and the move. She'd watched Glen create two stunning pieces; she'd watched him grow apart from her, and when she moved, the only pictures she'd brought with her had been of Henry. None of Glen. None of her mother. None of her sister, Laura, although she had called Laura twice from the phone in Chris's office to let her know she was all right.

At Laura's insistence, she'd finally given her the number at the office, but Laura hadn't felt that was enough. She'd cried on the phone, calling Mia "Mimi," as she had when they were children, reminding Mia of the early bond they'd once shared. She begged Mia to tell her where she was, but Mia couldn't take the chance of having Laura show up on her doorstep. She wouldn't let Laura and Glen into her life again. She truly felt apart from them here in Valle Rosa. Laura's shadow didn't extend this far north.

Mia knew before she began working on the sculpture of Henry that she would sculpt only his head. Bodies had suddenly become insignificant, cumbersome. She wasn't interested in them. From now on, she would focus only on faces, and she had proven to herself with Henry that she could convey all she needed to convey through his face alone.

For the first time since moving to Sugarbush, Mia pulled the shades before undressing for the night. Her isolation was no longer absolute. She took off her shorts and T-shirt, throwing them, clay-stained, into the laundry basket on the floor next to the dresser, then stepped out of her underpants and added them to the pile. She unhooked her bra and laid it on the dresser to open the pocket of the left cup, to remove the gel form. She had moved the mirror above the dresser a few inches higher on the wall, so that she could see only her face and her shoulders in it, nothing more. Carmen had offered to move a full-length mirror into Mia's cottage from one of the others, but Mia had told her not to bother.

She hadn't taken a good look at her body in the month and a half she'd been in Valle Rosa, and she didn't plan to do so in the four months she had left before the surgery that would give her back her breast. Four more months and the waiting would be over. Four more months and she could rejoin the world. She was holding herself in suspended animation until she could begin to live again, whole and healthy. Until then, sculpting was her salvation, her balm.

She had read somewhere that when the artist throws herself into her work, when her work becomes the reason for her existence, that she is using her art to protect herself from 'unrequited sexual feelings.' Was that what she was doing? When she woke up in the middle of the night with that unwelcome yearning, she'd fling off the sheet and go out to the living room where she'd pull the plastic from Henry, wet her hands in the pan of precious water, and run them over the slick clay until the feeling passed. Yes, she supposed that was exactly what she was doing.

She pulled her nightshirt over her head and turned out her bedroom light. Then she lifted the shade again to look outside. A light burned on Chris's porch, and he sat on a chair of rough-hewn wood, strumming a guitar. Through her open window, Mia heard snatches of music—enough to know he was singing as well as playing—but she couldn't place the song. Jeff Cabrio's cottage was dark, save for one dimly lit rear window. She pictured him inside in the darkness. He was mysterious. He was a lure. And he was going to make it rain.

Once in bed, she thought about the sculpture of Henry. She could have finished it any night this past week, perhaps even the week before, and suddenly she knew why she had been dragging her feet: she hadn't known what she would do next, what she could throw herself into to ward off unwelcome thoughts, unwelcome feelings. She hadn't known who her next subject would be. But now she knew. And he lived next door.

6.

The fourth car in her driveway had Ohio plates. Jeff Cabrio's. The alleged rainmaker. Carmen got out of her own car and walked around his, trying to peer inside it in the faint moonlight, but she could see nothing. The black Saab looked a bit battered, the right front fender dented. Who was this man who had conned Chris so easily? She didn't even know what he looked like. He could be a raving lunatic for all she knew. Maybe she shouldn't have agreed to let him live on her property.

Inside the adobe, the kitchen was cool and dark, and Carmen left the lights off, not certain which of her windows could be seen by the middle cottage. She locked the doors and checked the windows before going upstairs. She didn't usually bother to lock up the house at night, but then she'd never had a strange man living at Sugarbush before.

Her legs were tired as she climbed the stairs, and the smell of smoke seemed to emanate from her skin. The fires were dying, though. Sometime this afternoon, the army of fire fighters had managed to contain the last pocket of flame in one small section of the canyon, where they would leave it to burn itself out. Fine. She was sick of talking about demolished houses and dying children. Yet, what would she talk about when the fires were gone? They had given her the air time she needed, the exposure. For the first time since she'd been back at *News Nine*, her colleagues had treated her as something other than superfluous.

Dennis Ketchum, the general manager of *News Nine*, had initially been reluctant to take her back in any capacity. That had hurt and surprised her, because over the past five miserable years, he and the *News Nine* producers had talked about wanting her back, missing her skills. Every card she received from her former colleagues said something like 'It's just not the same without you here,' and Carmen had come to believe their words. But her colleagues were only being kind—she could see that now. They were only encouraging her to get well.

She had foolishly thought they would give her *San Diego Sunrise* again. No one had said as much, but everyone knew that *Sunrise* was her show, her creation. She'd figured they'd have her co-anchor the news for awhile to let her get her bearings, and then they'd dump Terrell Gates and reinstate her as anchor for *Sunrise*. Instead they'd given her the "light" portion of the *North County Report*, three times a week, the smallest assignment they could come up with that would still place her in front of the camera. She'd covered a library opening, a protest over a mural painted on the side of a bakery, and the ten-year anniversary celebration of a playground. She'd had to beg to be allowed to cover the fire, and now the fire was under control and she would have nothing of significance left to say.

Carmen's greatest fear was that they were right about her, although she would never, never let them know it. She had lost something these past few years, lost her ability to distance herself from her work. That weak, ineffectual interview she'd conducted with the mother of the children who died in the fire still haunted her. In the past she could have finished that interview and gone out for a drink with the rest of the crew. She wouldn't have let the magnitude of what had happened hit her until she got home, where she would talk it out with Chris. Now the very memory of that night could bring on a fresh bout of nausea.

Late that afternoon, she had gone into the lunchroom at the studio to heat a cup of coffee in the microwave. Bill Jackson and Terrell Gates were sitting at one of the tables. Terrell with her innocent blue eyes and creamy young skin and the short blond hair *San Diego Magazine* had described as "tame enough for the traditionalists, yet savvy enough to draw the younger, new-age sophisticates to *Sunrise*." Carmen had spoken with Terrell only a few times, and the younger woman never mentioned their connection, never even let on that she knew Carmen had once hosted *Sunrise*—that, in fact, the damn show wouldn't exist if it were not for her.

Carmen nodded a greeting to Terrell and Bill, and the three of them were quiet while she waited out the minute it took to heat the coffee. After leaving the room, she heard their soft burst of laughter, then Bill's muffled words—something about the "Carmen Perez fire report"—followed by Terrell saying, quite clearly, "I can't believe she's only thirty-nine. She's pushing fifty, if she's a day."

Carmen had no office of her own, no dressing room, and so she locked herself and her coffee in one of the stalls of the ladies' room and cried, vowing that this would be the last time she'd allow herself the weakness of tears, all the while knowing it wouldn't be.

Above the bed in her bedroom, the enormous skylight Chris had built let in the moonlight and the crisp, white glitter of stars. Carmen didn't bother with the overhead light. She turned off the air conditioner and opened one of the windows to let in the cool night air. And she heard something. Music. She could see the cottages from here. Mia's was dark, as was Jeff Cabrio's, but a light burned on Chris's front porch. He was sitting on one of the porch chairs, playing the guitar, singing. How long since she'd heard him sing? She strained her ears to catch a phrase, to place the song. *Catch the Wind.* He used to sing that one with Augie. She could picture them, father and son, sitting on the patio, their guitars and Augie's mournful harmonica filling the stillness of the Sugarbush night.

She opened the other windows in the room and sat down on the floor, leaning her head against the windowsill. Once, years ago, she had been helping Chris unpack after a long road trip. He was putting his toiletries away in the bathroom when she found, tucked into a side pocket of his suitcase, a small black notebook. The proverbial Little

Black Book. Her fear was so sudden she couldn't protect herself against it or against the quick tears that came with it. She wasn't naive; she knew what life was like on the road for baseball players. She knew there were women waiting for them in every town. And she knew Chris had lived life on the edge before he met her. But she had been so certain he'd grown above that.

She stood frozen, the book in her hand. Finally she opened it, and as she leafed through it she felt profound relief. At the top of each page, he'd written the name of a city, but instead of listing names of women beneath it, he had written the names and addresses of coffee houses and taverns where folk music was the norm, where he could take his guitar and make an impromptu appearance. While other players were reputed to drink, party, and womanize, Chris was known for showing up at clubs, guitar in hand, ready to play for a welcoming crowd. He wasn't a first-rate musician, but that hardly mattered. He was good with an audience. Relaxed and funny.

Carmen remembered how she'd walked to the open bathroom door, leaned against the jamb. Chris's back was to her; he was putting his toothpaste in the medicine cabinet.

"I found your little black book," she said.

He turned around, bewildered for a moment, then laughed when he saw the book in her hand. "Not very exciting, is it?" he asked.

She tried to laugh too, but found she couldn't. "For a minute there, I thought it was the real thing."

His smile faded. "Carmen."

She felt the tears again, this time spilling over, hot on her cheeks, and in two quick steps he was with her, his arms around her. The only place she'd ever felt safe enough to cry was in his arms.

"I miss you when you're on the road," she said. "I try not to let you know how much because I know you have no choice. I try to pretend I'm strong, but I'm not."

He stroked her hair. "You're very strong," he said.

"When I saw that book, I thought I'd lost you."

He'd leaned away from her then to look hard into her eyes, and she could see the hurt in his. "How could you even think I would do something like that?"

She hadn't bothered to answer him then, but now, as the final strains of *Catch the Wind* drifted through the open window into the bedroom, she whispered, "You tell me, Chris."

He stopped playing, and she waited, hoping he wasn't through for the night. In another minute, he began again with a song she didn't recognize, something soft and sweet, and she closed her eyes to listen.

7

"They're swarming," Mia said. "I locked the door, but it's still a little frightening."

Chris stood next to her desk, looking out the window at the sea of reporters and irate citizens of Valle Rosa who had assembled on the small, brown front yard of the office. Some of the crowd spilled into the street, others, into the minuscule, dusty park next door. Sam Braga from the *Valle Rosa Journal* stood above the gathering on a footstool he must have brought with him, and the cameras were trained on him. Chris knew what he was saying, since Sam had called earlier that morning to vent his ire over Chris's hiring of Jeff Cabrio.

"Where the hell do you get off making that kind of unilateral decision?" Sam had barked into the phone. Chris had never heard Sam angry before, hadn't known he was capable of growling. "We need new stoplights. There've been two accidents at the intersection of Fig and Jacaranda just this month. And Verde needs to be widened, and we've—"

"We need rain," Chris had interrupted him.

"What we need is someone at the helm of this ship

who doesn't have his head up his butt. I spoke with the National Meteorology Service to ask them if it's possible to make it rain here, and they laughed me off the phone."

Chris winced. It hadn't occurred to him to call anyone. He had made the decision to hire Cabrio on a whim. No, *more* than a whim. His decision had been based on a feeling so deep in his gut he couldn't name it or describe it.

He hadn't predicted this wrath, though, this outpouring of hostility. It was a lot like being booed off the mound.

From his vantage point at the window, Chris thought that Sam looked very tall up on that footstool—tall and slender and bespectacled and frail, just as he had looked as a boy. Chris and Sam had grown up in the same neighborhood in Valle Rosa, two of the handful of people who'd never left. Chris's love of Valle Rosa was matched only by Sam's.

"Someone dropped off a petition for you earlier." Mia lifted a few papers from her desk.

Chris turned away from the window. "A petition for what?"

"They want you to do something about the Mexican illegals who live in the canyons."

"I'm sure they do," he said, disgusted. "And they're Guatemalans. And Salvadorans. Not just Mexicans."

"Oh. Well, these people are complaining because they've had to put locks on their outside taps to keep the Mex . . . the undocumented workers from coming out of the canyons and using their water."

And they were the same people, he was certain, who hired the workers for ridiculous wages in the daytime hours. It was only at night, when the aliens were tired and hungry and thirsty, that they were asked to become invisible.

"There's no water for them in the canyons," Chris said wearily. "I guess we should just let them die, huh?"

Mia grimaced. "I think the signers of this petition would go along with that." She bit her lip, then spoke on a tentative note. "Chris?"

He smiled at her. "Give me some good news for a change, Mia, okay?"

"I'm afraid they've been putting stuff on the porch." Her voice was apologetic.

"What do you mean? What stuff?"

She nodded toward the window, and he stepped next to it at an angle, close enough to see out without being seen himself. The small porch of the office was littered with so much debris that at first he couldn't discern one object from another. Then he saw the avocados, small and dry and hard-looking, and the tiny, withered oranges, and the baskets of dehydrated strawberries and stunted ears of corn.

Mia moved next to him. "See the mice?" She wrinkled her nose.

"Mice?" Chris squinted into the rubble. It was a minute before he realized that the half-dozen or so clear plastic bags nestled among the fruits and vegetables were crammed with dead mice. "Shit," he said. "This is re-volting."

"There's Carmen." Mia pointed into the crowd.

Chris spotted her immediately. Dressed entirely in white, she stood out from the rest of the crowd. She was holding her microphone up to Braga; then she turned and spoke to one of the cameramen, her hands cutting through the air, her movements quick and sharp and assured.

"I guess I have to go out there," he said. At one time he'd had no fear of cameras, no fear of facing a mob of reporters. Carmen had groomed him for that part of public life, teaching him how to handle questions, how to modulate his voice. She'd denied having much to do with his success, though. "You have a natural presence in front of the camera," she'd told him. "You know how to make friends with it. It's a rare ability."

At the moment, he felt none of that old self-confidence. This crowd wasn't likely to be welcoming. His heart battered his rib cage, and the surge of fear he felt as he turned the doorknob reminded him of the day five years ago when he'd last faced a sea of reporters. He remembered struggling against tears that day— and failing.

The sun was blinding as he stepped onto the front porch, and he carefully cleared a space in the debris with his feet so he had a place to stand. The crowd turned in a wave, away from Sam Braga and his footstool, to face Chris. The reporters instantly began firing questions at him.

"What do you have to say to the transportation board?"

"Do you think you've made a wise decision?"

"What proof do you have that Cabrio can make it rain?"

Chris tried to smile, holding up his hands to still the crowd. He should have predicted this impromptu press conference today and worn something other than a T-shirt and shorts.

"Don't we already have enough problems?" a woman shouted from the street. "You're playing games with our lives and our livelihood."

The gathering responded with a fresh roar of indignation, and he held his hands up once again and waited for silence.

"I understand you have a lot of questions," he said when he thought he could be heard, "but for now, all I can tell you is that I take full responsibility for hiring Mr. Cabrio. I believe he'll succeed in helping Valle Rosa with its severe water problem, but I'm prepared to take the blame if he fails." He turned back to the door.

"Chris?"

He looked down to see that Carmen had elbowed her way to the front of the crowd. Her eyes were huge. Brown velvet. Mesmerizing.

"Where is Mr. Cabrio now?" she asked.

"He doesn't want to be disturbed," Chris said, and although he found it difficult to turn away from Carmen, he opened the door and walked inside.

He took a call at Mia's desk from the *Los Angeles Times*, telling the reporter exactly what he'd told the crowd. Then he walked back to his own office, opening the door to find Carmen sitting behind his desk.

"Jesus," he said, startled. "How did you get in?"

"Back door." She smiled. "You're lucky I was the only one who thought to check it. And look." She swept her arm through the air. "No cameras. No mikes. Just me."

"You've never needed a camera to be intimidating, Carmen." He sat down across the desk from her. Although the fire had nearly burned itself out, a papery chunk of ash clung to Carmen's hair where it curved softly over her shoulder. He resisted the temptation to reach over and brush it away.

"Where is he from?" she asked.

"I don't know."

"Come on, Chris. This is off the record."

He smiled. "Nothing's ever off the record with you."

She leaned forward. "I need a story, Chris. The fires are old news. Don't make me beg."

Her voice was strong, but there was a fear in her eyes he had never seen before. "I'm sorry, Carmen. I don't know anything about him to tell you."

"Where did he work before coming here?"

"I don't have any idea."

"I know you're not stupid enough to hire him without knowing *something* about him. Was he working in Ohio?"

Chris shrugged, suddenly glad he knew so little.

"Do you think I could interview him? Everybody's caught up in the *you* part of the story—you know, how Chris Garrett took one too many line drives to the head. So I could focus on *him*."

"He wants to be left alone." He smiled again. "And he's a little bit strange."

Carmen shuddered. "And you've invited him to live on my property. Thanks a lot."

He tried not to show any emotion when she called Sugarbush her property. "He's not dangerous. Actually, he's very likable."

"Look, Chris. I'm broke. They're paying me some sort of token salary at *News Nine*. I need to prove to them they need me."

"Why don't you go somewhere else? It'd be their loss."

"I spoke with Joe Simmons over at KCBJ. He was warm and friendly until he heard I was calling about work. He said, 'Let me be frank, Carmen. Forty would be one thing if you'd been working steadily on *Sunrise* and the ratings had stayed high. But to try to make a comeback at forty. Forget it.' He said he was surprised *News Nine* took me back at all."

Nice business she was in, Chris thought, although he knew that baseball hadn't been much better. "Maybe there's something else you could do. Some other kind of work?"

"Like what? Teaching high school?"

He sucked in his breath. "Low blow, Carmen."

She looked down at her hands, a rare blush staining her cheeks. "Sorry."

"I don't have a lot of money myself right now," he said. His money had been eaten up by medical bills. Carmen's. Dustin's. "But I can—"

"No."

"Just rent. You could be making money off that cottage if I wasn't in it."

She looked at her hands again, then cocked her head at him. "I'll tell you what you *could* do, if you think it's fair."

"What's that?"

"Well, the house needs work. I've got some plumbing problems, and the walls have really gotten dingy and can use a new coat of paint, and half the windows are stuck shut, and—"

"Yes." The idea delighted him. "I'd be happy to do some work in the house."

"When I'm not there," she added hastily.

"Fine. And let me at least pay for the paint and any materials I—"

"Chris." She groaned. "I don't want your money. Just give me Cabrio. Give me the story."

"I don't have a story to give you."

"Where is he now? Where's he holed up."

Chris hesitated. He saw that fear in her eyes again, passing through her like a spasm she couldn't control.

"In that abandoned warehouse by the reservation," he said.

She sat back, a triumphant gleam in her eye.

"Leave him alone, Carmen. Please. Let him work in peace."

She stood up to leave. "I won't disturb him," she said. "I promise."

8.

Jeff left his cottage before dawn and returned after dark, five days in a row. Mia watched him come and go. She'd be up early in the mornings, working on Henry, when she'd hear the banging of his screen door, and if she looked out her window she could barely make him out as he walked across Sugarbush through the lifting darkness. At night she watched for the beam of his flashlight as he walked from the driveway to his cottage. Inside his cottage, his lights stayed on no more than an hour before he turned them out, and she pictured him falling, exhausted, into bed. He hadn't been kidding when he told Chris he would give him all his waking hours.

Carmen had talked about him on the news. She hadn't improved his image, nor Chris's for having hired him. Jeff Cabrio was a loner, she reported, with no fixed address prior to his move to Valle Rosa. He was holed up in an abandoned warehouse on the rim of Cinnamon Canyon. There was one picture accompanying her report, a photograph obviously taken from a good distance away, of Jeff entering the warehouse.

Mia had had no opportunity to sketch him again, and

she was about to despair of ever getting the chance when he showed up at her door the sixth morning after his arrival. It was seven o'clock. She'd been working on Henry, and the sudden knock made her jump. She opened her door to find him standing there, the early morning gold of the sun lighting one half of his face and body.

"Didn't wake you, I hope," he began and then suddenly grabbed her arm. "What the hell did you do?" he asked.

For a moment, she was afraid. She pulled her arm away, holding it close to her chest. "What do you mean?"

He took her hand again, straightening her arm out in front of her. "What . . . God, it's paint!"

Mia looked down at the reddish stains on the inside of her forearm. "No," she said. "It's clay."

"*Clay*. I thought it was blood. Thought I had a suicide attempt on my hands." He shook his head, and she could see the relief in his face. "You know how it is, Mia. You try to keep a low profile, and you end up living on the property of a television journalist and a famous ex-ballplayer, and you innocently knock on your neighbor's door, thinking, what could be safer, and you end up spending the rest of the day in an emergency room with everyone asking you questions about yourself."

He was a madman. She drew her arm to her chest again. "You have an overactive imagination," she said.

"Maybe." He glanced toward the adobe, then back at her once more. "Could you do me a favor? Chris already left. He wanted me to stop by the office this morning, but I won't be able to. Sometime in the middle of the night I realized I'm off base with a few of my equations, and I need to get to the warehouse to work on them. Would you let him know that, please?"

"Sure." She had gotten his nose entirely wrong in her sketches. It was longer. There was the barest hint of a flare to his nostrils.

"Clay?" He peered behind her into the living room. "You're working with clay at seven in the morning?"

"Actually, I've been up since five."

He raised his eyebrows. "May I see?"

She stepped back to let him in. He walked across the plastic-covered carpet and sank to his knees in front of the orange crate. Henry grinned up at him. "Holy shit," he said softly, sitting back on his heels. "This is definitely not amateur hour."

"His name's Henry," she said.

He looked up at her. "You work down here on the floor?"

"Yes."

"You're going to destroy your back." He touched Henry's chin with tanned fingers. The hair on his arm was dark blond. "Terra cotta, right?"

She nodded, surprised.

"What did you use for an armature?"

She pointed to the wire armature on the coffee table.

Jeff ran his fingertips lightly over Henry's hair, and she knew he was hunting for a seam. "How did you get it out?"

She knelt on the floor next to him. "I cut him in two,

right where you're touching. Then I covered up my tracks."

He studied the top of Henry's head. "Excellent job," he said. "It's been a long time since I've seen something this realistic. It's not the kind of work most sculptors do these days, is it?"

"No. Figurative sculpting is not exactly 'in,' but I can't imagine doing anything else. Right now, though, I'm only into heads."

He touched Henry's rounded cheek. "You must have studied anatomy to be able to produce work like this."

"Yes." She'd had more figure study classes than she liked to remember. "How do you know so much about sculpting?"

He stood up again. "I know a little bit about a lot of things."

She pointed to the bulletin board covered with Henry's pictures. "He was a homeless man in San Diego. I paid him to let me shoot the pictures."

"Are you aware of how good you are?"

"Yes." She smiled.

"So why are you squirreled away out here in the middle of nowhere?"

"It's where I want to be."

His eyes narrowed as if he didn't believe her. "What will you work on next?"

Mia laughed as she got to her feet. "I was thinking about sculpting you."

A look of surprise crossed his features before he, too, laughed. "I wondered why you're always watching me.

You look at me as though you're trying to count the pores in my skin."

"Sorry." Her cheeks flushed, but she wasn't about to let this opportunity pass her by. "Would you consider it? Letting me sculpt you?"

"No, I don't think so."

"You wouldn't need to pose," she said quickly. "I could work from photographs, like I did with Henry."

He shook his head and began walking toward the door. "No, Mia. The thought of two dozen pictures of my face floating around is not too pleasant at the moment."

"They wouldn't float around, Jeff. They'd stay right here."

"Why not your boss?" he asked. "Why not sculpt Chris?"

"He's not right." Chris had boyish good looks and a roguish twinkle in his pale-blue eyes, but he wasn't a lure. "There isn't anything in his face."

"Maybe you're too young to remember this, Mia, but there were a lot of women who saw something in Chris Garrett's face over the years."

She frowned, annoyed. "It has nothing to do with being good-looking."

"Oh. Thanks."

"No, I mean, physical attractiveness is entirely beside the point. Have you ever really studied your face? They could use it to teach geometry. It's all rectangles and tri-angles and planes. The way Henry is all circles. Get it?"

Jeff dropped his gaze to Henry again, and she thought he actually did get it. He let out a sigh that seemed to drain him. "Are you sure you're not a plant for the dragon lady?" He nodded in the direction of the adobe, and it took Mia a moment to understand what he meant.

"I barely know Carmen," she said.

He opened the door and stepped onto her porch, turning back to face her. "This is against my better judgment, but you can take pictures of me in the warehouse if you like," he said. "It has to be within the next week or so, because after that we'll be using equipment that's too hazardous for you to be around." For a moment, he looked as though he might change his mind, and she plowed ahead.

"That's fine," she said. "I'll do it right away."

He hesitated again. "You'll tell absolutely no one what you see in there," he said, "and the pictures you take must never leave your hands. Understood?"

She wasted no time. On her way to work, she bought film, and during her lunch hour, drove the few miles to the warehouse. The building was low and huge and flat-roofed, the outside walls painted a dreary beige. It was surrounded by a few other colorless buildings, all of which looked as though they'd outlived their usefulness. There were no cars parked on the narrow street other than hers and Jeff's.

Rick unlocked the front door for her.

"Hey, Mia!" He was dressed only in baggy pink-and-yellow shorts. No shirt. No shoes. His skin was very dark in contrast to his blond-streaked hair. She had met him only once before, at Chris's office, but even then he had treated her as if they were old friends. "How's it going?" he asked.

"Fine, thanks." She stepped into the warehouse, her camera case over her shoulder and a peach in her hand. She followed Rick through a maze of bookcases and desks to the rear of the building. The warehouse was hot almost beyond endurance. It was a long shell of a building, made of metal and wood, with high, small windows scattered near the ceiling. A few of the windows held fans, which only served to drive home the fact that the air outside was scalding.

The warehouse was used for county storage, Rick explained as they walked. It was crammed full of file cabinets, desks, long tables, heavy wooden chairs, bookcases. There was nothing soft in the building, nothing to break the echo of her shoes clicking on the concrete floor or to absorb the low, constant hum of the fans.

She was surprised to see a flatbed truck parked along one wall of the building.

"How did it get in?" she asked, and Rick pointed to a huge garage door in front of the truck.

As they neared the rear of the warehouse, she saw that a space, perhaps thirty feet square, had been cleared of furniture, save one long table and two chairs. The table was littered with papers, and Jeff sat hunched over them, his back to Mia and Rick as they approached.

"Photographer's here," Rick announced, and Jeff looked up from the table. He was shirtless, too. She hadn't counted on that.

"Hi, Mia." He gave a faint nod in her direction before returning his attention to his work.

"You two go ahead with what you were doing," she said. "I'll be quiet." She set her peach on one of the desks.

Whatever they were doing wasn't what she'd expected. But then, what *had* she expected? Some sort of heavy labor, at the very least. How did you make it rain? At the edge of the cleared space stood six large rectangular boxes that looked like enormous stereo speakers. On the desk was a computer terminal which was absorbing Rick's attention. That was it. And paper. There was paper everywhere. Piles of it on the boxes. Disorganized heaps of it on the table. Jeff had a few sheets on his lap. It seemed that most of their work was on paper at this point, and those sheets she glimpsed appeared to be covered with equations. When Rick and Jeff spoke to each other, it was in numbers. Kilometers and liters and grams. If anyone had asked her under the threat of torture exactly what it was they were doing in the warehouse, she honestly couldn't have said.

For the most part, they ignored her, which was fine. She took off her shoes so she could walk around quietly, and discovered that the floor was surprisingly cool beneath her feet. This would be difficult, though. It wasn't like the other times she'd taken photographs of a model to use in her work. She'd posed those people, then circled them, snapping pictures, getting every angle of that particular pose. But Jeff was moving, fluid. It would take many more shots to get what she needed.

She was near the large boxes when a cat slipped by her legs, startling her, making her gasp.

"That's Eureka." Rick looked up. "My roommate. She hates staying home by herself."

Mia reached down to pet the cat, but Rick stopped her with a hand on her arm.

"I wouldn't do that if I were you," he said. "She's got a nasty streak. Scratches everyone but me."

Mia watched Eureka slink over to the table and leap into Jeff's lap. He kept his eyes on his work, but sank one hand into the cat's long white fur and began to stroke her. She could hear Eureka purring.

"Almost everyone," Rick said.

Mia used her zoom lens so she didn't need to disturb Jeff by getting too close to him, although she wasn't sure it would matter. He barely seemed aware of her presence. Her film was fast, yet the dim light of the warehouse demanded a slow shutter speed, and with every picture she took she was aware of the sluggish *click-whoosh* of the shutter.

Occasionally Jeff passed a sheet of paper across the table to Rick, sometimes saying a few words to the younger man, who then typed figures into the computer. The limp breeze from the fans caught edges of the papers, lifted their corners, and Mia closed her eyes now and then to listen to the humming of the fans, the quiet flutter of paper, the occasional soft, echoing voice. Once she dropped her lens cap and the sound reverberated around the walls. Jeff and Rick turned in her direction for a few seconds before bending their heads once more over the littered table.

The shirtlessness was a problem. She didn't want or need that much of him in her pictures. She focused on his head, the structure of the bones, the detail of his ear, the lines on his skin. But her old training soon took over and her eyes were drawn downward to his deltoids, lats, pectorals. They were not the muscles of a man accustomed to hard physical labor, yet they were well-defined; he had little fat on his body. The lines of his torso were sharp and angular, like the lines of his face, and before she knew it, she had taken a half dozen shots of his chest with its light smattering of golden-brown hair.

"So, how come that camera's never pointed at me, huh?" Rick asked, and Mia jerked her camera away from Jeff's body at the sound of his voice.

Rick was grinning, leaning away from the computer terminal. "What's he got that I don't have?"

"Maybe I'll do you next," she lied.

Jeff looked up from his papers, and for a second, his gaze locked with hers. There was exhaustion in his eyes, and something else. Some sadness. She couldn't turn away until he shut his eyes, taking his hand from Eureka to rub his left shoulder, rolling his head on his neck as if trying to ease some stiffness.

"We're going to have to turn these fans around," he said to Rick. "They'll do us more good blowing hot air out than in." He stood up, letting the cat jump to the floor. He stepped around the table and leaned over Rick's shoulder to study the terminal, his hands resting on the back of Rick's chair. Mia walked slowly behind them, snapping three more pictures before her film ran out, all the while incorporating his chest, his back, his arms, and a few inches of his khaki shorts into her imagined sculpture of him.

She put her camera in its case and picked up the peach. The men were engrossed in something on the terminal screen.

"Sorry to interrupt," she said, "but may I come back with another roll of film tomorrow?"

"Sure, Mia," Jeff said absently, not even bothering to shift his eyes from the screen.

But Rick lifted his head and grinned at her. "That's the roll for me, right?"

9.

It felt strange to give Chris a key to the adobe, and Carmen did it in an off-handed way, leaving it in an envelope with his mail on the steps of his cottage. She didn't want to humiliate him, didn't want to make a show of the fact that the house was hers and not his. Chris was suffering enough these days, although she'd once thought that all the suffering in the world was less than he deserved. Nevertheless, the way the media was tearing him apart distressed her. He'd asked for it, though, when he hired Cabrio. Perhaps now that she had regained her sanity, he was losing his.

Her suggestion that he do some work in the adobe had been impulsive, and she regretted making it when he so readily accepted. She wasn't certain how it would feel to allow him back into the house when she had so ferociously banished him from it. He loved that house. When they were first dating, he'd take her for long afternoon drives through the sprawling reaches of Valle Rosa, always going out of his way to pass Sugarbush and the run-down adobe at its core, always telling her his dream of owning it one day. He told her so often that the dream began to seem like her own. Now the property he had longed for was hers alone, but only in her weakest moments did she feel she had been cruel in keeping Sugarbush for herself.

He had said he would work in the house when she wasn't there, and so she didn't realize he'd started until one morning when she was dressing for a doctor's appointment and noticed the spackle on the walls of the bedroom. She walked around the house, and discovered he'd spackled the walls in the living room as well, and that the windows in the kitchen no longer protested when she tried to open them. The evidence of his presence warmed her one minute and gave her a chill the next, and she couldn't stop thinking about it until she'd pulled into the parking lot of the medical building in La Jolla.

There were two other women in the apricot-colored waiting room. They looked up from their magazines as Carmen walked in, and she saw the light of recognition in their eyes and heard the slight intake of breath. They quickly lowered their faces back to their magazines, smiles spreading, as they thought about the calls they would make later that day to their friends: *Guess who I saw at the plastic surgeon's this morning?*

She knew it was the streak of silver in her hair that gave her away. It began at her left temple and carved a sleek path through the jet-black of her long hair. She'd had the streak since her teens, when it had been a novelty, and through her twenties and early thirties, when it became a symbol of caricature. Once a political cartoonist had drawn a sketch of her after her rigorous *Sunrise* interview of former governor Jerry Brown, and there was that streak in the cartoon, as distinctive as ever. She cursed it now. It seemed to have doubled its width, like a testimony to the wretchedness of the last few years. She had thought of dyeing it, but then people would talk even more.

After signing in with the receptionist, Carmen took a seat on the opposite side of the room from the other women and pretended to lose herself in a magazine. She glanced at the women from time to time, trying to discern why they were there. One was small-breasted, although in any other setting she wouldn't have noticed. Was that the reason for her visit, or was it the slight knob on the bridge of her nose or the sagging line of her jaw?

God, was she really going to go through with this? She'd always looked at women who resorted to plastic surgery with disdain, thinking that she would graciously accept her own aging. She had been confident that her intelligence and skill would be enough to carry her through.

Yesterday, Tom Forrest, a retired reporter and a man she had long considered her mentor, visited her on the set of *News Nine*. Tom had taken her under his wing many years earlier, when she was a twenty-four-year-old intern at the station. She was too sweet, he'd told her then. Too soft, and entirely too subjective. He'd taught her how to mask her softness with a tough facade, how to keep her emotional distance when a story threatened to pull her too deeply under its spell. She had mastered everything he'd taught her, and then some.

She was surprised to see Tom, surprised by the sober, business-like way he greeted her. He had put on weight since the last time she'd seen him, and his teddy-bear frumpiness now had an unhealthy air to it. He took her out for a cup of coffee, since there was no place at the station where they could talk privately. And it was obvious that privacy was what he wanted.

"I've always given it to you straight, Carmen, and I'm not going to mince words with you now," he said, once they were seated in the restaurant. "I'm not going to tell you my sources, either, so don't ask."

"What are you talking about?"

He leaned forward, hands resting flat on the table. "Rumor has it that they were going to can you after the fires were out. No one saw much point to keeping you around."

She didn't let the shock register on her face. She studied the shape of his eyes, his graying eyebrows— something he had taught her to do a lifetime ago—to reduce the chance of her crying. Tom Forrest wouldn't respect her tears.

"It seems they're changing their minds, though," he continued. "At least they're holding off on making a decision."

"Why?" Her voice was barely audible.

"Because of the bits of info you're passing on about Jeff Cabrio. They're waiting to see how that story develops. They want to see what you'll do with it." He shook his head. "You've been away too long, Carmen. It shows, honey. I think Cabrio's your only chance."

Carmen had leaned back in her chair, trying to absorb his words. He had never, in all the years she'd known him, called her 'honey.' She must seem very small and powerless to him.

What else could she say about Jeff Cabrio? She had little to offer in the way of facts, but she had always excelled at embellishment. The night before, she'd shown a short film of Jeff and Rick unloading two large vats from a truck and rolling them into the warehouse, and she'd speculated over what possible use they might make of them in their avowed quest for rain.

"Milk the Cabrio story for all its worth, Carmen," Tom said, as they left the restaurant, but she had already made up her mind to do exactly that.

There were two doctors seeing patients, and so Carmen's wait wasn't very long. Lynn Sulley called her into a small office, the gently curving walls again a pale apricot, the carpet thick and deep green. Pictures of beautiful women lined the walls. Carmen wanted to look at them, but kept her eyes on Lynn's face instead, wondering which of them was older. Lynn Sulley looked no more than thirty-five.

Lynn offered her a warm smile, which Carmen tried to return, but the sensation felt unnatural to her face. She sat down in one of the black leather armchairs, while Lynn sat in the other.

"I'm very pleased to meet you, Ms. Perez," the doctor said. "I've been an admirer of yours for a long time. I'm so happy to see you back on the news."

"Thank you." Carmen folded her hands in her lap. "That's why I'm here, though. When I see myself on TV

these days, I'm shocked to see . . . well, I'm just shocked."
For a terrible moment, she thought she might cry.

Lynn Sulley rescued her. "You're an extraordinary-
looking woman," she said, her voice calm. "What spe-
cifically are you here for?"

"Well, I thought . . . a face-lift." She touched her hands
to her cheeks. "Just to . . . lose a few years."

Lynn sat back in her chair. She was still smiling, but
Carmen suddenly read condescension into the curve of
her lips. She rested her damp palms flat on her skirt,
waiting.

"You've had a very difficult few years, haven't you,"
she said.

"Yes. And every one of them shows on my face."

"Let me go over a little history with you, just to be sure
I have it straight from a medical standpoint. You had a
couple of miscarriages and then gave birth to a child who
suffered some sort of sudden illness, which resulted in
severe brain damage. Is that right?"

My God, was this woman going to make her go
through it all? Here? Now?

"Dr. Sulley," she said, striving for coolness in her
voice. "I don't see what that has to do with getting a face-
lift. I don't see why my history should matter more than
anyone else's."

"It doesn't. I would want to know these things about
any patient I'm considering treating because they factor
into how good a candidate you are for plastic surgery."

She would go someplace else. She could stand up now
and walk out of the office while her dignity was still intact.

But she couldn't move. Her arms and legs were leaden.

"For example," Lynn continued, "I know you suffered a major depression after your son's birth. You were hospitalized for quite a while, right?"

"The injustice," Carmen leaned forward, "is that you already know my history. Everyone does. The women in the waiting room, who are free to tell you what they choose about the past few years—even *they* know what's happened to me. Why can't you let me tell it?"

"Fine," she said. "Please go ahead."

Carmen looked down at her hands and felt some alarm to see she was clutching the fabric of her skirt in her fists. "Yes, I gave birth to a sick child, and I had severe postpartum depression that required a period of time in the hospital. Then I was divorced from my husband, and of course that was quite difficult. I took some time off from work to deal with all of that. Anyone would have had some trouble coping under those circumstances, don't you agree?"

"Of course. I'm not saying—"

"And now that I'm healthy and back on the job, I'm aware that I've aged during . . . the ordeal. So I want to do something about it."

"Forgive me." Lynn Sulley sat forward. "You're a public figure, and therefore I can't simply accept what you're telling me when I know there's more to it than that. I know you tried to kill yourself, and that you were addicted to pain medication. I know it's taken you four full years to be able to work again. I'm not saying this to upset you, but to help you see my position here. The addiction would rule out your being able to take any pain killers, and most women find them necessary after facial surgery."

"I can do without them."

She shook her head. "I believe this is the wrong time for you to make a decision about this type of surgery. I think your expectations may be too high. And you've just gotten back to work. Give yourself six months. You'll be less fragile then and—"

"I am not fragile." Carmen stood up. "What do I have to do to make people see that?"

Lynn Sulley stood up too and rested her hand on Carmen's arm. "You know," she said, "the first time I ever saw you on TV was after the plane crash back in '78. You were there just minutes after the plane went down, and I'll never forget how cool and calm you were with all that chaos going on around you. I remember saying to myself, 'That is one strong woman. How can she do it?' I wondered then if there was any softness in you at all. But there's a lot in there, isn't there? It's buried, but it's there. And that's okay. That's good."

Carmen withdrew her arm and picked up her purse from the floor. "Thank you for seeing me," she said.

"Go easy on yourself," Lynn said. "Give yourself a little more time."

She wanted a drink, a beer or two, something to numb her, but she hadn't given in to that urge in four years, and she wouldn't give in to it today. She forced herself to drive past the 7-Eleven without stopping on her way to the freeway. She could go home, get into bed and pull the covers over her head. That thought terrified her more than the temptation of a drink. She'd done that many times before—escaped into sleep—but not since she'd been well.

Traffic on the freeway was light and gave her time to think. She remembered back to the plane crash. A commercial jet and a small private plane had collided over North Park and dropped onto the houses below in a ball of fire. She had been one of the first reporters at the scene, and she hadn't been prepared for what she found. No one had. No caring human being could possibly have been prepared for that nightmare. When she'd stepped out of the van, she'd stepped directly on something that cracked beneath her foot. She'd looked down to see the severed hand of a child. And that had been only the beginning. She was surrounded by smoky carnage. Bodies had been torn apart, arms and legs caught in the limbs of trees above her head. Leaning against a nearby house was an airplane seat, the headless torso of a man still strapped securely to it by the seat belt. Already the stench of death was mixing with the smoke in the hot summer air.

The camera was on her in mere seconds, and she focused on it, on her job. She could do that easily back then; Tom Forrest had taught her well. That ability to shut down her feelings long enough to do what needed to be done, no matter how grisly the task, had been her finest skill. It wasn't until she got home that night that she allowed herself to fall apart, and it was Chris who pieced her back together again, Chris who held cool towels to the back of her neck while she battled nausea on the bathroom floor, Chris who comforted her when she couldn't sleep, when she woke up with nightmares. It was the knowledge that she would be going home to him after work that got her through those terrible few days.

Shortly before the crash, she had come up with the idea for *San Diego Sunrise*, but she hadn't been able to convince anyone at *News Nine* that she had the strength and guts it would take to pull off a show like that. Her coverage of the crash erased their doubts, and she was given the go-ahead within days. *News Nine* had been the beneficiary of her foresight and talent. Now, though, they were ready—anxious, it seemed—to get rid of her.

Carmen deliberately missed the exit that would take her out to Sugarbush. Instead she drove down Jacaranda, heading for the block-long "heart" of Valle Rosa. She turned onto Verde and parked across the street from the mayor's office. Chris's car was there. She opened her window and sat, keeping her eyes on the small, run-down building, feeling safe from the beer in the market, safe from the seductive lure of her bed and the sleep of a coward. She wouldn't go into the office. She wasn't about to let Chris know she still needed him. She wasn't even ready to admit it to herself.

10.

Mia was editing a letter when the phone rang. She picked up the receiver, tucking it between her chin and shoulder. "Mayor's office."

"Sunny?"

Stunned, she let the pencil fall from her grasp. "*Glen.*"

"You know, I don't understand your obstinacy, Sunny. Why won't you give Laura your home phone number?"

"I don't have a phone. I don't want one."

"You have an address, don't you? I mean, I can understand not wanting *me* to have it, but she's your sister, Sunny. She's all the family you have left. What if there was an emergency? What if she needed you?"

"She's never needed me. Besides, she has this number. Apparently you do, too."

He was quiet for a moment, and when he spoke again his voice had lost its bite. "Are you well?" he asked. "Are you keeping up with your doctor's visits?"

"I'm fine, and I'm going to get off now."

"No, Sunny, wait. I called you for a reason. You and I have been invited to be in the Lesser Gallery's local artisans show next month."

Mia was silent. It wasn't like Glen to tease, yet she found it hard to believe the Lesser would want either of them. She couldn't remember ever seeing their type of work in that show.

"You've been struck dumb." Glen laughed. "I was too, at first. Seems they're more open to figurative sculpting this year for some reason. So let's not fight it."

"But, me? I can understand them taking something of yours, but . . ."

"Let me tell you. The three committee members came here to my studio last week and they went straight to your stuff along the back wall. They simply gaped at it. To be honest, I was afraid they were going to select you and *not* me."

She felt a quick, unwanted rush of love for him. It was kind of him to say that, whether it was the truth or not.

"They were blown away by your mother and her yarn. Simply blown away. They kept walking back to it. One of the women came back the next day and took pictures of it to use in the brochure."

She closed her eyes. It had been so long since she'd seen that sculpture. All her work was still at Glen's studio. She missed working there, with the sunlight pouring through the skylights. She missed *him*.

"Which of yours did they like best?" she asked.

It was a moment before he answered. "The nude of you."

"Glen." She leaned forward on the desk. "Please don't put that in the show."

"Who's going to know it's you? Your hair was long

then, and you've got that hat on." He didn't mention the most significant difference between her body in the sculpture and her body now, but it was foremost in Mia's mind, and undoubtedly in his as well.

"*I'll* know," she said.

"They loved it, Sunny. I have to put it in. And you, my dear old friend, are going to have to come to San Diego for a few days in July to set up your work."

She felt the sharp unexpected sting of tears. "No. I can't do that. I'm settled in here."

"Don't be a lunatic, Mia. You can't pass up an opportunity like this. They want to use your work in their bloody brochure, for Christ's sake."

"Could you set it up for me? I know that's asking a lot, but . . ." She hesitated, biting her lower lip. "Glen, I just don't want to see you. I don't want to see Laura, either. I'm doing all right here. Please, Glen. Will you do it for me?"

He sighed. "Which pieces do you want?"

"You pick," she said, and she hung up the phone before he could say anything more.

It was past six when she arrived at the warehouse that evening, and Rick looked surprised to see her when he opened the door.

"I couldn't make it at noon," she said. "Is now okay?"

"Hey, anytime's okay with me, Mia." He lifted Eureka off the floor and draped her over his shoulder like a fluffy white boa as they walked to the rear of the building.

It was almost cool in the warehouse. Jeff was standing

on a chair set against the rear wall, working with the window fan.

"Jeff fixed the fans so we can bring the cool air in at night and blow out the hot during the day," Rick said.

Jeff stepped off the chair, glancing at her as he sat down on the edge of the long table. He lifted a stack of papers onto his thigh. "Can't stay away, huh?" he said. He was wearing a blue shirt, unbuttoned, but still covering all she had planned to concentrate on tonight. She was disappointed.

"I'm going to need a couple more rolls," she said. "It would be different if I just took them of you in one pose, the way I did with Henry. But here you're moving around and it's more difficult. Plus, I figured I should try a different speed film tonight." She was rambling, rather defensively, and he wasn't interested. He nodded at her and returned his concentration to the stack of papers, frowning, already lost in his work.

"We're in the middle of a problem here," Rick explained.

"I won't disturb you." She sat down on one of the desks to change lenses.

Jeff's eyes were lowered in nearly every one of the shots she had taken the day before, but she didn't feel she could ask him to raise his head. She was afraid of wearing out her welcome.

"No way around it," Jeff said to Rick. "These numbers won't work with this size trans-hydrator. Either we have to double the size, or double the amount we use. How big did you say that avocado grove by the gully is?"

"Ten acres," Rick said. "Maybe twelve."

Jeff walked over to a map they had tacked to the back of a bookcase. He rubbed his chin as he studied it.

"Jeff?" she said.

"Hmm?" He didn't turn to look at her.

"I'm sorry to ask this, but—"

"You apologize a lot, Mia, are you aware of that?" he asked, his eyes still fixed on the map. He traced a line with his finger across part of Valle Rosa.

"I . . . no, I didn't realize that. I'm sor—I mean, I was wondering if you would mind taking off your shirt."

Rick's head shot up, but still Jeff didn't look at her, although there was the faintest suggestion of a smile on his lips. "I thought you were just into heads these days," he said.

"Well, yes, I was. But I've changed my mind." She felt the heat creeping up her neck to her face.

Jeff slipped a yellow-headed pin into the map. "That blush must be a terrible liability, Mia."

How did he know she was blushing?

"I'm used to working with nude models," she said. "I mean, it's no huge deal to me. If you'd rather not, it's fine."

He turned to face her, the near smile warming the cool lock of his eyes. "It's chilly in here tonight," he said. "You'll have to come back during the day when it's warmer."

She nodded. "All right."

Jeff sat down again and took a long pull on a bottle of birch beer while she set about changing to another roll of film. Her hands were shaking, and she felt perspiration on her back. She would keep her idiotic mouth shut from now on.

She focused then on his hands, using the zoom, not daring to get too close. His hands were slender and dark, dusted with golden-brown hair, the nails clean and smooth. A second sculpture, she thought. It had been a long time since she'd done hands.

He stood up suddenly, and she lowered the camera. "Be back in a second," he said, more to Rick than to her. He walked through the maze of furniture toward the side of the building, and she gave Rick a questioning look.

"The can," he said.

"Oh."

Rick returned his attention to the keyboard, and Mia sat still, listening to the soft clicking of the keys against the background of humming fans.

"Oh no!" Rick said suddenly. "Oh shit." He grabbed his head with his hands, and looked up at Mia. "I went to save the data and I pushed the wrong key," he was nearly whispering. "I lost everything he was working on this afternoon. He'll kill me."

"With one key?" She leaned toward him, whispering too. "Is there any way to get it back?"

He shook his head and stared at the screen. "It's totally gone. I don't believe I did that. Oh, shit, man. I'm going to leave and you can tell him," he said, and she hoped he was joking.

They heard Jeff's footsteps returning across the concrete floor, and Rick looked at her with a resigned sort of panic in his eyes. Mia tensed as Jeff sat down on the table again.

"Jeff," Rick shook his head. "I'm sorry, man, I really blew it."

"What do you mean?"

"I mean I, like, created a catastrophe. I lost the sub-area data."

Jeff's eyes widened. She needed a shot of his eyes like that, but was too paralyzed to snap a picture. "All of it?" he asked.

Rick threw up his hands. "I just . . . I hit the wrong key."

Jeff walked around behind Rick to study the computer screen. He rested his hands on the younger man's shoulders.

"This is not a catastrophe," he said, studying the screen with narrowed eyes. "Catastrophes are when farmers lose everything they've worked for all their lives because there's no rain, or when little kids die in fires nobody can put out."

Mia thought she saw tears in Rick's eyes, and she lowered her own eyes to her camera.

"Let me sit here," Jeff said.

Rick moved, and Jeff quickly took his seat, pressing a few keys on the keyboard. When he paused to study the screen, lips pursed together, Mia lifted her camera to get a shot of his eyes. Through her lens, they looked very tired.

"You'll have to create it all over again," Rick said.

"There are worse things I've had to do in my life." Jeff

frowned at the screen. There was a crease between his eyebrows, a few lines at the corner of each eye. Mia snapped her shutter. She would never be able to settle on one expression for him.

Jeff pressed another key and sat back, smiling. "Look." He pointed to the screen and Rick broke into a grin.

"You got it back! I don't believe it. How the hell did you do that?"

"The data was still in there. It only needed some coaxing. I'll write down what I did so if it ever happens again you can take care of it yourself."

Rick sank into the other chair. "I'm drained, man. I was about to find a bridge to jump off."

"Hey." Jeff turned to grasp Rick's arm and give it a shake. "Don't talk like that," he said, with a seriousness that left Rick speechless. "Don't even joke about it, okay? Nothing in your life is ever going to be that bad."

The closest one-hour developing service was thirty miles away, but Mia didn't think twice about making the drive. She ate dinner at a sterile, family-style restaurant next door to the shop while she waited for the prints.

She barely managed to make it to her car before ripping open the packages and pulling out the photographs. Studying them in the overhead light of her car, she tore through them with what she refused to admit to herself was more than an artist's zeal. In an instant she knew the pose she wanted. He was standing up, his blue shirt open a few inches, a stack of papers in his hand. His eyes were raised upward to look at the map, and a few lines were carved deeply into his forehead. He looked tired. Troubled. He looked *afraid*. She hadn't noticed that before, but it was unmistakable. Afraid of what? That he would fail in this? She would leave out the stack of papers. Open the shirt wider. And she would give him a background, a context. A bas-relief of a window. He would look out the window, one hand on the sill, troubled by whatever it was he saw out there.

The photographs she had of him without the shirt were excellent. Perfect. No reason—or excuse—to make a nuisance of herself at the warehouse again. Fine. She would get started on this the following night.

Mia pulled into Sugarbush at nine-thirty. Carmen's Volvo was there, and Chris's Oldsmobile, but Jeff wasn't yet home. She pictured him and Rick still hunched over their endless sheets of numbers, and wondered if Carmen had said anything about him on the news that evening.

Under the good light in her kitchen, she studied the prints again, pulling out those she would use to guide her in the sculpture, piling the others separately. Jeff still hadn't gotten home by the time she went to bed. She opened her shade so that if she lay close to the edge of her bed, she could see his cottage. She didn't close her eyes. One lone coyote started his imploring howl, and she pulled her blanket tighter around her in the darkness, remembering Glen's phone call. For the first time since moving to Valle Rosa, she felt alone. Lonely. Ironic that having two people living closer to her only seemed to make her loneliness more apparent.

Was Jeff lonely? Was he married? Did he have a lover somewhere?

What if he came over when he got home? Maybe she should leave a light on in the living room to let him know she was still up. *Do you know how good you are?* They could talk about her sculpting. She could make him a cup of tea. He'd looked so tired at seven. By now he'd be exhausted. She could rub his shoulders.

The fantasy was unexpected, unsolicited. Completely unwanted, and yet tenacious. She pushed it from her mind, only to have it sneak in again when she let her thoughts wander.

All right, so he'd stop over. He'd walk into her living room, lean wearily against the wall. He wouldn't talk much. He'd just be a walking need. "I'm sick of being alone," he'd say, "And you looked pretty good to me tonight in the warehouse."

No. He didn't talk that way. And he hadn't really looked at her at all in the warehouse. He'd more or less simply tolerated her presence. She might as well have been snapping pictures of the furniture for all he'd responded to her.

So he wouldn't say much. Perhaps he would say nothing at all. He'd reach for her, hold her. A long embrace fed by exhaustion and the need to touch another human being.

That thought alone brought tears to Mia's eyes. Just to hold someone. To have someone hold her. It had been so long.

The coyote bayed again, miserably, and was answered

by no one. Mia brushed tears from her cheeks with her fingertips.

He would hold her, and then, not thinking, he'd kiss her. The kiss would be a little hard, a little desperate. She would feel the day's growth of beard on her cheeks and chin. She would open her mouth for him—she wouldn't be able to stop herself. And then . . .

And then what? There was no place for the fantasy to go but up in smoke.

She climbed out of bed, cursing herself, cursing her crazy imagination. She pulled the shades, blocking out Jeff's cottage, and stomped into the living room, where she sat on the floor and began slapping clay onto the board she would use for the bas-relief of the window. She kneaded the red clay, crammed her fingers into it, pounded it, and then, suddenly, stilled her hands to listen.

He was walking across Sugarbush. She heard him take a step onto the porch of his cottage. Then the footsteps started again, this time approaching her own cottage. She froze, her fingers in the clay.

He knocked at her door. "Mia?"

She was in her yellow cotton nightshirt, and her hands were caked with clay. She wiped them quickly on a rag and opened the door.

There were gray circles under his eyes. "It's after midnight and I saw your light was still on," he said. "Just wanted to be sure you're okay." He noticed the clay stains on her hands and shook his head with his tired half-smile. "You're driven, aren't you? When do you sleep?"

"You're a fine one to talk."

"Mmm," he said. "Right. Your neck's bothering you, huh?"

She started to shake her head no, but then realized she was holding her neck with her left hand as a way to keep her arm strategically placed over the flat left plane of her chest. "A little," she said.

"Shouldn't work down there on the floor."

"You're probably right." She thought about the cup of tea, the desperate embrace, the kiss that would leave her nowhere to go.

"Well, 'night," he said, turning.

"Thanks for stopping by," she said.

She closed the door softly, then walked into her bedroom and sat down on the floor by the window to watch him walk back to his own cottage. The coyote struck up his howling again, this time joined by a host of his friends, and Jeff looked out to the canyon before opening his cottage door and closing himself inside for the night. The lights flicked on in his cottage, and he walked past one of the windows. She raised her right hand to her lips. Her fingers smelled of clay, of earth. Closing her eyes, she let her hand trace a line over her cheeks, her chin, her throat, let it drift to her right breast, cupping its light weight in her palm.

She hadn't counted on him. She hadn't counted on her neediness. And she hadn't counted on the traitorous stirrings of a body she had tried to put in cold storage.

11.

Chris stood on the rim of the canyon, two miles from Sugarbush, looking down at what was left of the small neighborhood in which he'd grown up. The five houses had been leveled, except for their chimneys, which rose Stonehenge-like from the charred rubble, and the refrigerators and stoves, hulking and black. The manzanita trees which had graced this little valley were nothing more than eerie black skeletons against the red sky. The air hurt to breathe, and he tied his handkerchief over his nose and mouth.

It had been a freak set of circumstances, the fire chief had told him, that set off this newest fire and allowed it to jump the wall of the canyon to the pocket of five homes nestled together on the other side.

"First, you had the extremely high temperature," the fire chief had said, as he stood on Chris's cottage porch that morning. Behind him, the sun had been rising, filling the air with the terrible red glow of a recent, too-close fire. Puffs of ash had floated in the air around the fire chief's shoulders and littered Chris's cottage porch, and the chief's face had been black with soot and grime.

"Then you had the low humidity," he'd continued, "and the gusty winds." He'd described how the wind had carried embers from fires miles away, how once the chaparral around the houses was ignited, the wild blasts of wind fanned the flames into an inferno. "An electrical fire knocked out the pumping station around midnight," he'd added, "so the hydrants were dry. We just had to let the houses burn. It was a miracle no one was killed."

Chris tried to listen, tried to nod at the appropriate places in the fire chief's monologue, but he was thinking only of getting out to the little valley and seeing for himself what had become of his childhood home.

The house in which he'd grown up was the one closest to where he now stood. His father had built it, and Chris had always thought of the small ranch-style house—of this entire little tract of homes—as a tribute to Augie Garrett's pioneering spirit. Both of Chris's parents had grown up in the Midwest. When they married—very young—they headed for California, egging each other on with fantasies of adventure. They found San Francisco and Los Angeles, and even San Diego, too cosmopolitan for their tastes, however, and headed into the more rural areas until they reached Valle Rosa, where they encountered a network of similarly disillusioned city-dwellers. Augie came up with the idea of creating their own community outside the town. He found this little valley, and he and four other families worked together to build the small, functional houses that had rested there for forty-five years. The original families were long gone. As a matter of fact,

Chris and Sam Braga were the only people from the neighborhood still living in Valle Rosa.

Beyond the remains of the houses, Chris could see the horse pasture. From where he stood, it looked as though the fire hadn't touched it, although it was gray with a coating of ash. Why it was called the horse pasture, Chris didn't know. He had never seen a horse in it, and when he looked at that stretch of ash-covered earth, all he could see was himself out there as a boy, Augie coaching him in his pitching.

Frail little Sam Braga had practiced with them for a while. By the time Chris was eleven years old, though, his fast ball was so dangerous that Mrs. Braga forbade her son to play with him any longer. Sam's own father was a writer, erudite and serious and not much fun for a growing boy. Even at that age, Chris knew Sam was jealous of the relationship he had with Augie.

Mrs. Braga had many complaints about Chris and Augie. "A son should not call his father by his first name," she'd tell Augie in her attempts to reform him. "Chris should study more. Baseball is not the only thing in life. He's turning into a wild boy in a household without a woman's touch."

It *had* been a household without a woman's touch. Chris's parents had been married only three years when his mother died, and she hadn't had the chance to leave a lasting mark on the house. It became a male haven. Not dirty—Augie had too much pride in the house he'd built to let it go to seed—but he and Chris ate whatever they felt like eating whenever they felt like eating it, and they talked baseball day and night, Augie grilling his son on statistics the way other parents grilled their children on the times tables. Sometimes Augie would let Chris skip school so they could practice out in the horse pasture, and in the spring he'd pull him completely out of his classes for a week so they could go to Arizona to watch the Padres at training camp.

As Chris got older, he began to make his own rules for when he should skip school, and he was in trouble with his teachers more often than not.

"You come by your wildness naturally," Augie once told him. "Even your mother was a crazy lady. We were both drunk off our asses the night of the accident. At least I can tell myself she felt no pain."

Augie had been pitching in the minor leagues at the time of the accident, and his leg was destroyed, shattered, leaving him with a permanent limp. He'd been a promising pitcher, and he rued his missed opportunities. He tried to make up for them through his son, doing everything he could to build Chris's confidence in himself as a ball player. When he'd stop in Chris's bedroom at night, he'd tell him, "You're going to be the best there is, son," and out in the horse pasture, he'd jump up and down and whistle and yell every time Chris pitched something so fast and so smooth that Augie couldn't even see it whisk past him.

By the time Chris was seventeen, though, Augie Garrett had changed his tune. Chris was playing baseball both in high school and in a local league, and he told

Augie he no longer felt nervous before a game, that he knew he was the best there was.

"There's such a thing as being too confident," Augie warned him, but by that time nothing could hurt Chris's image of himself.

The press picked up on it later, painting him not as conceited exactly, but as very sure of himself. "The fans relax whenever Garrett takes to the mound," one sportscaster said of him. "He is simply nerveless out there." The fans loved being able to depend on him. They loved *him.* The problem was, the more they loved a ballplayer, the more they invested in him, the more bitter their disappointment when he let them down.

Did anyone remember him as confident? He had forgotten the feeling himself. It had been replaced by guilt. He'd failed the people in his life. Not only his fans, but Carmen and his father and his son. And now he was the scapegoat for all that was wrong with Valle Rosa. Somehow, that didn't seem unreasonable. It felt like a perfectly logical role for him to play these days.

Chris had been standing on the rim of the canyon for several minutes before he realized that someone was down there, digging in the rubble of the house farthest from him. It was a woman, her dark hair and black shorts and sooty T-shirt blending into the charred remains of the house. Only the white mask over her nose and mouth had caught his eye.

He walked toward her through the burned chaparral.

"Hello!" he called when he reached what would have

been the outside wall of the house. It seemed rude to step inside without an invitation.

She was kneeling near the center of the house, a cardboard box at her side, and she turned to look at him. "Do I know you?" she asked, her voice muffled by the mask.

"No." He stepped over the burned wall into what had once been the kitchen, skirting the blackened refrigerator that lay on its side in front of him. "I was up on the ridge there and spotted you. Can you use some help?"

She laughed a low bitter laugh. "I need more help than you can give me." She wore blackened gardening gloves, and she dug carefully through a pile of ashes. In the box, he could see sooty, knobby disks of some sort. He bent down and ran his fingers over one of them to discover a cut-glass plate.

"Fostoria," she said. "They've been in my family a long time—belonged to my grandparents—and I've found exactly three unbroken plates so far out of a set of sixteen."

"Let me help." He tightened the handkerchief over his face and knelt next to her.

"There are cups and bowls and saucers, too." She held up a charred glass cup and sighed. "Gary's in the hospital for smoke inhalation, and my husband broke his collarbone trying to help the fire fighters. We don't have insurance, and now we don't have a house, either."

"I'm sorry."

"And I'm not the sort of person who cares a lot about material things, you know? But these dishes . . ." She shook her head. "They were always really special to me. They were all I had of my grandparents."

They worked together quietly, Chris's bare hands blackening quickly with soot. "I lived in one of these houses when I was a boy," he said after a while.

She wasn't impressed. "Back when there was water, right? Back when Valle Rosa wasn't hell on earth." She shook her head again, a flurry of ash falling from her hair. "We're going to move away from here as soon as my boy's out of the hospital. I used to love this place. I came here when I was sixteen and I thought it was paradise. But now I'm going to get as far from Valle Rosa as I can." Tears glistened in her dark eyes.

"Maybe things will get better here," he suggested.

"Yeah, right, with that turkey of a mayor we've got."

Chris grimaced beneath the mask. "Well, there'll be an election in November," he said. Sam Braga's most recent op-ed piece in the *Journal* had suggested that Valle Rosa's experience with Chris underscored the need to take the upcoming mayoral election very seriously. Chris couldn't agree more.

"November's not soon enough." The woman pulled a broken chunk of a plate from the ashes and slipped it into her box.

Chris was quiet again, glad of the anonymity the handkerchief across his face afforded him. After a few minutes, his fingers caught on something, and he carefully pulled it from beneath a pile of charred wood. It was a Fostoria platter, huge and heavy and perfect, except for the soot. "Look!" He held it out to her, and she caught her breath. He watched her eyes tear up again.

"I never even dreamed that would still be in one piece," she said. She took the platter from him, reverently, then looked him directly in the eye. "Thanks," she said. "You've made my day."

12.

Carmen sat at her kitchen table over half a grapefruit and an English muffin, sitting through the stack of bills next to her coffee cup. She had avoided looking at them for weeks. Nothing extravagant: insurance, telephone, and, of course, water. And yet she would barely be able to pay them. Cosmetic surgery was completely out of the question. She had thought about asking for a raise, but now that she knew they were keeping her around merely out of charity, she didn't dare make waves. If, God forbid, *News Nine* let her go, she would have to put Sugarbush on the market. She would have no choice. The thought made her panicky. Sugarbush was all she had.

There was absolutely nothing of substance to report on the news tonight. No new tidbits to pass on about Jeff Cabrio, nothing she could use to further build an air of mystery around him. She had wanted to do a story on the undocumented workers living in the canyon, focusing on how they were affected by the drought, but Dennis Ketchum had vetoed the idea. "There's no sympathy for them right now," he'd said. "People have their own problems to worry about."

Carmen still left the hose attached to her outside tap, as she had for years, knowing that at night the workers would steal into her yard for a shower and a few buckets of water to take back to their camp. Every once in a while she would find a few coins left behind in payment, but she never touched their money. There had been a time when she knew the workers by name, knew each of their stories and the hardships they'd endured. She'd give them work in her yard and food from her kitchen. It could have been her, she'd thought; it could have been someone in her own family. There were too many of them now for her to learn their names, and far too many stories to hear, but she let them have her water. It was all she could offer right now.

So covering the workers in the canyon wasn't an option, and she had no other brilliant ideas for stories. She would have to go out to the newest fires, see what she could dredge up there. "The Carmen Perez Fire Report." The words made her cringe.

After breakfast, she dressed in jeans and a long-sleeved white shirt and was on her way out the door when Jeff appeared around the side of the house.

He stopped short when he saw her, standing a few yards away as though she might bite if he got closer. "There's a screen missing from one of the windows in the living room," he said. "Do you have a spare?"

"Can it wait until tonight?"

He nodded. "I'm on my way to the warehouse, so no rush."

They walked toward their cars, that space still between them. "So, Jeff," she said, "how about an interview?"

"No thanks."

"I hear you're quite a fascinating guy."

He looked out toward the canyon. "People think what they want to think."

"And they believe what they want to believe. It seems like I'm the only one who thinks you're a charlatan."

"You'd be an idiot to think anything else at this point."

"Are you dangerous?"

He glanced sideways at her. "What do you mean?"

"I mean, do I need to be afraid of you? Because I'm going to do everything in my power to expose you."

"Well, then, I guess I'm the one who should be afraid."

"Where did you work last?"

He smiled. "Do you honestly expect me to answer that?"

"Who did you con last? Was it an individual or another town full of desperate people? Was it rain you promised them, or oil, or a successful harvest, or homes for the homeless and jobs for the unemployed?"

"Carmen," he said, "I wouldn't dare tell you for fear of spoiling your fun."

She looked at his car. "Your license plate is from Ohio," she said. "Is that where you're from?"

"Maybe."

"Okay, so you're from Ohio. Are you married? Do you have kids?"

He opened his car door and looked directly at her for the first time, his eyes a dark blue. "Give it up, Carmen," he said. "I don't like your line of work. I don't like the way you shove your way into people's private lives."

"Chris says you're an environmental engineer. Where did you get your degree?"

"I'd like to have that screen by tonight, please." He got into the car, but Carmen caught the door.

"Look. Just tell me where you were born. That can't be asking too much."

He sighed, looking back toward his cottage. "Springfield," he said. "May I go now?"

For a moment, she was stunned into silence that he had given her an answer; albeit one that was fairly useless. "Springfield where?" she asked. "There's a Springfield in practically every state."

"Hmm." He half-smiled. "Is there, now?"

She watched him pull out of the driveway. Springfield, Ohio? Illinois? He was probably lying, but at least it gave her a place to start.

Late that evening she carried the screen over to his cottage. The screens for these old outbuildings were nothing more than wire mesh suspended between two lengths of wood. They were flimsy and not secured to the sides of the window frame, but they offered enough protection for Valle Rosa. It kept out the moths and the flies. There were no mosquitoes.

Her knock wasn't answered, and she turned to see if Jeff's car was in the driveway, but the view was blocked by the adobe. She tried the door. It was unlocked, and as she slipped into the living room she felt a thrill of excitement at being in his house, of being surrounded by potential clues about him. This wasn't trespassing, she told herself. She was the landlord; he needed a screen.

It wasn't until she had opened the rear window of the living room that she heard the sound of running water. He was in the shower.

For a moment, she froze, her hands on the screen. Then her eyes fell on the small table in the corner, where a wallet lay open next to the old wrought-iron lamp. She glanced toward the hallway.

She fastened the screen to the bottom of the window frame, then walked to the table. The wallet was made of dark leather, worn to a shiny finish. His driver's license was tucked into a clear plastic pocket and completely exposed to her view. He looked pale in the picture, with at least two days' growth of beard, and his expression was flat, his eyes nearly closed. She wished Chris could see this picture. He wouldn't be able to think of Cabrio as anything other than a common criminal.

The license was indeed from Ohio. She memorized his address—500 Kenyon Street, Columbus—and his birth date—3-12-56.

The water was still running. She could search the wallet if she wanted to. Her heart began to beat audibly in her ears, playing against the background music of the running water. She would have to talk to him about letting the water run so long. He was from Ohio. He didn't understand the need to turn the water off to soap, on again to rinse. Then again, what did he care if her water bill was outrageous?

Five hundred Kenyon Street.

There was cash. She could see that without even touching the wallet. Quite a wad of it, too. Did he have more stashed somewhere else in the cottage? Did the fact that he was obviously behaving like a criminal give her the right to search the rooms when he wasn't there?

March-twelve, nineteen-fifty-six.

Perspiration broke out on her forehead.

She carefully lifted one edge of the inside pocket of the wallet, her hand shaking.

Don't do this, Carmen.

There was a newspaper clipping. It slipped out easily between the tips of her fingers. The thump of her heartbeat nearly masked the sound of the shower as she opened the yellowed clipping, which threatened to fall apart at its well-worn creases. Inside was a newspaper picture of two little blond-haired girls sitting on top of an elephant. The caption read: "Cleo gives Katie and Holly Blackwell a ride."

The water stopped. Carmen quickly refolded the clipping and slipped it back into the wallet. She took a few steps down the hallway toward the bathroom, trying to slow her breathing.

"Jeff?"

"Who's there?"

"It's Carmen, Jeff. I put the screen in for you."

There was a beat of silence before he answered. "Okay," he said. "Thanks."

"And Jeff? You shouldn't let the water run that long. You should turn it off while you—"

He opened the bathroom door, a blue towel around his waist. Soap-scented steam poured into the hallway. Surely he could read the guilt in her face. Her heart began to race again.

"Come in, Carmen," he said. Drops of water fell from his dark hair to his shoulders.

She hesitated.

"Come on," he said.

She took a step into the bathroom and saw that the claw-foot tub had a couple of inches of water in it and that he had rigged up some sort of siphoning system from the tub to a bucket on the floor.

"I'm using the water to flush the toilet," he said, pointing to the bucket. "And I'm going to use it for my laundry, too. Does that meet your approval?"

She couldn't help a sudden smile. "Yes," she said, "that's fine." She thought of asking him to rig up a similar system for the adobe, but quickly bit her tongue.

Once she was walking back to the adobe, though, she wished he had been completely, malevolently wasteful of the water. She wanted him to be one hundred percent evil. It was the only way she could justify what she had done, and the only way she could justify what she was going to do next.

500 Kenyon Street was the address of a motel in Columbus, Ohio, and she was disappointed. She spoke by phone with the manager, who had no memory of a man fitting Jeff's description having stayed there recently.

"But, uh, this is the kind of place you don't take much

notice of who comes and goes, if you know what I mean."
The manager gave a greasy chuckle. "Most people who
come here would just as soon you took their money and
gave them a key and turned your head the other way."

There was a Springfield in Ohio, but there were
Springfields in more than a dozen other states as well.
Carmen spent an hour in the lunchroom at *News Nine* with
a paper and pencil and map, trying to use logic to narrow
down her search. Ohio was most likely, of course. She
ruled out New Hampshire and Maine and Massachusetts,
since he had no trace of a New England accent. Of course
he may have been born in one of those states and moved
someplace else the next day. Or, more likely, he was lying
about Springfield in the first place. She ruled out the
South and the West, narrowing it down to Ohio, Illinois,
New Jersey, New York, Minnesota, and Missouri. Now
what? She needed contacts in those states to check birth
records. A former colleague worked in Chicago. She had
never been too close to him, but she could grovel a little,
promise something in return. First, though, she called
Tom Forrest, and read off her list of states.

"Do you know anyone who might be able to check
those records?"

Tom sighed. "You're working on some pretty slim
leads, Carmen."

"I know, but they're all I have. Please, Tom? The
name's Jeff—Jeffrey, I suppose—Cabrio, born March 12,
1956 in Springfield."

"He told you his date of birth, too?"

"I happened to see his driver's license." She thought of

what else she'd seen in her guilty little perusal of his wallet. "Tom? I just had a thought. If 'Cabrio' doesn't work, try 'Blackwell.'"

"You think he's using an alias?"

"It would make sense if he's on the run, wouldn't it?"

"Where did you get 'Blackwell' from?"

"Doesn't matter." She couldn't admit to Tom how she had learned that name. She didn't even like admitting it to herself.

"This will probably take a couple of days," Tom said.

"No problem, as long as the fires hold out." She grimaced at her own insensitivity, thinking of Chris's old neighborhood. He'd looked pretty glum when he'd brought over a few gallons of paint early that morning. She was probably the only person in Valle Rosa who woke up hoping there'd be a new fire burning someplace.

Her colleague in Chicago was willing, but wouldn't be able to check the records for her until the following week. Tom, however, called back the next day.

"It's New Jersey," he said.

"Really? You found something?"

"There was nothing under Cabrio on that date, but you were right about Blackwell. A Robert Blackwell was born on March 12, 1956, in Springfield, New Jersey."

Carmen bit her lip. "Robert Blackwell." She tried to connect the name to Jeff. "It could be a completely different person."

"I think not," Tom said. "He was born to a Steven Blackwell and an Elizabeth Cabrio."

"Oh, my." Carmen covered her mouth with her hand, smiling. This was entirely too easy. She almost felt sorry for Jeff, that he was no better than this at covering his tracks. What the hell was this man's game? He was only getting money for supplies, Chris had said. So was he actually buying supplies, or was he pocketing the money? She thought of the wad of cash in his wallet.

"Well," she said. "I guess with his real name I can learn all there is to know."

"Yes, you probably can, if you want to screw things up for yourself."

She frowned. "What do you mean?"

"Show me you're as bright as you always were, Carmen. You tell me what I mean."

She was quiet for a moment, thinking. Undoubtedly, Jeff was wanted for something. There was a good chance that with his real name, she could find out what that was and turn him in. She'd save the citizens of Valle Rosa from pouring more money and energy into his scam, when they could be searching for real solutions to the water problem. Chris would look bad, but better to look bad now than after months of dumping Valle Rosa's financial resources into Cabrio's pocket.

And she would look like a hero.

But it would be short-lived. Tom was right. Carmen Perez saved the day. Big deal. Her flame would burn like wildfire for a week or two, and then fizzle out to nothing.

"No one else knows his real name," Tom prompted her. "No one except me, and I can guarantee you I'm not going to utter a word. This one's yours."

Carmen smiled to herself. No one else knew, and it was unlikely that anyone else could find out. She could take her time, then. She could learn the facts about him slowly, feed information to her audience piecemeal, like Scheherezade, keeping her king so hungry for the next installment of the story that he forgot he had wanted her dead. It would be elegant. Once she knew the truth, though, she would tell Chris before she told anyone else. She would give Chris a chance to save face.

"You're right, Tom," she said. "I've got it."

She was late getting home that evening, but Jeff was even later. It was after eleven when his Saab pulled into the driveway. She watched from her kitchen window as he set out on foot across Sugarbush, quickly disappearing into the darkness. When she saw a light go on inside his cottage, she picked up her flashlight and followed him.

He answered the door on her second knock. He seemed suddenly taller than her memory of him, and with the light coming from the room behind him, his features were nearly impossible to see. That unnerved her, and she had to remind herself that she was the one with the advantage here. She was the one in control.

She looked past him into the living room. His briefcase was on the coffee table, papers spilling over its edges. In the middle of the room stood a tall, four-legged yellow stool, a saw lying across its seat.

Her palms were damp, and she pressed them together as she drew in a breath. "I wanted to make sure your quarters are comfortable, Robert," she said.

Even in the dim light, she thought she could see the color drain from his face.

"That's not my name," he said.

"No?"

"No. And if you suggest to anyone, on the air or off, that it is, I'll leave Valle Rosa immediately." He took a step toward her, and she glanced again at the saw, fighting the urge to back away from him.

"Maybe that's not such a bad idea," she said.

"Fine. You can put out your goddamned fires by yourself."

She stepped off the porch. "You don't need to worry. I won't tell anyone your name, Jeff." She emphasized the word "Jeff." "Good night, now."

The following night, she prepared her *North County Report* with great care.

"All eyes in Valle Rosa continue to focus on the rainmaker," she said, exaggerating, but knowing that by making that pronouncement, it would begin to come true. "*News Nine* has learned that Valle Rosa's mystery man, Jeff Cabrio, was born in Springfield, New Jersey, and lived most recently in Columbus, Ohio."

After her report, Dennis Ketchum stopped her in the hall. "Where are you getting this stuff?" he grinned, sucking on a cigarette. "Is Cabrio talking to you?"

"I have my sources," she said, smiling, and she felt a power inside her she hadn't known in years.

Mia would have used any excuse to see Jeff again, so when Chris said he needed to take some order forms over to the warehouse, she volunteered to do it for him after work.

Rick opened the warehouse door for her. "Hey, Mia," he said.

She handed him the forms, peering toward the rear of the long building, realizing she had no reason to walk back there.

"I'm starving," Rick said. "You up for some pizza? We'll see if we can get the workaholic to join us." He nodded toward the back of the warehouse.

"Sounds great," she answered, pleased.

She followed Rick through the maze of furniture to the rear of the building, where Jeff was working at the computer. A lamp burned on the bookcase above the table, and the light that spilled from it was sharp and beautiful on the angles of his face.

Rick stood at the end of the table. "How about a break?" he asked Jeff. "We'll go out for pizza."

Mia held her breath, waiting for his answer. Jeff

pushed another few keys on the computer. The hum of the window fans was hypnotic, and she wasn't sure how many seconds had passed by the time he looked up from his work. "I'll be here another couple of hours," he said.

Rick picked up a set of car keys from the table, tossed them high in the air and caught them with a flourish. "Looks like it's you and me, Mia."

He didn't seem disappointed, but she was. The bas-relief of the window was waiting for her at home, and she was tempted to back out of the invitation. But she was hungry. Her work could wait.

They drove to Valle Rosa's one small, uncrowded pizzeria, where they sat at a corner table. Mia had no problem at all talking Rick into ordering the vegetarian pizza.

"So," he said after the waitress had served Mia's lemonade and his beer. "Jeff says you're a pretty good sculptor. 'Accomplished' was the word he used."

"You mean he actually talks about something other than work?" she asked. "He's always so quiet." She wished she could have heard those words come out of Jeff's mouth herself. Had he said anything else about her?

"He's thinking." Rick sprinkled some salt on the red tabletop and began drawing a pattern in it with his fingertip. "At first I thought, this guy's pretty weird. I even felt scared the first day I worked with him. We were alone in that warehouse, and I thought, What the hell are you doing, Smythe? You don't know this dude. He could be a depraved ax murderer, for all you know." Rick rolled his eyes. "At first I was trying to make conversation with him. We were clearing that space in the warehouse and his silence was making me nervous, so I started filling it with all sorts of mundane shit, but he didn't say a word back to me. I don't even think he was listening. Finally he sat down at the table with a pad and pencil and got this faraway look in his eyes, and I knew I'd better not disturb him."

Rick paused for breath, and Mia realized she didn't know this young man sitting across from her at all. He was far more animated than she'd expected, far more wired. He doodled in the salt as he spoke, every once in a while glancing up at her, and each time she was surprised by the Caribbean blue of his eyes.

"So I sort of walked around the warehouse feeling like a jerk, you know?" He shook his head and took a swallow of beer. "Completely useless. After—God—two hours maybe, he called me over, and he had twenty or thirty sheets covered with figures and equations and stuff I'd never seen before. I had to admit to him it was all over my head. And he said, 'No, it's not. You're extremely bright.'" Rick laughed. "And I said, 'How do you know that? All you've seen me do is push goddamned furniture around.' And he smiled—*finally*—like I wasn't sure the dude had any smile muscles, you know? And he said that he could *feel* my intelligence and that he was certain I have what it takes to work on this project." Rick sat back, a little smugly, and raised his glass again to his lips.

"So," she said slowly, "I guess you two are working well together, then." She couldn't imagine a more mismatched duo than Jeff Cabrio and Rick Smythe. Jeff, who was bright and cerebral and sullen and mysterious, and Rick, with his ebullient, child-like openness and his— there was no other word for it—simplicity.

"Oh," he said, "we're awesome together."

Their pizza was delivered and she looked at it dubiously. The cheese was thick. Pure fat. She should have ordered a salad. She took a slice onto her plate and blotted the oil from it with her napkin. When she looked up, Rick was smiling at her.

"You are not ordinary," he said.

"And you are?" She pointed to the salt on the table, and he laughed.

Taking a triangle of pizza onto his own plate, Rick continued with his story. "So anyhow, Jeff sat there and taught me what he was working out. I swear to you, Mia. I mean, I've got a master's degree—I'm no imbecile—but this guy . . ." He shook his head. "I've never seen anything like it. Somehow he's got me understanding what he's coming up with. Once he explained it, I could follow it. He's creating concepts that never existed before. He's putting two and two together and getting five, and he can prove to you why he's right." He lifted the slice of pizza to his mouth, but set it down again without taking a bite. "It's going to work, Mia. I mean, I lay in bed at night, and I can't sleep 'cause I just keep thinking, God, this is actually going to work."

She swallowed her mouthful of pizza. "You're in awe of him," she said.

"Hell, yes, I'm in awe. I'm so fucking excited I haven't even gone to the beach since he got here." He finally took a bite of his pizza, wiping his mouth with his napkin before he spoke again. "God, I can't stop talking. You're going to think I took an upper or something."

"It's interesting." She wasn't lying. She liked hearing about Jeff from the person in Valle Rosa who probably knew him best.

"Well, speaking of the beach, I was wondering if you might like to go tomorrow. It's Saturday. I can afford a couple of hours off, and you look like you could use some sun."

She sat back, surprised, and for the first time since arriving at the restaurant, a little uncomfortable. Was he asking her out? Until this moment, she had thought of him as nothing more than her link to Jeff. She didn't want to think of him in any other way. He was attractive, yes. A good-looking California boy, the kind of guy Laura liked. Used to like.

"I'm in Valle Rosa to work, I'm afraid," she said, as if it were something outside her control. "I need to sculpt tomorrow, but thanks for asking." The thought of her body in a bathing suit nearly brought tears to her eyes, and she swept the image quickly from her mind.

"You and Jeff are so alike," he said. "All work and no play is not a healthy way to live, girl."

She laughed, enjoying the comparison to Jeff.

"Well, if you decide you'd like a break, let me know." He took another slice of pizza and sat back on the bench. "So, what's happening with Chris and Carmen? Everyone's agog, you know? Everyone thinks it's pretty fascinating that Chris is living back at Sugarbush."

She looked at him blankly. As far as she knew, nothing was happening with Chris and Carmen.

"You know they were married, don't you?"

She nodded.

"They were San Diego's hot couple. On all the magazine covers. You know Chris was a Padre, right?"

"Of course." Chris Garrett was a famous name from her teens and her early twenties, although it had taken her more than a few days to place it when she first started working for him, and a little longer to remember that Carmen had once been his wife. She couldn't see them as a couple. She pictured Carmen in a flouncy, white, off-the-shoulder Mexican dress, a blood-red rose between her teeth, and Chris with his Birkenstocks and T-shirt and those all-American-boy looks that seemed to make it hard for anyone to take him seriously as mayor.

"I don't think anything's happening between them now," she said. "I don't see them talking much. You'd never know they were once husband and wife."

"Well, she dumped him pretty good."

Mia stopped her glass halfway to her lips. "Dumped him? Why would she do that? He's so nice."

"*Too* nice. Chris screwed up his arm back in '87 and that was the end of his career. So she dumped him."

Mia cut herself another slice of pizza and pressed her napkin to the cheesy surface. "You're saying she left him because of his arm?" She thought, uncomfortably, of the chilly parallel that scenario had to her own life.

"You tell me." Rick set down his pizza, and took off on another one of his rapid-fire monologues. "Take a look at Sugarbush," he said. "Worth a couple million bucks, wouldn't you say? Chris was loaded. Carmen made a fair amount of money herself, true, but Chris was far wealthier in his own right. That came to a screeching halt when he got sacked."

"So, you're suggesting it boiled down to greed? Neither of them seem particularly interested in money." She didn't want to hear any of this. She didn't want to know that Carmen was capable of cruelty, or that Chris had been hurt at her hands. "And people don't get divorced when one partner is injured or loses a job. That's when he would have needed her most, right?"

Rick grinned at her. "Are you as sweet and naive as you seem Mia, or is it all an act? Wake up, girl. It's another world we're talking about here. Marriage for someone like Carmen was just a means to an end, a rung on the ladder. She stuck with Chris as long as he made her look good and could bring home the bucks, and they could fly off to Puerto Vallarta or wherever for the weekend." He handed her another napkin. "Still have a pocket of grease right there." He pointed to her pizza, and she rested the napkin on top of the cheese. She was no longer very hungry.

"Carmen was pregnant when Chris screwed up his arm," Rick continued, "and she held onto him until after the baby was born and then gave him his walking papers."

A *baby*? Mia felt thoroughly thick-headed. Chris had never mentioned being a father. "They have a child?" she asked.

"Not really. They have a vegetable." Rick winced at his own words, and smacked the side of his face with his hand. "Whoa, Smythe, unkind," he said. "I shouldn't have said that." He looked apologetically at Mia. "Yeah, they had a baby boy, and he got really sick a week or so after he was born. He's in an institution. Carmen ignores him, but Chris visits him every week."

"I had no idea Chris had a son." Mia shook her head, bewildered. "And I absolutely cannot picture Carmen ignoring her own child. She's been so good to me. She cut the rent on my cottage in half when she realized I couldn't afford it, and she's the one who told me about my job. And she can't be all bad if she's let Chris live at Sugarbush."

"Yeah—in a fucking outbuilding." Rick pushed his empty plate away from him. "It's for show. She knows the press eats that sort of thing up. 'Carmen Perez lets Chris Garrett come home after his house burns down.' She's cleaning up her public image. She's as shrewd as they come, trying to kiss up to the people who still think of her as a bitch for dumping Chris."

Mia scowled. "I don't see how anyone can look at someone else's life and make those sorts of judgments." She thought of the woman who had given her the tour of Sugarbush, who had wanted to make her comfortable. Carmen did seem a little cool, perhaps. Aloof. But she was thoroughly different from the spirited, controlling woman Mia remembered from *San Diego Sunrise*. This new Carmen had struggled against something big, something threatening. Maybe it took one woman to recognize those signs in another. "I'm sure there's more to the whole thing than meets the eye," Mia said. "I'm sure there's plenty the press doesn't know."

"Look what she's doing with Jeff," Rick argued. "He's asked to work in privacy, and she's badgering him with questions. It really bugs him."

Mia shrugged. "He's news and she's a reporter."

"God, women." Rick shook his head, but he was smiling. "You always stick together."

Outside the restaurant, A boy of about eight or nine sat on the sidewalk, cradling a cardboard box filled with kittens between his knees.

"Hold on." Rick stopped Mia with a hand on her arm. "I know a man who needs a cat to call his own. What do you think?" He knelt next to the box and drew out a small gray tabby.

Mia knelt next to him and lifted a sleek black kitten from the box. "I don't know," she said. "He's not home much."

Rick brushed a strand of long blond hair from his eyes. "This will give him something to come home to, and with the mouse problem in this town, how could he say no?" He looked into the hopeful face of the young boy. "Are they free?"

The boy nodded.

"This one or that?" Rick asked Mia, holding out the tabby.

She raised the black kitten into the air and imagined the dark air of mystery it would possess as a full-grown cat. "This one," she said.

They bought litter and a litter box and a few cans of food.

"We could take it over to the warehouse," Rick said, as they got into his car, "but he really hates being interrupted."

"I'll take it with me," she offered, as if she were doing Rick a favor. "I'll give it to him when he gets home tonight."

In the back of her closet hung a storage bag filled with clothes she hadn't worn since before the surgery. She removed a short-sleeved, pale-blue sweater from the bag and grimaced as she pulled it over her head. It was going to be obvious, she thought; she should stick with the oversized T-shirts she usually wore.

She had to stand on her bed in order to see her chest in the wall mirror, and she spent five minutes turning this way and that. He wouldn't know. The prosthesis looked surprisingly natural.

The kitten slept quietly on her thigh as Mia sat on the floor, watching for Jeff's arrival from her bedroom window. She thought again of Rick inviting her to the beach. If Laura had been sitting next to her, he wouldn't have given Mia a second look. It had always been that way, even when they were very small. She could still remember overhearing her kindergarten teacher, a woman who had taught Laura two years earlier, whispering to a classroom aide: "It's hard to believe they're sisters. Laura is such a beautiful child, and Mia's so plain, although she's certainly a cheery little thing."

Laura had been very popular in school. Mia had her own circle of friends, but until Glen, rarely dated at all. At the dinner table, her mother and Laura would giggle as they commiserated over who they could fix Mia up with, and Mia would laugh along with them, wanting to feel a part of that beautiful mother–daughter team. She supposed it was her own fault that she hadn't dated. Even when Laura hadn't been standing next to her, she'd felt her sister there, neat and polished, tossing her hair, smiling with a coquettish self-confidence Mia could only imagine.

Jeff arrived at his cottage close to ten, and Mia sat by the window a few minutes longer to give him time to settle in. She looked down at the sleeping kitten. Pretty impulsive, she thought. What had she and Rick been thinking? She knew why she'd done it: it was her chance to see Jeff tonight. But perhaps dropping an unsolicited cat in his lap wasn't the best way to go about it.

She gathered together the bag of food, the litter box and the kitten itself and set out for Jeff's cottage. The night air was cool, and stars filled the sky. The crickets were strangely quiet, though, and she could hear nothing from the shadowy canyon other than an eerie, rustling breeze.

Jeff must have seen her coming. He turned on the porch light before she had a chance to knock and opened the door, staring at the kitten in her arms.

"That's not for me, I hope."

Mia laughed. "Afraid so. Rick and I thought you might like some company." She held the skinny black kitten out to him as if trying to tempt him with a piece of candy.

After a long moment, he reached out to take the kitten

from her, lifting it into the air and looking into its yellow eyes.

"I don't want any attachments," he said, but he drew the cat close to him, nuzzling its head beneath his chin. The kitten let out a long, squawky meow.

Mia smiled at the contradiction between Jeff's words and his actions and held up the shopping bag. "We bought you a litter box and some food."

He shook his head, a resigned look on his face as he stepped back to let her into the cottage. She set the litter box on the living-room floor and began tearing open the bag of litter.

"I was just about to have a glass of wine," he said. "Want one?"

She emptied the litter into the box. "A little late for that, isn't it?"

"Well," he said, pouring wine into a glass on the dining-room table. "I've gotten into the probably dangerous habit of having a glass before bed. Helps me sleep. I don't sleep too well these days."

"Neither do I." She took the glass he offered and sat down in one of the old upholstered chairs in the living room. The room was clean, spartan; the blue walls looked freshly painted.

Jeff put the kitten on the floor and disappeared into the kitchen. When he returned, he was wadding up a length of tin foil into a small ball. He winked at Mia as he sat down on the floor, his back against the sofa.

"Let's see what you're made of," he said to the kitten. He threw the ball of foil across the room, and the cat scampered after it, batting the foil around on the carpet for a moment before picking it up in its mouth and carrying it back to Jeff.

Mia stared, open-mouthed, and Jeff smiled his almost smile. "Good cat, Mia," he said, throwing the foil ball across the room again.

"I've never seen a cat fetch before," she said.

"Animals are like people. They live up to your expectations of them."

She thought of Rick, of Jeff telling him he was extremely bright.

"You have to name her," she said.

Jeff scooped the cat up and lifted its lanky tail to peer underneath. "Him," he said. "And I'm not going to name him. You name something and suddenly you're responsible for it. I'll just call him 'the cat.'"

"Well, he'll have to be an indoor cat or the coyotes will get him."

He looked up at her sharply, then shook his head. "This is a bad idea," he said. "I don't want to have to worry about him. And I'll be leaving here as soon as I get things rolling."

She suddenly felt guilty. "Maybe it was a bad idea," she said. "Do you want me to take him back?"

He lifted the cat and pressed the silky black fur against his cheek. The kitten purred audibly in response. "Nah," he said. "I'll hang onto him for a while. When I leave, though, I'll probably need to give him to you."

"All right." She would worry about that when the time came.

"So." He stretched out his legs in front of him and rested the kitten in his lap. "How did the pictures come out?"

"Very well." She took a big swallow of wine. "I'm trying to settle on an angle that catches the true emotions in your face."

He looked amused, swirling the wine in his glass. "Exactly what do you think my true emotions are? I don't think I let much of anything show."

"I know that," she said. "And you probably would be a mystery to someone who's not accustomed to reading faces, but that's something you learn to do when you're an artist."

"Uh huh," he said skeptically. "So, go ahead, I'm waiting. What do you think you see in my face?"

"Well." She rested her glass on the end table and sat forward, using her hands to help in her description. "The angles are rigid. You're scared. I don't know of what, but it's your primary emotion. Fear."

He set his own glass on the floor next to him and frowned at her. "How can you possibly say you see fear? The only place you've seen me is in the warehouse, where I've been concentrating on my work."

"It underlies whatever else you're feeling. It's like throwing a slipcover over a raggedy old chair. You can hide it, but it's still there, just below the surface."

He took in a long breath. "Uh huh. And what else do you think you see?"

"Anger. I get the feeling there's a deep, festering rage in you."

He laughed.

"I do. I wouldn't want to cross you. Also, there's hurt. Grief. Sadness."

He attempted a smile, but didn't quite succeed.

"And when you smile, it doesn't work as a smile because the rest of your face—your forehead, your jaw— is saying, 'I'm not happy.' It doesn't matter what your mouth is doing. Or maybe it's pain. Physical pain. Are you in pain anywhere?"

"Mia." He slumped lower against the couch and looked at her from under heavy-lidded eyes. "Do you know what projection is?"

She frowned, not certain what he was getting at.

"I think you're projecting your own feelings onto other people. Maybe what you see in any given person at any given time is just a mirror of what's inside yourself."

The tables were turning on her, and she stiffened. "I don't know what you're talking about."

"*You're* the one who's scared," he said. "What are *you* afraid of? What are *you* angry about?"

She felt the color creep into her cheeks. "Nothing."

"There's nothing wrong with it," he said. "It's actually more intriguing to think that you're expressing your own feelings through the faces of others. Or maybe it's only that you're drawn to models who suit your current mood."

She thought of how she had gravitated toward Henry and his smile at a time when she had felt carefree and loved.

Jeff threw the foil ball across the floor, and the cat leaped after it.

"Well," he said, "I've made you quiet if nothing else."

"Mmm." She shifted uncomfortably in the chair. "The wine's slowing me down."

He suddenly leaned toward her. "It's only when you're working that you feel completely at peace, isn't it?" he asked. "It's the one thing that's wholly yours—your work. It's the one thing no one can ever take from you."

His gaze seemed to burn into her as he waited for her reply. "Yes," she said, and for another moment, she couldn't turn away from his eyes.

He stood up then, and the spell was broken. She knew he was telling her it was time to go. She stood too, and immediately felt the effect of the wine. She hadn't had anything to drink in so long.

"You all right?" he asked, opening the door, keeping the kitten inside with his foot.

"Yes, but it's definitely bedtime." She stepped onto his porch. "Let me know if the cat becomes a problem."

"All right. And Mia?"

She turned to look at him.

"I understand how it feels to have only your work," he said. "I understand that completely."

She nodded slowly, wondering if there were any limits at all to how easily he could see through her. "Good night," she said.

She walked across the ridge of the canyon to her cottage, knowing he was watching her from his doorway, but when she turned to wave, he did not lift his hand.

14.

Chris turned off his cottage lights before carrying his guitar onto the porch. He liked the darkness, liked being able to feel the canyon more than see it. The air was thick with the smell of soot and eucalyptus. He turned his chair so that the lights from Mia's cottage and the adobe were blocked from his view. Stretching out in front of him, the black canyon hummed softly with the sound of crickets, and as he began to sing, his voice seemed to travel for miles before losing itself in the abyss.

He sang ballads, too tired for anything more energetic. He'd spent the evening in the adobe, removing the wallpaper from the room they had used as the nursery. Years ago, he had emptied that room of its furniture, but he doubted Carmen had set foot in there since the day Dustin left the house. Chris had worked quickly tonight, blocking from his mind the memory of the few joyous days they'd had with their seemingly healthy son, as well as the memory of that long, frightening night, when it was apparent that Dusty was desperately ill. Chris pulled and scraped and tore at the wallpaper, as if trying to destroy all the pain embedded in its yellow-and-blue flowered print.

He'd had another reason to be angry as he worked on the room. A new fire had cropped up today. It had been small and fairly easily controlled, but he considered it particularly abhorrent. This one had been set intentionally by someone who wanted to drive the undocumented workers from the canyon. The fire had started early that morning, and by noon all that was left of that particular camp on the north side were the charred sheets of corrugated metal that had served as roofs for their plywood and cardboard shelters. No one had been hurt; no one had even been seen. The workers had simply disappeared, no doubt slipping deeper into the canyon to start over. If anyone running for mayor came up with a plan to provide the undocumented workers with decent housing, they would get his vote. He stopped singing "The Water Is Wide" in the middle of a verse and began singing "De Colores," on the whimsical chance that the workers had moved to a section of the canyon from which they could hear him.

Sam Braga had run a piece on the mayoral election in yesterday's *Gazette*. It seemed that the two contenders, Joyce DeLuis and John Burrows, were in agreement on absolutely nothing, except that Chris Garrett's hiring of the "alleged rainmaker" had been irresponsible at best. "On that," Braga wrote, "the two candidates are in complete accord."

Chris heard a sound from behind him and stilled his hands on the guitar as the beam of a flashlight played over the porch.

"Don't stop." Jeff turned off his light and sat down on the step.

Chris started to play again, but he was thinking that it was nearly eleven, and Jeff was only now getting home. Jeff had worked similar hours every day since arriving in Valle Rosa. He had to be exhausted.

"Bravo," Jeff said quietly when Chris had finished the song.

Chris couldn't easily see Jeff's face in the darkness, but he heard the smile in his voice. "Thanks," he said.

Jeff sighed, stretching his legs out on the porch. "Once I was at this coffee house in Philadelphia with a group of people," he said, "and you showed up."

"The Rising Sun," Chris said, surprised not so much that Jeff had seen him at a club, but that he was talking about it, offering a morsel of information about himself. He wanted to ask Jeff if he'd lived in Philadelphia, but thought better of it.

"You sang that song," Jeff said. "Your trademark song."

"'Center Field.'"

"Right. I remember thinking how strange it was. The crowd was very hot on the Phillies and very down on the Padres, but the second you walked in, they turned non-partisan."

Chris strummed the guitar, softly. "Well, that type of place was pretty safe to go," he said. "People were there for the music. The receptions I got were usually good."

"You still sound good. I could hear you all the way from the driveway. Do you perform anywhere these days?"

"Hell, no." Chris laughed, but he felt an involuntary shudder at the thought of climbing onto a stage in front of an audience. "That'd take guts I don't have anymore. Once you've been pulverized by the fans that supposedly loved you, it's hard to risk going back for more." He could still remember the agony of being booed at his last game for the Padres. Other players had been regular recipients of the crowd's disdain, but not Chris. It had stung him badly, and he'd been glad of the isolation of the mound, glad no one was near enough to him to read the pain in his face. "Getting everyone's wrath as mayor is enough for now. I'm not the most popular guy in town, in case you haven't noticed."

"It's hard to miss." Jeff stretched his arms above his head, yawning.

"You must be wiped out," Chris said. "Please take some time off when you need it."

"The sooner I get this done, the sooner I can leave." Jeff shifted his position on the porch step to face Chris more directly. "You know, it's been two weeks and you haven't asked me a thing about how my work's going."

Chris laughed. "Well, I figure when you hire someone to perform a miracle it's a little banal to ask him how it's coming along."

"It's going all right," Jeff volunteered, "but it's difficult, since I don't have any of my data with me. I'm starting from scratch with everything."

"Where is the data? Can you send for it?"

"It doesn't exist any more, except in here." He touched his fingertips to his temple.

Chris could see only Jeff's eyes, and they were wide and riveted on his own.

"But it's coming back to me pretty easily," Jeff continued. "I've crammed what took me five years to figure out into the past two weeks. Two or three more and we'll be ready for a small-scale experiment. Then I'll know if I'm headed in the right direction. I need a few more things, though." He sounded apologetic.

"You name it."

"First of all, some kind of warning signs. 'Danger—Keep Out.' Something like that."

"To keep people from hounding you?"

"No. We'll be moving into a phase soon where there really may be some danger. The risk is extremely small, but I don't want to take the chance of anyone getting hurt."

For the first time, Chris felt a wave of uncertainty over hiring this stranger to help Valle Rosa. "What are we talking about here?" he asked. "There's nothing radioactive or—"

Jeff chuckled. "Nothing like that. I've discussed it with Rick to be sure he understands the risks, and he's okay with it." He hesitated when Chris didn't respond. "Do you need to know more?"

"No." Chris made a quick decision to continue operating on trust. "What else do you need?"

"A couple more vats. Very specialized. Little plastic pockets on the inside. Two hundred gallons. Air-tight. I know where I can get them, but I'd like to do some research to find another source. Not too many people need exactly what I'm looking for, and I'd rather they didn't put two and two together and figure out who's doing the ordering."

"Okay."

"They're expensive. Sorry."

Chris shrugged and smiled. "What else?"

"That's it for now."

A breeze slipped across the porch, dropping a few powdery ashes on the guitar. Chris blew them off and stood up. "How about a beer?" he asked.

This time he could see Jeff's smile. "Love one," he said.

Inside the house, Chris switched on the living-room light and went into the kitchen for the beer. When he returned to the living room, Jeff was sitting on the couch, pulling a sooty baseball bat out of one of the boxes Chris had brought from his house.

"This looks like an interesting collection." Jeff peered into the box.

"Memorabilia," Chris said, embarrassed. His ego was in that box.

Jeff balanced the bat across his hands, ignoring the soot it deposited on his palms. "What makes the bat special?" he asked.

Chris placed Jeff's beer on the coffee table and sat down in the chair nearest the sofa. "Well,"—he twisted the cap off his beer—"when you're known for your pitching, nobody takes you too seriously as a hitter. But in this one game—against the Phillies, as a matter of fact—they had me batting ninth, and as usual, told me to bunt.

Something got into me, though, and I told myself to ignore them and just let it rip." He took a swallow of beer and smiled at the memory. "Got a home run. I wasn't about to part with the bat."

Jeff pulled a handkerchief from his pocket and wiped the soot from the bat and his hands. "I remember reading about that in *Throwing Smoke*," he said.

"You read *Throwing Smoke*?" He hadn't taken Jeff Cabrio for a baseball fan.

"Yeah. I enjoyed it."

Chris shook his head. "That book embarrasses the hell out of me now."

"How come?"

"A biography about someone who's only thirty-five years old seems ridiculous. Pretentious."

He hadn't thought so at the time, though. He'd felt worthy of having an entire book written about him, and he'd thought that the author had captured him well. The tone of the biography had been flattering, with Augie seen as his best friend and driving force. Chris's early excesses and escapades were described in entertaining, almost comical terms, and his marriage to the country's least typical baseball wife was seen as a testimony to the unpredictability of love. The book sold very well, but Chris quickly realized that it had been written prematurely.

"Here it is, only five years later," he said to Jeff, "and if I read that book again, I wouldn't even recognize myself."

Jeff nodded. "Well, I doubt the Chris Garrett in *Throwing Smoke* would ever say he was afraid to perform in front of a crowd."

Chris's mouth twisted in a sad half-smile at the memory of his former, crowd-loving self.

Jeff raised his beer to his lips and took a long drink before setting the bottle on the table again. "I remember something about you turning down offers to coach in the majors after you hurt your arm," he said. "Why didn't you stay in baseball?"

Chris sighed. "It would have meant leaving Valle Rosa. Carmen and I had separated by then, but I still didn't want to desert her because she was . . . pretty sick at the time. And I didn't want to be too far from my son." Chris knew he wasn't offering much—just cryptic pieces of information—but it was far more than he usually said. Still, he wasn't sure if Jeff was following him.

Jeff nodded, though, as though he heard all that Chris wasn't saying. He must know then, Chris thought, about Carmen's depression, and about Dustin. He probably knew the story from Rick. Or at least, he knew the story as Rick understood it.

"Also, I wasn't sure I could stomach being behind the lines in baseball. You know, being involved as a coach without being able to play." It wasn't a lie, but not the truth either. Quitting baseball and staying in Valle Rosa had, in many ways, been the easy way out.

Jeff pulled the box closer to him. "Tell me about the stuff in here."

Chris couldn't resist the invitation. He moved to the floor and began pulling his treasures from the box, describing each of them to his rapt audience. There was a baseball in a sooty plastic holder from the first major league game he'd pitched in, and another from the game that marked his hundredth win. He showed Jeff a few of his trophies. At the bottom of the box, the Cy Young award was wrapped in a towel.

"Wow." Jeff held the plaque with appropriate respect. "You must be relieved this didn't get ruined in the fire. It's got to be one of your most prized possessions."

"Yes and no." Chris studied the plaque himself. He always felt a strange combination of satisfaction and sorrow when he looked at it. "It was the greatest honor of my life," he said, "but my father died right after I received it, and the two events are sort of tied forever in my head."

"Oh, yeah." Jeff nodded. "I know how that happens."

Chris set the plaque on the coffee table. "Would you like to go to a Padres game sometime?" he asked, impulsively. The thought terrified him. "I haven't been to a game myself since I retired, but maybe it's about time."

Jeff's eyes lit up, but the rest of his face was reserved. "I'd be afraid that being with you would make me too visible," he said.

"Well, the truth is, I don't feel like being all that visible myself at the moment." Chris laughed. "We can sit in the nosebleed seats. No one will give us a second look."

"Let me think about it a while." Jeff stood up and yawned. "Right now, though, I'd better get some sleep."

He walked to the front door and turned to face Chris again. "I know you're taking a lot of heat for hiring me," he said. It was almost an apology.

Chris shrugged. "I can handle it."

Jeff shook his head. "You still have guts, Chris," he said. "Don't let anyone tell you anything different."

Jeff left the cottage, and Chris watched him walk across the yard. Jeff may have said he wasn't interested in making friends in Valle Rosa, but his actions tonight contradicted his words.

Clearly, he wasn't a man who enjoyed being alone. Then again, Chris thought, neither was he.

He slowly repacked his memorabilia, saving the Cy Young award for last, wrapping it carefully in the towel before setting it on top of the other items.

The day he'd received the Cy Young award had also been Augie's sixty-second birthday. Carmen had insisted on throwing a party to celebrate both events, despite the fact that she was five months pregnant. Chris had tried to talk her out of it, worried about the stress it might cause her. Stress, he was certain, had been the culprit when she lost their first baby nearly two years earlier, the day after her cousin's wedding. Carmen had insisted on having the reception for the wedding at Sugarbush, hoping that with that gesture, she might be able to heal the long-standing rift between herself and her aunt and uncle. But that wasn't to be. On the day of the reception, her relatives shunned her in her own home, taking advantage of her hospitality and talking about her when her back was turned—and, sometimes, when it wasn't. All that night, Carmen cried with the pain of wanting a family that didn't want her. When she miscarried the next day—a miscarriage followed by a dark, crippling depression— Chris had no doubt at all of the cause.

At the time he won the Cy Young award, though, Carmen felt very well, and very confident that she would carry this baby to term. So confident, in fact, that she planned to announce her pregnancy on *Sunrise* the following week.

Chris watched her during the party. There was an unmistakable glow about her. It radiated from her, touching everyone in the room, and he felt very proud that she was his wife. All was right with his world: he was surrounded by friends, by the woman he admired and loved, by his father who had coached and guided and nurtured him. And in a few months he was going to be a father himself.

In bed that night, though, he felt Carmen trembling in his arms and knew she was crying. She tried to deny it.

"Just chilly," she said, but he touched her cheek and felt the tears.

"What is it?" he asked.

She was quiet a moment, and he could hear her breathing deeply, trying to gain some control over her emotions, something she could usually do quickly, easily. "I wish you didn't have to go tomorrow," she said.

He was leaving on a road trip, a long one.

"I know." He pulled her closer. "I wish you could come with me, at least for part of the time." Even though she didn't fit in well with the other wives, Chris loved having her with him. There was nothing in the world he enjoyed more than the way she rubbed his arm after a game, the way she would pretend to swoon when her hands kneaded his sore muscles. Ordinarily, she would have joined him for a weekend or two during a trip of this length, but her doctor had advised against traveling.

There was little he could do to take away the source of her unhappiness, so he settled for holding her through that night, while she cried off and on and chastised herself fiercely for the tears.

When he got into his hotel room the following night, there were three messages for him to call her. That alarmed him. She rarely called when he was on the road; she hated to appear that needy.

She answered the phone quickly when he dialed the number for Sugarbush.

"Are you all right?" he asked.

"I'm fine," she said. "And I think everything's going to be okay, but I wanted to let you know Augie's in the hospital."

"Augie? Why?"

"He woke up this morning with chest pain, but it seems it was just a false alarm. He's okay now. They're keeping him overnight and if all's well in the morning, they'll release him."

Chris's own heart was pumping hard. "What caused it, though?" he asked.

"He said he had a little indigestion from my cooking last night." She laughed, and Chris smiled. His father felt well enough to joke. That was a good sign.

"I should come home."

"Absolutely not. He was adamant about that, Chris. It's too late for you to call him now, or he could tell you that himself."

"Well, did you get a chance to talk with his doctor?"

"Uh huh. All the tests on his heart were perfectly normal. He's fine, Chris."

"I just wish I could talk to him."

"Tomorrow."

"And how about you?" he asked. "You took it easy today, I hope?"

"Didn't lift a finger. Lolled around all day with my feet up. The *bebito* on the other hand has been a little hellion. I don't think he's going to play baseball, Chris. It's going to have to be hockey or soccer or something where he'll be moving all the time. He's got a ton of energy."

He could picture her lying in their bed as she talked to him, stroking her swollen belly with her long, dark fingers.

"I'll call Augie at the hospital in the morning," he said.

"I love you, Chris. I wish you were here beside me."

"Wish I was there, too, Car."

He didn't sleep well that night, and when he called his father's room early the following morning, there was no answer. A clerk at the nurses' station told him Augie was in the bathroom, and he left a teasing message for him, something about the length he'd go to for a little pampering and TLC, a message that would haunt him for years to come.

It was evening by the time he returned to his hotel, and he was stunned to find Carmen there. She'd been sitting on the edge of the bed, but she rose quickly to her feet when he let himself into the room.

"Carmen." He froze in front of the door. "What are you doing here?"

Her face was ashen. "I didn't want to tell you over the phone," she said.

"Augie?"

She pressed her hands together in front of her. "I'm sorry, Chris."

He felt his heart slip away from his body, leaving him momentarily numb. "When?" he asked. "How?"

She took a step toward him. "It was this morning. He—"

"But you said he was fine." He heard the childlike tone of his voice, the unfounded sense of betrayal. Suddenly furious, he pounded his fist into the door. "He can't be dead. You said I didn't need to come home."

She moved close enough to put her arms around him, and he had a fleeting thought that she was brave to do that. She was unafraid of him when he was, at that moment, afraid of himself. He buried his head in her shoulder and clung to her.

"It wasn't his heart," she said. "His heart was fine, and they were going to release him today. It was an embolism, very sudden. No one suspected it."

He couldn't speak. Carmen tightened her arms around him and only then did he realize he was shaking with deep, gut-wrenching sobs.

"Oh, baby," she said. "I'm so sorry. I feel terrible about telling you not to come home last night."

"I know." He spoke into her shoulder. "I only wish I could have talked to him one last time."

She leaned away from him, looked him squarely in the eyes. "There was nothing you didn't say to him, Chris. No secrets, no feelings held back between the two of you, ever. He always knew how much you loved him."

He nodded slowly and pulled her back into his arms. "I should be mad at you for coming here," he said, "but I'm so glad you did."

They flew home that night, quiet with one another on the plane, but close, holding hands. He felt her strength, and he gave in to his need for it, letting her take care of him once they reached Sugarbush, letting her make the phone calls, run his bath, settle him in bed.

In the middle of the night, he woke up to find himself alone in the room. For a moment, he couldn't remember where he was. Then he saw the moon through the skylight above him, and Augie's death drifted back to him like the threads of a bad dream.

He sat up in the bed. "Carmen?"

He ran his hand over her side of the mattress and cringed at the cold wetness there, and he pulled back the blanket to reveal the dark stain.

God, no, not again.

He raced into the bathroom, where he found Carmen shivering, crying, bleeding. Later that night, as he sat next to her hospital bed, and felt the lifelessness in her hand and saw the opaque blackness of her eyes, he knew the depression that was settling over her would be even worse than the last time.

Her obstetrician was sympathetic but stern when Chris dragged Carmen to the follow-up appointment two weeks after the miscarriage. "I wasn't speaking lightly when I said 'no undue stress,'" she said.

Carmen looked out the window. She didn't seem to care what her doctor was saying. She didn't even seem to hear. Yet the tears were there. Chris saw one shimmer in the light as it slipped over her chin. The tears were constant, and terribly silent.

"My father died," Chris said. "We could hardly control that."

"But she didn't have to throw a party. That's what triggered her last miscarriage, having to entertain a house full of people." The doctor sighed, leaning forward, her elbows on the desk. "Listen you two," she said. "Carmen. Look at me, Carmen."

Carmen turned her head slowly to face the woman on the other side of the desk. Chris was no longer sure if her sluggishness was from the antidepressant she was taking or from the depression itself.

"Any pregnancy you have is going to be extremely high-risk," the doctor said. "We don't know what causes you to spontaneously abort, but next time I'll insist on complete bed rest. That will at least rule out excessive activity as a cause."

"There won't be a next time," Chris said, impulsively.

Carmen jerked her head toward him, and although the suddenness of her response surprised him, he was pleased to see any reaction out of her at all.

"I don't want you to go through this again," he said to her.

She didn't seem to have the strength to argue, although he knew what she wanted to say: She couldn't imagine her life without a child in it. Children had always been part of their plan. He knew that if Carmen pulled out of this depression, and if she was still motivated and willing to follow her doctor's orders to the letter, he would agree to try once more.

He never guessed how fervently he would one day regret that decision.

15.

Carmen found no Cabrios listed in the Springfield, New Jersey, telephone directory, although there were two Blackwells. Women answered at both those numbers, and neither of them had heard of a Steven or Robert Blackwell, so Carmen widened her search. She actually spoke with a Robert Blackwell in Roselle Park, but he was ten years older than Jeff, and he knew of no other man with his name.

She found one single Cabrio—Cabrio, S. G.—listed in New Providence. Her call to the number was answered by a machine. The message, delivered in a soft, feminine voice with a mild, but unmistakable New Jersey accent, was succinct: "Hello, there. Leave a message, please."

Carmen wouldn't chance leaving a message, which could be ignored or lost. Besides, what could she say?

She called the number regularly for four days in a row without success. Finally, while loading the dishes in her dishwasher one evening, she tried again. It would be close to eleven o'clock in New Jersey. Maybe by now S. G. would be home.

The voice that answered with its expectant "Hello,

there," sounded exactly as it did on the tape, and Carmen nearly hung up before realizing she had reached a live human being.

She quickly shut the door of the dishwasher and gave the phone her full attention. "Excuse me for disturbing you at this hour," she said. "My name is Carmen Perez, and I'm calling from television station KTVA in California." She would leave out the city. She would get as much information as she could while revealing as little as possible. "I'm trying to reach S. G. Cabrio. Is that you?"

"This is Susan, yes." The woman seemed hesitant, but Carmen detected curiosity in her voice.

"Susan," she asked, "do you know of an Elizabeth Cabrio?"

There was a sharp intake of breath from the other end of the line, then silence, and Carmen knew she'd hit pay dirt. She grabbed a notepad from a kitchen drawer and sat down at the table. This call should be taped, but she couldn't take the chance of scaring Susan Cabrio off by telling her she was being recorded

"Ms. Cabrio?" she prompted.

"Who did you say you are again?"

Carmen repeated her name. "I'm from television station KTVA in Mira Mesa, California." Ordinarily she would tell someone that KTVA was in San Diego, even though it was physically located in Mira Mesa. She was hoping the latter would be a more forgettable name.

"And why do you want to know if I know Elizabeth?"

Carmen laughed, trying to convey a lightness, an embarrassment. Trying to keep Susan Cabrio at bay until she understood better how her players fit together. "I know this will sound strange, but I'm calling you cold. I'm not exactly sure yet what I'm looking for. I'm following up on a story out here, and her name has come up."

There was another moment of silence on the other end of the line, and Carmen bit her lip. Susan Cabrio was struggling to determine how to handle this call, and Carmen felt sorry for her. Still, she could use this woman's curiosity to her advantage.

"What kind of story?" Susan asked finally.

"I'm sorry, Ms. Cabrio, but I don't know the answer to that myself. And I realize it's not fair for me to ask you questions when I'm not even sure yet why I'm looking for the answers. What if I call you back when I have a clearer sense of what I need?"

"No, wait!" Susan paused, but only for a second. "Beth is my older sister. Do you know where she is?"

Carmen smiled to herself, and wrote "E. C.'s sister" beneath Susan's name and number. "No, I don't," she said. "I was hoping you might be able to put me in touch with her."

She sensed Susan Cabrio's hesitancy once again. "There's nothing I'd like better than to speak with her myself," Susan said finally, "but I haven't seen her since I was fourteen. I think you should at least tell me if she's in some kind of trouble."

"No, I'm certain it's nothing like that, but as you can tell, Susan, right now I'm grasping at straws. I promise you, though, if I do manage to learn her whereabouts, I'll let you know."

"Don't get off!" Susan said quickly, although Carmen had no intention of hanging up yet.

"Would you like to tell me about Elizabeth?" she coaxed.

Despite Susan's reluctance to get off the phone, she seemed even more reluctant to speak.

"I don't think I should," she said. "It was a family matter. A private matter. I—"

"But the more I know about her, the more likely it is that I can find her."

Susan seemed to hold her breath for a moment before letting it out in a long sigh. Carmen imagined her sitting down, settling in, finally ready to talk.

"Well," Susan said, "Beth left home when she was fifteen."

Carmen did some quick arithmetic in her head and was surprised to realize that Susan Cabrio was close to fifty. She sounded much younger.

"Really?" Carmen said. "And you haven't seen her since then?"

"No. She didn't leave on her own, exactly. My parents kicked her out because . . . how much of this do you want to hear?"

"I'd like to hear anything you're willing to tell me."

"Well, Beth was pregnant."

Carmen closed her eyes. *Yes.*

"That was punishable by death back then, especially in my family. None of us ever heard from her again. She simply fell off the face of the earth. I cried myself to sleep at night for about a year before I began to accept that she was never coming back."

"Maybe she got married?" Carmen suggested. "Maybe she ran off with the baby's father?"

"I don't think so. She refused to tell my parents who it was, and she really never talked about having a boyfriend, at least not anyone in particular."

"Does the name Steven Blackwell mean anything to you?"

"Who's that? You're not saying that's the father, are you?" Susan's voice rose with excitement. "Do you know something about . . ."

"No, no." Carmen interrupted her. "That name's cropped up, and I wondered if he might be connected in some way."

Susan was quiet for a moment. "You've got names cropping up all over the place, don't you?" she asked.

Carmen cringed, but let out a small laugh. "It must seem that way, I guess." She liked Susan Cabrio. She wished she could tell her the little she knew, but it would be a mistake. And what could she say? *I think I know where your nephew is, but it looks like he's involved in criminal activity, which I'm trying to uncover?*

"Well," Susan said, "I've never heard of a Steven Blackwell. I guess it's possible that Beth mentioned the name of the baby's father to me at some time and I've forgotten it." She paused for a long time. "I tried to find Beth myself a few years ago," she said finally. "Sometimes I get so angry with her. She cut me out of her life."

"Can you tell me about the search you mounted for her? What did you learn?"

That long sigh again. "Not much. I did find out that, after she was kicked out of our house, she moved into the home of a woman who lived in Newark. I spoke with her. Beth cooked and kept house for her in exchange for room and board. Once the baby was born, though, the woman told Beth to find another place to live. She couldn't handle having a baby in the house. She wasn't certain where Beth went, but she thought it might have been some sort of home for wayward girls. Something along that line. I gave up then, because I figured it would be almost impossible to get into the records of a place like that, and I really didn't know where to begin."

"You must wonder what happened to the baby."

"Oh, I do," she said. "I never got married, never had any kids of my own, and every once in a while I think of that little one and . . . I just hope Beth was able to take care of her."

Carmen dropped her pencil on the table. "The baby was a girl?"

"Oh." Susan laughed. "Only in my imagination. I don't know what it was, and the woman Beth worked for didn't remember."

"Do you think I might be able to speak with the woman?"

"I'm afraid not. She died a few years ago. She was pretty old even when Beth was with her."

Carmen looked down at her scribbled notes. "Is there anything else you can tell me?"

"I can't think of anything." Susan laughed. "This has been a pretty weird phone call."

"I know," Carmen said. "And I appreciate how open you've been."

"It's been good talking about Beth." There was another moment of hesitation before Susan spoke again. "She would be fifty-one now, and I bet she's still beautiful. Oh, please, please let me know if you find her."

"I will," Carmen promised, and she meant it absolutely. "You'll be the first to know."

16.

"Glad you're here." Tina, one of the nurses at the Children's Home, smiled as Chris approached the unit desk. "Dusty's been a royal pain in the butt all week."

"Yeah?" Chris grinned as though she'd complimented him. They all complained about Dustin—he could be a demanding child from the confines of his soundless, sightless world—but Chris enjoyed their tales of his four-year-old son's stubborn opposition. He liked that Dustin was a fighter, that he didn't submit easily to the cross he'd been given to bear.

Chris sat on the edge of the desk. "What's he been up to?"

Tina closed the chart on which she was working and stood to put it in the circular rack. "He yanked out his feeding tube yesterday."

Chris's eyes widened. "You mean he used his hands?"

"Oh, no." Tina looked chagrined at having misled him. "You know he'll never be able to do that, don't you Chris?"

He nodded.

"No. He rolled around on the beanbag chair until it came out."

"Oh. What else?"

"The crying." Tina sounded almost apologetic as she leaned back against the counter. She drew her brown hair up into a ponytail, fastening it with a rubber band she'd had around her wrist. "You know how bad it gets sometimes. Tuesday and Wednesday we thought he'd never stop."

More than anything Chris hated the crying. No one knew the reason for it, and Dustin had no means to communicate the source of his discomfort. On the few occasions it happened during one of his visits, Chris would desperately try to still the heartrending sobs. He'd change his son's diaper, adjust his feeding tube, walk him down the halls in the wheelchair, rock him, sing to him, and Dustin would continue to cry. Chris would often end up in tears himself from the frustration and pain of seeing his son in such unrelenting anguish. Dustin wasn't the only child here who could cry for twenty-four hours straight. Chris had nothing but respect for Tina and the other high-energy women—and a few men—who had chosen to work with these kids. The rewards were few.

He found Dustin in his room curled up on his bed. He was facing the window, the one with the view of Mission Valley that he could never appreciate. Sunlight poured into the room, bouncing off the yellow walls and lighting up the colorful balloons on the ruffled curtains. This wasn't a sterile place. Chris had wanted someplace homey, someplace warm and as unlike an institution as it could be. Dustin would never know the difference, but he would.

"Hey, Dusty," Chris said, resting his hand on Dustin's

back. The little boy jumped, startled, and Chris leaned close. "It's Daddy." He let his lips linger on the warm, almost febrile skin of Dustin's temple and noticed how clean his skin and his hair smelled. The care here was excellent.

Dustin grunted and tried to roll over, and Chris carefully picked him up, pulling him into his arms. Dustin rocked his head, so vigorously that Chris had to cup his hand around the boy's forehead to prevent it from smashing into his jaw.

Chris sat down in the armless rocker, which he had bought for Carmen during her first pregnancy, and let his son thrash and struggle to get comfortable, all the while crooning to him in words Dustin couldn't hear, but which Chris knew he picked up on at some level. The vibrations, they'd told him. He feels the vibrations in your chest, your throat. In the air.

"How's my boy?" Chris asked, rocking.

He never allowed himself to think beyond the moment, to wonder how he would be able to hold Dustin this way when the boy got older. *If* he got older. His heart wasn't good, and Chris wouldn't allow the tests to determine the extent of the damage, tests that could only add to Dustin's suffering and do nothing to improve the quality of his life. Sometimes he wished his son looked worse than he did. It was hard to convince himself of the severity of Dustin's condition when, except for his eyes, he was beautiful. He was of average build for his age; his useless limbs were well-formed. His hair was thick and very dark, his features perfect. Would Chris still be able to pick him up, sing to him, rock him, when Dustin was ten? Fifteen?

"He'll never be able to know the difference between you and anyone else," one of the staff had told him long ago, in an effort to be kind, to let him know that his regular visits were not really necessary. But Dustin *did* know. By the time he was two, even the staff had to admit that his spirits seemed to lift when Chris arrived. Only recently did one of them tell Chris that Dustin sometimes cried when he left.

Dustin's thumb jerked up to his mouth, and he sucked hungrily, his eyes open, the corneas silvered over, like the milky backing of an old mirror. He made small humming sounds deep in his throat, sounds Chris had long ago decided were Dustin's way of showing contentment. Chris rocked, shutting his own eyes, resting his chin against his son's sweet-smelling hair. He began to sing, quietly.

Tell me why the stars do shine
Tell me why the ivy twine
Tell me why the sky's so blue
And I will tell you just why I love you.

When Chris stopped singing, Dustin pulled his thumb from his mouth and begin to rock—his agitated, frustrated rock—making wild sounds: "Nah! Nah! Nah! Unh! Unh!" Chris began to sing again.

Sometimes he stopped intentionally just to get Dustin's reaction, just to feel as though there was some sort of communication between them.

"Would you like to know what your mother is up to?"

he asked when he had finished his song. "She's really cooking, Dusty."

He remembered Carmen on *News Nine* the night before. She'd said that Jeff Cabrio refused to make a statement to the press—Carmen could make a "no comment" sound like a major news event—but that Mayor Chris Garrett reported "good progress" on the rainmaking project. No one had a clue what that meant, but it didn't matter. From very little information, Carmen, in her old, inimitable style, was creating a mystique around Jeff. She described the long hours he spent in the warehouse, how he sent out for food to avoid seeing other people, how he returned home to his cottage long after dark and was up again before dawn.

"There was a blurb in the paper today," Chris told his son. "It said that *News Nine*'s ratings are up a bit on the nights your mom makes her *North County Report.* What do you think of that?"

Dustin was still. Nearly asleep.

"And I painted your old room the other day."

Dustin's head was heavy against his chest. Chris stood up slowly and lowered his son back to the bed.

"Unh! Unh! Unh!" Dustin sprang to life. And then the crying began, and with it the wrenching pain deep in Chris's chest. He set his hand on the little boy's back again.

"Dustin, don't do that. Please, don't."

"I'll stay with him."

Chris turned to see Tina standing in the doorway. He

looked down at his son, whose little shoulders heaved with his sobs.

"I hate when he does this," he said.

Tina nodded. She pushed past Chris and began fiddling with Dustin's covers, as though what she was doing was more important than anything Chris could possibly do right now. It was a game they played, Chris knew. A game designed to give him permission to leave, guilt-free. Although nothing regarding Dustin would ever leave Chris guilt-free.

It was nearly three o'clock when he arrived at Sugarbush. Carmen was about to get into her car as he was getting out of his. He was certain she knew where he'd been, that he went to San Diego to see Dustin every Saturday.

"Hi," she said.

"Hi."

She looked toward the cottages, squinting against the sun. "How long is the drive?" she asked.

"An hour and a half."

"Oh," she said, simply, disinterestedly. She said nothing more to him as she opened her car door and slipped in behind the steering wheel. But before she started the engine, she smoothed her thick hair back from her face, and in her huge eyes he could see the unmistakable shimmer of tears.

17.

She was kneeling in the rose garden, kneeling in the dust. Chris watched her from the edge of his bed, where the misleading early morning chill made a slow sweep over his body. Carmen's tawny skin, tawny shorts and shirt blended in with the earth and brush of Sugarbush, and only the dark shine of her hair stood out against the muted colors of the yard. The sun lit up her hands and the white-tipped vermilion roses that had always been her favorites. She knelt near the one leggy rose bush at the center of the garden. Those bushes farthest from her were dead and crumbling; those closer, still clinging to life, still showing some green in their stems.

Next to her was a beige bucket, so close in color to the earth that, until she picked it up, Chris hadn't realized it was there. She poured water over the ground around the rosebush. Her gray water, he was certain. Carmen, breaking the law to save this one pinch of color in her yard.

The sleeves of her blouse were rolled up; she didn't know anyone was watching. From this distance, though, Chris couldn't see the scars. Even now, certain images from that long-ago morning remained vivid in his memory: the swirling pattern of blood on the floor and walls of the bathroom she had decorated entirely in white; the sharp precision with which she'd opened her veins. He'd pressed the thick white terry towels to her arms, pressed as hard as he could until his own arms shook with the effort, and the ambulance siren neared. They took her away, leaving him crying and shaking and sick, and wondering how, in such a short span of time, such a mere heartbeat, they had gone from happiness to the total destruction of a marriage they had both treasured.

Carmen stood up, leaning over to smell the fullest rose, straightening once again. She looked to either side of her, to all she'd lost, and she seemed to sag, her shoulders drooping. Reaching for the bucket, lifting it, seemed almost too much effort for her.

"Hang in there, Carmen," he said softly to himself.

He watched her until she disappeared once again inside the house. Then he took a shower, saving his own gray water in a large earthenware bowl he found in the kitchen. And once Carmen had left for work, he carried the water outside and gave it to her vermilion roses.

18.

He was home. It wasn't yet dark, and already he was there, kicking against the porch step to rid his shoes of dust before walking into the cottage. Mia could see him through the window of her living room, where she sat on the sofa, eating her steamed vegetables. She hadn't spoken to him since the night she'd given him the kitten. He had intimidated her then, the way he saw through her, the way he seemed to know more about her than she knew about herself.

She was putting the leftover vegetables in the refrigerator when Jeff knocked on her door, and he opened it a few inches before she had a chance to get to it herself.

"May I come in?" he asked.

"Of course." She wiped her hands on a dish towel as he stepped into the room, carrying what looked like a yellow stool with a wide circular seat.

"What's that?" she asked.

"I made it for you," he said. "It's to save your back."

He rested the stool on the plastic sheeting in the center of the living room and smiled at her confusion. He moved one of the kitchen chairs next to the stool and motioned her toward it. "Sit down," he said. "I want to see if it's the right height."

She sat down on the chair, and he whisked his hand along the edge of the stool's circular top, making it spin like a lazy Susan. "You put your work on here and you're all set."

"It's perfect," she said, pleased. "Thank you."

"Will it be sturdy enough?"

She leaned forward, resting her arms on the circle of wood, and nodded.

"Good." He put his hands on his hips, looked around the room. "It smells great in here," he said.

"Have you had dinner? I have leftovers."

He sniffed the air. "Onions. Carrots—no, sweet potatoes, right?"

"Both," she said.

"And something else. Cabbage?"

"Close. Brussels sprouts. I'm impressed."

"No meat?"

"Just vegetables. Would you like some?"

"Please."

He followed her into the kitchen, where she took the bowl of vegetables from the refrigerator and put it in the microwave she'd brought from home.

"Vegetarian?" he asked.

"Yes."

"Moral or health reasons?"

She hesitated, turning away to take a plate from the cupboard. "I just think it's better for all concerned." She glanced at him and knew he didn't quite buy the explanation, but he didn't seem inclined to push her.

"Have a seat." She motioned toward the small kitchen table. When the microwave beeped, she handed him the bowl of vegetables. "How's the cat?" she asked.

"Smart. And fortunately very independent. He takes what I can give him and doesn't ask for anything more. And he's turning out to be a watch cat. He sits on the windowsill and guards the place." He took a bite of sweet potato. "So where are the pictures you took of me?"

"I'll get them." She walked into the living room and picked up the pictures from the coffee table, along with the sketches she was making of the pose she would use for her sculpture. Back in the kitchen, she laid the pictures next to his plate.

Jeff set down his fork, and his eyes widened. He picked up the top photograph, one of him standing, shirtless, next to the computer.

"My God," he said. "I'm falling apart." He touched his hair, his abdomen, just below the ribs, and she was surprised by his reaction, by the sudden vulnerability she saw in him when he had seemed so thoroughly invulnerable.

"You're excellent," she reassured him. "You're a perfect subject."

His face was still creased with worry. "It's been so long since I've really gotten a look at myself. I need to do a few sit-ups or something."

Mia shook her head and took the photograph from his fingers. "The real beauty in this body," she said, "is that it's not the body of some young student model paying his way through college. There's a maturity to it. Your pectorals and abdominal muscles are still defined, but with a certain softening."

"You're not making me feel any better."

"It's very subtle, the softening, and it gives you character. It makes you a lure to an artist, Jeff. It makes you irresistible."

He raised his eyebrows, a half-smile on his lips.

"To an artist," she repeated firmly.

"Well, Mia," he said. "At least I know right where I stand with you, huh? All you want is my body, and you don't even try to cover up your dishonorable intentions."

She laughed, but she could see he was still disconcerted as he fanned through the rest of the photographs. "Who is this stranger?" he asked, more to himself than to her. "Who the hell is this guy?"

She showed him the nearly finished bas-relief of the window she planned to use as the backdrop for his sculpture. He admired her work, then suddenly looked up at her.

"Could you make a fountain?" he asked.

"A fountain?"

"Yes. Wouldn't it be nice if—once there's some water to spare—Valle Rosa had a small fountain to celebrate? Maybe in the little park next to Chris's office?"

She smiled slowly. "You're nuts, you know. Water to spare?"

"Could you do it?"

"It's not the kind of thing I usually do, but it might be

fun. I could do it in clay, then make a plaster mold and pour concrete into it." She was as crazy as he was.

"That sounds great." He pushed his chair back from the table, and stretched his arms above his head. "Do you know what time the coyotes start up?" he asked.

"Close to eleven, I'd say. Why?"

He looked at his watch. "I plan to tape them tonight."

"You mean, on video?"

"Just audio."

"From your cottage?"

He shook his head. "The canyon. I'll walk out a ways."

"It'll be eerie," she said. "Scary."

"No. I like the way they sound. It's a natural sound. It's other noises I'm afraid of."

She felt a surprising surge of envy at the thought of him walking in the cool darkness of the canyon.

"I can see the idea appeals to you," he said. "Would you like to join me?"

She hesitated only a second or two. "All right."

At ten-thirty she met him on the porch of his cottage and they set out in darkness, down into the canyon. From somewhere in the distance came the faint but unmistakable smell of smoke.

Jeff carried a flashlight with him, but he didn't turn it on, not wanting to disturb the wildlife any more than he had to. The half-moon spilled enough light on the chaparral to help them negotiate the steep drop into the canyon. At one point, though, she began to slip and had to grab his arm to steady herself. She let go quickly.

"Here," Jeff said finally. He climbed onto a broad flat

boulder, white-lit in the moonlight, and nodded for her to follow him up.

The boulder still held some of the warmth of the day. She sat next to him as he stretched out on his back, resting the recorder on his stomach.

"Ah," he said. "This is nice. This is complete freedom. Not a soul knows I'm out here. No one. Not even Miz Perez."

"I know," she said.

He turned his head toward her, and she could see the moonlight on the sharp lines of his temple, his cheek, his jaw. "Yes," he said, "but you don't count."

"What do you mean?"

"You don't count because you're on the run, too." He circled her wrist with his fingers, and although it sent a chill up her spine, there was nothing romantic, nothing suggestive, in his touch. He squeezed his fingers closed around her skin. "You value freedom as much as I do," he said. "I don't know your reasons, and I don't need to know. But we're kindred spirits, Mia."

She drew her wrist away with the pretense of smoothing her hair from her cheek, but she lay down on the boulder, not too close to him. Above her, the sky was a dome of stars. "For me, though, it's temporary," she said. "It's not my choice."

He laughed. "It's not my choice either. I didn't decide one morning that I'd enjoy the life of a fugitive."

"What will you do with the tape of the coyotes?"

"Take it with me wherever I go."

"Why?"

"Because they're free." His voice was soft. Mia had to strain to hear him. "They're adaptable. They can live where it's fifty degrees below zero or a hundred and twenty in the shade. They're loners, but they're smart enough to band together to catch something fast and big, like an antelope or a jack rabbit. Which is why I'm not out here taping antelopes and jack rabbits." He chuckled. "And they're clever. When they dig a den for themselves, they always make sure to dig an escape tunnel out the back."

"Do you have an escape tunnel?" she asked softly.

He was quiet for so long she wondered if he had understood her question.

"I had one," he said finally, "but it's getting a bit muddy, a bit impassable, and I don't seem to have the motivation any more to clear it out."

"Why not?"

"Because I'm being seduced," he said. "By Valle Rosa. By the water problem. By the challenge. It's all clouding my judgment and I . . . Shh."

He closed his fingers around her wrist again, and she heard the soft, distant yips that had caught his attention. They came from the north. Jeff let go of her to turn on the recorder.

The yipping grew to a high-pitched whine, and then into the familiar, chilling howl that cut across the moonlit canyon. Mia shut her eyes and shivered, closing her arms across her chest. From far behind them, a second howling began, and a third joined in from the east. The sound filled Mia's head and wrapped itself around her body, and she felt the threat of inexplicable tears. She wanted to touch Jeff, to remind herself that she wasn't alone, to still the quickening of her heartbeat, but she kept her hands locked tightly over her arms.

It was several minutes before the howling faded away. Jeff clicked off the recorder, but for another moment or two they lay still, not speaking, barely breathing.

"Does it sound like joy or sorrow to you?" he asked finally.

"Sorrow," she answered quickly.

"Ah," he said, and she heard a smile in his voice. "Perhaps you and I are not kindred spirits after all."

19.

Barbara Roland, a handsome woman in her early fifties, sat across the coffee table from Carmen, balancing her Lenox teacup on her linen-draped lap. They were in her house in Summit, New Jersey. It was a beautiful house, a stunning colonial, well aged but thoroughly renovated. The hardwood floors shimmered where they weren't concealed by thick oriental carpets; the walls of the high-ceilinged rooms were covered in richly detailed wallpaper.

She'd found Barbara's name after flying to New Jersey, at her own expense—an expense she could ill-afford—and searching through libraries and public records until she came across information on the old "home for unwed mothers" run by the Catholic diocese in Maplewood, New Jersey, outside of New York City. She was able to track down a woman who had been involved in running the home, but who told her flatly she couldn't provide her with information that was clearly confidential. She did, however, suggest that Carmen get in touch with Barbara Roland, the woman who was now director of a statewide program for pregnant adolescent girls. Carmen saw no point in speaking with someone involved in a program currently in operation, but she had no other leads and so called Barbara Roland, who immediately agreed to see her. As she sat in Barbara's comfortable living room, she was beginning to understand why.

"It was old Sister Frances you spoke with," Barbara said, smiling. "And she put you in touch with me for a very good reason. I was one of the girls at the home when Beth Cabrio was there."

"Oh." Carmen sat forward, resting her teacup on the glass-topped coffee table and trying to quickly reassess the elegant, silver-haired woman sitting opposite her.

"My past is no secret," Barbara said. "Everyone knows that the reason I care so much about the girls in my program is that I was once one of them myself."

"And you knew Beth?" Carmen had already made it clear she wasn't prepared to divulge the exact nature of the story on which she was working, only that it had something to do with Beth Cabrio's son.

"Beth and I were best friends," Barbara said. "She was an inspiration. She'd already had her baby by the time she moved into Saint Mary's, while most of us were still expecting. A lot of us, myself included, had planned on giving up our babies for adoption and going back to our former lives as though nothing had happened. But Robbie was such a beautiful baby that several of us changed our minds." Her eyes quickly misted over. "Thank God I never gave up David, my son," she said. "My husband, Al, is David's father. We were married when David was a few years old, and we'll be celebrating our thirty-second anniversary next week."

ughtful for a moment, and then chuckled again
recollection. When her expression cleared of
, she continued. "Once Robbie was old enough to
hool, I let Beth use our address so that, no matter
he was living with, Robbie would have one con-
t school. As you can well imagine, that little boy had
eat deal of trouble academically. His teachers were
stantly calling Beth in to meet with them. They'd call
y house, and I'd pretend to be Beth and set up a meet-
ng between her and the teacher. Then I'd track Beth
down and make certain she kept the appointment."
Barbara shook her head. "It was all rather amazing, in
retrospect."

"What do you mean?"

"Well, the school thought Robbie was 'backwards.'
Even in kindergarten, his teacher recommended special
remedial classes for him. Beth absolutely refused to hear
of it. She was furious when she got the notice telling her
they were going to make him repeat kindergarten."

"Repeat kindergarten?" Carmen was incredulous.

"Yes, indeed. I went up to the school with her—something I vowed never to do again. She made an incredible
scene, and Al said it would reflect poorly on David if the
principal thought I was friends with her. Anyway, she flew
into that principal's office with a chip on her shoulder the
size of Mount Rushmore. She could be a very . . . i
appropriate person." Barbara smiled. "She never see
to understand proper decorum, if you know what I

Carmen nodded.

"She was wearing a skirt I will never f

Carmen smiled. "Congratulations." She liked this
woman and would have enjoyed hearing more about her
clearly unusual life, but it was time to shift the conversation back to Beth Cabrio. "Did you know Steven
Blackwell?" she asked.

Barbara laughed. "Was that the name? Steven? I'd
forgotten. There *was* no Steven Blackwell. Beth fabricated
that name for the birth certificate. To be frank, she didn't
have a clue who the baby's father was, so she simply
picked a name she liked and used it." Barbara looked
thoughtful as she tapped a finger to her lips. "Beth was a
reckless sort of girl. Not bad, by any means, but fun-
loving and spirited, and she couldn't leave the boys alone.
I don't think she'd ever gotten enough love at home, if
you know what I mean."

Carmen nodded. She knew.

"She'd even sneak boys into her room at Saint Mary's,
which I assure you was a mortal sin. The nuns were going
to ask her to leave, but then she met a man and left on her
own with him." Barbara sighed and stared out the window
toward the full weeping willow in the garden. Carmen
said nothing. She wasn't certain what to ask next. She
wished she knew more clearly what she was looking for.

"I left the home around the same time," Barbara continued, "and moved into my brother's home in Maplewood, but I always kept in touch with Beth. I worried
about her and about the baby. She attracted a rough sort of
person. She stayed with that first man for no more than a
week or so before he threw her and the baby back on the
street. Then she'd move from one man's apartment to

another, whoever would take her in. This went on for years. She lived out of a suitcase. As Robbie got a little older, he'd try to treat the men in Beth's life as if they were his father." Barbara took a sip of tea and shook her head. "It was pathetic. My heart would break for that little boy, but Beth saw no other way to live. The men used her, one way or another. A few of them abused her physically, and she'd endure it until they'd lay a hand on Robbie. That, she wouldn't tolerate. Then she'd have to find someone else to live with for a while. I remember one man who treated her fairly well, and she was optimistic that their relationship might turn into something lasting. But then Robbie broke his leg falling out of a tree." Barbara laughed again. "He had his mother's wild streak, I'm afraid. The gentleman they were living with couldn't deal with Robbie's cast and carting him around everywhere, so he asked them to leave. Life was such a trial for her. Do you know people like that? Life throws one obstacle after another in their face, and they never seem able to get ahead?"

"Yes," Carmen said, thinking of the struggles of her own youth. She had made different choices than Beth Cabrio, though. Better choices. But she hadn't had a baby to worry about. Perhaps Beth had done the best she could.

"You and Beth sound very different," she said. "It seems unlikely that you'd ever be friends."

"Yes, you're right. We were nothing alike. Al would say that I always took up for the underdog, but it was much more than that." Barbara leaned over to straighten a tapestry pillow at the end of the sofa. "Beth was a good friend," she said, "and a good person. She had no money,

but she'd always be there⟨...⟩ through all my trials a⟨...⟩ right there to listen to me,⟨...⟩ her ear for hours on end."⟨...⟩

Carmen tried to picture the t⟨...⟩ ing with one another about men a⟨...⟩

"Beth would listen and give me he⟨...⟩ advice." Barbara chuckled as she lea⟨...⟩ herself more tea from the silver pot on⟨...⟩ offered some to Carmen, who declined. "A⟨...⟩ Barbara said. "She'd cry because I was in⟨...⟩ friend, she was a real treasure."

Carmen nodded. "Go on," she said. "Please t⟨...⟩ more."

"Well, I married Al when David was three." Barb⟨...⟩ stirred sugar into her tea and sat back on the plush so⟨...⟩ again. "Al never cared for Beth. She was very pretty, bu⟨...⟩ she wore too much make-up, and she simply didn't look healthy or well kept. She did the best she could with Robbie, though, making certain his vaccinations were up to date, that sort of thing. She loved him very much, but I used to think she treated him more like a playmate than a son. He called her 'Beth' instead of 'Mom.'" Barbara shook her head. "She was still a child herself. I think Al was threatened by her, to be honest. I think he was afraid that Beth would be a bad influence on me, and that I'd start acting as wild as she did.

"I assume that didn't happen," Carmen said with a smile.

"No, but I didn't exactly rub off on her, either." Barbara

suede. Tight as a glove. Her hair, which was a pale, pale blond, was up in a beehive, and she was carrying a lit cigarette. Can you picture this?"

Carmen laughed at the image.

"I remember looking at her and wondering how it was I'd come to be her friend," Barbara said. "Like you were saying, how could I love her so much when we were so different?" She looked at Carmen, as if for the answer.

"I think you're the type of woman who doesn't judge people," Carmen said, with some admiration.

"I hope so." Barbara looked into the teacup on her lap. "Well, as I said, Robbie was held back, and even by the time he got into the first grade, he was still failing subjects. Poor little guy. He was one of those children who simply couldn't sit still, who couldn't concentrate very long on one thing. I think he was labeled a difficult child from day one, and then no one expected anything from him but trouble." Barbara set her empty cup on the coffee table. "Ah," she said, slapping her hands on her thighs, "but then Beth met Jefferson Watts, and everything changed."

Carmen was struck instantly by the name. "Jefferson?"

"That's right." Whoever Jefferson Watts was, it was obvious that Barbara Roland approved of him. "Jefferson was a big, tall handsome man—a black man—with a deep booming voice that you could feel inside your ribcage when he spoke. I remember Beth telling me that the first time she and Robbie went to Jefferson's apartment, Robbie hid under the bed, he was so afraid of him. Jefferson was much older than Beth. She was about twenty-two then. Jefferson must have been close to forty, and he was quite well-off." Barbara raised her hands dramatically into the air. "Suddenly, Beth had lovely clothes to wear, and she could buy things for Robbie. She even bought me something—a pair of beautiful silver earrings, which I still own. She started wearing her hair in the natural style that was popular back then—perfectly straight, with long bangs. It was very attractive on her. She was eating regularly, no one was hurting her, and she was finally in love, for real this time, with someone who loved her, too. You could see how much Jefferson cared about her when they were together. It created some problems between Al and myself, since Jefferson was black. It wouldn't have mattered if Jefferson were president, Al wouldn't have approved."

Carmen tried not to frown, although bigotry always touched a deep and tender nerve in her. She had been its victim often enough. She wondered how this marriage between a liberal do-gooder and her narrow-minded husband had survived for thirty-two years.

Barbara poured herself more tea, and this time Carmen accepted some in her own cup.

"After a few months," Barbara continued, "Beth started using Jefferson's address for Robbie, and she was then able to move him to a different school. I don't know whether it was moving him into a school where they didn't already have their minds made up that he was a problem, or whether it was having Jefferson around, but after only a few weeks, Robbie's teacher called Beth in for a meeting and told her, 'Your son is very bright and needs special classes.' Well! Of course, Beth didn't argue with her, and Robbie began to do extremely well."

Carmen felt, oddly, like cheering, but Barbara's smile faded quickly.

"And then I lost touch with them," she said.

Carmen was taken by surprise. "Why?" she asked.

"I don't really know." Barbara shook her head, a perplexed frown on her face. "Beth was finally genuinely happy. Jefferson treated Robbie like his own son. Even Al was starting to come around. He was talking to Beth about taking the high-school equivalency exam and going into accounting. She was sharp with numbers. She came across as a dumb blond, but once you knew her, you could see there was more there. Much more. Al had gotten her some study guides, and he started tutoring her."

Al immediately redeemed himself in Carmen's eyes. Maybe he had mellowed over time.

"Then, one day, they disappeared." Barbara turned her hands out in a gesture of confusion. "Beth stopped by late one night. She hugged me. She was crying. She just wanted to say goodbye, she said. They were leaving town, and she couldn't say where they were going, but she'd get in touch when she could. The next morning, Robbie didn't show up at school. Davey was heartbroken. He and Robbie had been best friends since they were little."

"Why would they leave so suddenly?"

Barbara smoothed her skirt over her knees. "Looking back now, I think Jefferson must have been in some kind of trouble and they needed to get away quickly. I got a

Christmas card from Beth a few years later. She said they were well and happy, and that Robbie had skipped a grade, and they thought he was so smart that he might skip another."

"No return address?"

"No, but I did notice that the postmark was from Plainfield. That was the last I heard of her." Barbara sighed. "I still find myself thinking about Beth, trying to figure out if there's some way I can get in touch with her. Do you know? Can you at least tell me that much?"

"I'm sorry," Carmen said. "I'd love to speak with her myself, but I don't know her whereabouts. I promise, though, to let you know when I find out."

"What about Robbie? I assume you know where he is, since you said your story has something to do with him."

Carmen thought about the request. It seemed harmless to put Jeff in touch with this kind and caring woman, but it was clear that Barbara Roland expected nothing but good from that little boy. How would she feel if she knew Carmen was trying to hang him? "Let me have some time to develop my story before I hook up the two of you," she said.

"Well." Barbara rested her cup on the silver tray. "I know how it is with you reporters. Whatever you're working on is your story, your scoop, isn't that right? You have to protect it until you have everything in place." Her tone was almost sympathetic. Carmen felt no accusation in it.

Carmen reached down to turn off the tape player where it rested on the black-and-red oriental rug. "It must have been frustrating, losing touch with her like that," she said.

"It certainly was." Barbara rearranged the empty cups on the tray and stood up. "Do you have a few more minutes?" she asked.

Carmen looked at her watch. "Yes." Her flight wasn't until later that evening.

She followed Barbara upstairs to a room the older woman used as an office. Barbara showed her the numerous pictures of Al and David that graced her desk and a scrapbook of articles on the state's program for unwed mothers. Then, from the back of a dusty album, she pulled a yellowing, faded color photograph. The young blond woman in the picture grinned at the camera as she held the hands of a tow-headed toddler who seemed to be taking his first steps.

"Beth and Robbie," Barbara said.

"That's Robbie?" Carmen asked, stunned. She scanned the child's features, hunting for some resemblance to Jeff Cabrio, but finding little. "He was so blond."

"Oh, yes. And Beth's hair was natural. The envy of all of us at the home." Barbara slipped the picture out of the small black corners that held it in place and handed it to her. "I'd like it back when you're done with it," she said, and Carmen nodded.

She walked Carmen downstairs again. At the front door, she took her hand, squeezed it. "If you do see Robbie, please tell him I'd adore hearing from him. Tell him I'd give anything to know how his mother's doing."

*

While waiting for her plane at the Newark airport, Carmen used her earphones to listen to the tape of her interview with Barbara. She took notes on a yellow pad balanced on her knees, trying to decide what pieces of information she would pass on to her audience the following day and what she would save until later. She would need to decide on the tone of her report, as well. That was becoming a real dilemma. The cynical approach had worked at first, but it no longer seemed to fit the information she was discovering about Jeff. The facts she'd learned so far could only elicit compassion for him, and if she were moving toward uncovering his possibly criminal past, she couldn't risk making him into an object of sympathy.

Toward the end of the tape, she listened again to Barbara's description of Beth's tearful goodbye and sudden disappearance. Maybe Carmen could focus on that unexplained, apparent escape Beth and her family had made, an early allusion to Jeff's life as a fugitive. But she would need further verification of that story before she could use it. She didn't even *want* to use it. The truth was, she had found herself rooting for Beth Cabrio and her son as Barbara recounted their tale. She'd felt nothing but sympathy for their plight.

Carmen turned off the recorder and removed the earphones from her head, then looked at her watch. Still another hour. She rested her head against the wall and closed her eyes, thinking.

Beth had been a young girl, fighting the heartache of her family's rejection and the practical battle of physical survival for herself and her child. She'd fought that battle inelegantly, perhaps, but with strength and vitality and determination. She'd been tough. Very tough. Carmen wanted to meet her. She wanted to know that Beth had found a peaceful existence in middle age, that she had no fear of whatever hardship life might hand her next. In some way that Carmen couldn't explain even to herself, she felt Beth Cabrio's struggle almost as keenly as if it had been her own.

20.

Mia was always waiting. She awoke in the morning, and if Jeff wasn't her first thought, he was no further away than her second. Sometimes he was in her dreams. Once she dreamt that he was kneeling in the yard where she had seen him with the tarantula, and when he stood up, he was holding the tarantula on his arm, staring at it eye to eye.

She was waiting for the daytime hours to run their course so she could be with him, because in the five days since they'd listened together to the coyotes, he seemed to seek her out. It wasn't her imagination. When he called Chris's office, he spent so long with her on the phone, that once she forgot to put the call through. He could talk about anything. Anything except himself. When she asked him questions, she geared them carefully toward his cottage, or the cat, or the promised rain.

They ate together at night, Mia purposely changing her routine so that she didn't begin cooking until nearly sunset, when she knew he would be home. He was no longer working into the dark hours of the night, and he didn't even pretend that his early arrival at Sugarbush was an accident. He'd come over, the cat tagging along, and eat Mia's steamed vegetables as if they were filet mignon. On one occasion, he brought over his own set of vegetables and made her eggplant stuffed with rice and spinach, assuring her the recipe contained not a drop of fat. "Although," he said, "you sure look as if you could use some."

She began to hope that Rick was wrong, that Jeff wouldn't succeed in producing rain, at least not any time soon. He would have to stay in Valle Rosa, wrestling with the problem for months. She began to relish the breath-stealing heat, the crackling dry leaves of the scrub oaks and the scent of newborn fires, all symbols of the drought that kept him close.

After dinner she would work with her clay or on the design of the fountain, while he'd sit on the sofa with the kitten at his side, a pencil in his hand, and his usual pile of papers resting on his lap. Occasionally she'd catch him watching her, his smile open and genuine, and she'd return to her work with a delicious warmth inside her and a telltale wash of color in her cheeks.

Sometimes they would talk, sometimes not, but she was surprised by the ease she felt sharing parts of her life with him. She told him about Glen—not everything, of course—but about how he had taught her sculpting, how he'd called her Sunny, and a little bit of how she'd loved him.

"And why did it end?" Jeff asked her, leaning forward on the couch, the intensity in his eyes almost too much to bear.

"I can't talk about it," she answered, and he smiled.

"I understand that feeling."

He returned to his own work, and she wished he hadn't let her off the hook quite so easily.

Her fantasies pulsed with new life. Maybe he would stay in Valle Rosa so long that she would have her reconstructive surgery. Or maybe he would have to leave, but he would tell her—trust only her to know—where he was going, and she could find him after the surgery. But then, reality would settle over her like a suffocating cloud of smoke. She would remember Glen. She would remember her mother, and she'd explore her right breast gingerly, reluctantly, terrified of finding something that would set her back that much further.

At ten o'clock on the fifth night after they'd taped the coyotes, Mia turned on the television to watch the news. Jeff, sprawled on the couch, barely glanced up from his work until the anchor with the patent-leather hair introduced Carmen and her *North County Report*. Jeff raised his head then, setting his pencil on the coffee table, and folded his arms across his chest.

There was something magical about Carmen on television. The color in her face was vibrant; her eyes were huge, dark and exotic. Ordinarily, Mia enjoyed simply looking at her, but tonight she picked up Jeff's tension, and stilled her hands on her clay.

"More information now about Valle Rosa's mystery man, Jeff Cabrio," Carmen began. "*News Nine* has learned that Mr. Cabrio was the illegitimate son of a very young homeless mother who lived in or near Newark, New

Jersey, and who struggled to keep her son fed and clothed." While Carmen spoke, a photograph of a blond girl and a toddler appeared behind her. Jeff sucked in his breath and sat up on the sofa.

"Once in school," Carmen continued, "young Jeff Cabrio's brightness was at first misinterpreted, and he was held back a grade. Later though, his superior intelligence was recognized and he skipped two grades."

"Three," Jeff said quietly. "Get your goddamned facts straight."

Mia looked at him as the camera swept back to the anchorman. Jeff's cheeks had reddened; a vein pulsed at his temple. Suddenly, he raised his fists and brought them down hard on the table. "Where the hell is she getting this stuff?" He was on his feet, papers flying. The cat leapt away from him onto the floor, then up to the windowsill. Jeff ran his hands through his hair. "Where did she get that picture? *I've* never even seen it before."

"Is she . . . I mean, is what she's saying . . . accurate?"

"Close enough. Accurate enough to tell me she's got a source. She's got a bead on me."

Mia leaned back in her chair. "What does it matter? Do you honestly care what people think? Do you think anybody gives a damn if you were illegitimate or—"

"That's not it."

"Well, what is it then, Jeff?" she asked gently. "What are you so afraid of?"

He walked across the room to the window that faced the dark adobe. "Don't ask, Mia, all right? I like that you don't ask me questions." He turned to look at her. "I like sitting here with you in the evening. It reminds me of . . ." His smile was sudden. Small. Wry. He turned back to the window again. "It's just comforting, and I find that I need that sort of comfort more than I expected. I need other people more than I thought I did. Please though, don't ask me questions you know I can't answer."

"I only want to console you," she said, "and I don't know how to do that because I don't understand—"

"She's going to do me in, bit by bit. I should get out of here. Out of Valle Rosa." He rubbed his hand slowly across his chin, his eyes never leaving the window. "But I'm so close. And it's going to work."

"Maybe you should just leave Sugarbush," Mia said, panicked by the thought of him leaving Valle Rosa altogether. "There must be someplace else you could live. Chris could—"

"No. As long as I'm in Valle Rosa, I need to stay here. Carmen Perez is one scared woman, and her fear makes her very dangerous, but as long as I'm living on her property, no other reporter can get to me. It's symbiosis, pure and simple. She protects me from other predators, and in exchange she gets to feed off me. It won't be much longer. I only wish I knew who her source is." He shuddered. "I don't know what she'll say in her next report, or the report after that."

He stared out into the darkness, and Mia saw the real-life image of her sculpture—Jeff and the bas-relief of a window—in front of her.

"What do you mean, she's scared?" she asked. "What is she afraid of?"

"Losing," he said. "Losing everything she's worked for." He turned to face her. "She could unveil me now, Mia. She has enough knowledge, enough power, that if she wanted to, she could move in for the kill. But she's playing some sort of game. Did you see the gleam in her eyes?"

Mia nodded, but Jeff had already turned back to the window. "She loves this," he said. "And it's really my own fault."

"How is it your fault?" She wasn't following him at all.

"I told her where I was born. I told her in a cryptic way, and I never thought she'd be able to figure out all of this"—he waved toward the television—"from that little piece of information." He sighed. "Maybe I wanted her to. Maybe I'm sick and tired of running."

Running from what, she wanted to ask, but knew better.

Jeff walked to the sofa and gathered up his papers. The cat came running when he called him, and he reached down to pick him up. He stopped behind Mia's chair as he was walking toward the door. Leaning over, he slipped his arm across her chest from shoulder to shoulder, surprising her. He touched his cheek to the top of her head, and she stiffened at the weight of his arm on her breast. She could feel her heart beating against the prosthesis.

"See you tomorrow," he said, letting go. "Dinner will be on me."

Mia didn't let out her breath until he had closed the door behind him. She listened to his footsteps on the porch, and in a moment she heard his own cottage door open and close. Then she looked down at the sculpture on the stool in front of her. Right now it was nothing more than clay over an armature, a vaguely human form, the head and face a smooth, featureless sphere that gave nothing away. She hadn't yet settled on an expression, an emotion for him, but she knew that in the next few days she would begin to shape the clay, to carve it, until its secrets gave way bit by bit beneath the patient, careful touch of her hands.

21.

Jeff stopped Carmen as she was pulling out of the Sugarbush driveway the following morning. She didn't notice him until he pounded on her right front fender to get her attention. She'd been imagining her next step in researching his life, and it jarred her to see him in the flesh. He had started to seem almost like fiction to her.

He came around to her side of the car and motioned for her to roll down the window.

"You're putting people in danger," he said.

"What do you mean?"

"The people you're getting your information from. You're putting them in jeopardy."

"Why, Jeff?" She turned off the ignition and leaned her arm on the windowsill. "Why would talking to me cause a problem for anyone, with the possible exception of you?"

He looked tired. He hadn't shaved yet this morning; fine lines fanned out from the corners of his eyes. She tried not to feel sympathy for him.

"Just keep in mind that it could," he said. "Although I suppose that wouldn't make much difference to you."

"If I honestly thought I was hurting innocent people, of course I would care."

"Sure you would," he said. "Where did you get that picture you showed on the news last night?"

She shook her head. "I can't say, Jeff, but I learned a lot about your mother from the person who gave it to me. She sounds like a very impressive woman. I'd like to meet her."

Jeff stared at her so hard she had to look away, out to the cottages.

"Well," he said, "I'll have to have the two of you over for dinner sometime."

She ignored his sarcasm. "Where does she live?"

"Go to hell, Carmen." He started to walk away from the car, but turned back after a few steps. "You'd let me stay here for free, now, wouldn't you?" he asked. "Just to have exclusive access to me?"

She smiled. "I've got to get to work," she said, rolling up the window again. "Have a good day."

As she pulled out of the driveway, she gritted her teeth in self-disgust. God, she could be a bitch! Had she always been this haughty, this self-righteous? And what if he was right? What if she was putting people in jeopardy in a way she didn't yet understand? She wouldn't want harm to come to either Barbara Roland or the elusive Beth Cabrio.

More likely, though, Jeff was merely attempting to throw her off the trail. He's on the run from something, she reminded herself as she negotiated the curving road above the nearly empty reservoir. Law-abiding citizens don't adopt an alias and move from town to town. They don't use a motel as the address on their driver's license. And they don't con desperate people into believing they can do something that is clearly impossible.

Plainfield, New Jersey. From her desk at *News Nine*, in the large, open room she shared with a dozen other *News Nine* peons, Carmen spoke with directory assistance. She was trying to track down any Cabrios living in that city. There were none. There were ten numbers under the name Watts, however, and she tried them all. No one knew of a Jefferson; no one recognized the name Beth Cabrio.

The Christmas card had only been *postmarked* Plainfield, Barbara Roland had said. Maybe Beth had gone out of her way to make certain the card was sent from a town other than the one in which she was living. Still, it was a place to start.

She called directory assistance once more and got the names of all the elementary and junior high schools in Plainfield. Over lunch, she pondered the list, trying to figure out what to do next. How old had Jeff been when he moved to Plainfield? Surely he'd only been in elementary school, but that particular list of schools was formidable, and she didn't know how to begin to track down a student who might have attended one of them nearly thirty years earlier.

There were only two junior high schools, though, and she decided to tackle them in alphabetical order.

After lunch, she called the number for Hubbard Junior High. Summer school was in session, and the receptionist who answered the phone tried to persuade her to call back in September, but Carmen was persistent. She wanted to speak with the librarian, she said, and no, it didn't matter if it was the "summer librarian." The receptionist finally put her through.

The librarian, though, was no more agreeable. Carmen asked if she would mind looking through the yearbooks for the years Jeff might have attended Hubbard to see if the name Robert Blackwell appeared in any of them.

There was a long pause before the librarian responded to her request. "You've got to be joking," she said finally. "You think I've got nothing better to do with my time? It's summer session and these kids are wild."

Carmen spent a few futile minutes trying to persuade her. Finally the woman agreed to give her the names of the class presidents for the five-year stretch Carmen had targeted as the dates Jeff would most likely have attended the school.

She hung up the phone, frustrated. Now she had a list of names as well as a list of schools. Great. She dialed directory assistance again, searching for the numbers of the class officers and wondering how likely it was, that after twenty-some years, any of them would still live in their hometown.

But one of them did, it seemed. One woman who had blessedly not changed her name. President of her eighth grade class, Gail Evelyn Vidovich. The phone was listed under Gail E. Vidovich. Surely there couldn't be two women by that name.

Carmen took the telephone number home with her

and tried calling Gail Vidovich late in the evening, New Jersey time.

"Do I remember Robert Blackwell?" the former class president laughed into the phone. She had the same slightly gritty New Jersey accent as Susan Cabrio. "You could have called anybody who attended Hubbard Junior High while he was there and they'd remember Robbie. He was one of those kids you never forget."

Carmen held the phone to her ear as she dug through her briefcase in search of the tape recorder and the suction cup device that would allow her to tape over the phone. She hadn't been prepared for this. She hadn't expected success. "Well," she said, inserting a new tape into the recorder and sitting down at the kitchen table, "I'm researching his background for a story I'm working on out here in southern California, and—"

"Really? What's the story about?" Gail was a manic speaker, quick and eager.

"I'm not at liberty to talk about it yet. It's an exclusive, and so I have to keep it quiet right now, but I hope you'll still be willing to tell me a little bit of what you remember about him." She thought about her conversation with Jeff that morning, how she might be endangering the people she was interviewing. "Your name won't be used in any way," she added.

"This is so wild," Gail said. "I was thinking about Robbie just the other day because—"

"Excuse me," Carmen interrupted her. "Would you mind if I recorded our conversation?"

"Record it? Sure. Whatever."

Carmen attached the small suction cup to the side of the phone receiver. "Okay," she said. "Please go on."

"I was thinking about him, because at work the other day—I work in a hair salon—this woman was talking about her fourteen-year-old son who had somehow rigged up the phones in their house so that long-distance calls were being charged to a neighbor's phone. It had been going on for months, and they just caught up to him. He's in a ton of trouble."

Carmen frowned, wondering what that could possibly have to do with Jeff. Perhaps Gail Vidovich had been breathing the chemicals in her hair salon for too long. "Why did that remind you of Jeff?" she asked.

"Jeff who?"

"I mean, Robert. Robbie. You said that reminded you of him."

"Right. It's exactly the kind of thing Robbie would have done." Gail laughed again. "Do you know what he did once?"

"What?"

"He somehow got all the clocks in the school—I am not making this up, every one of them—running fast, so that our periods were only forty-five minutes long instead of fifty, and by the end of the day we got out at something like two-thirty instead of three."

Carmen smiled. "You're kidding."

"No. And it took them two days to figure out what was going on. See what I mean about him being memorable?"

"I do. What happened to him when he got caught, though?"

"Hmm." Gail paused. "I don't remember that part. Probably not much. I'm sure the administrators thought he should be punished, but they were so amazed that he could do something like that, that it was hard for them to discipline him. I mean, how do you punish a thirteen-year-old kid for doing something no adult in the school could begin to figure out how to do?"

"I can see the problem," Carmen said. She wondered how Beth Cabrio would have reacted to her son's antics. "Did you ever happen to meet his mother?"

"His mother? No. I don't think I met any of his family."

"What else can you tell me about him?"

"Well, he was cute. A charmer. Kind of skinny and a little younger than most of us—if I remember, he skipped a grade—but all the girls thought he was adorable. And, obviously, he was very smart, probably the smartest kid in the school, but he didn't necessarily get the best grades because he acted like a lot of the work was beneath him." Gail paused for breath. "They were always pulling him out of class to make him take special tests, and the teachers made a fuss over him. When they'd hear about something he did, like the clocks, they'd try to look disapproving, but you could see they were laughing inside."

"So, he got away with a lot."

For the first time, Gail hesitated. "Well, that makes him sound like a bad kid, and he wasn't. He was a nice person, and even though he got all this attention for being smart, he didn't have a swelled head."

Naturally, Carmen thought. *He was a saint.*

"You called him a 'charmer,'" she said. "Was he someone who would use his charm to his own advantage?"

"Hmm. Not with girls, if that's what you mean, but we were all pretty young then. As I said, though, he could charm the socks off adults. He was in my English class, and he really had no earthly interest in diagramming sentences, you know? It wasn't his thing at all. But he could always convince the teacher to let him do something else, something on his own instead. I doubt anyone but Robbie would have gotten that special treatment."

"Didn't the other kids resent him for that?"

"Oh, no. He was different and everyone simply accepted it."

An entire school full of saints.

"What was he like in high school?" Carmen asked.

"Actually, he didn't go on to PHS—Plainfield High School—with the rest of us. Now that I think about it, I remember something about his mother dying and him moving away."

"His mother died?" Carmen tightened her grip on the phone. An almost personal sense of loss swept over her. Her clear vision of the young, homeless Beth Cabrio, struggling to find a stable life for herself and her son filled her head. She cringed when she remembered asking Jeff about his mother that morning. "Are you sure?" she asked. "Do you know how she died?"

"I'm not a hundred percent sure, but that seems right, and I don't have the faintest notion how she died. All I know is that Robbie moved out of Plainfield."

"Where did he go?"

"I don't know that either, but you know who might? Danny Grace."

"Who's that?" Carmen pulled her notepad from the briefcase and jotted down the name.

"Danny was Robbie's best friend."

"So he would know about his home life, too? That sort of thing?"

"Oh, sure. They were always over each other's houses."

"Does Danny still live in Plainfield?"

Gail laughed. "No. He got out long ago and never came back. He's a lawyer now, somewhere in Maryland. Probably goes by Daniel. He was an idiot in high school, though. Straight D's."

The eighth-grade class president was now a beautician, the class idiot, an attorney. So much for junior high school being a predictor of the future.

Carmen wished Dan Grace were anything but a lawyer. So far, everyone with whom she'd spoken had been easy to probe for information. A lawyer would give her story greater credibility, but he was bound to ask questions, bound to be suspicious. "Is there anyone else who might know about Robbie's family?"

"Hmm. No one I can think of. Give Danny a call. Tell him I said 'Hi, and how're ya doing?'"

Carmen hung up the phone and turned off her recorder. She stared at the notepad, where she'd written Daniel Grace, atty, MD. Probably the Bar Association could put her in touch with him. She could call them in the morning. Maybe not, though. She had to remember not to move too quickly.

She rifled through her briefcase, setting aside a few nerve-wracking unpaid bills, until she found the memo Craig had slipped on her desk before she'd left the station that afternoon. She'd been on the phone at the time, and Craig had given her a wink and a thumbs-up sign before disappearing back into the hall, and she'd known that the memo contained good news.

She set it on her kitchen table to re-read it. *News Nine*'s ratings had climbed yet another notch on the nights she was on. That was all it said. Very brief. Brief, and beautiful.

It was working, her slow methodical unraveling of Jeff's story from the ground up. There was something incredibly satisfying in feeding him to her audience in bits and pieces, keeping his story alive, despite the fact that he hadn't delivered a drop of rain. She was certain he never would. Nevertheless, she found herself reading the weather report each morning, praying for rain. Just a shower. Just a mist. Something to make people continue to think that Jeff Cabrio was worthy of their curiosity.

She pulled a sheet of stationery from her briefcase and wrote a quick letter to *News Nine*'s general manager, Dennis Ketchum, requesting that her portion of *North County Report* be increased to five days a week. Her hand shook as she attached the letter to the memo detailing the new ratings. She slipped them both into an envelope, wondering if, in the morning, she would still possess the courage she'd need to deliver it to Dennis. No doubt, he had been among those wanting to get rid of her. Surely, he now realized that would have been a mistake.

She would get *San Diego Sunrise* back, she thought, as she sealed the envelope, and she would have as her guests the people she was interviewing. Perfect! All at once? Yes. Susan Cabrio. Barbara Roland. Gail Vidovich. This lawyer, Daniel Grace, if he was willing to talk. She would never be able to get Jeff himself to appear, but this would be even better. His portrait would be painted by the memories of others, painted in layers, far more complex than it could ever have been by having him on alone.

And the others were sure to tell things that Jeff himself never would.

22.

There were five of them. Three men, a woman, and an infant, huddled at the side of the adobe. Chris watched them from the window of the master bedroom, where he was painting the walls the soft salmon color Carmen favored for most of the house. He'd heard a noise from outside, and when he'd turned off the light, he'd seen them filling empty plastic milk jugs with water from the hose. The undocumented workers from the canyon.

The men were small and stripped to the waist. Their bodies, caught partially in the light coming from the back of the house, were tight, the muscles well-defined. The woman was a little heavier; the child she held was wrapped in a blanket or towel—from this distance, Chris couldn't tell which.

If they were speaking to one another, he couldn't hear them. He'd closed all the windows in the adobe because soot from a new fire on the other side of the canyon was sifting through the screens, and he was afraid it would layer itself on the freshly painted walls. Besides, he was tired—very tired—of the smell of smoke.

So Carmen still did this, he thought, still let the

workers living in the canyon use her water. No wonder her bill was astronomical.

It was rare to see women and children among the men. Usually it was the men who risked the journey north across the border, who did the hard labor and sent the money home to their families.

One of the men held the hose for the woman as she leaned over to wash her long, dark hair with a bar of soap. When she straightened up again, she unwrapped the child and soaped his small body, while the man poured water over him from a plastic jug. The child howled. It was cool outside, and Chris could imagine how the cold tap water felt on the baby's skin. He thought of hurrying downstairs to fill a basin with warm water, but he knew what Carmen would say: "I never go out to talk with them anymore. They can pretend it isn't charity if they don't have to see me. They can keep their pride."

Carmen could give and ask nothing in return. It was a side of her she allowed so few people to see, a side of her he didn't want to forget existed.

As the woman dried her baby, the man plucked a prairie blanket flower from the earth and handed it to her. With a pang of loneliness, Chris walked away from the window and turned on the light again. He needed to finish his painting and be out of the adobe before Carmen arrived home.

23

Looking back, Mia knew that Glen had been frightened to see how her body had changed, although at the time he hadn't let on. Even now she felt some gratitude toward him for hiding his fear, for allowing her to think he could see the worst she had to offer and still love her. Back then, she couldn't have taken the blow. It was bad enough when it finally came.

Karen Barker, the social worker in Dr. Bella's office, had counseled her. Was there a man in her life? Yes, Mia had said, she was engaged. She and Glen had planned the wedding for that very month, but they had put it off until she was feeling well again.

"Has he seen the incision?" Karen asked, and Mia started to cry, realizing how desperately she needed him to do exactly that, and how afraid she was of his reaction. It was hard enough to look at the scar herself.

Karen asked her what Glen was like, and Mia told her how he had helped her care for her mother, how he had even stayed with the older woman one night a week while Mia took a class. She told her how, when Laura had moved home devastated after breaking up with Luke, her boyfriend of several years, Glen had worked to cheer her up.

"He sounds like a sensitive man," Karen said. "A caring man. He'll be fine. You have to trust him. You're trying to be very strong for him, but he sounds like someone who likes taking care of people. Let yourself be taken care of for a change, Mia. Give him the chance to do that. Give him the chance to show how much he loves you."

She and Glen were in her bedroom that evening. Since her mother's death a year earlier, Glen had lived in the house with her, had slept with her every night. After the surgery, though, he'd started sleeping in her mother's old room. "What if I roll over and accidentally hurt you?" he asked, and she hadn't been able to tell him that mattered to her far less than having him close.

She had taken a shower and had put on her white chenille robe, and she stood close to him, near the bedroom window. "I'd like you to see—" She couldn't find the word. Her chest? Her incision? "My scar," she said.

Glen nodded. "Good." He sat down on the bed. "I wasn't sure if I should ask or not. I didn't want to push you."

She undid the tie of her robe, wishing the lights were dimmer. The skin of her hands had a bluish cast to them in the stark overhead light. She could see every vein. She didn't like the idea that the skin of her chest would look so translucent, so deathlike. She opened the robe, but left it on, her eyes on Glen's face.

"Just for a year," she said. "It'll only be like this for a year. Then I can have the reconstruction surgery and it won't look so—"

"It's fine, Sunny," he interrupted her. "It's not so horrid." He reached up to touch the taut skin covering her chest, and she flinched, pulled away. "Does it hurt?" he asked.

"No." She laughed. "You surprised me, that's all. It burns a little when you touch it, but it doesn't actually hurt."

"Do you feel . . . off balance?" He smiled at her.

"A little." For the first time in weeks she felt a surge of happiness. The poison was gone from her body. The danger. And Glen could handle this.

He reached up to tie the sides of her robe together again, then he stood and held her. "I love you." He kissed her temple.

"I'd like you to sleep in here tonight," she said.

She felt him nod against her head. "All right."

The next day she stopped by Dr. Bella's office, although she had no appointment. She poked her head into the social worker's cubicle. "You were right," she said. "Glen was great."

For several days everything seemed as though it would return to normal. She felt strong enough to work with clay again. Glen spent his mornings at his studio, but despite the fact that she insisted she wanted to cook, he came home early enough each night to make dinner for her and Laura. Laura was working as an assistant buyer for a large department store, and she was starting to laugh again; Luke's name came up less and less in conversation.

Then Laura started helping Glen cook, both of them gleefully banishing her from the kitchen when she tried to participate. They told her she was still recovering. She needed to be cared for, pampered, and she tried to ignore the feeling of being left out.

Glen didn't bring up sex, and Mia figured it was up to her to let him know she was ready to make love again. More than ready. She'd put in her diaphragm for three nights in a row in the hope that he would suggest it, but there was a distance between them in bed that she tried to deny. He was afraid of hurting her, she thought.

On the fourth night, she told him that her diaphragm was in.

"Ah," he said. "You must really be feeling better."

She got into bed wearing her cotton nightshirt and pushed her way close to him. He wrapped his arms loosely around her.

"I'm okay," she said. "I won't break."

He kissed her, but there was no passion in the kiss, no fire, and she nuzzled closer to him, close enough to feel the softness of his penis through his boxer shorts. After a moment he drew back from her. "I'm wiped out tonight," he said, stroking her hair. "Sorry."

"That's okay." She had never been that close to him when he wasn't hard and ready for her.

The following night was a repeat performance, and on the third night when he rolled away from her, he sounded truly upset. "I don't know what's wrong with me," he said.

"It's my breast."

"No, no, Sunny." He put his arm around her, pulling her head to his shoulder. "It's me. Maybe I need a physical myself." He laughed. "Have you ever known me to strike out three nights in a row?"

She had never known him to strike out even once, but she said nothing.

He wasn't in the bed when she woke up the following morning, although it was quite early. She got up and went to the closet for her clothes. Through the air-conditioning shaft that ran through the rear of the closet, she heard voices. Glen, talking to Laura. She could hear them clearly; she didn't even have to rest her ear against the shaft to make out their words.

"I nearly retched when I saw it," he was saying. "I know I'm a shit for feeling that way, but it's grotesque. She's damaged beyond repair. She looks like a freak. I try to block it out of my mind when I'm sleeping with her, but I can't. I can't even . . . perform."

Laura said something too soft to hear, then her voice grew louder. "She's still the same person, Glen," she said. "She's still Mimi."

There was a long silence, and when Glen began speaking again, Mia knew he'd been crying. She had seen him cry only once—when they were traveling in Rome together and visited the Pieta.

"I tell myself she's the same person, but she's not. Sunny's gone. My bubbly, giggly, happy, radiant Sunny. They destroyed her when they destroyed her body."

"Glen." Laura sounded almost desperate. "She's still

recovering, for Christ's sake. You can't expect her to be kicking up her heels. Every day, she's a little more like her old self, don't you see that?"

"I can never, ever get used to that one breast staring at me."

"She'll have reconstruction."

Mia heard the scrape of a chair on the floor, and when Glen spoke again, his voice sounded very close. "I'm not proud of myself for reacting this way," he said. "I can't let her know how I feel. But, God! Every night she's hoping we'll make love, and I can't even get the bloody thing up when I'm near her."

Mia stepped out of the closet, shutting the door behind her and leaning back against it. She thought she might get sick. Closing her eyes, she tried to block out the pain and humiliation roiling inside her and focus on what she should do next. It would be best if she told him she'd heard, that she knew how he felt. She could suggest they both see the social worker, that they get counseling. But she couldn't bring herself to confront him. Not now, not yet.

She didn't go downstairs until she was certain Laura had left for work and Glen had gone to his studio. Throughout the day and into the night, his words pulsed in her head: She was damaged. *Grotesque. A freak.*

She called Dr. Bella to ask him if she might have reconstructive surgery sooner, but he was adamant about waiting and chastised her for having unrealistic expectations. "It will never be exactly like your old breast, Mia," he warned her. "You mustn't expect it to be."

To her face, Glen continued to be kind. He said loving things to her she no longer believed. She was careful not to undress in front of him, careful to seem like the old, untarnished Mia he had fallen in love with in the hope that he would fall all over again, and his discomfort with her body would gradually disappear. She no longer bothered with her diaphragm at night, though, and in bed, she didn't ask him to hold her or touch her. She allowed him his distance, until it felt as though they were not even sleeping in the same bed at all.

24

Carmen had little problem tracking down Daniel Grace. She called the Bar Association in Maryland, hoping he'd be listed in their directory, but the woman who answered the phone recognized his name.

"Everyone knows Dan Grace," she said to Carmen. "He's the finest criminal defense attorney in the state."

After a morning of telephone tag, she managed to catch up with him in his Baltimore office. It was two o'clock, eastern time. She worded her request warily, expecting him to be on his guard. Suspicious. But once he found out the topic of her interview—and that Gail Vidovich had suggested she call him—he was most forthcoming. Still, she didn't want to push her luck by asking his permission to tape the call. Instead, she settled down with her notepad at the desk in her study at Sugarbush.

"Do you mind if I eat my lunch in your ear?" he began.

"Not at all."

"Well, let's see what I can tell you about Robbie Blackwell," he said, and Carmen heard what sounded like the crinkling of plastic in the background. "To begin with,

Robbie was a kid who really didn't fit into any one group in junior high," he said. "His friendships cut across the whole gamut. We were pretty young—and he was younger than the rest of us—but even so, the girls liked him a lot, and the guys couldn't understand the attraction. He was so different from most of them that they couldn't figure out a way to compete."

"Different how?"

"Well, he was bright beyond belief. Light years ahead of the rest of us. And he was different in the way he treated other kids. He was tolerant of everyone. Nice to everyone. It didn't matter whether a kid was popular or a complete nerd, black or white, they were all the same to him."

Carmen groaned out loud. "Could you tell me something rotten about him, please? What's the worst thing you can say?"

Daniel Grace laughed. "You're only getting the good stuff, huh?"

"Right. Help me round out the picture, Mr. Grace."

"Dan. And there's not much bad stuff to tell. There were always a lot of rumors about him, though. Someone like that, who stands out from the crowd, generates a lot of speculation. You know what I mean?"

"Yes." She knew. "What sort of rumors?"

"Oh, that his mother was a prostitute, that he was a mulatto." Dan laughed again. "This blond kid. Ridiculous. Not that it mattered one way or the other."

"He was blond?" Carmen asked, surprised. "I knew he

was blond when he was very young, but even in junior high school?"

Dan bit into something that snapped in her ear. "He's not blond now?" he asked.

Carmen pictured Jeff's nearly black hair, and thought she'd better answer prudently. "I wouldn't really call it blond."

"I wish I could see him. Can't picture him without that mop of yellow hair."

For a brief moment, she wondered if she might be digging up information on the wrong Robert Blackwell after all.

"What else do you remember about him?" She opted for the open-ended question, since Dan Grace seemed to be enjoying this. She pictured him leaning back in his chair in his poshly decorated office, a carrot stick in his hand, and his feet, in their Italian leather shoes, propped up on the desk.

"He liked baseball and he wrestled for a while, but he wasn't very good. He wasn't aggressive enough—although, wow, if you stepped on the toes of a friend of his, watch out."

"What do you mean?"

"Well, it was like he was always taking up for the little guy. He could handle a lot of abuse himself—I mean, he'd let the rumors roll off his back—but he couldn't stand to see someone else get dumped on. I remember one incident. There was this really nerdy girl in our class. I mean, beyond nerdy. Strange. Not groomed well. Had a little . . . aroma to her. And you know how junior high kids are. They picked on her unmercifully, like she wasn't even human."

He paused for a moment, and Carmen heard him take a drink of something.

"I'm sure *I* even made fun of her from time to time," he continued. "She was the class scapegoat. The sacrificial lamb. Phyllis, her name was. We called her Syphillis, although I'm sure ninety-five percent of us didn't even know what the word meant." Dan chuckled. "Anyhow, she sat behind Robbie in science class, and during a test one day I noticed he was holding his paper on his desk in a way that she could copy from it."

"You mean he was intentionally letting her copy?" Carmen jotted down the anecdote, wondering if it could be interpreted as an early disregard of rules and authority. It hardly seemed to fit.

"That's right," Dan said. "I couldn't believe it. I don't think he even knew her well enough to talk to her, but he felt sorry for her. Then a few months later, this group of kids was taunting her out on the sidewalk in front of the school. Robbie and I were walking past them, and when he saw what was happening, he told the kid who was the ringleader, 'You'd better stop it, or else.' Of course the kid laughed at him and kept on tormenting Phyllis. So, the next day, Rob mixed up some concoction and put it in a little capsule and set it on the kid's chair in homeroom. When the kid sat down on the capsule, it broke, and for the rest of the day he smelled as though he'd messed his pants. No one would get near him." Dan laughed. "Whew.

This is a real memory test. Haven't thought about this stuff in years."

"He had a vindictive streak, then."

"That's stretching it, Ms. Perez," Dan said, dryly. "What he did have was a sense of what was fair and what wasn't, and an intolerance for anyone who'd try to make himself look or feel good at someone else's expense."

Carmen was quiet as she wrote down his words. Then she took a deep breath. "Gail Vidovich thought his mother died." She bit her lip, waiting for his response.

"Yes, she did," Dan said. "Some sort of accident. Car, I guess, but to be honest, I'm not sure if I ever really knew what happened." He took another bite of something. "Excuse me," he said. "This must sound pretty obnoxious."

"No problem," Carmen said. "Did you know her? What was she like?"

"She was very pretty. Younger than most of my other friends' mothers, and maybe because she was younger, she understood better what it was like to be a kid. So she and Rob were very close."

"That must have been terrible for him. Losing her, I mean."

"Yeah. She was all the family he had. Blood family, anyhow. They lived with a black man, although I don't think his mother ever married him. She went by Cabrio and the man's name was Watts. Robbie called him Dad. I spent a fair amount of time over there, and Mr. Watts acted like he was Rob's father. He'd make rules for him and that sort of thing, and he'd buy him all these kits— you know, chemistry sets, telescopes. Made me jealous, actually. He was very proud of Rob, too. I remember him coming to the science fair when Rob won first place, and he was beaming."

"What was Rob's science-fair project?"

"Oh, something I didn't understand." Dan sounded as if he were yawning. "Science wasn't my thing. It was some sort of ecosystem, I think. Some sort of enclosed life space, with plants and things in it, in which he somehow controlled the atmosphere. He adjusted something to make light and warmth and rain. I didn't get it, but the judges certainly did. He went on to compete in the state and national competition, if I remember correctly."

Carmen closed her eyes. A chill started low on her spine and the hair on the nape of her neck stood on end. She definitely had the right man. If he could do something like that at the age of thirteen, what could he do now?

"Rob's family always had money," Dan continued. "Not a ton. Not old money. But they were a lot better off than my family, although they didn't own a house. They rented the top story of one of the big houses on Seventh Street. The driveway was always filled with Mr. Watts's old cars. He loved fixing them up. He drove a Model T, and he used to give us rides in it."

Carmen was still shaken by the realization that Jeff might be for real. She tried to collect herself, to focus on what Dan was saying and keep up with her note-taking. Her hand ached from writing so quickly. "What did Mr. Watts do for a living?" she asked.

"He worked on other people's cars, though I used to hear my parents saying they didn't understand how that would bring in so much money. Beth—Rob's mother—worked at Teppers, but Mr. Watts was usually home. He cooked supper every night, and I remember thinking that was strange. It wasn't the division of labor I was accustomed to at home."

Dan was quiet for a minute, and Carmen waited for him to speak again.

"Rob was with my family when his mother was killed," he said finally. "We were down the shore, and he got a call from Mr. Watts telling him about the accident. I remember watching him on the phone, all the color draining out of his face. He wouldn't say a word when he got off, just sat in the living room staring out the window. He wouldn't tell us what was wrong. My mother was sitting there with him, trying to draw it out of him, but he wouldn't even look at her. Mr. Watts drove down and picked him up, and he's the one who told my parents Beth was dead. Robbie got into the car without saying a word, without even saying goodbye." Dan sighed. "I didn't know what to say to him myself. It's one of those things I wish I could do over, now that I've had a little more life experience. Know what I mean? Especially if I'd known it would be the last time I saw him."

"The last time?"

"Yes. It was the summer before high school, and I thought I'd see him in a few weeks. But when I got home from the shore and tried to call him, I found out that he and Mr. Watts had moved."

Once again, the disappearing act. Had Jeff been on the run his entire life?

"Do you know where they went?" she asked.

"It was somewhere in south Jersey. Cherry Hill, if I remember correctly. My mother found that out from the woman who owned the house they'd rented, but she had no street address. Somewhere along the line we stopped trying to track him down. I never heard from him again."

"Shall I give him your number?"

"Hell, yes." There was a grin in his voice. "And it's your turn now. Tell me how he is? Is he married? Does he have kids? I bet he's a rocket scientist, huh?"

"To be honest, Mr. Grace, I don't know that much about him." She grimaced, not wanting to be coy. She wanted to tell him more, but she would have to be careful. "He's very reserved," she said, "and he's working on a project of a scientific nature that he hopes will help a lot of people."

"Well, tell him to get in touch, please," Dan said. "I'd love to talk with him."

Carmen agonized over her script for that evening's news report. She studied her notes, and her eyes were drawn again and again to the one line of all Dan Grace's words that haunted her most. *He had an intolerance for anyone who'd try to make himself look or feel good at someone else's expense.*

But the facts were simple. The meatier she made her reports, the higher the ratings would climb. *What choice do I have, Jeff?* she thought. *You're my job.*

In the end, though, her script was calculated, restrained. Her wording was gentle. Her characterization of

Jeff was, for once, kind and compassionate, and although she said nothing about his childhood science-fair project, for the first time there was no skepticism in her tone when she described his work in the warehouse.

She arrived at Sugarbush after midnight. A light burned in Mia's cottage, but Jeff's and Chris's cottages were dark. At her kitchen table, she penned a note on a scrap of paper. "Forgive me for questioning you about your mother the other morning," she wrote. "I know what it's like to grow up with loss. I'm sorry."

She walked outside, and the coyotes' song made her shiver as she slipped the note under the windshield wiper of Jeff's car.

25.

Chris wanted to go to this game. He wanted to conquer the fear of facing the stadium again, of facing old fans he'd disappointed, of being on the outside looking in. He wanted to recapture the pleasure he'd once taken from the best sport in the world. For far too long now, he'd cut himself off from that joy.

More than anything, though, he wanted to see a good baseball game. He wanted to smell hot dogs and drink beer, to hear the crack of a bat and the roar of the crowd. He wanted to watch his old team play, to see how his old friends were holding up, how the new players were fitting in.

Jeff sat next to him as they drove to the stadium in San Diego, and they had spent the entire last hour talking about baseball—what games they'd seen when they were kids, what players they had worshipped. Jeff had been a serious fan. The only difference in their stories was that Chris had attended the professional games with Augie, and occasionally another friend or two. Jeff didn't elaborate on who he'd gone with, and Chris knew better than to probe.

"Rick and I are planning an experiment," Jeff said after a break in the conversation.

"Oh, yeah?"

"We'll need two-way radios."

"All right." Chris made a mental note to stop by the electronics shop in Escondido the following week.

"And is it possible to get a TV in the warehouse?"

Chris glanced at him. "You want to catch Carmen's news reports, huh?"

Jeff rubbed his temple with the palm of his hand. "Don't talk to me about your wife," he said. "She dissects me for public consumption and then tries to make it up to me by leaving vague notes of apology on my windshield."

"Ex-wife," Chris said. "She left you a note?" He remembered what Carmen had said about Jeff on the news the night before. She'd spoken to one of his childhood friends who had described Jeff as an extremely bright boy—this wasn't news—who took up for the underdog and occasionally played pranks on other kids in junior high school. She'd added that he'd been very affected by the death of his mother, which occurred when he was thirteen.

"Yes, she left me a note," Jeff said, in a voice that was closing the subject.

Chris switched on the radio to the sports station for the pre-game chatter. He started humming *Take Me Out to the Ball Game.*

"You're up for this," Jeff said.

"Yeah."

"I thought you said going to a game scared the shit out of you, or something to that effect?"

Chris pressed his palms against the steering wheel. "Yeah, it does."

"What's the worst that could happen?"

Chris sighed. "Oh, that someone will recognize me and make some crack about what an asshole I was when I left, and he'll, you know, alert the thousands of other people in the stadium to the fact that I'm there, and I'll become your basic object of scorn. Nothing serious." He laughed. "But as long as I'm incognito and walk in there as Joe Fan and nothing more, I think it'll be fine."

They found a parking space in the outer reaches of the crowded stadium lot. Daylight was fading quickly, but Chris decided to leave his sunglasses on for the walk across the parking lot. He opened the trunk of his car and produced two old brown-and-orange Padre caps.

"Camouflage," he said, handing one of them to Jeff. "Everyone will have them on. We'll blend in."

Jeff laughed, setting the cap on his head, and there was a sudden, dramatic change in his appearance. For the first time, he didn't seem so much the outsider. He looked like a born-and-bred San Diegan.

They walked across the parking lot toward the stadium, making their way through the maze of parked cars and the cleanup detail from tailgate parties. Chris breathed in the scent of fried chicken and beer and summer stadium air, caught off guard by a pang of nostalgia.

He could feel his heart pounding against his ribs by the time they reached the ticket window. They stood next to each other in line, quietly. Chris was too anxious to talk. It was going to be all right, though. He caught a glimpse of his reflection, with sunglasses and cap, in the glass of the ticket window and hardly recognized himself.

But the grizzled, middle-aged man behind the glass had no problem at all.

"Chris Garrett!" he exclaimed, exposing a set of perfect dentures in a wide grin.

Chris tensed, his smile freezing in place. Behind him, a ripple of recognition passed through the line, and conversations stopped, only to begin again with new enthusiasm.

"How are you doing?" he asked the man, as though they were old friends. He slid enough money for two tickets under the glass shield of the window.

"Great!" Still grinning, the man passed the tickets back to him. "Good to see ya, fella," he said. "The game hasn't been the same since you were out there."

"Thanks," Chris said, surprised by the compliment. He stepped out of the line without glancing at the people behind him, and only then realized that Jeff was no longer with him. He spotted him several yards away, standing alone, facing the parking lot.

Chris walked over to hand him a ticket. Jeff touched the brim of Chris's cap.

"Effective disguise," he said.

"That was a fluke," Chris said, unable to suppress his sense of delight in that early reception.

They walked under the broad concrete overhang of the stadium and through the gate. Chris took off his sunglasses. The smell of hot dogs was suddenly inescapable and seductive, and the clamor of fans already in their seats filled the air. Chris glanced at his ticket to be sure they were walking in the right direction.

"You know," he said, eying the concessions, "I never eat hot dogs, but there's something about a baseball game that makes me feel like I'm breaking the law if I don't have one."

Jeff grunted a response. He seemed preoccupied. His walk was stiff and wired. He was, Chris thought, ready to bolt.

"How about a dog and a beer before we find our seats?" Chris suggested, more directly this time.

"Hmm?" Jeff frowned. "Oh, sure. Right."

They stood in one of the four lines leading to the concession stand, and Chris quickly became aware of the whispering on his left. People were staring, pointing. After five years away from this world, he hadn't expected to be so easily recognizable. He lifted his chin, squared his shoulders. He wouldn't allow himself to be thrown by anything anyone might say to him.

One of the men in the line to his left nudged him, lightly. "Haven't been able to get my wife to come to a game since you left," the man said, smiling.

Chris heard the compliment behind the words. He grinned. "That's funny," he said. "I never had any trouble getting her to come." He cringed at his own brashness. It had been a hell of a long time since he'd let loose with that sort of innuendo, but the man let out a burst of laughter, and his friend—a man with a dark ponytail and a small hoop in one ear—joined in.

"You look good, Garrett," said a third man, from further down the line. "Politics must agree with you. How's the arm?"

Chris raised his right arm into the air. "It's dynamite at pushing papers across my desk." He glanced at Jeff, who stared straight ahead from under the visor of his cap, pretending for all intents and purposes not to know him.

The men—and a couple of women—were starting to form something of a circle around him. The lines were disintegrating. He was used to this, but it hadn't happened in a long, long time. "They don't appreciate you out in Valle Rosa," said an older man, who was wearing a El Cajon Little League jacket. "Come back to the Padres where you belong."

The man with the earring touched Chris's arm. "I met you once when I lived in New York. It was at a Mets game. I was a big Mets fan back then, no offense. I was hoping you'd get hurt or something and not be able to play, 'cause I knew we didn't stand a chance if you were pitching."

Chris laughed. "Thanks, I guess."

A boy of about ten squeezed through the crowd. He plucked a baseball card from the stack in his hand and offered it to Chris, along with a pen. "Could I have your autograph, Mr. Garrett?" he asked.

Chris dusted the top of the boy's head with his hand. Then he signed the card, leaning it against the back of the man from New York. He couldn't remember the last time he'd autographed a baseball card.

He was about to hand the card back to the boy when a woman popped out of the circle of people, coming to a stop directly in front of him. She was blond. Young. Pert. "Hi, Chris," she said.

He looked at her blankly. She was with a dark-haired friend who was trying vainly to tug her away from him.

"You don't remember me, do you?" the woman asked.

He shook his head. "No, sorry."

"Kim Rickert," she said. "It's been a long time. I was from your pre-Carmen Perez days—if you know what I mean."

The man from New York let out a hoot, and Chris colored. He had no memory of her whatsoever, but he doubted she was lying. Most likely he had slept with her once, maybe more.

Her friend groaned, tugging at her arm. "Come on, Kim."

Kim allowed herself to be dragged away. "We miss you, Chris!" she called over her shoulder.

The men snickered as Chris put his hands over the little boy's ears. "You didn't hear any of that, did you?" he asked, laughing himself.

"Uh uh." The boy grinned as he took the card and disappeared back into the throng.

Chris and Jeff had reached the front of the misshapen line. Chris noticed that three policemen who'd been served several minutes earlier were still milling around at the edge of the concession stand, obviously waiting for him. They were grinning and laughing.

"Can you handle one more autograph?" one of them asked, handing him a napkin. "It's for my kid," he winked.

"Yeah," said another. "A forty-five-year-old kid."

"I'm only forty-two," said the first officer indignantly. He watched over Chris's shoulder as he wrote.

When Chris looked up again, he saw that one of the other officers was staring at Jeff with narrowed eyes.

"Aren't you that rainmaker guy?" he asked.

Chris hadn't seen fear in Jeff's face before, but he had no problem recognizing it now. For the first time since he'd met him, Jeff seemed at a loss for words. It was painful to see that uncertainty in him. Painful to see him afraid.

"Shit!" Chris said suddenly, and the policemen turned to look at him. "I left the binoculars in the car."

He locked eyes with Jeff, who suffered only one brief moment of bewilderment before a look of understanding crossed his face.

"We can get by without them," Jeff said.

"No way!" Chris said. "I'd rather get by without the beer." He stepped out of line and turned to the police with a wave. "We'll be back. Nice seeing you guys."

Jeff fell into step beside him as they walked toward the exit.

Outside the stadium, the air suddenly lost its compressed, superheated quality, and Jeff drew in a long, long breath.

"Joe Fan," he said dryly.

"Sorry. I really had no idea."

It had grown dark outside in the short time they'd been in the stadium, and the parking lot was a mixture of light and shadow.

"I assume there are no binoculars in the car?" Jeff's voice was flat. Tired.

"Right."

"So what exactly is the plan here?"

Chris put his arm across Jeff's shoulders, a little self-consciously. "We're going to get in the car and drive back to Valle Rosa and reinstate you firmly in your hideaway at Sugarbush."

Jeff was quiet for a moment, but Chris felt his relief.

"I could go to a movie or something and come back to pick you up," Jeff offered. "You were really psyched for the game."

Chris lowered his arm back to his side. "There'll be other games," he said, and he knew there would be. He would never be afraid of going to a game again.

They continued walking in silence, the sound of their footsteps growing louder as the roar of the crowd fell behind them.

Chris got into the car and reached over to open the door for Jeff, who was still looking uncertainly at the stadium.

"Are you sure . . . ?" Jeff asked.

Chris nodded toward the passenger seat. "Get in," he said to his friend. "We're out of here."

Neither of them spoke until they'd driven out of

Mission Valley and had turned onto the freeway. Then Jeff shook his head. "Your basic object of scorn," he teased.

Chris smiled to himself. No one had uttered a negative word about him, at least not to his face. They seemed to remember only his achievements, as if they'd developed a collective amnesia regarding his humiliating last season with the Padres.

"Would you mind pulling off?" Jeff asked suddenly, pointing to the first exit.

"Here?" Chris glanced at him in confusion.

"Uh huh."

Chris shrugged and turned off the freeway. The ramp took them onto a road above Mission Valley.

"Stop here." Jeff pointed to a 7-Eleven, and Chris obediently pulled into the parking lot.

"Anything you want?" Jeff asked as he got out of the car.

Shaking his head, Chris settled down to wait for him.

In a few minutes, Jeff returned with a fairly large brown bag. "Thanks," he said, fastening his seat belt. "Now how about driving around this area for a while?"

Chris looked at him skeptically. "Is there a point to this?"

Jeff half-smiled. "Trust me."

Chris drove for nearly a mile on the winding residential streets above the Valley. Finally, Jeff pointed to a small apartment complex. "Pull in to that parking lot," he said.

Chris did as he was told.

"All the way to the rear. That's right." Jeff was smiling

now, and as Chris neared the far edge of the parking lot, he began to understand. They were high above Mission Valley. The stadium was below them in a circle of starry lights.

He looked at Jeff, who reached over and turned off the ignition.

"Push your seat back till you're comfortable," Jeff said, adjusting his own seat. Then he opened his bag. The aroma of hot dogs quickly filled the car, and Chris laughed.

Jeff pulled the hot dogs from the bag, along with two beers, a bag of unshelled peanuts and a box of Cracker Jacks. He leaned over to turn the key in the ignition. The radio came on, and he raised the volume until the roar of the crowd surrounded them.

He handed a beer to Chris.

"Cabrio, you are too fucking much," Chris said, still laughing.

Jeff twisted the cap from his own beer and tapped his bottle to Chris's. "To the Padres," he said.

"To the rainmaker," Chris responded, and settled back in his seat to listen for the crack of the bat.

26.

It was late, but Carmen was still at the station when she received the call from Dennis Ketchum. He wanted to see her in his office, he said. Tonight. Now.

She felt only slight trepidation as she knocked on his door. It couldn't be bad news. All the feedback she'd received on her reports lately had been positive.

"Sit down, Carmen." Dennis stubbed out a cigarette and let loose with one of his thick, frightening, smoker's coughs as Carmen lowered herself into the chair near the door.

"Well." He was almost smiling as he swiveled his chair around to face her. "I think we'd be crazy not to give you five days a week at this point."

A surge of joy shot through her, but she kept her face impassive. "Right," she said. "You would be."

Dennis reached for a stack of mail on his desk and dropped it into her lap. She lifted her hands quickly to keep the letters from spilling onto the floor.

"All those viewers are asking for you," he said, nodding toward the letters. "It's a little like the old days."

She had some difficulty keeping her smile in check. She wouldn't appear too eager.

Dennis coughed again, then shook his head, a look of mild amazement on his face. Amazement, and something else. Admiration? "You've managed to turn nothing into something, Carmen," he said. "I don't mind saying that I was worried about you—about your ability to do your job after the past few years. But you're impressing the hell out of me, kid."

She crossed her legs, fully composed now. "So, does that mean *News Nine* will pick up the tab if I need to travel again to further the story?"

"I'll arrange it." He leaned forward, elbows on knees, and looked hard into her eyes. "There's some real dirt on this guy, isn't there?" he asked. "How close are you?"

"I'm not sure," she hedged. She had no idea what she might find on Jeff, and she was no longer certain she would ever find anything of significance.

"Well, you're doing fine with it. Keep the screws good and tight on Cabrio. Take your time. Just be sure you're the first to get the scoop." He sat up straight again and lit another cigarette. "The other stations are frustrated as hell," he continued, blowing two streams of smoke from his nose. "They're in the dark, and their ratings are falling day by day. Don't let them get to it before you do, Carmen. I'm trusting you to time this right."

Late the following afternoon, as ashes from a new fire danced outside her *News Nine* office window, Carmen reached one of Jeff's high-school teachers.

"I taught chemistry for forty years," Frank Howell

said, over the phone. "There are exactly three students who stayed in my mind, and Rob Blackwell is at the top of the list."

With the receiver clutched in her hand, Carmen breathed a sigh of relief. The librarian at the high school in Cherry Hill, New Jersey, had been most cooperative. The yearbooks indicated that Robert Blackwell had attended the school for three years, graduating in 1973 at the age of sixteen. The librarian had given her the names of some of the teachers pictured in the yearbook, and Carmen spent the rest of the day trying to track down phone numbers for them, with little success. She finally reached Lillian Phelps, an elderly woman who had taught English during the years Jeff attended the school, but who didn't remember him at all.

"He probably would have been more into science than English," Carmen had told her, and Lillian Phelps suggested she try Frank Howell, who had retired from teaching chemistry only a few years earlier.

Frank Howell was an enthusiastic, clear-thinking historian. For the first time, Carmen decided to give her interviewee a taste of the truth behind her questioning. She had to know if there was a chance Jeff was for real.

"Robert Blackwell has suggested he might be able to ease the drought here by producing rain," she said, careful to keep her voice neutral, to keep the cynicism in check.

Howell chuckled. "Cloud-seeding?"

"No. Some other way."

"Well," Howell said slowly. "I can't say that surprises

me. Rob had a real feel for science. A gift. Although he could be a reckless son of a gun." He chuckled again.

"Reckless?"

"Yes. He caused an explosion in the chemistry lab one day. I'm sure he used to lay awake at nights and think of experiments that weren't in the book." He drew a long breath. "Truth was, by the middle of Rob's sophomore year, he was way ahead of me. I went to the board and told them we needed something to challenge this kid or we'd lose him. So, they worked up a special program for him through Rutgers. Let him take some college courses in math and science for a few hours each day. It cost the family something, but Rob's father—stepfather, I guess it was—paid for it."

For the first time, Carmen could truly picture Jeff as a teenager. Serious, brilliant, far above his fellow students. Far above his teachers. Probably, he hadn't fit in well.

"What was he like socially?" she asked.

"Socially? That's something I didn't pay much attention to. That wasn't the part of him that intrigued me."

"Well, I was wondering if he was perceived by the other students as a goody-two-shoes or a . . . a nerd because of his intelligence."

"Neither," Howell said. "He wasn't a goody-two-shoes by any stretch of the imagination. He got into his share of trouble."

"Like what?"

"Hmm. Always had to push the limits. If you said to the class, 'No talking or else,' he'd have to talk just to find out what the 'or else' was. Or if you told him to add two grams of a particular compound to a beaker, he'd have to see what would happen if he added three."

"You make him sound irresponsible and impulsive."

"Oh, not really." There was a smile in Howell's voice. He had clearly felt some affection as well as respect for young Robert Blackwell. "He was just curious. Think where we'd be today if our inventors and scientists hadn't been curious."

"You said the other students didn't see him as a nerd?"

"Not that I knew of. Seems as though he always had girls around him. I don't know if there was anyone special, though. He did have a good friend who was another top chemistry student. Kent someone or other. I can't recall his full name, but he was sharp too, and they were always trying to outdo each other. Talk about reckless! Kent lost a couple of fingers when he tried to plant a little homemade bomb in another kid's locker."

"Nice," Carmen said. Lovely kids Jeff hung out with.

"They suspended him, but not for long. Guess they figured losing half his hand was punishment enough. He and Rob weren't much alike outside of their interest in science, though. Kent was always a little strange, where Robbie was just a good-looking, normal kid who happened to excel in everything he did."

Carmen wondered if it would be worth the bother to call the librarian back and beg her to look through the yearbook for a "Kent." She doubted the request would be appreciated. "You mentioned his stepfather," she prompted.

"Yes. At least I assume it was a stepfather. I don't

actually remember, but the man was black, and I'm sure Rob didn't have a speck of black blood in him."

"Rob was quite blond?"

"Yes, well, what they call dirty-blond, I guess. Anyway, there was some sort of scandal."

"A scandal?" Carmen pulled her notepad closer to her on the desk and jotted down the word, even though she was taping the conversation.

"Right. I'm not sure I remember the details, but this stepfather of his was put in jail. Something to do with drugs. Seems to me there was a death involved because he was locked away for a long time, and Robbie got put in a foster family for his senior year. I even considered taking him in, but my wife wouldn't hear of it. The whole mess hurt him academically, I remember. He couldn't pay for the college courses anymore, and his grades really dropped that year. I was worried about him, about seeing all that potential go down the drain." He fell suddenly quiet, as if trying to decide if he should tell her more. "Once I called him in to talk about his situation," he said, after a moment, "but he didn't want to talk about it. He kept trying to steer me back to an experiment we'd done the day before in class. But I kept pushing. I regretted it later. Probably it wasn't the right thing to do, because he started to cry. It embarrassed him, and I let him go. Tore me apart, though. He was a kid in a lot of pain, and there didn't seem to be a way to help him."

Carmen felt an unwelcome surge of compassion for Jeff. She leaned back in her chair. She was going to have to think long and hard about how to present this information in her report. She liked the reckless, bad-boy stuff, but the underlying theme of struggle and misfortune that seemed so much a part of Jeff's life could only gain him sympathy. That was the problem of gathering facts, of building a story. You couldn't make it go the way you wanted it to. She could twist things a little, yes, but no matter how she colored the information for her audience, she would know the adversity that lay behind Jeff Cabrio's grand bravado, she would know the losses he'd endured, the hardships he'd overcome.

"Well," said Frank Howell, obviously summing up, "it was a joy to teach a student like Robbie. If he says he can make it rain, I'd buy an umbrella."

She was getting into her car in the station parking lot that evening when she heard someone call her name. She turned to see Terrell Gates standing next to her own car—a silver Mercedes—blowing puffs of ash from the convertible roof.

"I understand congratulations are in order." Terrell dusted her hands together as she walked toward Carmen. "You're going to get a little more air time."

Carmen opened her car door. "Yes," she said.

"That's terrific." Terrell smiled brightly, but the condescension in her voice was impossible to miss. It was as if she were talking to a kindergartner about her first finger painting. "I know they've been getting a lot of mail on you," she continued. "Apparently you're quite the rage with the older viewers. Lucky there are so many retirees out here."

Carmen closed the car door again and put her hands on her hips. "Do you have to practice being a bitch, Terrell, or does it come naturally to you?"

Terrell didn't lose her smile, not for an instant. "Listen, Carmen." She brushed a strand of gold hair from her eyes. "Things change very quickly in this business, and you've been away quite a while. Even some of the technology's changed, and I'm sure it can be overwhelming when you've been out of the action for so long. Probably makes you feel a little insecure. You let me know if there's anything I can do to help, okay?"

Carmen stared at her young nemesis. Terrell knew exactly what she was doing. Carmen recognized the manipulation, the innuendoes, the subtle taunting that preceded moving in for the kill. She had once been a master of the very same techniques.

She folded her arms across her chest. "Let's tell it like it is, Terrell." There was a wonderful strength in her voice. "You and I both know that I was a name in this business when you were still in diapers, and we both know you wouldn't be sitting in that *San Diego Sunrise* chair if it weren't for me. So don't you dare patronize me, and don't you dare kid yourself into thinking you have anything to teach me."

Terrell seemed at a sudden loss for words. There was a quiver in her lower lip, the suggestion of a crease between her perfectly shaped eyebrows.

Carmen had said all she planned to. She got into her car and drove out of the lot, but by the time she reached the service road leading to the freeway, she had to pull over. Rolling down her window, she leaned back against the headrest and closed her eyes.

Any pleasure she'd taken in lashing out at Terrell Gates had quickly disappeared. She'd been given a glimpse into the woman behind the tough veneer. She'd seen the panic in the younger woman's eyes, and she knew that panic well.

It can happen to you too, Terrell. You're young and on top now, but just wait a few years.

Could she ever handle *Sunrise* again? Could she ever again go the extra, sometimes vicious, mile necessary to make that show come alive in the way that she used to, in the way that Terrell did now?

Keep the screws good and tight on Cabrio.

She would have to. Whatever it took, she would have to do it. Put on that tough-gal mask. Go after the grittiest news, blind to how much it might cost someone, how much it might cost herself. Right now, she had no other choice.

27

From where she stood in the art supply store with Jeff, Mia could feel the pull of the Lesser Gallery. They'd driven to San Diego to get some materials for the fountain and while she'd been piling clay into her cart, her gaze had drifted to the front window of the store. In the distance, she could just make out the corner of the pink stucco building that housed the gallery. The local artisans' show in which her own work was to be displayed had opened there the day before.

She was loading her supplies onto the checkout counter when she realized she hadn't picked up the steel rods she would need for the armature. "I can't believe I forgot them, of all things," she said to Jeff as they made their way to the back of the store again.

"You're distracted," Jeff said. "You've been distracted since we walked in here."

"I should have made a list of what I needed." She pulled the rods from a bin. "I usually make a list."

Once back at the checkout counter, she insisted on paying for the materials. Jeff protested, but she ignored him as she wrote out the check.

"Wrong amount." Jeff peered over her shoulder.

He was right. The supplies came to $87.78; she'd written the check for $78.78. She tore it up and started over again.

She was quiet as they left the store, but once in his car, Jeff turned to face her. "Okay, Mia," he said. "Where exactly is your head today?"

She tapped her fingers mindlessly on the windowsill, debating with herself over whether or not to tell him. "Well," she said finally, "we're about two blocks from the Lesser Gallery. There's a showing of local sculptors' work there, including some of my own."

He followed her gaze in the direction of the pink stucco building. "Why didn't you say anything?" he asked. "Let's go."

She shook her head. "I'd rather not."

"Well, I want to go. You can stay in the car, if you like." He turned the key in the ignition and pointed toward the gallery. "That way?"

She squirmed lower in her seat. "Yes."

A blue Volvo was pulling out of a spot in front of the gallery and Jeff slipped in after it. Mia looked at the broad arched front door of the building. A few people were milling around on the steps, some walking into the gallery, some out. She felt torn. She longed to see her work again, to see how they had displayed it, but she had cut herself off from this life. She didn't belong here.

Jeff unfastened his seat belt. "Okay, let's have it," he said. "Tell me what's wrong."

She looked at him squarely. "I don't want to see

anyone I know. And some of Glen's work will be in the show. He might be here. I don't want to see him. I *can't* see him."

"Ah, the old boyfriend, right?"

She nodded.

Jeff reached behind his seat and extracted a brown Padre cap from the floor. He set it on her head, pulling the brim low. "This is a great disguise," he said. "Trust me. I've used it myself."

Mia turned the rear-view mirror so that she could study her reflection. Undoubtedly, she would be the only person in the gallery wearing a baseball cap, but as a disguise, it might work. She tucked the ends of her hair up inside the cap and returned the mirror to its original position.

"All right," she said. "Let's do it."

She was pleased by the size of the crowd inside the gallery, pleased by the anonymity it offered. Jeff picked up a brochure at the door, and Mia did a double take as she noticed the cover. It was the sculpture of her mother.

"That's mine," she said, casually touching the brochure.

Jeff looked down at the photograph. The bronze sculpture was of a woman holding a basket of yarn between her knees. "Sure," he said.

"Honestly. It is. Look." She pointed toward the central hall in front of them, where the sculpture had been given prominent stature, and felt the burn of pride in her cheeks, the sharp sting of tears. It was overwhelming, seeing something she had created displayed so beautifully. If it had been another one of her pieces, something less personal than her mother, she might have been able to convince herself it wasn't hers at all.

They joined the group of people circling the sculpture and the marble pedestal on which it rested. The statue was twenty-three inches high. Liz Tanner sat on a stool, a scarf wrapped around her head, her face drawn, but smiling and beautiful and alive. She wore a loose-fitting blouse and a long skirt pulled up above her knees. A basket filled with balls of yarn was cradled in her hands. A few strands of yarn fell over the edge of the basket; one curled gently over her bare calf and foot. She wore large hoop earrings. She looked like a gypsy.

Jeff bent close to the pedestal to study the small brass plaque. "Liz and yarn," he read out loud. "Terra cotta cast in bronze. Mia Tanner." He turned to face her, eyes wide, and she shrugged and smiled, blinking hard against the tears.

"Just a little something I threw together," she said.

"Mia." He touched his fingertip lightly to her mother's cheek. "How did you do this? How did you get this expression? Why is she wearing the turban?"

Mia walked around the sculpture. Above her, the ceiling was high and filled with windows and the light poured over Liz Tanner like honey.

"She had cancer," Mia answered. "She posed for this while she was recovering. Although she never actually did."

"She died?"

"Yes."

"I'm sorry. She looks very young."

"She was only forty-eight."

"What kind of cancer?" Jeff didn't take his eyes from the sculpture.

"Breast." She stopped circling the sculpture to stand next to him. "Then she had a stroke. Her body didn't handle the chemotherapy well. The cancer eventually spread to her lungs."

Jeff squeezed her arm in a gesture of comfort, but let go immediately. "Sorry," he said, his head close to hers. "I know you don't like to be touched."

"What makes you say that?" she asked, surprised.

"The other night at your cottage, I hugged you and you went cold. You froze up."

Mia stared at the basket of yarn in her mother's lap. She had never thought of herself as cold. Jeff had no idea how much she longed to be touched.

He ignored her silence. "Was your mother artistic, too?"

"No. She knitted, but that was about it. She was more like my sister than she was like me. More the cheerleader type. I was odd-man-out in my family."

"You were the lucky one. Your talent will last a lot longer than leading cheers."

Mia grazed her fingertips over her mother's foot. "One day, when I was a teenager, I was rummaging around in the attic and found some charcoal drawings my father had made before he died. They were of my mother, mostly, and they were extraordinary. For the first time, I understood how I came to be the way I am." She had felt complete that day, validated by a father she had never really known. Her life would have been very different if he'd lived; she would have had him in her corner.

"Your mother's name was Elizabeth?" Jeff asked, as they walked into the next room.

"Yes." This room was crowded with people milling through a maze of sculptures. Mia recognized the work of some of her colleagues.

"Mine, too," he said.

"How did she die?" Mia glanced up at him. Carmen had said only that his mother had died when he was in his early teens.

Jeff sighed as he leaned over to read a plaque on a delicate bronze school of fish. "She died from a combination of failed technology and human ignorance." He straightened up and moved on to the next sculpture without looking at her. She didn't understand his answer, but knew better than to press him for more.

They moved around the gallery separately for a while, Mia looking for the works of her friends while furtively checking the crowd for the friends themselves. She didn't want to see anyone she knew. She didn't want to have to explain her absence from San Diego, or to answer their questions about her health or to introduce them to Jeff.

After a few minutes, she spotted Jeff in the third room and began walking toward him, stopping short when she noticed the sculpture he was studying so intently: Glen's nude of her. He wouldn't know, though. Her hair was longer. She looked entirely different.

She started walking toward him again as he leaned

over to read the plaque, and she knew what it would say: *Sunny: Terra cotta cast in bronze. Glen Jesperson.*

He straightened up when she neared him. "Well, Sunny." He gestured toward the plaque, smiling. "I suddenly feel as though I know you rather intimately."

She wrinkled her nose, tugging the brim of her cap lower over her eyes. "Would you have recognized me without the plaque?"

"Well." Jeff crossed his arms in front of him and cocked his head at the statue. "Your hair's different, and you had a little more meat on your bones. But yes, I think I would have."

Her conical breasts seemed like two beacons. Glen might as well have named the sculpture *Sunny's Breasts*. She wondered how Jeff could see anything else.

"You look happy, Mia," he said.

"I was." She observed the cocky smile, the sly look in her eyes. Everything had been new then, with no history to get in the way of the future.

"There's a playfulness to you here that I don't see in you now."

She lifted her hand to cover his eyes. "I think you've dissected this sculpture quite enough," she said. "Can we move on?"

"Sure." He laughed and turned toward the door leading to the next room, but Mia froze. Glen stood in the doorway, leaning against the jamb, talking with a red-haired woman dressed in a short, tight black dress. Glen looked tall and blond and handsome in a caramel-colored suit Mia had never seen before. He seemed full of laughter and completely absorbed in his conversation with the woman.

Mia spun around to face Jeff. "Glen's here," she said quietly. "Can we go, please?"

Jeff looked past her toward the doorway, but she was already carving her way through the crowd toward the entrance. She was outside, leaning breathlessly against his car by the time he caught up to her.

"You look as though you've had a near-death experience," he said, unlocking the door for her.

She got into the car and stared out the window at the buildings, the people, trying to erase from her mind the image of Glen, laughing and handsome and looking perfectly content with his life.

Jeff said nothing more until they'd turned onto the freeway.

"Okay," he said then, as if he were continuing a conversation they'd been having for minutes. "My best guess is that Glen ran off with another guy."

She couldn't suppress a laugh.

"How close did I come?" he asked.

Mia sighed and looked out the window toward the skyline. "Actually, he ran off with my sister," she said.

"Oh. Nasty."

He had no idea how nasty.

"We were engaged to be married," she said. "Then Laura came home after living in Santa Barbara for several years. She'd broken up with her boyfriend, and she was very depressed. Glen was really nice about it, including her in almost everything we did. I'd always been jealous of her when we were growing up. She was beautiful, and I was plain. She got the guys, and I got my mother to take care of. Then, what do you know, she got Glen, too." She bit her lip, surprised by the hostility in her voice. She had never said any of this out loud.

Jeff kept his eyes on the road. "You loved him a lot?" he asked.

"Yes. I'd been sick for awhile and was feeling better and looking for a job to support my sculpting habit. I finally found one through a temporary agency, but when I showed up for work the first day, they said they didn't need me and sent me home. When I walked into the house, there were Glen and Laura, together on the living-room floor."

"You mean"—he glanced at her—"making love?"

"No," she said. "Fucking."

Jeff stared at the road again, the lines of a frown creasing his forehead. "What cruelty," he said. "What a betrayal."

Mia sighed in agreement.

"Are they still together?"

"Oh, yes. Laura and Glen. Glen and Laura."

"Pond scum."

She laughed. "So you ran away to Valle Rosa and became a hermit."

"Right."

"And how long do you plan to keep running?"

She shrugged.

"Mia," he said. "This is not a good reason to run away, and certainly not to some little hamlet like Valle Rosa.

You need to live somewhere where you can meet other people, people who'll let you know you're a worthwhile person who didn't deserve to be treated like shit."

"Look, Jeff." She wanted him to stop talking about this. "I'm not badgering *you* about running away, so please don't badger me, okay? And I'm hungry."

Jeff smiled and swerved the car into the right lane to exit the freeway. "The lady's hungry," he said, pulling onto the off-ramp, "and suddenly feisty. Unpredictable. Timid one minute, brassy the next. She allows men to sculpt her in the nude, but turns to ice when you touch her. She—"

"Please don't," she said. If he uttered one more word, she thought she might explode.

He had pulled up at a stop sign, and he didn't cross the intersection until she looked at him.

"I'm sorry," he said, when she met his eyes.

"It's okay." She regretted her sudden bitchiness, but at least it had put an end to his teasing.

They stopped at a delicatessen and picked up subs— vegetarian for Mia, turkey for Jeff. When Jeff took a bottle of wine from the shelf, Mia grabbed another. She wanted to get drunk tonight.

They picked up the cat at Jeff's cottage, then walked over to hers. She rolled up the sheet of plastic from the carpet, and they sat on the floor, their backs against the sofa, while they ate. And drank. Mia was on her second glass of wine when Jeff dared speak to her of anything substantive again.

"So," he said, "did Glen make that sculpture from

pictures of you or did you pose? Or would you rather not talk about it?"

"I posed." She rewrapped the remaining half of her sandwich and set it on the coffee table.

"Was it awkward?"

She shook her head and took a long drink of wine. "It seemed like a perfectly natural thing to do at the time. But I was a lot younger then."

He laughed. "You're only twenty-eight now." He poured more wine into his own glass. "Though I have to admit it surprises me that you would do that."

"Why?"

He swallowed a bite of his sandwich before speaking again. "Because you're a very closed person, physically," he said. "You keep this enormous personal space between you and other people. I don't think it's just me, is it?"

She shook her head and stared at her bare feet. They looked pale against the nut-brown carpet. How long since she'd been out in the sun? "I didn't use to be that way," she said. "At the time I posed for Glen, I wasn't that way at all."

"Did losing him to Laura do that to you?"

She shrugged, non-committal.

Jeff finished his sandwich and rested his head against the cushions on the sofa, staring at the ceiling. "I don't think you're plain," he said.

Mia leaned her head back, too. The room had a little spin to it. "Well," she said, "it's just that Laura is extremely beautiful."

"You said she got all the boys and that you took care of

your mother." Jeff tipped his head forward again to take a sip of wine. "Does that mean Glen was your first?"

She turned her head on the cushion, looking at him from under a lock of blond hair. "Are we talking first boyfriend or first lover?"

He shrugged. "Your choice."

"He was both, actually." She nearly giggled, and she took another swallow of wine before resting her head on the cushion again. "I was a late bloomer."

"So he was very significant. Very important in your life."

"Mmm." There was a brown water stain on the ceiling from some long-ago rain. "How about you?" she asked. "Who was your first?"

"I was very young."

"How young?"

"Thirteen."

"Thirteen!" Her head shot up, and she winced at the sudden vertigo. "How old was the girl?"

"Seventeen. It was a dare. She was very sexy and very . . . carefree, shall we say. It sounds better than 'loose.' Some of my friends bet me ten bucks to do it with her."

"That's disgusting." Mia poured more wine into her glass.

"Do you think you need that?" Jeff pointed toward the glass, and she nodded.

"Yup," she said stubbornly. "I certainly do."

"Well, you're right." Jeff returned to the conversation. "I guess it was disgusting, in retrospect. It backfired on me anyway. They demanded a report from her before they'd pay up, and she told them I was the lousiest lay she'd ever had. She said, and this is one quote I'll never forget, 'He doesn't know his dick from a doorknob.'"

Jeff shuddered, and Mia laughed. The wine was definitely taking hold of her, the giddiness warm and inviting.

"So, that was ego-deflating enough to make me wait a few long years before I tried again." He smiled at her as he wadded up the wrapper from his sandwich. Then he reached behind him to take her sketch pad from the sofa. Resting it on his knees, he began drawing a crude-looking version of the two-tiered fountain. "I was wondering if you could make this part wider." He pointed to the upper tier. "What do you think?"

He held the sketch toward her, and she laughed again.

"Finally, something you're no good at," she said. "You can't draw at all."

He pulled the drawing away from her, an insulted look on his face, and tossed the balled wrapper at her cheek. Then he propped the sketch pad against the coffee table and leaned his arms on his knees. "Well, Mia," he said, "do you think I'm going to make it rain?"

She giggled. "No."

"How come you bought all that stuff for the fountain then?"

"I thought I should humor you."

"Carmen probably had her spies following us all over San Diego. You'll be on the news tonight." He began speaking with a Spanish accent, far stronger than Carmen's. "Valle Rosa's mystery man, the elusive Jeff Cabrio, was spotted today in San Diego with Mayor Chris Garrett's winsome secretary, Mia Tanner. The alleged rainmaker, Mr. Cabrio, seems to have engaged Ms. Tanner in his delusion that he can make it rain."

"Oh, God, I don't want to be on the news," Mia said. There was real alarm in the thought, but she couldn't quite grasp the source of it.

"Mr. Cabrio was seen contemplating a nude sculpture of Ms. Tanner," Jeff continued. Then he laughed. "I can see the headlines in tomorrow's paper: *Secretary Poses in Nothing but Scarf and Fedora while Rainmaker Looks On.*"

"Oh, no," she groaned.

"Carmen's spies are probably right outside your window as we speak." Jeff gestured toward the evening sky, a splash of orange at the living-room window. "And I think we should give them something to take back to the dragon lady."

He leaned over to pull her to him, softly, by her shoulders. Mia felt herself stiffen, felt the urge to slip her arms protectively between their bodies. But he was already too close to her for that, and his mouth was on hers, pressing and eager. When she felt his tongue slip between her lips, the battle inside her began in earnest, the hunger in her own body fighting the impossibility of letting this go any further.

She pulled away from him, pressing her hands lightly but firmly against his chest. A wave of nausea washed over her, and she tasted the wine in the back of her throat. "Please don't," she said. "Please go."

After a moment, he stood up, but only to move to the

sofa. He reached for her hand. "Come here, friend," he said, pulling her up from the floor and gently onto his lap.

She felt too weak and sick to fight him and she let herself lean against him, her arms held close to her body, wrists crossed above her chest. She squeezed her eyes shut as he rubbed her back.

"Holding you is like holding a giant prickly pear," he said, softly. "Was he abusive to you? Glen?"

She shook her head. His hand was warm on her back.

"Do you really want me to go?" he asked.

She bit her lip. "Could we just sit like this for another few minutes?"

"No," he said, "not like this, we can't. Loosen up a little, Mia. I won't kiss you. That's better."

She felt her body begin to relax, and with the thawing of her muscles came her tears. He held her, rubbing her arms, smoothing his fingers over the skin of her hands, while she cried quietly against his chest.

"Oh, Mia," he whispered. "There's a pain in you as big as the world, isn't there?" He pressed his lips against her shoulder, and she felt their warmth through her shirt. "There's a pain in you as big as my own."

She lifted her head to look at him. "I want you to kiss me," she said. "But that's all. I need to know that's all you'll do."

"All right," he said, and with that promise in her ears, Mia opened herself to him. Jeff kissed her slowly, deeply, with a tenderness that gave her courage. She rose to her knees and straddled him, and at his look of surprise, said, "I want to touch your face."

Shutting her eyes, she rested her palms against his cheeks, then slowly glided her fingers over the warm angles of jaw, his nose, his temples. The skin was satin-smooth on his forehead, rough with a day's growth of beard on his chin.

"Feels good," he said.

She moved her hands to his shoulders and shifted her weight until she could feel the heat of his erection through the denim of his jeans and the thin fabric of her shorts. She kissed him, pressing her hips against him, and was jolted by the beginning electric promise of an orgasm—an orgasm that would be unexpected and very welcome, but impossible to accept in this miserable, dishonest, hazardous fashion.

Jeff groaned, and kissed her harder, pulling her shirt from her shorts with one quick tug. She panicked as he slipped his hands beneath the shirt, as she felt them glide over the bare skin on her back.

Quickly, she sat up and grabbed his wrists, pressing them down hard on her thighs. "*Now*," she said. "You really have to go now."

He watched her through the narrowed eyes of a skeptic as she stood to tuck in her shirt. The room swirled slightly, but for the most part, she felt clear-headed and sober.

Jeff rose from the couch, placed his hands on his hips and stared at her until she had no choice but to raise her eyes to his.

"I'd be wrong to assume you're merely a tease, wouldn't I?" he asked.

She winced at the sound of the word. "Yes," she said, surprised by the huskiness of her voice. "You'd be wrong."

He leaned over to kiss her lightly on the cheek.

"What you are, Mia, is a liar," he said. "A kiss is definitely not all you want."

He lifted his glass and drained the last of the wine before giving her his half-smile and heading for the door.

From the window in her darkened bedroom, she watched him walk back to his cottage, the cat scampering after him in the moonlight, and the memory she'd been fighting much of the day flooded over her.

She'd had a difficult time finding a job after recovering from the mastectomy. Her depression over her loss, and over what she knew to be Glen's true feelings about her body, must have come through during her interviews. Or maybe the interviewers could see that her enthusiasm would always lie at home with her clay and not at some tiresome desk job. The temporary agency was her last hope. When she showed up for work that first day and was told she wasn't needed, she wasn't disappointed. She would go home and go back to bed. Glen would be at his studio, Laura at work. There would be no one to chastise her or try to cheer her up.

She'd been surprised to see their cars in the driveway, but not nearly as surprised as when she walked in the front door. It was like stepping inside a dream. A nightmare. Her sister and Glen were in front of the fireplace, naked, Laura's legs wrapped high around Glen's waist as he thrust into her. Mia stood frozen, her hand on the doorknob.

Laura was first to see her.

"Mia!" She pushed Glen away from her and sat up, her perfect breasts glistening in the sunlight. Glen turned to face the door, his erection full and painfully familiar.

Mia spun around and ran out to her car. She drove blindly, with no sense of destination. Glen was behind her, though, in his old Rover. He caught up to her at the first corner and jumped out of his car wearing only his jeans. He was still zipping them up as he climbed into the passenger seat beside her.

"*Bastard*," she said. "Get out!"

"No, Sunny. Pull over."

She drove across the intersection and pulled up to the curb but didn't turn off the ignition. Staring straight ahead of her, she spoke quietly. "Get out of my car, Glen. Leave me alone."

He leaned over to turn the key in the ignition, and silence filled the car.

"Sunny." He tried to pull her toward him, to hold her, but she flailed at him with her arms.

"Go to hell!" She pressed herself against the car door, as far from him as she could get. She was surprised she felt no urge to cry. There was far more rage inside her than sorrow. She longed for the satisfaction of hitting him.

"I'm sorry," he said. "I'm so sorry. Laura and I were sort of thrown together, taking care of you."

She scowled at him. "Please come up with something better than that. That's so simplistic, it's insulting."

"We didn't intend to fall in love. It simply happened. Sometimes these things are unpredic—"

"Shut up!"

"We wanted to wait until you were strong and well again before we told you."

"How very considerate of you both."

Glen was quiet a moment. "I still love you, Sunny," he said, his voice thick. "But it's simply not the same as it used to be."

She swallowed a sarcastic reply. Right now, she needed to deal in the truth. "I repulse you," she said quietly.

"No."

"You can't make love to me, but apparently you have no problem at all making love to my sister."

She pulled the diamond engagement ring from her finger. He tried to grab it from her, but she opened the car window and threw the ring as far as she could into the road.

"Sunny! You're bloody crazy!" Glen opened the door and ran into the street to hunt for his precious diamond, and Mia took that opportunity to drive off, knowing that, except to get her clothes and some sculpting supplies, she wouldn't return to her house again.

She stopped looking at herself in the mirror after that day. This wasn't her real body, she told herself. It was a shell. A temporary shell.

After the lights flicked off in Jeff's cottage, she lifted the mirror from the wall above the dresser and rested it against the headboard of her bed, so that as she sat in front of it, she was reflected from waist to chin in the pale moonlight coming through the window. She began un-buttoning her shirt, slowly, the way she thought a man might, the way Jeff might.

Could she tell Jeff? He wasn't at all like Glen. Maybe he would respond warmly. Not with pity, but compassion. Maybe he could see past the damage in a way that Glen could not.

She slipped the shirt from her shoulders, but found it difficult to look at her image. Even in the hazy moonlight, even wearing a bra, it was obvious that she wasn't nor-mal. Her right breast was full where it met the bra. The left side of her chest gave her the look of a child dressed in her mother's underwear. She forced herself to unhook the bra, let it fall.

She pressed the tips of her fingers hard against her lips. It was worse than in her memory. The skin was a smooth, white plane, unbroken by a nipple, but crossed with the pink line of the scar.

Mia lowered the mirror face down on the bed and closed her eyes.

She would take his friendship. Settle for that. She wouldn't kiss him again or let him hold her or touch her. She wouldn't take the chance of frightening him away. She couldn't expect anyone else to love her when she couldn't even love herself.

28.

The avocado grove covered a little more than two acres on the sloping rim of Cinnamon Canyon. Carmen parked her car on the crest of a hill and got out, shading her eyes to survey the land below her. In the distance, smoke rose above the horizon, the latest in a string of fires burning their way toward Valle Rosa. Last night, the blaze had destroyed six homes and killed a teenaged girl who had apparently slept through the warnings to evacuate. In the middle of the night, Carmen visited the neighborhood with a camera crew. The people looked exhausted. "Don't know how much more of this we can take," one woman said into Carmen's microphone.

Carmen had slept poorly after that midnight outing, haunted by the vision of the fire fighters dragging the charred body of the girl from the ruins of one of the houses, so she had been awake when Jeff started his car in the driveway of the adobe. It wasn't quite five o'clock. She put on her robe and looked out the bedroom window to see his tail lights disappear around the first curve in the road. Her curiosity wouldn't allow her to go back to sleep. She got dressed and drove to the warehouse, stopping the car a block away to watch as Jeff and Rick pulled the two flatbed trucks out into the street. She followed them at a distance as they drove to the grove, then used her car phone to call the station, requesting they send a camera crew to this little corner of Cinnamon Canyon as quickly as possible.

Rick had parked his truck at the south end of the grove, closest to where Carmen stood, while Jeff had parked his to the north, a good distance away. The arrangement of the trucks seemed important, and the men had shifted them back and forth on their respective roads in a peculiar *pas de deux* before being satisfied with their resting spots. It wasn't until Rick got out of the truck that Carmen realized they were communicating with one another by two-way radios. Rick spoke into the little box in his hand, and Jeff waved to him from the other side of the grove.

She wished she had binoculars. From this distance, each truck looked identical. Each carried what appeared to be something like a satellite dish, surrounded by three tall, broad white cylinders. There were several black boxes on the floor of the trucks, boxes which must have had buttons or knobs on them, because Rick and Jeff knelt next to them, pressing or pulling or turning things, talking all the while into the radios in their hands.

Suddenly, Rick turned around, and Carmen knew she'd been spotted. Jeff stood on the flatbed of his truck, one hand on his hip, the other holding the radio. Obviously, he and Rick were discussing her presence. In another minute, Rick jumped off the back of his truck and started walking up the canyon toward her, working his way through the thick, leathery chaparral. She was glad it was Rick she would have to deal with and not Jeff.

The *News Nine* van arrived on the road behind her just as Rick neared the crest. Jake Carney and Toby Wells sauntered lazily out of the van, laughing.

"They only sent two of you?" she asked, disappointed. No one was taking this very seriously.

"Right," Jake said, opening the rear of the van for his equipment. He stopped to wipe his forehead with a red bandana pulled from his pocket. "Christ, it's hotter than blazes out here already."

"Well, come on," Carmen said. "We're going to have to try to get closer."

"You can't." Rick skirted a withered scrub oak on the ridge and came to a stop in front of her. He was winded. Sweat matted his blond hair to his forehead. "Jeff says for you to keep your distance."

"What exactly are you doing?" Carmen asked.

Rick looked across the grove at Jeff, as though wondering how much the older man would want him to say. "It's an experiment." He spoke with cautious apprehension, but the boyish excitement in his eyes was unmistakable.

"I'd like the cameras to get a little closer, please," Carmen said. "We need a better look at the trucks."

"No," Rick said with some force in his voice. "You can't come any closer than this. It'll interfere, okay? This is delicate stuff." He started walking back toward the canyon.

"What if one of the cameramen came down on foot?" Carmen called after him.

Rick faced her again with a groan and an exaggerated slump of his shoulders. He said something into the radio, then took a few steps toward her, holding the little box in front of him. "He wants to talk to you," he said.

She took the device from Rick's hand and held it to her ear. She looked to the north, where Jeff stood facing her from the truck. "Hello?" she said.

"Do you want to see rain fall over Valle Rosa, Carmen?" Jeff's voice crackled in her ear.

She thought she could actually *feel* his eyes locking with hers across the expanse of the grove.

"Yes," she said.

"Then stay right where you are. No closer. All right?"

"All right," she said, defeated.

Rick took the radio from her hand, and as he made his way back into the canyon, Carmen turned to Jake and Toby.

"We'll film it from here," she said.

"Film *what* from here?" Toby asked.

"Typical Valle Rosa footage," Jake said, sitting down on the crest. "Blue sky, yellow sun, dead avocado trees." He pulled the red bandana from his pocket again and wiped it across his forehead.

An hour later, Jake and Toby were sprawled on the dusty earth, sweating profusely and drinking orange soda out of cans. Carmen had refused their offers of something to drink, although she was very hot. Her blouse was stuck to her back with sweat; she wished she could roll up the long sleeves. Walking back and forth along the rim of the canyon, she watched as Rick and Jeff fiddled with their equipment, spoke into their radios, and gestured to one another with broad sweeps of their arms.

"Nice little wild goose chase, Carmo," Jake said, yawning. The van radio sputtered behind them, and Toby slowly got to his feet. He paced back to the van, and a few minutes later came to stand next to Carmen.

"We're wanted in Escondido," he said. "Four alarm fire and they—"

"Shh!" Carmen held her hand up to stop him. She raised her chin, turned her head, struggling to hear . . . what? Something different, something very faint. A high-pitched hum. Soft, but growing louder, so loud that Jake got up off the ground to join them on the ridge, staring in the direction of the trucks.

And then it happened. At first it was a mere hint of gray in the sky over the grove. Carmen thought it was her imagination, but then the gray deepened—and spread. Rick spoke into his radio, and he and Jeff knelt next to their black boxes, pressing buttons, turning knobs, as the blue of the sky between the two trucks gradually gave way to the thickening gray shadow.

"Holy shit," said Toby.

"Get the cameras!" Carmen ordered, and in a minute the phenomenon was being caught on film. The cloud spread across the sky, slowly, like syrup, its color now an opaque, ominous near-black. There was a churning at its core, a slow-moving, dark tumble of mist, suspended directly above the center of the grove. The churning spread as the ends of the roiling cloud reached toward the trucks, and the grove was blanketed in thick, cool shadow.

And then the rain began. Not a mist, not a shower, but a pelting, teeming rain that beat against the dying leaves of the avocado trees, while Carmen and Jake and Toby stood awestruck on the sunlit ridge of the canyon.

Carmen told Toby to film her as she took a few steps into the canyon. When she'd reached the rain, she turned to face the camera, laughing out loud, holding her arms out to her sides, palms up.

"This is Carmen Perez," she said to the camera. "I'm standing on the rim of Cinnamon Canyon, where a small miracle is taking place." She brushed a thick, wet strand of hair from her cheek. "On what is otherwise a typically dry, sunny southern California day, rain is falling over this heat-ravaged avocado grove behind me. In an experimental test of their rainmaking technology, Valle Rosa's mystery man, Jeff Cabrio, and his assistant, Rick Smythe, have succeeded in producing rain. So don't believe whatever weather reports you heard this morning. It's pouring in Valle Rosa!"

Chris left his office around eleven the morning after the experiment, a stack of phone messages for Jeff in his shirt pocket. He had fielded most of them, thanking the callers for their congratulations, putting off those who wanted to know how they could get in touch with Jeff. Could he come to their drought-worn town next? Could he teach others to do what he was doing in Valle Rosa? Chris explained to each of them that, for now, Jeff was working only for Valle Rosa, but he assured them he would pass along their messages.

Even Sam Braga had called with a guarded apology. "I'll hold my fire until I see what else Cabrio can do," he said.

Chris was glad Carmen had followed Jeff and Rick out to the avocado grove the day before, glad she had gotten that mesmerizing footage of the mini-rainstorm, because if he had heard about it only from Jeff himself, he wasn't at all sure he would have believed it.

As he drove through one of the residential tracts of Valle Rosa, he spotted the first umbrella. It was bright yellow, open, and it hung upside down from a mailbox next to the street. He thought little of it until he saw the second, this one blue, hanging from the limb of a manzanita tree in the yard of the house next door. There were three umbrellas hanging in the third yard, and a huge red-and-white striped umbrella hanging from the porch of the fourth. Chris felt a chill up his spine. Somehow this symbol of hope had taken hold of Valle Rosa overnight, as though everyone had awakened this morning after dreaming the same dream.

News vans lined the street across from the warehouse, and Chris had to park around the corner. A group of children and a few adults sat on the retaining wall by the side of the warehouse, probably hoping to steal a glimpse of the rainmaker. A couple of young men were trying to peek in the high windows, but even standing on one another's shoulders, they couldn't get a good look inside.

An alert cameraman must have recognized him, because he started his camera rolling as Chris walked quickly toward the front door of the warehouse.

"All right, Mayor Garrett!" someone called out, and a smattering of applause broke out among the spectators.

Chris let himself in with his own key. Inside, he gave his eyes a moment to adjust to the dim light before walking toward the rear. Rick was on one of the trucks, Jeff at the computer. He looked up as Chris neared him and smiled.

"How did you like our little squall yesterday?" he asked.

Chris shook his head as he sat down across the table from him. "Incredible," he said.

"We made friggin' history." Rick leaned against one of the vats on the truck.

"And everybody wants a part of it." Chris pulled the stack of phone messages from his pocket and set them on the table. "Fifty calls this morning from people who want to interview you, or pick your brain, or have you come to their town next."

Jeff lifted the top message and read it, his face sober.

"And there are umbrellas hanging from mailboxes and tree limbs. Everyone's caught up in what you're doing. Everyone believes you can do it." Chris pursed his lips together in something of an apology. "And I'm afraid the vultures are outside."

Jeff raised wide eyes to his. "What do you mean?"

"Reporters," Chris said. "Fans. The excited citizenry of Valle Rosa. They're all waiting for a glimpse of you."

Jeff groaned and leaned back in his chair. "You've got to help me, Chris. Please. Do whatever you can to keep them away from me." He pushed the stack of messages back across the table. "And is there anything you can do to get your ex-wife off my back?"

Chris remembered Carmen on TV the evening before, for the first time in many years, the undisputed star of *News Nine*. He'd felt a mixture of relief and profound joy as he watched her shine. He had nearly forgotten that her success was at the expense of the man sitting across the table from him.

"She's on a roll now," he said. "I'll talk to her, but I doubt there's much I can do to stop her."

"I'm afraid she might stop *me*." Jeff stood up and stretched. "I need another month," he said. "I'll move in here if I have to to avoid the press, and I'll send Rick out for food."

Chris shook his head. "No. I'll hire some security." He had made that decision earlier that morning. "The equipment should be watched when you're not here anyway." Chris took a small notepad from his shirt pocket and set it on the table. "What more do you need in the way of supplies?"

Jeff studied the map on the back of the bookcase. "One more truck should do it."

"That's all?" Chris was almost disappointed. "I mean, you only covered a tiny area with the two."

Jeff smiled again. "Did you hear that Rick?"

Rick laughed. "You better fill him in on the facts."

Jeff turned from the map to face him. "We were

only using about two percent of our power, Chris," he said. "You'd better make sure your flood insurance is paid up."

29

When the knock came on her door very early in the morning, Mia expected it to be Jeff. She'd been up for hours already, doing her laundry in the bathtub and working on the sculpture. But she wasn't yet dressed. She wiped her hands on the clay-stained rag and loosened the folds of her blue robe across her chest to make the absence of her breast as unnoticeable as possible.

When she opened the door, though, it wasn't Jeff, but Carmen who stood on her front porch. Behind her, Sugarbush lay spread out in breathless beauty, the dry earth rose-colored in the fire-charged air of the sunrise. She wore an off-white pants suit, and the rose color glowed on one side of her face and body. For a moment, Mia simply drank in the scene with the rapture of an artist viewing a lure.

"May I come in for a minute, please?" Carmen asked.

Mia took a step backward to let her in, reflexively raising her hand to her neck, covering the left part of her chest with her forearm.

Carmen closed the door behind her. The warm, pink sunlight poured through the windows, illuminating the shadows and lines on her face and shimmering in the gray streak of her hair.

Yet there was no denying Carmen's beauty—a tired sort of beauty, somehow made even more extraordinary by its gentle aging.

Carmen glanced at the plastic on the floor and at the terra cotta sculpture taking shape on the stool. "You're working," she said. "I'll only take a minute of your time."

Mia folded her arms across her chest, a stiffness to her body that was beginning to feel all too natural. She remembered Jeff saying she was protective of herself physically, that she was careful to keep others out of her personal space. He was right. Perhaps this cool rigidity had become so much a part of her that she would never be able to lose it, not even once her body was whole again. She would remain forever tense and hyper-alert, always turning away, trying to hide herself from the eyes of others.

Right now, though, her tension was only partially related to her body. She felt nervous having Carmen see how she had transformed the cottage. She had moved the furniture around and covered the floor with plastic. The laundry she'd done that morning hung on lines stretched across the hallway. It looked like a community of ghosts. Would Carmen mind? Would she feel Mia had taken undue liberties with a space she was merely renting?

"That was something else yesterday, wasn't it?" Carmen walked across the living room and leaned against the arm of the sofa. "The rain?"

"Yes," Mia said. The owner of the avocado grove had

sent Chris a bouquet of flowers. Suddenly, Chris was being viewed as some sort of hero.

Carmen folded her own arms beneath her breasts. "Did you know all along that he'd succeed? Did you have some sixth sense?"

Mia smiled. "I was probably every bit as astonished as you were." She'd cried when she saw the footage of that remarkable rain. She'd cried from happiness for Jeff and for his success and his vindication. And she'd cried from the realization that he was nearing his goal, nearing the time he would leave Valle Rosa.

Carmen looked down at the sketch pad on the sofa, idly running her fingertips across the drawing Jeff had made of the fountain. "You've become good friends with him," she said. It was almost an accusation.

Mia sat down behind the stool. She knew now what Carmen was after this morning, and she felt suddenly powerful, suddenly superior. She had something Carmen wanted, and she also had the integrity to keep it from her.

"Yes," she said. "We're friends."

"So, what is he like?" Carmen lowered herself to the sofa. "I can't get near him. All he does is bark at me. What has he told you about himself?"

"Nothing. And I don't question him, either."

Carmen's eyes suddenly fell on the bulletin board propped up against the coffee table. "Oh!" she said, reaching over to lift the board to her knees. She studied the layer of photographs. "These were taken inside the warehouse!"

"Yes."

"Why do you have them?" She glanced at the sculpture on the stool in front of Mia. "You're sculpting him!" She rested the bulletin board against the back of the sofa and stood up, circling the stool, studying the emerging sculpture. It didn't yet resemble anyone in particular. The pose was in place—a man standing, shirt open, one hand raised to draw back a curtain that didn't yet exist—but he lacked identifying features, and the bas-relief of the window was still wrapped in plastic on the coffee table. Carmen continued to walk around the stool, and Mia thought of a hungry wolf circling its prey.

"You're working from the pictures?" Carmen asked.

"Yes."

"I'll pay you for those pictures, Mia." Carmen gestured toward the bulletin board. "A month's free rent."

Mia laughed, shaking her head.

"Just one picture, then. You can pick which one." Carmen returned to the sofa and plucked one of the pictures—Jeff and Rick poring over the computer—from the board. She frowned at it. "What's it like inside? What are they doing in there?"

"Honestly, Carmen, I don't have the vaguest idea." She must have conveyed some annoyance in her voice, because Carmen's shoulders suddenly drooped and she bit her lip.

"I know I'm intruding," she said. "I know I'm being unfair, but I need to learn more about him."

"I doubt I know any more than you do. Even if I did, he's my friend."

Carmen nodded, the look on her face one of resignation

as she handed the photograph over to Mia. "Well," she said, "he's lucky to have you." She sighed and glanced around the room again, her eyes falling on the laundry hanging in the hallway. "Oh, Mia, you poor thing!" She walked toward the hall with its crisscrossed lines of underwear and over-sized T-shirts. "This is ridiculous. You can't even walk down the hall. And how are you washing it—in the sink?" She peered into the bathroom, and Mia tried to imagine what she was seeing: towels hung from the shower-curtain rod, buckets of clay-laced water in the tub, the prosthesis on the edge of the sink.

Carmen disappeared into the bathroom. Mia took a deep breath and followed her in, clutching her robe tightly around her. Carmen was tapping a loose wall tile into place above the tub.

"From now on," she said, standing straight again, "you're using my washer and dryer. Any time, okay? The spare key is under the potted lemon tree on the patio."

Mia must have looked suspicious of her motives, because Carmen said, "No obligation, Mia. Really." She pointed toward the damp laundry in the hallway. "This is crazy."

"Okay. Thanks." Mia took a step into the hall, hoping to lure Carmen out of the bathroom, out of the cottage, but the older woman's eyes had fallen on the sink.

"What's that?" she asked. "Some sort of—?" She stopped short, and Mia saw the realization dawning on her.

"It's a breast prosthesis," Mia said, with a sense of doom. Carmen was a woman capable of using people to her own gain, a woman always on the lookout for other people's secrets. For a panicky moment, Mia thought of offering her Jeff's pictures in exchange for her silence.

Carmen shut her eyes, pressing her fingertips to her mouth. "Oh, Mia," she said quietly. "I'm so sorry."

Mia was shaken by the sincerity in her voice. "I don't need . . . I don't want pity," she said.

Carmen opened her eyes again. There was sympathy in them, sympathy that could only be construed as genuine. "I had no idea," she said. "I was jealous of you. I *am* jealous of you. I know you don't need pity."

"Jealous of me?"

"Of your youth. Your talent. Of the lovely life you've created for yourself—coming way out here to pursue your art. Your passion. And I envied how easily you seemed to fall into a relationship with a man no one else can get close to."

"I'm Jeff's friend. I don't want anything else from him. He knows he can trust me."

"And he knows he can't trust me for a minute, huh?" Carmen's smile was wistful.

"Not for a second."

Carmen nodded toward the prosthesis. "How long has it been?" she asked. "Are you all right now?"

"The surgery was in January, and I'm fine. I'll have reconstructive surgery next year." She walked back into the living room, Carmen close behind her, but at the front door, the older woman stopped.

"I mean it about the laundry," she said. "And if there's anything else you need, please let me know."

"Just don't mention me in your reports on Jeff, all right?" Mia asked. "The next thing you'll say is that he's befriended a one-breasted woman."

Carmen looked stricken. "Do you think I would do that? Do you think I'm that cruel?"

Mia answered her with silence. She knelt down on the plastic and began organizing the pictures on the bulletin board.

"I'm sorry for what you've gone through." Carmen stepped closer, touching Mia's shoulder, bending low, and with some horror Mia realized she meant to embrace her. She folded her arms across her chest again and stood up, and Carmen dropped her own hands to her sides.

"I'm not a mean person, Mia," she said. "Really I'm not."

Mia felt herself color. She was the mean one. Instantly, she knew that it was Carmen in need of the comfort an embrace would provide. Carmen needed it far more than she did.

Tell me about your son, Mia thought. *Tell me what's made you so hard.*

"I know you're not cruel," she said, walking toward the door again. "You've been good to me. But you're hurting Jeff."

Carmen nodded, slowly. "Well." She reached for the doorknob, "if it's any consolation, I don't like myself much either these days."

She offered Mia a cheerless smile and left the cottage, slipping quietly once more into the rose-colored morning.

30.

Chris's palm perspired on the handle of his tool kit as he waited in the darkness outside Carmen's kitchen door. He'd asked her if he could work on the leak in the bathroom while she was home, telling her it might take him a few days before he could get to it at a time she would be gone from the adobe. It was a lie; he could have fixed the leak while she was at work the following day. But he needed this time with her. He needed the opportunity to talk with her about Jeff. He had to ask her to leave Jeff alone.

Yet when Carmen opened the door for him, when she ushered him up the stairs and into the master bedroom they had shared, he knew the source of his nerves had nothing to do with his deception, but rather with being near Carmen in the bedroom that held so many memories for him, good and bad.

"I've appreciated all you've done in the house," she said, leading him into the master bath.

"I've enjoyed it." He set his tool case carefully on the tiled countertop.

Carmen pointed to the dripping tap in the white

whirlpool tub. "It doesn't seem that bad right now, but I swear, at night the noise keeps me awake. Even with the door closed."

He remembered how lightly she slept, how anytime he would awaken in the middle of the night, she would already be awake, usually holding him, snuggling close to him.

As he hunted in the tool case for a screwdriver, she took a folded green towel from the chrome étagère near the tub, fluffed it open and hung it on the towel rack. She stepped back to admire it, and he realized this bathroom was nothing more than one more room in the house to her. Of course. She couldn't possibly share his memory of this room—the blood everywhere, the splashes of red in the tub, on the towels. She had been nude when he found her, and more than anything else, that had told him she'd been serious about killing herself, that she truly no longer cared about anything, not even what people thought of her.

She surprised him by sitting down on the white-tiled tub surround as he worked on the faucet.

"Have you thought about running, Chris?"

The question surprised him. He was wearing shorts, and he glanced down at his legs. His muscle tone wasn't what it used to be.

"I know I should," he said, prying off the gold-toned handle of the faucet. "I don't work out at all any more. Just don't have the time."

Her face registered confusion, and then she laughed. "I meant run for *mayor*."

He gave her an incredulous stare. "Are you out of your mind? Every morning I count the days until the election when I can turn this mess over to someone else."

She was quiet for a moment. "I think you should consider it."

"DeLuis and Burrows are far better qualified."

"But they're such . . . politicians. Their primary interest is power. They don't really care about Valle Rosa. No one loves Valle Rosa the way you do, Chris."

He removed the screw holding the old washer in place. "And it would make a good story, huh? You could get a lot of mileage out of good ol' Chris Garrett running for office."

She let out her breath. "That wasn't what I was thinking about at all."

"Sorry."

"Oh, Chris, don't you get it?" She rested her elbows on the tub surround to lean close to him. "You're doing something miraculous for Valle Rosa. You've got everybody excited, everybody full of hope, hanging their umbrellas from the treetops. You've got everybody in this little hamlet working together for a change. Whether or not Jeff succeeds in making it rain is almost immaterial at this point. This is the toughest thing Valle Rosa's ever going to face. If you can handle this, you can handle anything."

He thought of Sam Braga's editorial in the *Journal* the day before. Sam had—at some cost to himself—eaten his words. "The *Journal* has been critical of Mayor Garrett in the past," he wrote. "In light of the recent rainmaking experiment, that criticism must be reconsidered. Christopher Garrett may well emerge from this ordeal as a visionary." In the same edition, someone called for the start of a fund to keep Jeff Cabrio working without sacrificing the transportation needs of Valle Rosa. The residents of the town were indeed working together with a spirit of community Chris hadn't seen since he was a child.

Chris replaced the handle, pushing its decorative ceramic cap into place. "I don't have a political bone in my body, Carmen," he said, closing the tool chest.

"I know." She stood up. "That's why you'd be perfect."

They left the bathroom and walked together into the bedroom. Chris pointed to the skylight above the bed.

"Speaking of leaks," he said, smiling, "how's the skylight holding up?"

She laughed. He saw her try to stop it, but she couldn't.

"That was really funny," she said.

"How long did it take us to realize it was leaking?" he asked, although he knew the answer. They had been making love while a cold winter rain fell outside and a fire burned in the bedroom fireplace. Carmen had been above him, and he remembered the glow of the firelight in the slim stream of water that slipped over her shoulder, her breast. Even then she didn't seem to notice, and he wasn't about to bring it to her attention and risk destroying the pure, pleasured concentration in her face. They had exaggerated that leak over the years when they recounted the story to friends. What had begun as a trickle became a deluge.

"Well, I knew it right away," she said, "but you were lost in ecstasy." She looked away from him, almost shyly, and he wanted to touch her, to pull her into a hug, but he didn't dare. Instead he stared at the bed. In that bed, he hadn't been a pitching ace and Carmen hadn't been the star of *San Diego Sunrise*. They'd been nothing more than two human beings in need of one another.

A sudden, soft breeze blew through the open window, bringing with it the smell of eucalyptus, strong and familiar. He felt a wave of longing, not to make love so much as to recapture the closeness he and Carmen had shared in this bed. He wanted the warmth of her body next to him, wanted to see the tangle of her dark hair in the moonlight spilling from the skylight above them.

He looked at her now. "I'm sorry I ruined everything," he said.

She bent over to smooth an imaginary wrinkle on the floral bedspread. "So, seriously now, what do you think about running?"

He smiled at her abrupt change of topic and changed it again. "I think you and I need to talk about Jeff."

She sat down on the bed. "What about him?"

Chris folded his arms across his chest. "Well, I was hoping you could lay off his story for a while. Let him get his work done and get out of here before you reveal anything else about him."

"You know I can't do that. This is the biggest story in Valle Rosa right now. It's the biggest story in southern California." She looked up at the skylight with a sigh. "They're finally paying some attention to me at work,

Chris. What do you think they'd do with me if I suddenly stopped reporting on him?"

He knew she was right. Her dilemma was real. "I'm just afraid you're going to scare him off," he said.

She frowned at him. "Doesn't it bother you that he's obviously hiding something? For all you know, you could be harboring a murderer. Or has he told you something I don't know? Has he told you what he's running from?"

"No, and frankly, I don't care. It doesn't matter to me what he did before he came here. All I know is that he can help us in a way no one else can."

Carmen smoothed her hand again over the spread. When she spoke, her voice was soft. Confidential. "Sometimes I appall myself." She looked at him, her eyes dark and wide. "All I can think about is getting more information about him. It's obsessive. I wake up in the morning trying to figure out whose brain I can pick next, who can tell me something about him I don't already know."

She hadn't spoken to him—*confided* in him—like this in so long. He wished he could hold her. He sat down on the bed himself, but left a space between them.

"They were laughing at me at *News Nine*, Chris," Carmen continued. "They were literally ready to get rid of me. Now, they're taking me seriously again. Jeff is big news, and I have him in my back pocket. Am I supposed to let that opportunity slip through my fingers?"

He started to speak but was interrupted by a knocking from downstairs. Carmen immediately got to her feet. Disappointed, he followed her down to the kitchen, where Mia stood at the screen door.

"Sorry to disturb you." She seemed to be speaking only to him. "Jeff wants to know if you could come to his cottage to talk about some more equipment he needs."

"Now?"

Mia nodded. "He said it's important. He needs to get the stuff soon." She smiled. "And he asked if you could bring your guitar and a bottle of wine, too."

Chris looked at Carmen. He wasn't ready to leave the adobe, not when they were finally talking like something other than adversaries. The image of the white bathroom, blood-streaked, flashed through his mind. *Irrational,* he told himself. *She's all right. She's all right because she has Jeff's story.*

"I guess I should go," he said to her, wondering if his tone conveyed his reluctance.

Picking up a sponge, Carmen began wiping the already clean kitchen counter. "No problem. Thanks for fixing the leak." There was a formality in her voice, telling him that, even if he were to stay, the spell had been broken.

Still, as he walked across Sugarbush with Mia at his side, he couldn't help but picture Carmen, standing alone in the kitchen of the adobe, with only her obsession as company.

31.

It took her several days and some help from Tom Forrest—who apparently had a tight-lipped connection in New Jersey—for Carmen to find the name and phone number of the foster parents with whom Jeff had lived during his senior year of high school.

Only the foster father, Walter Hunt, was still living. Carmen called him one evening from her kitchen. She had decided to downplay who she was and where she was from in order to prevent him from discerning that Robert Blackwell was the rainmaker in southern California. She had to be particularly careful now; the reclusive Valle Rosa rainmaker was becoming national news.

But Walter Hunt wasn't going to be a threat. He sounded very old, his voice tired and soft. He had some trouble following her as she explained that she was doing a profile on Robert Blackwell. He didn't seem the least bit interested in her reasons, and she was pleased when he simply began to talk.

"We took in a hundred and twelve kids over the years," he said, a certain pride in his raspy voice. "But I remember the one you're talking about. The county told us he was a genius, but the truth is, he was too smart for his own good. He wasn't a real happy kid, either. Who could blame him? His stepfather was locked up and his mother died a few years earlier having an abortion."

"An abortion?" Carmen guessed Walter Hunt had Jeff mixed up with one of the other hundred or so kids he'd taken care of. "I thought she died in a car accident."

"That's what the kid told everyone. Abortions weren't legal back then, you know—and they shouldn't be legal now, if you ask me—so of course he and his stepfather tried to cover it up. The county social worker said it had been done in a back alley somewhere, and the police found her in the parking lot of a church. She'd bled to death."

"Oh, God." Carmen closed her eyes, wishing she could block out the image of Beth's suffering. At some point she was going to have to tell Susan Cabrio what had become of her sister. She wished she didn't know quite so much.

She drew in a breath. "When did Rob come to you?"

"After they arrested his stepfather. Watts, his name was."

"And why was he arrested?"

Walter Hunt sounded as though he were yawning. "Well, I think a couple of people got killed during one of his drug deals, even though it was an old case. He'd stopped pushing drugs long before. Not fair, I guess, for a man to go straight and then get put away for something that happened long ago. But that's the way the law works. Rob was real defensive about him. Amazing the kid never got into drugs himself, 'cause he really loved that man. He visited him as often as he could, taking off without telling us where he was going. That was typical of him."

"Where was Mr. Watts incarcerated?"

"Hmm. Good question. I don't recall, except that Rob used to take a bus to get there. We knew when he'd disappear he was either out seeing his convict stepfather or having sex with some girl." Walter Hunt laughed. "He was fast. We heard that from the other kids. They said he'd move from girl to girl, that he'd done it with practically every girl in the senior class by the time he graduated."

"I see." Carmen wasn't certain how to respond to that particular piece of information. "What else can you tell me?"

"Well, I remember this friend of his—a boy—who was always hanging around. Felt like we'd taken in two kids, sometimes. He was another brainy type."

"Was his name Kent?"

"Yes! That's it. Kent Reed. Real tall. Bad skin. Had a few fingers missing on one hand. He and Rob could scare the living daylights out of you when they got together. One of those brains that was always cooking up something was enough. Put two of them together and you could have a real catastrophe on your hands. You never knew what they were going to do next." Walter Hunt paused for a moment. "Anyway, Kent gave the other kids at the house the willies. He was always over, always wanting to be with Rob—even Rob would get annoyed with him. So, the wife and I made some rules about when he could come over, how long he could stay, that sort of thing."

Carmen had written the name Kent Reed down on her notepad and drawn three circles around it.

"Do you have any idea at all where Kent Reed might be now?" she asked.

Mr. Hunt yawned again. "Interesting question. I'd guess either a top-secret government agency where they cook up futuristic weapons, or an insane asylum. Take your pick."

"How about Rob? Do you know where he ended up?"

"Can't say that I do. When he graduated, though, the schools were falling all over each other to get him. Don't remember which one he picked. MIT, might have been. One of those technology schools."

She jotted "MIT?" down on her notepad. "Well, thank you, Mr. Hunt. You've been very helpful."

"Sure." He didn't sound ready to say goodbye. "I'll tell you something," he said. "I remember Rob as one of the most difficult kids we had, though that's odd in a way. We had kids who got high or who didn't know right from wrong. We had ones who were borderline retarded, others who broke the law. Robbie wasn't any of those things, but he was sad and angry and hard to reach, and none of our rules mattered to him if he wanted to break them. He wasn't a mean boy, just single-minded. When he left for college, the wife and I thought, good riddance. We told the county we didn't want any more kids with genius IQs."

Carmen got off the phone. She poured herself a glass

of iced tea, then sat at the table again, tapping the tip of her pen on the notepad. Where the hell was she going with this? She felt like disregarding Tom Forrest's advice to move slowly. She wanted to call the FBI to see if Jeff was wanted for something. She was tired of working in the dark, tired of trying to decide what was significant and what wasn't. Lately, she'd found herself studying the wanted posters in the post office, examining the features of the shifty-looking men for some resemblance to the man living on her property.

She thought back to her conversation from the day before with Tom Forrest. He was proud of the way she was handling the Cabrio story, he said. "You're incredible, Carmen!" he'd told her. "They're eating it up. Keep those tidbits flowing."

She had hesitated in her response, not certain how to word it, not certain how it would be received.

"Sometimes I feel like I'm using him," she said softly. "Exploiting him."

There was dead silence on the line.

"Tom?"

"I can't believe what I'm hearing." Tom's voice conveyed something like disgust. "This is your *job*, Carmen, and there was a time you were better at it than anyone else I know."

"Right," she said. "I'll be fine."

There was no point in trying to explain her feelings to him. Tom's skin had grown thick and calloused over the years. He didn't know what it was like to suddenly wake up one morning with your skin full of tender spots. He wouldn't be able to understand how easily she bruised.

She thought of Mia's allusions to her cruelty, Jeff's complete disdain for her. Only Chris seemed to understand.

He always had.

32.

The moment Carmen appeared on the television screen, Mia set down the wire cutters and stood to turn up the volume. Carmen was wearing an aquamarine dress tonight. Every night this week, she'd worn something new, something bright and bold. There had definitely been a change in her on-screen presence lately. She held her head a little higher; her smile was sure and confident. Tonight, though, Carmen wasn't smiling. Her demeanor was serious and Mia guessed she was about to divulge some piece of information about Jeff to her audience, undoubtedly something Jeff would rather the world not know. Mia sat down again behind the wire armature for the fountain and waited, tense and frowning, for Carmen's first words.

"*News Nine* has learned that Jeff Cabrio's stepfather was arrested during Jeff's senior year of high school," Carmen said. "The charge was a murder committed several years earlier related to a drug deal. Jeff was then placed in foster care. I had the opportunity today to speak with his foster father in New Jersey. He stated that Jeff had been one of the most difficult youngsters he and his wife had ever taken in, a genius whose tumultuous family life made it hard for him to find happiness. He described Jeff as single-minded, sad, angry and unreachable."

Mia's eyes were drawn to the coffee table, where the unfinished sculpture of Jeff rested under a sheet of plastic. He hadn't changed much over the years, she thought. He hadn't changed at all.

She was getting out of the tub a few hours later when she heard Jeff calling the kitten. Wrapping a towel around herself, she peered out the bathroom window. She couldn't see him, but she heard that high-pitched questioning whistle he always used with the cat.

"Hey cat!" he called. "Come here, kitty."

She put on her underwear and the sundress she'd worn that day and went outside.

He stood on the rim of the canyon, hands on his hips.

"Jeff?"

He turned to watch her walking toward him. "The cat's missing," he said, when she was standing next to him. "He was gone this morning. You know how he loves to play 'watch cat' and sit on the windowsill in my living room?"

She nodded.

"Well, he must have slipped out the side of the screen where it isn't fastened to anything. I was hoping he'd come home sometime during the day."

He looked away from her, probably reading her thoughts. Surely he'd heard it too last night—the too-close howling of the coyotes.

She began calling for the kitten, walking a few yards down into the canyon to join Jeff in a search she felt certain was futile, sensing his desperate need of the ruse. She listened in vain for the squawky little meow. Darkness was falling rapidly over the canyon. The chaparral and scrub oak sent long shadows across the earth, every shadow as dark and black as the cat.

Suddenly, Jeff turned and stalked out of the canyon, walking toward his cottage. Mia heard him step onto the porch, but continued her search. Most likely, he was coming up with some wonderful Jeff-like solution to the problem. He would emerge from the cottage with a whistle carved from the limb of a tree or some magical piece of equipment designed to pinpoint the cat's whereabouts. At the very least, she expected him to bring out the box of kibble, which they could shake in the hope of luring the kitten home.

When he didn't return after several minutes, however, Mia left the canyon herself and walked to his cottage. The front door was open. He wasn't in the living room, where his usual stacks of papers rested on the coffee table, nor was he in the kitchen.

"Jeff?" She walked slowly down the hallway toward the one bedroom, where she found him lying on the bed, staring at the ceiling. The back of his arm rested across his forehead, and she thought of how Carmen had described him on television earlier that evening: sad, angry, and unreachable.

She leaned against the doorjamb. "Maybe he's okay," she said. "Maybe someone found him and took him in."

He looked at her from under his arm. "Did you see the dragon lady on the news tonight?" he asked as if he hadn't heard her words of consolation.

"Yes." Mia hesitated, but Jeff seemed to want her to continue. "It made me very sad," she said. "Growing up was so difficult for you."

He nearly smiled at her. "I wish Carmen Perez had a fraction of your compassion." He patted the bed next to him and, against her better judgment, Mia stepped into the room and lowered herself to the mattress. Jeff took her hand, but let go quickly. Since that night in her cottage, he hadn't touched her. Right now, though, Mia wanted the warmth of his fingers on hers. She pulled his hand to her lap, locking both of her own hands around it.

"I'm jinxed, Mia." Jeff tightened his lips, the smile gone. "People should avoid me. I'm a danger to everyone. I can't even take care of a goddamned cat. You should go back to your cottage and stay there. Lock the door and don't let me in no matter how long or how hard I beg."

"You're talking nonsense."

"I wish I were."

There was a rustling noise from outside. "Shh." She let go of his hand and turned off the lamp next to the bed. Raising herself to her knees, she leaned close to the window screen, searching the darkness outside for the sleek black kitten.

"Do you see anything?"

"No," she whispered, pressing her forehead to the screen. "But it would be hard to see a black cat out there."

At first, Jeff's touch on the back of her thigh was so

light she barely noticed it. It might have been accidental, a random pass of his fingers across the skirt of her sundress. But she knew it was no accident. He didn't even feign subtlety as he circled the back of her thigh with his palm. Mia froze. She had to stop him, but there was no part of her willing to lose the delicious sensation of his touch.

He rolled toward her, raising the skirt of her dress just enough to let him press his mouth against her knee, and she closed her eyes and gripped the headboard of the bed in her hands. She was safe, she calculated quickly. He was lying down; he couldn't possibly reach the left side of her chest. So, she surrendered to the pleasure as he stroked her thighs through her cotton dress, surrendered to it as his touch grew more probing and intimate. From the canyon, she heard the hum of crickets on the soft summer air. Other than that, the only sound was her breathing. It was deep and quick by the time Jeff slipped his hand beneath her dress, jagged when he touched her between her bare thighs.

Was he watching her? Could he see the need in her face in the darkness? He stroked her through the wet silk, then inside, and she lost track of what he was doing to her body. His fingers seemed everywhere at once, and she rocked against them, abandoning any last remnant of inhibition. She clutched his shoulder as she came and heard her own voice slip out into the canyon in a moan of pleasure.

Jeff sat up then, quickly drawing her into his arms and

kissing her hard as he reached for the top button of her dress.

"No." She held him away from her, her hands flat on his chest. The muscles in her thighs quivered.

"Mia, for Christ's sake!" He leaned away from her. "What's with you?"

She held her arms in her usual protective position across her chest, her fingers locked over the top button of her dress. He was so close, his eyes so piercing. She looked down into her lap, while he smoothed his fingertips over her cheeks, cupped her face in his palm.

"You've got to tell me," he insisted. "What are you afraid of?"

She hesitated only a second or two, then looked him squarely in the eye. "I had cancer," she said. "I've had a mastectomy."

His face registered stunned surprise, then he shut his eyes, pulling her into his arms again. "*Too young*," he said.

She savored the way he was holding her, tightly, with no fear of her or her body. It was a moment before she realized he was rocking her, and another before she became aware of her tears. She leaned hard against him and let herself cry like a child.

"Suddenly everything makes sense," Jeff said.

She wiped her cheek with the back of her hand. "What do you mean?"

"Why you've frozen up on me every other time I've touched you, but now, when I was touching you far more intimately than I ever have before, you were completely receptive. I didn't expect that response out of you."

Mia colored at the memory.

"I liked it a lot," he said. "Your response."

"Me too."

"And the mastectomy explains why you're out here in Valle Rosa, doesn't it? It explains what you're running away from."

She lifted her head to look at him. "In October I can have reconstructive surgery. I'm hibernating."

"Your left side, am I right?"

She frowned, alarmed. "How could you tell?"

"You're protective of your left side." He lowered his head to kiss her slowly, but suddenly pulled away.

"*Glen*," he said. "How does he fit into this?"

She sighed. "He was repulsed. He said I was grotesque."

"Cad."

"He was right, though. It's hideous."

He pulled away from her, reaching for the top button of her dress.

She caught his hand. "No, Jeff, please."

He looked her in the eye. "Do you want to be friends or lovers?" he asked.

"Both," she whispered.

"Then you have to let me do this."

"But I'm afraid once you do, we won't be *able* to be lovers. After he saw my scar, Glen said that he couldn't get"—she hunted for a word—"he couldn't get aroused around me."

Jeff was unbuttoning her dress as she spoke, but when she'd finished speaking he stilled his fingers and looked thoughtful for a moment. Then he leaned back on his elbow to unbuckle his belt, unzip his jeans. He took her hand and drew it inside, pressing it around his erection, and she sucked in her breath at his brazenness.

"Our litmus test," he said, nodding southward. "Let's see what happens." He finished unbuttoning her dress. "Raise your arms."

She had to let go of him to do so, but after he had lifted the dress over her head and dropped it behind him on the bed, she returned her hand to the steely warmth inside his jeans, smiling to herself as he responded with a groan.

He reached behind her to unfasten her bra, and she held her breath as he slipped it from her shoulders. It fell onto her wrist, heavy with the weight of the prosthesis, but she wasn't about to let go of him now. The image of her body as it had looked in the mirror the other day flashed through her mind and she shut her eyes in distress, fighting the urge to cover herself from his gaze.

"Mia," he said, and she heard the amusement in his voice. "You're hanging on for dear life down there. Can you relax?"

She shook her head.

"It's okay," he said. "I've seen your chest, and I'm still here."

"Glen said it was okay, too. I only realized he was repulsed when I overheard him talking to my sister about it."

"I'm not Glen." Jeff gently withdrew her hand from his jeans and stood to take off his jeans,. He motioned her to stand up, and she clung to his shoulders as he lowered her dress over her hips.

"We . . . I used to use a diaphragm," she said, "but I didn't bring it with me to Valle Rosa."

"I've had a vasectomy. Which is something I regretted until right this minute, because I really wouldn't want to have to put this off until tomorrow." He bent low to kiss her, to hold her tightly, and she thought she would never be able to get close enough to him.

"No one's held me in so long," she said.

He drew away and she saw concern in his eyes. "I need your guidance," he said.

"What do you mean?"

"I don't know if I should ignore your right breast or not."

"Oh." She closed her eyes, her breast nearly aching for his touch. "Please don't ignore any part of me."

He pulled her onto the bed again, and she lost herself once more to the gifts he offered, offering some of her own in return. He was above her; inside her, when they heard a sudden rapping on the front door. Jeff raised his head, the look in his face nothing short of terror. The knock came again, and he pulled out of her swiftly, reaching for his jeans as he got off the bed. She caught his terror although she didn't understand it. She pulled her dress over her head, forgetting her bra and her underpants, and followed him out to the living room. He motioned her to move back into the hallway, then seemed to brace himself before opening the door.

Chris stood on the porch, holding the kitten in his

arms. "I found him in the crawl space under my cottage," he said, stepping into the living room.

Jeff started to laugh, the relief in his face, in the entire room, nearly palpable. Chris looked from him to Mia, where she stood in the hallway, and back again, and his expression showed instant understanding of what she was doing there. Mia's feet were bare, and she'd managed to button only three of the buttons on her dress; Jeff wore no shirt and, in his rush, had forgotten to snap his jeans.

Jeff reached for the cat, who squawked hoarsely as he nestled into a dark ball against his owner's bare chest. "I thought he was a goner," he said. "You want to come in?"

"Uh, no." Chris grinned. "I get the distinct feeling I'm intruding."

Jeff didn't argue with him. He held the cat up in the air. "Thanks for bringing him home," he said.

Jeff closed the door on Chris, hit the lock, then turned to face Mia, still smiling. "Could you look a little guiltier, please? I don't think he got the picture."

"*Me.*" She laughed. "You answered the door with your pants falling off."

"Well." He put his arm around her and began walking her back toward the bedroom. "As long as Chris thinks we've already completed the dirty deed, we might as well go through with it."

"You know what you are, Mia?" he asked later, when they lay in his bed, tired and full of each other and, as far as Mia could discern, content.

"What?"

"You are a wood sprite who's gotten herself trapped in a jar."

"Oh," she said, sadly. "I think maybe I can come out every once in a while now."

Jeff drew in a long breath, squeezing her tightly as he let it out. "Listen to me Mia," he said. "I've . . . you've been good for me. I didn't expect to find a friend here. And I find that I need you in a way I never expected to need anyone ever again. I need you in a way I haven't wanted to need anyone, because it complicates things."

He was quiet for a moment, and Mia said nothing, breathing in the soap-and-sweat smell of his chest.

"But you have to understand something," he said finally. "I can't offer you anything. I can't stay here much longer, and I can't even answer your questions about why I have to go. I know it's unfair to you. Completely unfair."

She listened to his words without believing them. "I want to be with you as long as you're here." She heard the lack of conviction in her voice. He wouldn't leave now. He couldn't.

"And you understand that the fact that you've lost your breast will have nothing to do with me going, right?"

She nodded against his chest.

"Tell me about it," he said. "Tell me about the cancer."

She spoke softly. She had avoided thinking about cancer, she told him, despite her mother's experience and the statistical probability that she too would contract the disease. She had decided she would begin worrying about it when she was thirty-five.

"I never checked myself. I closed my eyes to the entire

possibility. I found the lump when I was showering one day, and even then I tried to ignore it."

"You don't strike me as that irrational."

"Only when it comes to breast cancer. They did a lumpectomy, but couldn't get clean margins, and because of the type of cancer it was, they decided they'd better take the entire breast. I worry now that I'll get it in my other breast."

"I think I'd want to have my other breast removed, too, so I wouldn't have to think about it."

"You wouldn't say that if you were a woman."

"Maybe not." He leaned up on an elbow to look at her, resting one warm hand on the flat plane of her chest. "You've put your life on hold until you can have the reconstruction surgery, but you've survived, Mia. You're alive *now*. You shouldn't waste this time."

She looked up at him for a moment. "Okay," she said finally, reaching for him, wrapping her leg over his hip and pulling him close to her. "Let's not waste a minute."

They were lying exhausted in each other's arms an hour later when they heard the faint strains of Chris's guitar. Mia lifted her head to listen.

"*Fire and Rain*," Jeff said. His voice was muffled against her chest.

"What?" she asked.

"The song he's singing."

"Oh." She let her head fall to the pillow again as he stroked her hair. The muscles in her arms and thighs were weak and tremulous. She'd given them more of a workout in the past few hours than they'd had in a year.

"Jeff?" She stroked the tips of her fingers across his chest. "How come the hair on your chest and arms is so much lighter than the hair on your head?"

He chuckled. "That's none of your business." His tone was light, but she knew he was serious, and she swallowed the hurt. He would trust her only so far.

He sat up and stretched. "Let's get a bottle of wine from the fridge and join Chris on his porch," he said.

"Okay." She got to her knees and began searching at the foot of the moonlit bed for her dress, but he caught her hand, and when she looked down at him she saw the fear in his face, the damage.

"Hold me again," he said. "Please."

She wrapped her arms around him, feeling a strength inside her she had forgotten she possessed. After a few long minutes, Jeff pulled away.

"Thanks," he said. His smile was almost sheepish. "And Mia?"

"Hmm?" She stroked her fingers across his knee.

"The hair on my head is actually a few shades darker than yours."

Carmen was undressing in her bedroom when she heard the music. She turned off the light and knelt by the window. All three of them sat on Chris's porch—Chris and Mia on the rough-hewn chairs and Jeff on the top porch step, leaning against the post. Chris was playing the guitar, and Jeff hit something against his knee. At first she thought it was a tambourine, but then realized he was playing spoons. The three of them were singing, stumbling over the words to *Puff the Magic Dragon*. Mia was laughing so hard she was nearly doubled over.

Carmen folded her arms across her chest to comfort herself. She could put on her jeans, go over and join them, but she knew what would happen then. The easy-going rapport between the three of them would dissolve, and they would resent her more than they already did.

She stayed by the window for a long time, as long as she could stand it. Then, when the loneliness seemed too much to bear, she closed the window on the music and went to bed.

33

The house was tiny—a diminutive, white, Spanish-style stucco on a postage-stamp lot one block from the Santa Monica beach. Carmen checked the address in her notebook. This was it. Janet Safer. The woman Jeff had dated during his years at MIT.

Carmen had used her yearbook ruse with one of the librarians at MIT, but this particular librarian's husband had attended the school during the same period as Jeff. He had been friends with Janet Safer and knew her current address in Santa Monica. Carmen had been delighted. As a Californian, though, Janet Safer was quite likely to have heard of the Valle Rosa rainmaker, and Carmen had been extremely discreet in describing the reason for her interest in Robert Blackwell. Having a referral from an old friend of Janet's had given her an edge.

Sure enough, Janet had greeted Carmen's request for an interview with enthusiasm.

"Rob Blackwell!" she'd exclaimed. "I always wondered what happened to him."

Carmen walked cautiously on the crumbling sidewalk leading up to the house. The yard had a neat, cared-for appearance, but the house itself looked as though it had been through one too many earthquakes. The stucco was cracked; the roof was missing a few of its red clay tiles. Still, this close to the beach the house was probably worth a good deal of money.

A woman opened the door before Carmen had a chance to ring the bell.

"Carmen Perez?" Janet Safer was tall and attractive, her dark hair pulled back in a ponytail. Deep dimples appeared in her cheeks when she smiled.

"Yes. And you're Janet Safer?"

"Sure am." The woman stepped back into the room to let her in, and Carmen nearly stumbled over the little girl hanging onto Janet's leg. Carmen cupped the child's head in her palm as she passed her and was startled to look down into the face of a child with unmistakable Down's syndrome. Something froze in her heart. She should not have come here. She should have conducted this interview by phone.

"This is Kelly," Janet said.

"Hi." Kelly grinned up at her.

"Hi, Kelly." Carmen smiled at the little girl, her heart pounding. Kelly was no more than four or five, with the telltale square build and almond eyes of a Down's child. Carmen couldn't look at her long. She felt a sick fear, the kind of fear another person might experience when told they would have to cross a raging river in a fragile canoe. In the past few years, she had turned away from damaged children—*all* children, really—when she passed them on the street and blocked the memory of their image from her mind. Still, they would find their way into her dreams.

Janet led Carmen into the small kitchen where she settled Kelly at the table with a coloring book and a box of fat crayons. Carmen wished the child didn't have to sit with them. She would have liked it if Kelly could be safely locked away in another room for the next hour.

Carmen took a seat at the battered, drop-leaf oak table. The kitchen looked like a hundred others she had seen in these small, aging, California homes. Old cabinets sported what was probably their tenth coat of paint, this one a cobalt blue. Chipped white tile covered the counter tops.

"Perrier?" Janet asked, producing the bottle from the harvest-gold refrigerator.

"That would be great." Carmen watched Kelly page through her coloring book until she settled on the line drawing of a bird in a tree.

"Rob Blackwell," Janet said again, shaking her head as she poured. "Flash from the past." She set Carmen's glass in front of her and took a seat on the other side of the table, next to her daughter. The ponytail made her look very young. She wore triangular-shaped silver earrings in both ears, and three small silver hoops through the upper lobe of her left ear. There was color in her cheeks that hadn't been there a moment ago, and Carmen thought it must be the memory of Jeff that put it there.

"Here, darlin'." Janet helped Kelly open the box of crayons, as Carmen set her tape recorder in the center of the table and turned it on.

"So," Janet said, scooting her daughter's chair closer to the table. "What would you like to know about him?"

"Tell me anything you remember. Tell me about your relationship with him."

"Well." Janet pulled her bare feet up onto her chair and hugged her knees. "Rob wasn't your regular sort of guy, if you know what I mean."

Carmen took a sip from her glass and nodded. "I've gotten that impression from other people I've spoken to." She didn't want to admit to her own personal knowledge of him.

"He was exceptional in just about every way," Janet said. "Though the one place he really was a little screwed up was in relationships. He was one of those people who was afraid to get close. He'd sabotage closeness. I mean, things would be going well, and then he'd go out with some other girl and make sure I knew about it. I didn't understand at first. Was he trying to make me jealous or what?" She smiled into her glass. "Eventually I caught on. He was afraid when things started getting serious. He really liked me, and it scared him. He'd lost his mother. Then he lost the man he thought of as his father. So naturally he was afraid he'd lose anybody else he loved."

Carmen frowned. Jeff had lost his stepfather?

Kelly tried to push one of the buttons on the tape recorder, but her mother caught her hand and returned it to the coloring book without a word.

"You said he lost his father," Carmen said. "Do you mean he died, or just that he was still in prison when you and Rob were dating?"

"He was in jail. You know all about that?"

"A bit."

"What was his name?" Janet asked. "Jefferson?"

"Jefferson Watts."

Janet shook her head. "Rob had a lot of admiration for him. Somehow he managed to reconcile himself to the fact that Jefferson had broken the law—big time—and had even killed a couple of people."

"A couple of people?"

"Yeah. I don't remember the details. Rob never really told me because he didn't think it was important. His father had gone straight by the time they caught up with him, and I guess that was all that mattered to Rob. I never met his father. Rob used to write to him a lot. He'd hear back from him every once in a while."

"Mommy." Kelly looked up from her paper with its thick waxy brown-and-blue lines. "Breaked." She held up the blue crayon which she had worked down to the paper wrapper.

"I'll fix it for you, buttercup." Janet peeled off an inch of wrapper and handed the crayon back to her daughter, and suddenly Carmen wanted to change the focus of this interview. How did you feel when she was born? she wanted to ask. Did you fall into a depression you thought you'd never get out of? Do you know why she was born that way? Is there someone—anyone—to blame?

"Anyhow," Janet continued, "once Rob read me a letter he'd gotten from Jefferson. He wrote that Rob should work hard in school, that he had a lot of promise and could really make something of himself. He said Rob should live within the law and not make the kinds of mistakes he had made, and so on."

"And did he? Live within the law?"

"Rob? Oh, God, yes." Janet laughed, her glass halfway to her mouth. She set it on the table again. "He was very straight-arrow. It was always hard for me to believe he grew up with a criminal in the house." She winced. "It would really have upset him to hear me talk about Jefferson that way."

"How long did the two of you date?"

"Nearly three years. Our last three at MIT. I'm the one who ended it." She stood to get another ice cube from the freezer and dropped it into her glass. "God, I felt so bad." She took her seat again. "I got scared when he started talking about marriage and kids. Here I'd persuaded him to date me exclusively, to take our relationship seriously, and then when he did, I backed away."

"Why did you do that?"

"Well, as I said before, Rob wasn't a regular sort of guy. When I thought of actually settling down for a lifetime with someone so . . . out of the norm, it terrified me." Janet knit her brows together. "He was so intense. Plus, he had no money. He was on a scholarship and working as a teaching assistant to be able to feed himself. I started thinking about raising kids with him, with no money and with his attachment to an old drug-dealing murderer and to this weird friend of his, Kent Reed."

"He was still friends with Kent Reed when he was at MIT?"

"You know about Kent?" Janet asked.

"A little." Carmen wondered if the librarian's husband might have some idea where the peculiar Mr. Reed was living these days.

"God, what a weirdo." Janet shuddered. "And yes, unfortunately Rob was still friends with him then. Kent followed him from their high school to MIT, where Rob thought it would be great fun for me to fix him up with my girlfriends. I told him to forget it—I valued my friends too much to do that to them."

Kelly tapped her mother's arm. "Dooce?" she asked.

"Apple or orange?" Janet stood again and opened the refrigerator.

"Appa." Kelly put down her crayon and folded her hands neatly on top of her drawing, waiting while her mother poured the juice into a glass. Something about the gesture—those chunky little hands, folded, patient—touched Carmen in a way that was almost painful. She tried to tear her gaze away from the child, but the sheen of the little girl's dark hair and the dimples, so much like her mother's, were captivating.

I don't want to feel this, she thought. *I don't want to feel anything.*

She watched Kelly take a long drink from the glass her mother handed her, then forced her attention once more to Janet. "What was Kent like?"

"Oh, wow." Janet took her seat again and swept her bangs off her forehead. "He was very tall. Gangly, like Ichabod Crane. He'd make a point of shocking people with his deformed hand. And he whined. Complained from sunup to sundown, I swear. He'd get under your skin—or at least under my skin—real fast. And he could be mean, too." She narrowed her eyes to make her point. "I remember he was president of the chess club and he got kicked out of a tournament for 'poor sportsmanship' after he threw the board in his opponent's face."

"Why on earth was Rob friends with him?"

"I used to wonder that myself. He'd deny it, but I think it was at least partly the hand."

"You mean he felt sorry for Kent because of his hand?" That would make some sense. Jeff Cabrio and his underdogs.

"Well, no, I mean he felt guilty since he was the cause of it."

Carmen glanced quickly at her recorder to make sure the tape was still running. "I didn't know that," she said, selecting her words with care. "I thought Kent lost his fingers in high school, when he planted a bomb in another boy's locker."

Janet hesitated. "Hmm," she said. "I thought you knew. I feel kind of funny telling you."

"Use your own judgment, Janet." Carmen kept her voice even, but she was squeezing her glass between her fingers.

"Well, it's true that Kent lost his fingers when he tried to plant the bomb, but it was Rob who made the bomb. He never intended it to be stuck in someone's locker, and it went off before it was supposed to."

"My God." Carmen set her glass down, truly shaken.

"Right. So I think that's part of why Rob hung out with Kent, but also, there's no denying that Rob was simply fascinated by Kent's mind. No one else liked Kent, but Rob was never the type to pick his friends based on their popularity. He was very secure that way." Janet let out her breath as though she was exhausted by all she had revealed. "Anyway, while I could respect him for caring about his stepfather and Kent, I couldn't see marrying into that mess and bringing my kids up with it." She looked at Carmen, almost apologetically. "I couldn't see having a future with him."

Carmen nodded, noticing a mist of tears in Janet's eyes.

"It was a very hard choice for me to make," Janet said. "I was down for a long time after we broke up. Sometimes I still think about him, about how my life would be different. I wouldn't have this one, for example." She rested her hand on her daughter's back, and Carmen nodded again in sympathy before realizing it wasn't regret she heard in Janet's voice. Janet was *glad* she had made the choices which resulted in her daughter. "I can't imagine my life without her," she said.

Carmen murmured something, something she hoped sounded appropriate and gracious, all the while wondering where Janet had found the strength, the depth of love, she'd needed to welcome this child into her life.

They spoke for a few more minutes, but Carmen was anxious to escape. As they walked to the door, Janet asked, "Someday can you let me know what this is all about?"

"Yes," Carmen said. "I'll be in touch as soon as I'm free to talk about it." She rested her hand on the doorknob and turned to look at Janet. "There must not have been too many women at MIT when you were there," she said.

"Not many. I got my doctorate there, too."

Carmen studied this ponytailed woman with admiration. "You've accomplished a lot," she said.

Janet laughed. "Well, I was ambitious back in those days. Right now a PhD in physics seems a little unimportant. I worked for a few years after I got it. Then Kelly was born, and I knew she needed me more than my job did. So here I am." She followed Carmen out into the sunny front yard. "Do you have kids?" she asked as they walked down the decrepit sidewalk.

Carmen shook her head, grateful she had reached her car. She walked around it to the driver's side. "Thanks so much for your time," she said, getting in behind the wheel.

"Hey!" Janet called after her. "Give Rob a hug for me!"

She drove to a 7-Eleven where she eyed the beer. It would take a lot of beer to numb her at that moment, a lot of beer to block out little Kelly Safer's face from her mind, a lot to block out Janet Safer's loving touch on her daughter's hair. And more alcohol than she could consume to block out the memory of her response to Janet's question—that quick shake of her head. *No, I have no children.*

She bought a large coffee and sat in her car to drink it. If only she could crawl into bed and go to sleep. But she had a two-hour drive ahead of her. Two hours to think. Her eyes fell on the pay phone in the corner of the parking lot.

She rested the coffee on the floor of the car as she got out and began walking toward the phone. She seemed to be moving on automatic pilot, something trying to hold her back, something stronger pushing her forward.

Mia answered when she dialed the number for Chris's office, and Carmen was relieved when she put her through without trying to make small talk.

"Where are you?" Chris asked. "I hear traffic."

"Santa Monica. I just did an interview up here." She spoke quietly, pressing the metal cord between her fingers.

"Carmen? Are you all right?"

"Yes."

"Well . . . why are you calling?"

She squeezed her eyes closed. "I was wondering if you could tell me about Dustin."

Chris hesitated. "About Dustin? Do you mean . . ."

"Just anything. Tell me anything about him. Whatever comes into your mind."

"Hang on a second."

She heard him walk across the room, heard the closing of his office door. Then he was back on the phone.

"Well, do you remember his dark hair? How much he had when he was born?"

"Yes."

"It's beautiful. Very thick, with a little wave to it. He has your coloring. He looks a lot like you, actually. He's a handsome kid, except for his eyes."

A truck squealed around the corner next to the phone booth, and she put her finger in her ear to block the sound. "Tell me about his eyes," she said. "Tell me the worst."

"His eyes have a milky sort of look to them. And they don't track."

"And they don't see."

"No. And you know he can't hear, either, right?"

"Does he look . . . I mean, the rest of him. How . . . normal does he look?"

Chris hesitated again. "Carmen, why don't we have this conversation in person instead of—"

"No. Please, Chris. Tell me."

Chris sighed. "He looks much closer to normal than you'd expect, but he's not. And his facial expressions aren't what you'd usually see in a boy his age. I guess that's something you learn socially, and he's never had the chance."

She began to cry and hoped he couldn't tell. "What is his life like? Is he in terrible pain?"

"Carmen . . ."

"Please, Chris."

"I don't know if he's in pain. He cries a lot, but there's no way to know why. He gets angry and throws little tantrums, but when I visit him, he lets me hold him and rock him, and sometimes he gets very calm."

She covered the mouthpiece of the phone to take in a shaky breath.

"Do you want me to come up there?"

"No."

"I shouldn't have told you all this over the phone. Are

you depressed? I mean, things are looking up for you, Carmen. Keep that in mind, okay? Don't dwell on—"

"I'm all right," she interrupted him. He was afraid she would try to hurt herself again. She could hear the fear in his voice. The guilt. "I just wanted to know about Dustin."

"I have a lot of pictures of him, and you're welcome to look at them. With or without me. Whatever's easier for—"

"No." She didn't want to see pictures. The image of Dustin forming in her head was torture enough. "I can't do that."

"All right. Are you on your way back to San Diego now?"

"Yes."

"Call me when you get in, okay? Let me know you made it safely."

34.

Chris stopped three times on the way to the Children's Home. The first time was when Jeff asked him to pull off the freeway so he could get a better look at a dry, cracked lake bed and the gaunt cows feeding on the barely existent grass at its rim. Then, as they were about to get back onto the freeway, Jeff spotted a stalled car on the ramp and ordered Chris to pull up behind it.

Chris watched while Jeff calmed the panicky teenaged boy at the wheel, peered under the hood and worked his usual magic on whatever he found there. In minutes, he had the car purring.

The third stop—the only one they had planned—was at an auto-parts store in a strip mall on the northern outskirts of San Diego. The store was the closest outlet for some specialized equipment Jeff needed in the warehouse. Chris had suggested they drive to San Diego together, as long as Jeff didn't mind waiting while he paid his usual Saturday visit to Dustin.

Once in the parking lot of the strip mall, Jeff eyed the customers walking in and out of the auto-parts store and shook his head.

"Would you mind going in for me?" he asked. He pulled a pen from the pocket of his red-and-brown Hawaiian-print shirt and a scrap of paper from his briefcase. "I'll write down what I need. It's sort of an unconventional assortment of goods. I'd rather not have to deal with anyone's questions."

"Fine." Chris watched him make out the list, which covered both sides of the paper. Jeff handed it to him, and Chris shook his head as he read it. "If it hadn't been for that experiment, Cabrio, I'd think you were off your rocker." The list ranged from racing spark plugs and oil coolers to a hubcap.

"I'll be in there." Jeff pointed halfway down the strip to Caprice and Company, a chain of stores known for their silky and sexy lingerie. There was a time when Chris had depended on that store—he knew he could buy Carmen anything within its walls, and she would love it.

But Jeff in Caprice and Company? Something for Mia, no doubt.

It took him half an hour and a few glib explanations to the sales people before Chris managed to collect the items Jeff had requested. By the time he emerged from the store, Jeff was already in the car. He opened the back door to put in his three bags of purchases and saw the gift box wrapped in green paper lying on the seat.

"How'd it go?" Jeff asked.

"Got it all."

"Great." Jeff sounded relieved.

Chris got in behind the wheel. "The check-out guy

thought I was pretty strange, but other than that it was no problem."

"Thanks for taking care of it."

Chris turned the key in the ignition and pointed into the back seat. "For Mia?" he asked.

Jeff smiled. "Who else?"

Chris didn't know what more to say on that subject. He had been surprised at first to realize that Jeff and Mia were something more than friends. Yet after he thought about it—and after spending some time with them, singing and laughing on his cottage porch at Sugarbush— he knew their attraction to one another made sense. Both of them were creative and imaginative, both of them saw people in a way others didn't. He could picture them together easily now, and he envied their closeness.

When they were a mile or so from the Children's Home, Chris began wondering if he should ask Jeff to wait outside while he saw Dustin.

After a few minutes of silence, Jeff said, "Why don't you tell me about your son?"

Chris feigned a look of surprise, as though he hadn't been thinking of his son at all. How did Jeff always seem to know what was going on in his head? "Would you like to meet him?" he asked.

"Of course."

"Okay. But . . . I guess I'd better prepare you." He rubbed his palms on the steering wheel. "It might shock you to see him." He glanced at Jeff, then drew in a breath and blew it out. "He got really sick shortly after he was born," he said. "They expected him to die. He didn't, but he was left with severe brain damage, as well as a lot of other physical problems. He's deaf and blind. He can't speak and he doesn't have much control over any part of his body."

Silence filled the car again, and Chris felt his description of his son hanging in the air between himself and Jeff.

Finally, Jeff spoke. "This may be way too personal a question," he said, "but Rick said that Carmen never visits him. I thought maybe Dustin was your son from a previous marriage or—"

"No, no," Chris interrupted. "Dustin is definitely Carmen's son."

Jeff shook his head. "No offense, Chris, but I can't picture Carmen as a mother to anyone."

Chris chewed his lower lip as he took the exit to the Children's Home. He understood Jeff's lack of sympathy toward Carmen. Still, he felt compelled to try to soften his reaction to her. "You've got Carmen figured wrong," he said.

Jeff made a sharp sound of disgust. "Why are you always so quick to defend her? From what I've heard, she treated you pretty shabbily."

"What do you mean?"

"Rick said she wanted a divorce as soon as she found out you couldn't play ball any longer."

Chris bristled. "Rick Smythe doesn't know shit about my life." He pulled into the parking lot of the Children's Home and turned off the ignition. The air in the car quickly heated. He looked toward the small, park-like side yard of the home and pointed to a bench. "Let's sit there a while," he said. "I'd rather you heard the facts from me than a bunch of crap from people who don't know what they're talking about."

Jeff stared at him. "You don't owe me any explanations."

Chris opened his car door. "I know that," he said, "but it's time. It's way past time for me to talk about it."

The heat of the day weighed heavily on him as he walked across the parking lot with Jeff at his side. He had told no one, save Carmen's psychiatrist and Dustin's primary physician, what he was about to tell Jeff, and he knew it was more than a desire to defend Carmen that made him want to pour out the story now.

They sat at opposite ends of the bench, and Chris was grateful for the shade provided by the fig tree behind them.

He started slowly, not looking at Jeff, but keeping his eyes locked on the other side of Mission Valley, far in the distance. He told him about injuring his arm. "I had trouble accepting . . . I just couldn't accept how serious it was, that it might mean the end of my career. Baseball was my life. It was all I ever wanted to do, and I was flying high back then. I was really peaking."

"I remember."

"Carmen was on top, too, although it had been a struggle for her to get there. It was more than the usual climb up the career ladder." He described how Carmen's Mexican parents had sent her to live with her aunt and uncle in California, how the aunt and uncle had raised her to be a good wife and mother, despite Carmen's academic excellence and desire for a career. "It caused nothing but conflict in her family, and her relatives eventually wrote her off because of it."

"That's what she meant by loss, I guess," Jeff said.

"What?" Chris looked at him, not following.

"Nothing. Go on."

"Well, anyhow, Carmen wanted a career, but she also wanted a family. We both wanted kids. She could have pulled it off, too, I think, having both motherhood and a demanding career." Chris was quiet a moment, remembering Carmen's indefatigable energy and drive.

"But . . . ?" Jeff prompted.

"We'd been married a couple of years when she got pregnant," Chris continued. "Everything seemed great, and she announced it on her show and to the press. In the fourth month, though, she miscarried and sank into this all-consuming depression. It was hormonal, her doctor said. Postpartum depression, she called it, even though Carmen had only been pregnant a few months." Chris closed his eyes at the memory of his suddenly unreachable wife. "I'd never seen anything like it. She'd spend hours staring into space. She wouldn't eat. Wouldn't talk to me. She finally snapped out of it, but it took months. She wanted to try again, which we did. I figured it couldn't happen twice. Anyway, she got pregnant pretty quickly. She was supposed to take it real easy—no stress, no exertion. Then my father died. He and Carmen were close. She miscarried again, this time after five months."

"And she got depressed again?"

"Big time." Chris sighed. "It was terrible, and frustrating as hell because there was nothing I could do to pull her out of it. Even medication didn't help, and she couldn't work for a few months."

A woman pushing a stroller walked past their bench. The child in the stroller was probably Dustin's age, four or five, but his arms and legs were withered, and his neck was bent at such an awkward angle that Chris couldn't see his face at all. The woman smiled at them. Chris waited until she was out of earshot before he began speaking again.

"So, she eventually got better. I was ready to forget about having kids at that point, but once she was back on her feet, she started talking about it again. She was constantly visiting her friends who had children. She loved kids." He looked at Jeff. "It's a side to her you haven't seen."

"You're right." Jeff sounded unmoved and somewhat disbelieving. "I haven't."

"Then she got pregnant with Dustin."

"Was he born prematurely? Was that the problem?"

Chris drew another long breath. "No. And Carmen was good as gold. She followed her doctor's orders to a T, and Dustin was born one day shy of his due date." He pictured Dustin inside the home behind them, alone in his room, alone as he always was and always would be, no matter how many people were around him. "No," he said, "the blame for what's wrong with him lies entirely on my shoulders."

"What do you mean?" Jeff asked.

Chris struggled with where to begin. "You know, I was pretty wild before I met Carmen."

"Well, yeah, you had a bit of a reputation."

"But once I met Carmen, I put all of that behind me. She always came first. I was faithful to her, on the road and off."

Jeff nodded.

"But the arm thing got me down. I couldn't let anyone know how bad it was. I didn't want to be told I couldn't play, and I didn't want to worry Carmen. I was thirty-five years old, for Christ's sake. Ancient. Other guys my age were already rolling along in their careers. I had a degree in physical education, but I couldn't imagine teaching after what I'd been used to. I was really down, but I pretended everything was fine for Carmen's sake. Her doctor was saying, 'no stress,' and my career was turning to garbage." Chris rubbed a hand over his forehead. Even in the shade, it was too damn hot. "So anyhow," he continued, "early that season I went on a road trip. It was obvious to everyone that I was having trouble, but I still wouldn't give in. I worked with a physical therapist, and I got out there on the mound even though my shoulder felt like it had a hatchet in it. We hit a major losing streak, and it looked like I was the cause of it, which"—he laughed, without mirth—"in retrospect, I know I was. I'd get booed when I'd go out to pitch. That had never happened to me before."

"I remember reading about that in the papers."

"I was hoping Carmen wasn't following the news. I'd call her from the road and tell her I was fine. I'd fabricate all kinds of reasons for why we were losing. She was about seven months along and doing well, but she was on bed rest, and her doctor had told her to read only books with happy endings and to watch nothing but sitcoms on TV."

Jeff laughed.

"The final blow came when we got back to San Diego, and I got booed at a home game. They even threw stuff at me." Chris's hands tightened into fists at the memory. "I was used to respect—God, I was used to *adulation*—and suddenly they were treating me like a pile of manure." He shook his head. "I can see now that I just didn't know when it was time to bow out gracefully, to call it a day and walk away with some dignity left. Anyhow, that was one of the shittiest nights of my life. Even my buddies wouldn't talk to me. All I could think about was how much I wanted to talk to Carmen, but I knew I couldn't lay my problems on her without risking another miscarriage. I got as far as calling her from a phone booth in the stadium, but in the end . . . well, you know how it is. I kept it to myself and felt even worse when I hung up the phone." He paused, his hands clenching the edge of the wooden bench. "There was this woman waiting for me," he said. "I knew her. Actually, about two thirds of the team knew her better than I did, if you know what I mean." He glanced at Jeff, who nodded, his face sober.

"She used to follow us around during the season," he continued. "She always seemed to have a thing for me, but I had no interest whatsoever in her. Until that night, anyhow."

Jeff studied him for a moment. "You slept with her?"

Chris nodded. "When I left the phone booth, she put her arm through mine and said, 'They're never going to be able to replace you, Chris,' and I thought . . . well, I guess I didn't think at all. I just took what she was offering as a way to make myself feel better. The next morning, it was all over the papers about my miserable final performance in the stadium. And Carmen was great." She had told him to hold his head high, that she didn't care if he played pro ball or pumped gas, and those words had meant more to him than he'd been able to express. "She didn't know what I'd done, though, and—I swear this is the truth—I put it out of my mind. I felt like I'd been given a second chance. We forgot about baseball for a while and focused on the baby and the future. In a way, those last two months of her pregnancy were some of the best times of our marriage."

Jeff was quiet, but as Chris kept his eyes riveted on the other side of Mission Valley, he felt acceptance rather than condemnation in the silence.

Finally, he drew in a breath and turned to Jeff. "Did you know you could have herpes but not have any symptoms?"

Jeff frowned. "Yeah, I've heard that, but . . . Oh, no." He literally recoiled, leaning away from Chris on the bench.

"Oh, yes. One of my teammates who knew I'd slept with Cory—that was the woman's name—told me he thought he'd gotten herpes from her the previous year. I was worried at first, but when I didn't develop any symptoms, I thought I'd lucked out. But I *did* have it, and

I passed it on to Carmen, who also had no symptoms, and she passed it on to Dustin. If we'd known she was infected, she could have had a C-section and Dustin would have been all right. Or at least he could have been treated right after he was born. But we didn't know until his symptoms started, and then it was too late."

Jeff hesitated. "God, Chris . . . I'm sorry," he said, his voice subdued. Chris could barely hear him.

"Carmen was already slipping into that postpartum depression again, but at least this time she had a beautiful baby to think about. Once Dusty was diagnosed, though, and my part in his condition was out in the open, she completely shut down. She told me to leave the house; she couldn't stand the sight of me. I got an apartment and called one of her cousins to come stay with her." Chris groaned. "That was a mistake. The cousin took decent care of her physically—at that point Carmen wasn't even eating or getting dressed in the morning, and the cousin was a drill sergeant. But she'd tell Carmen that Dustin's condition was her punishment for going against her role as a female."

"You're kidding."

"Wish I were. That's the way her entire family thought. As far as I know, Carmen never told any of them the truth."

"What about psychiatric help?"

Chris shrugged. "I tried getting her to go, but she wouldn't listen to anything I said. One day, her cousin called me to say that Carmen had locked herself in the bathroom and wouldn't come out. I went flying over there and had to take the door off the hinges. She was unconscious, in the tub, blood everywhere."

Jeff's eyes widened. "She cut her wrists?"

He nodded. "And one ankle. I think she would have opened every vein in her body if she hadn't lost consciousness first."

"Jesus."

Carmen would be furious, Chris thought, if she knew he was recounting this story to Jeff. Yet he knew of no other way to make Jeff understand. "They hospitalized her for a long time. She wouldn't see me. She essentially pretended Dustin had never been born. Had never been conceived. They didn't want to release her but finally had to because she was no longer considered a suicidal risk. That's because she was so doped up on antidepressants she didn't have the energy to hurt herself. She went back to Sugarbush alone. The very first night back, she was so woozy from the drugs that she fell and broke her arm. They gave her painkillers for the arm and she became addicted to them."

"Good God."

"Anyhow," Chris went on, "she was such a mess by then that I didn't have much trouble getting her into a rehab program." Carmen had gone into the program without a hint of protest. She had no fight left in her by then. "She was in rehab for months, slowly getting better. I could see the gradual change in her each time I'd visit. She'd never talk to me, though. I was supposed to go in for these 'conjoint' sessions, but I was the only one doing the talking. Then finally, during one of the sessions, she started screaming at me, saying she hated me, she wished I'd die." Chris smiled ruefully. "They said that was the turning point for her, that after she started yelling at me, she got better. Shortly after that, she filed for divorce."

Jeff was quiet. In the silence, Chris became aware of his own exhaustion. He was drained. Drained and very sad.

Finally, Jeff shifted on the bench, leaning forward, his forearms across the top of his thighs. He shook his head slowly. "Well, if you'd asked me to fabricate the worst possible explanation of why Carmen is the way she is, I couldn't even have come close. God, what a nightmare."

Chris leaned toward him. "Do you see why Carmen's feistiness now pleases me so much? I did speak to her about leaving you alone, but she's going to do what she thinks she has to do. And I have to admit, my loyalties are divided. It's so good to see her going after a story again. It's a sign she's getting better. This past year she's been free of all drugs—she doesn't even drink. She's been getting some exercise. She's even trying to get her garden growing again. Going back to work was the final step, and she was devastated to find out they weren't waiting with baited breath for her to get there." He thought back to her phone call the other day, when she'd asked him questions about Dustin. "I'm worried about her. She's still shaky. She's just trying to keep her head above water. Maybe she's not going about it exactly the right way, but it's the only way she knows how, and it's working for her. I only wish it wasn't at your expense."

Jeff sighed and stood up, shaking his head with a sad

half-smile. "Come on," he said. "I want to meet your son."

The air conditioning inside the Children's Home was cool and welcoming.

"I'm sorry, Chris," Tina said, when she met them at the nurses' station. "We were hoping to get him quieted down before you got here, but he's been inconsolable today. We've tried everything."

Chris nodded, and held the hall door open for Jeff to pass through ahead of him.

"What is she talking about?" Jeff asked, as they walked down the long corridor.

"Crying. Sometimes he cries, and no matter what you do, he won't stop. You change him, hold him, sit him in his beanbag chair, sing to him, and nothing makes a difference."

Three doors from Dustin's room, they could already hear the little boy's sobs.

Dustin was propped up in his bed, arms tight to his sides, chin lowered to his chest. His whole body shook with his crying, and his blue T-shirt had two dark, wet patches down his chest from his tears.

Chris pulled a chair close to the bed and leaned forward to hug Dustin's unresponsive body. "What's the problem, Dusty?" he asked.

Jeff stood at the head of the bed. "If I'd waited until I'd seen him, I wouldn't have needed to ask if Carmen was his mother, would I?" He ran one hand over Dustin's thick, dark hair. "He's a gorgeous kid," he said. "Can he see anything at all?" He held his hand in front of Dustin's face. "Shadows? Light?"

Chris shook his head.

"Can he hear anything? Certain tones? Can he be startled by sound?"

"No."

Jeff moved to the side of the bed and lifted Dustin's small, well-formed hand and placed it palm down on his own. "Touch," he said. "That's all he has."

Chris watched as Jeff slowly reached up to cup Dustin's face with his hands. Dustin looked surprised. The crying stopped, as Jeff smoothly, methodically, wiped the tears from the little boy's cheeks with his thumbs. Chris held his breath, and for the first time in over four years, felt a quickening of hope. This was a man who could work magic, a man who could work miracles. He leaned away from Jeff and his son. Leaned away and watched, but as suddenly as Dustin's tears had stopped, they started again, spilling over Jeff's thumbs, over the back of his hands. Jeff lowered his hands to the boy's shoulders, let them slip down the rigid little arms. He cupped Dustin's hands in his own, squeezed them, stroked them, and then finally let go.

"There are some things," he said, "that can never be made right."

Chris said nothing. His disappointment was intense, although he knew the nameless stab of hope he'd felt had been unrealistic and unfounded. He stood up, bending over to lift his son into his arms, and settled down in the rocker. Shutting his eyes, he drew Dustin's head to his chin and began to sing. "Tell me why the stars do shine. Tell me why the ivy twine."

He finished the song, and only then, only when Dustin began his grunting verbal protests to make him start again, did he realize the little boy had stopped crying. Chris opened his eyes and looked at Jeff, who was sitting on the floor, his back against the wall, smiling.

Chris hugged Dustin close to him, ignoring the wired rigidity in the little body. "Can we stay a while longer?" he asked Jeff. "Do you mind?"

Jeff shook his head. "We can stay all day if you like."

They were nearly back to Sugarbush when Chris began thinking about the ease with which Jeff had touched Dustin.

"Do you have any children?" he asked.

Jeff turned his head to look out the window as if Chris hadn't spoken, and Chris wished he could take the question back. He'd broken the cardinal rule Jeff had set in place between them.

Neither of them spoke as Chris drove into the parking area next to the adobe. They got out of the car, and he opened the back door.

Jeff lifted the bags of supplies into his arms, but made no move to leave. "I need to ask you something . . . awkward," he said.

Chris looked at him in surprise. He couldn't imagine anything more awkward to discuss than the story he had told Jeff that afternoon. "Shoot," he said.

Jeff shifted the bags in his arms. "How did you live with yourself?" he asked, then added quickly. "I'm not trying to be flip. I really need to know how you got up every morning without wanting to run away."

Chris knew he was being complimented. He had done something this remarkable man didn't see himself capable of doing.

"I *did* want to run away," he answered honestly, then smiled, thinking of how he longed for the mayoral election in November. "Sometimes I still do."

"Well." Jeff didn't look satisfied with the answer, but he seemed disinclined to press for more. "Thanks for the ride," he said.

"Right," Chris said. "Glad you came with me."

Jeff started toward the cottages, but turned before he reached the edge of the parking area.

"Chris?"

Chris closed the car door and shaded his eyes to look at him.

"I had three children," Jeff said. "Perfectly healthy, whole children. But I lost them all." He turned away again, and as he walked toward the cottages, Chris saw for the first time the laborious world-weary set of his gait.

35

Although it was Saturday, Mia went into the office early in the morning. She had gotten little work accomplished that week and thought she should take advantage of the fact that both Jeff and Chris were in San Diego and she'd be able to work undisturbed by either of them. Her desk was piled high with the letters Jeff's experiment had inspired. As she inserted a piece of paper into the typewriter to respond to the first letter, however, she knew her concentration would be no better today than it had been during the week. No matter how she tried to shift her thoughts to the task at hand, they slipped back again and again to Jeff and the magical turn her life seemed to have taken.

Even Chris was treating her with a new awareness, a new affection. He seemed pleased by her link to Jeff. "I know you don't need any lectures, Mia," he said, in what sounded like a fatherly tone, "but be careful, okay?" He said it with such genuine worry that she felt herself tearing up at his concern.

"Maybe you can make him stay?" she had asked him, hoping Chris knew something about Jeff's plans which she did not.

"No one can make him do anything," he'd replied, and she knew he was absolutely right.

The week since she and Jeff had become lovers had been one of the best in her life—at least when she could prevent herself from thinking into the treacherous future. Jeff made it easy for her. He had stopped talking about leaving and in that way had fed her fantasy that he might not.

Not only had her work at the office suffered, but she'd gotten nothing done on the sculpture or the fountain either. Her evenings were spent with Jeff, her nights in his bed or hers. It looked as if the year she had planned to be alone and sexless might turn out to be quite the opposite. "You've been sublimating your sexual needs in your clay," he'd said to her the other night. "Sublimate them in me instead. Really, it's all right. I volunteer to take them on."

He cooked her pasta with roasted vegetables and bought heavy wholegrain breads for her. "You're all bones, girl," he'd say, watching her eat. He told her regularly, with a twist in his voice each time, that he loved her. He told her often enough that she was beginning to believe him. And yet, no matter how close she got to him, there was always a part of him she couldn't touch.

She left the office around two. Back at Sugarbush, she did Jeff's laundry as well as her own in Carmen's washer and dryer. She had folded his clean T-shirts and was slipping them into his dresser drawer when her fingers caught on something hard. She drew it out from the back of the drawer and set it on the dresser. It was a jewelry box, a black ring box. She opened the lid slowly to reveal a worn gold band. She took the ring out of the box and held it in her palm. It was heavy. Plain. The gold was scratched in a few places. She slipped it on her finger and it hung loosely, like a gold bangle bracelet might hang from her wrist. It had to be his. Either he was married now, or he had been married, or . . . or what? Could she ask him? Who was the woman? Was she waiting for him? Was she the reason he would have to leave Valle Rosa? Leave her?

A sudden flame of jealousy burned inside her, and it hadn't subsided by the time Jeff returned from San Diego late that afternoon. She was sitting in her living room, her hands slipping idly over the clay she would use for the fountain, when he walked in the front door. He was wearing the red-and-brown Hawaiian shirt he'd had on that first day in Chris's office. All she'd wanted from him that day was a chance to sculpt a lure. He had given her far more than that.

He was carrying a box wrapped in green paper. If he said hello, she didn't hear him. As he sat down on her sofa, she felt a distance slip between them that she hadn't known this past week.

He let out a long sigh, resting his head against the back of the couch, and closed his eyes.

"Jeff?" she asked, "are you all right?"

"Hmm?" He opened his eyes to look at her. "Yes. I'm fine." His smile was weak and distracted, and she wasn't reassured. "Oh." He suddenly leaned forward to rest the box on the coffee table. "This is for you."

She covered the clay and went into the kitchen to wash her hands. Back in the living room, she sat next to him on the sofa, careful to leave a space between them. He wanted that distance, she thought. He barely seemed to be in the room with her at all.

She unwrapped the box. Inside, was a jade-green satin chemise. She lifted it up by the delicate shoulder straps.

"It's beautiful," she said, although she felt the color creeping into her cheeks. The chemise was blatantly sexy. She would look ridiculous in it right now.

"I thought the green would be good on you."

"I love it. Thank you." She lowered it back into the box in a pile of green satin.

Jeff grew quiet again, his head resting against the back of the sofa, his eyes staring into space.

"Did you get what you needed in San Diego?" she asked.

He smiled again, this time ruefully. "I got more than I needed, thank you."

"What do you mean?"

He shook his head. "Nothing, really." He stood up and walked toward the door. "I'm afraid I've got some work to do, Mia. I've spent the whole day riding all over the county. Have to make up for it now."

She frowned at him. "What about dinner? I could make us something."

"What?" He looked puzzled by the question. "Oh. No, thanks. I'm not hungry."

She couldn't bring herself to ask if she would see him at all that night. She couldn't ask him if, for the first time in a week, they would be sleeping separately. She was afraid to hear his answers.

It was nearly midnight, and she was in bed, crying softly, when she heard him open the door to her living room. She quickly dried her eyes in the darkness, and she lay still as he undressed and slipped into the bed next to her. He put his arms around her, rested his head in the crook of her shoulder, and she could feel the exhaustion in his body. He would want to sleep, not talk, not make love. That was all right. He was here.

"I was afraid you didn't want to sleep with me tonight," she whispered, and he whispered something in return, something muffled inaudibly by her shoulder, but which she thought sounded very much like "I love you."

She woke up sometime during the night. Her room was dark and still, but the coyotes were howling so loudly she thought they must be just outside her window. She rolled over to reach for Jeff, but her hand felt only the empty expanse of sheet next to her.

She got out of bed, pulling on her robe, and walked through the cottage. He wasn't in the bathroom, and the living room was dark except for the small, white squares of moonlight thrown across the carpet from the windows. The front door was open, though. She walked out onto the porch.

He was sitting on the steps, and he didn't even glance at her when she sat down next to him. The coyotes howled from the canyon, and she shivered. Jeff's face was turned away from her, but she could see the grim set of his jaw, and on his cheek, the shine of perspiration. Or perhaps, tears.

She tentatively put her arm around him, resting her cheek against his shoulder. "Do you want to talk?"

She felt him shake his head.

"No," he said, but he reached for her arm and clutched the sleeve of her robe in his fist. She relaxed. He wanted her there.

The coyotes howled again, and when they had finished he spoke.

"It was a dream," he said. "A nightmare. I saw the faces of those children who died in the fire. I saw them burning. I could hear them crying. Screaming."

"The coyotes," she said.

"Maybe. Yes, maybe that's what made me dream it."

He pressed his lips to her temple and she closed her eyes. She wouldn't ask him about his wife. Not now. Not ever. He was with her now. Nothing else mattered.

36

Carmen pruned the leggy rosebushes, then rested on her heels and looked at her watch. In another hour she would have to leave, and she dreaded what lay ahead of her. Craig Morrow had called before she'd even gotten out of bed that morning to tell her about the accident. A school bus—one of the small ones that carried handicapped kids to their summer program—had skidded off the road above the reservoir and tumbled into the canyon, killing the driver and three children. Craig wanted her to meet him at the scene of the accident at ten o'clock, when a crane was scheduled to lift the bus out of the canyon. Then she was to talk with some of the families and put together the human-interest side of the tragedy.

It felt like a test, one she wasn't certain she could pass. For the first time since returning to work, she thought she had reached her limit. She couldn't do this, couldn't look at the scorched earth where the children had died, couldn't talk to three families whose grief was still fresh and alive. But she'd agreed to meet Craig, forcing the words calmly out of her mouth in the hope that, once the initial terror wore off, she would be able to carry through on her promise. She'd thought the roses might calm her, but every movement she made was greeted by a new wave of nausea.

The sun seemed hotter than usual. It stung her cheeks as she clipped the branches. She raised one hand to tilt her wide-brimmed hat lower on her forehead and as she did so noticed Jeff walking toward her. He was crossing the barren stretch of Sugarbush between his cottage and the garden, his stride long but unhurried. She self-consciously rolled down her sleeves and was buttoning them at the wrists when he reached her.

He sat down on one of the boulders and seemed to be assessing the garden.

"You've done a good job with the roses," he said. "It's almost impossible to grow them under the conditions you've had here."

She studied him skeptically. In the distance behind him, the sky was red from a new fire burning on Mount Palomar, and with that as his background, Jeff looked as if he'd been plucked from some surrealistic painting.

"Thank you," she said.

He picked up the pruning shears and leaned forward to snip a branch she had missed. Then he sat back again, squinting against the sun as he looked at her.

"I met Dustin yesterday," he said.

Involuntarily, her hand flew to her throat. "You . . . what do you mean?"

"I had to go into San Diego for something, and Chris invited me to ride along with him. We stopped at the Children's Home and spent some time with your son."

Her cheeks burned. She lowered her head. No one ever referred to Dustin as her son. No one other than Chris ever mentioned him to her at all.

"I see." She smoothed her gloved hand across the dusty earth around one of the rose bushes. "Did Chris tell you why he's the way he is?"

"Yes."

She let out her breath, feeling betrayed by Chris's sudden candor. "The man has no shame."

Jeff shaded his eyes. "He's full of shame," he said.

She shot Jeff a look from under the brim of her hat. "He shouldn't have told you anything. My life is absolutely none of your business."

"And mine is public property, right?"

She sighed, feeling the barest hint of a smile cross her lips. "Touché."

He leaned toward her. "You know, they may have told you Dustin would die, but he didn't. And frankly, he doesn't look like he will anytime soon."

She held up her hands to ward him off. "Look, Jeff, I cannot deal with this right now. In less than an hour, I'm supposed to exploit a few devastated families, and I can't think about anything else, so please pick some other time to deliver your lecture on motherhood."

Jeff stared at her, a look of disbelief forming in his eyes. "Are you talking about the bus accident?" he asked.

"Yes."

"You're going to badger those parents who lost their kids just a few hours ago?" His voice rose.

"I don't have any goddamned choice!" She sucked in a

quick breath, stunned by how close she was to snapping, to simply losing it. Steadying herself, she spoke more calmly. "It's the last thing I feel like doing, I can assure you of that. I feel sick when I think about it." She felt the crack in her voice and hoped he hadn't noticed.

But he had.

"Then don't do it," he said softly.

She pulled off her gloves. "They'll can me." She looked him in the eye, leveling with him. "'She's gone soft,' they'll say. I'll lose everything again."

"Make up an excuse. Tell them you're sick."

"I'd have to be on my deathbed before that would work," she scoffed. "This is the hot story right now."

She smoothed the gloves, one on top of the other, as a few seconds of silence stretched between them. Jeff looked out toward the canyon. Behind his head, the fiery red of the sky had softened.

Finally, he spoke again. "You're not a bitch, you know it?" he said. "You're still human, but you've beaten down your ability to feel compassion for another person until it's practically nonexistent."

Carmen shook her head. "No one—least of all a woman—gets very far in this business by being compassionate. I've only done what I had to do to get the job done."

"Mmm." Jeff ran his hand over the sunlit boulder. "But at what cost?"

Carmen's throat tightened. She couldn't handle this now. "Please leave me alone," she said.

He pursed his lips, nodding. "Right." Getting to his

feet, he looked down at her. "Try putting yourself in those parents' shoes when you conduct your interviews," he said.

He started to turn away, but Carmen found she couldn't let him go. "Do you hate me?" she asked.

Jeff put his hands on his hips. "Hate's the wrong word, Carmen. I'm *afraid* of you, of what you can do to me. You hold all the cards. Are you planning to give me some warning before you show your hand?"

"How can I answer that?" she said, shaking her head. "I don't know how things will unfold."

He gave her one of his half-smiles, this one tinged with the bitter disdain she was accustomed to receiving from him. "Just doing your job, right?" He started striding toward his cottage, but suddenly turned on his heel and walked back to her.

She put the last of the clippings in a plastic bag and stood up as he neared the garden again.

"Rick and I are going to be moving some of the equipment onto the roof of the warehouse this morning," he said. "It's the next step in preparing to drench Valle Rosa. I think you should be there, don't you?"

It took her a moment to catch on. She couldn't cover both the bus crash and the events at the warehouse; she would have to pick between the stories.

"Yes," she said, and she couldn't stop her smile. "I think I'd better."

She went into the house after finishing up in the garden. For some reason, she walked upstairs and opened the door to the old nursery. She hadn't been inside that room in years, and she wouldn't have recognized it. There was no furniture, of course; the crib and dresser had long ago been put in storage. And although Chris had told her he'd taken down the wallpaper, she was still unprepared for the echoing emptiness in the room and for the bland expanse of the flat white walls.

Stepping inside, she circled the room, her tennis shoes squeaking on the wooden floor. She stopped at the double windows, from which she had a sweeping view of Sugarbush. The rose garden was a distant patch of reddish-orange against the pale earth.

The children on the bus had been killed instantly, she thought. They were far too young to die, yes, but at least those parents would be able to take some comfort in knowing that it had been quick. Their children hadn't suffered. Not like her child. Not like Dustin.

Carmen rested her forehead against the warm pane of glass in the window. Dustin should have died. That night in his room, when he cried and stiffened and stopped breathing in her trembling arms—that night should have been his last. If only she had never learned CPR. If only she hadn't had the presence of mind to breathe for her baby. If only the ambulance hadn't arrived so quickly.

Oh, Dusty.

He cries a lot, Chris had said.

Carmen pressed her fist to her mouth and backed away from the window and out of the room. Once in the hallway, she took in a deep breath, straightened her spine, and swept her hair back from her face with her hands.

She glanced at her watch as she walked toward the

bedroom. She would have to call Craig to tell him she wouldn't be covering the accident. Then she would head out to the warehouse.

She had a job to do.

37

Mia was leaving the cottage to go to the office when she came face to face with Laura. Her sister stood on the bottom step of the porch, and Mia reflexively started to back into the cottage again, as if she'd opened her door to find a growling dog waiting for her.

"Wait, Mimi! Don't slam the door on me. Please."

Mia stepped onto the porch, folding her arms across her chest and leaning back against the wall. "How did you find me?" she asked.

"It wasn't hard. The number you gave me was a Valle Rosa exchange. Glen said that when he called you there, you answered the phone 'mayor's office.' So, I asked around town. A waitress at that catfish restaurant knew you lived out here. She even knew which cottage was yours." Laura began to cry. "Oh, Mimi," she said. "I'm so sorry. I've been so terrible."

Mia steeled herself against Laura's tears. "Why are you here?" she asked. "What's wrong?"

"*Everything's* wrong." Laura began crying in earnest, and Mia couldn't help but feel some sympathy for her sister. They had never been the closest of friends, but they hadn't always been enemies. "Please, can I come in?"

She didn't want Laura in her cottage. Closing the door behind her, she sat down on the porch step. Laura dusted the step off with her hand before sitting next to her. She wiped her eyes with a tissue she had wadded in her fist.

"What's going on?" Mia asked, more gently now.

"Well, to start with, he ditched me."

"Who? Glen?"

Laura nodded, a fresh stream of tears slipping down her cheeks. "Oh, Mimi, how can you ever forgive me? He ditched me for some little slut who works at the Lesser Gallery."

"Oh." She remembered the woman in the tight black dress she had seen Glen talking to at the gallery.

"The bastard!" Laura pounded a fist into the wooden step. "He said it was mostly physical, that there never really was much depth to our relationship."

Mia sighed. "There isn't much depth to *Glen*, Laura," she said.

"He ditched me on my thirtieth birthday." She shook her head, a rueful smile on her lips. "But somehow it snapped some sense into me. I suddenly realized what I'd done to you." Laura shifted on the step to face her, taking her hand. "I'm so sorry for everything I did, Mia. I thought it was real between Glen and me. I thought it was fated and that justified hurting you. Can you ever forgive me?"

Mia smiled. "You saved me from him," she said. "I guess I owe you for that."

Laura clutched Mia's hand harder. "Let me stay with you a day or two, Mia, please? Let me try to make up to you for what a shit I've been."

Mia looked out toward the canyon. So much of her energy had gone into escaping from her sister. It had been a close call, but she'd gotten out in time. Now Laura was here, at Sugarbush, in the little corner of the world Mia had carved out for herself.

"I don't know," she said. "I don't think I'm ready to spend time with you."

"Please, Mimi?"

Mia glanced at her watch. She needed to let Chris know she was going to be late. "Let me call my office," she said. "Wait here. I'll be back in a minute."

She walked across Sugarbush to the adobe, feeling only slightly guilty for making Laura wait on her porch instead of in the cottage. She extracted the key from under the potted lemon tree on Carmen's patio, let herself into the house and dialed Chris's office on the kitchen phone.

Chris was in a good mood. When she told him her sister had shown up on her doorstep, he suggested she take the day off. She didn't bother to tell him she would rather work than spend the day with Laura.

Then she called Jeff at the warehouse.

"My sister's here," she said.

It took a moment for her words to register. "Laura?" he asked.

"Yes. She appeared on my doorstep a half hour ago, crying her eyes out because Glen broke up with her."

There was another beat of silence from Jeff's end of

the line. "Wow," he said. "What happened? Did she get a zit or something and he couldn't handle it?"

Mia laughed in spite of her poor humor. "She wants to stay with me for a couple of days. She said she wants to make up to me for what she did. I actually feel sorry for her. She's being sweet. I think she's sincere, but she's *not* staying in my house."

"Let her stay, Mia," Jeff said.

She was surprised. She'd expected his support in telling Laura to leave. "Why?"

Jeff sighed. "I know what she did was pretty unforgivable, but everybody screws up once or twice in their lives. Why don't you give her a chance to redeem herself? Family's important. Maybe you'll get some resolution out of her visit."

"But I want to see *you* tonight."

"And you can. Invite me over for dinner."

Mia looked at the beamed ceiling of the adobe. She didn't want Laura to meet Jeff. And she knew by the sudden, frantic beating of her heart that she was afraid to have Jeff meet the always-beautiful, always-alluring Laura. The image of Laura in the green chemise Jeff had given her slipped into her mind. Laura would fill it out easily. She would look lovely in it.

"All right," she said, refusing to give in to her insecurity. "She can stay for one night. If she hasn't redeemed herself by morning, she's lost her chance."

Jeff laughed. "Atta girl."

Laura looked small and helpless where she sat on the porch step as Mia approached her cottage again. "All I have is a lumpy sofa," Mia said, "but it's yours for tonight if you want it."

Laura jumped up to hug her. "Oh, Mia," she said, "you're the best!"

Mia stepped back to study her sister's face. Laura's eyes were puffy and red, the diminutive bulb of her nose a little swollen. Yet she was still pretty, her silky eyelashes glistening with tears. Mia put her arm around her. "Well," she said, "let me show you my little home."

Laura wiped her cheeks with the backs of her hands, the tissue by now useless. "Can we get my suitcase first?"

"All right."

They walked to the driveway where Laura's silver Mazda stood next to Mia's green Rabbit. Laura opened the passenger door of the car and lifted a small beige-and-mauve floral suitcase from the seat.

Walking back toward the cottage, Laura seemed to notice Sugarbush—its vastness, its primitiveness— for the first time. "Could you get any farther from civilization, Mimi?" she asked. "This is nowhere. It's so wild. I can't believe you're actually living alone out here. Aren't you terrified at night?"

"Not at all." Mia felt an unfamiliar surge of superiority over her sister.

"Are there any malls around here? I want to take you shopping. I want to buy you things."

"Not too close."

By the time they reached the cottage, Laura was crying again. It gave Mia an opportunity to move the bulletin board and Jeff's pictures into her closet. The last thing

Jeff had said to her before getting off the phone was, "If it's possible to keep Laura from figuring out that I'm Valle Rosa's so-called mystery man, I'd appreciate it."

She and Laura spent much of the day talking, but there was little give-and-take in their conversation. Laura tried. Mia could see her struggling to find things to say about the finished sculpture of Henry, and the work in progress of Jeff, and the massive wire armature for the fountain standing in the corner of the cluttered dining room. But the effort was simply too much for her. Laura was clearly obsessed with her loss and able to talk about little other than Glen. She moved through the rooms of the cottage in slow motion, a perpetual frown on her face broken only by sudden, intractable spells of weeping.

Mia managed to drag her into town for lunch, and then for a walk through the canyon, which Laura didn't enjoy, especially after Mia mentioned the coyotes. But Mia was more relaxed with her sister outside the cottage. Inside, Laura was an overwhelming presence. She filled the rooms with the scent of expensive perfume. Her white shorts and peach-colored blouse were pressed and perfect, her nails carefully shaped and polished a deep coral. Her long hair was streaked with pale blond, and she glittered with gold rings and bracelets. Every movement of her hands sent a blur of gold through the air.

Several times during the day, she checked her reflection in the bathroom mirror. "God, look at my eyes," she would say. "They're so swollen and red. I look hideous. And I'm *thirty*. Why couldn't he have left me when I was still twenty-nine?"

Late in the afternoon, they sat in the living room drinking white wine. Soon Mia would have to tell her sister that Jeff would be joining them for dinner, and she was trying to figure out how she would describe him, how she would define his presence in her life.

Laura suddenly interrupted her thoughts. "Do you know how guilty I felt during those years when you were taking care of Mom and I was at school?" she asked.

Mia raised her eyebrows. "No," she said. "I didn't know."

Laura groaned. "I look back now and I can't believe how selfish I was. I can't believe I let you do all that without lifting a finger to help you."

Mia stared into her wine, her cheeks hot. She simply didn't feel ready to forgive her sister for any of her transgressions. "It's in the past," she said. It was the most she could manage.

"You're so lucky, Mia." Laura shook her head.

"I am?"

"You always knew what you wanted, from the time you were small. You wanted to be an artist, and you went ahead and did it. I'm very proud of you. When I saw that piece you did of Mom in the Lesser Gallery, I cried."

Mia was surprised. "Thanks."

"Everyone who ever met you liked you."

Mia frowned. "You're a fine one to talk. You were always the most popular kid in school."

"Yeah, but they liked me because I was pretty. They liked you because of who you were."

"Hmm." Mia guessed that was supposed to be a compliment.

Laura was quiet for a moment, taking a few delicate sips from her wine glass. "Do you still see Dr. Bella?" she asked finally, her eyes huge over the rim of the glass.

"When I have to." Mia looked directly at her sister. "You're examining yourself, Laura, aren't you?"

"Constantly. I feel like a time bomb, like there's no way I can escape it." She swirled the wine in her glass and didn't look at Mia when she spoke again. "I think that was the real reason Glen left me. He was afraid it would happen to me too. He wanted to get out while I was still . . . intact."

"He said that?"

"No. But I'm sure that's what he was thinking." Laura grimaced. "I couldn't handle it if it happened to me, Mia. You're much stronger than I am. And you never cared much about how you looked or anything. But for me, it would be the end."

"No, it wouldn't. You'd be all right."

"I can't stand talking about it." Laura shuddered. "I can't stand thinking it could ever happen to me." She leaned forward. "Listen, Mimi, after you get the reconstruction, we can go out. Like sisters. I want us to be friends. We can do the singles scene together."

Mia felt an old sick feeling inside her. She remembered too well what it was like to be out socially with Laura, how invisible she felt. "I don't have much interest in the singles scene," she said.

"Yeah, and that's always been your problem. We'll get you dating again. Both of us. It'll be fun."

"I'm dating now."

"What?" Laura nearly spilled her wine. "Who?"

"A man who lives in one of the other cottages."

Laura looked as though this news was too much to be believed. "You *are*? Are you just friends, or . . . how serious? I mean . . . does he know about your breast?"

"Yes. And he doesn't care."

Laura slouched down in the sofa. "God," she said, "Glen was a pig."

"He's coming over for dinner tonight. The man I'm seeing."

"He is? What time? We should straighten up this place."

Mia laughed. "He's not that kind of man."

Laura checked herself in the mirror more frequently as the hour neared for Jeff's arrival. She was helping Mia cut vegetables in the kitchen, when every once in a while she would disappear from the room. In a moment, Mia would hear the click of her sister's shoes on the tiled bathroom floor.

Jeff knocked on the door while Mia was stir-frying the vegetables.

"Would you get it, Laura?" she asked, and she clutched the spatula in her hand as if she expected the next few minutes to turn her world upside down.

She heard Laura and Jeff exchange greetings. Jeff said something she couldn't quite make out. Laura laughed in response, and Mia dug at the vegetables in her wok with a new vengeance, annoyed with herself for her lack of faith in Jeff.

"Hi." He walked into the kitchen, Laura close on his heels. He had showered. He smelled of soap and shampoo, and his hair was still damp. He wore khaki pants, a gray-and-blue striped shirt open at the neck, a brown braided leather belt. She wished he didn't look quite so beautiful.

She pretended to be absorbed in her work on the stove when he bent over to kiss her cheek.

"Brought some wine." He slipped the bottle between her eyes and the wok. "Want me to open it?"

"That'd be great," Mia said. Her cheeks felt hot.

There was a different sort of energy coming from Laura with Jeff in the cottage. Her scent seemed to over-shadow the aroma of Mia's cooking. Where she had been mopey and weepy throughout much of the day, now she glowed and glittered, her smile radiant.

Mia felt herself sinking down. Disappearing.

"That's my favorite wine," Laura said as Jeff pulled the cork from the neck of the bottle. "You have great taste."

"Thanks." He poured them each a glass, then rested a hand on Mia's back. "What can we do to help?"

"Everything's under control." She glanced up at him. "Just keep me company, okay?"

"So, Jeff." Laura leaned back against the counter. "What kind of work do you do?"

"Engineering." Jeff answered quickly, and Mia knew he had rehearsed this. "I work for Valle Rosa's water con-servation program."

"Oh, that sounds interesting. Isn't this where that rainmaker guy is? Have you met him?"

Jeff reached into the cabinet above Mia's head for the napkins. "Once or twice," he said.

"How does he do it?"

Jeff shrugged, setting the napkins on a tray. "He's very secretive."

"Well, I saw the film of that so-called rain on TV." Laura rested her glass on the counter and folded her arms beneath her ample breasts. "It looked fake to me."

"I thought so, too," Jeff said. "The way those clouds were boiling up like that. I've never seen anything like that outside of the movies." He reached into the wok and plucked out a pea pod, slipping it into his mouth. "So, Laura," he asked, "how long are you staying?"

"Just till tomorrow. I was hoping maybe I could take Mia shopping before I leave, though. My little baby sister." Laura put her arm around Mia, and Mia could feel the awkwardness in the gesture. "How close is the nearest mall?"

"Escondido," Mia said.

"Well, that's not too terrible, and I don't mind driving. And I'm buying—I'm sure I'm making more money than you are. You could use some new clothes, Mimi. I remember that skirt you're wearing from when you were in school, for heaven's sake."

"It's very comfortable," Mia said. Laura was right, though. The skirt was at least a decade old.

"Maybe, but nobody wears long skirts like that anymore."

"Your sister sets her own trends," Jeff said to Laura.

"Wouldn't it be fun to go to one of those make-over places where they take glamorous pictures of you?" Laura asked. "I think—now that I'm thirty—I should make some changes in my make-up or something. And you could get the works, Mimi. Wouldn't she look great in bangs, Jeff?"

"I think she looks great just as she is," Jeff answered gallantly.

Mia rolled her eyes above the wok, hoping neither of them could see her. "This is done," she said, pulling a bowl close to the stove.

"Let me help you with it." Jeff lifted the wok and tipped it toward the bowl while she scraped out the vegetables. "Smells good," he said.

They carried the vegetables and rice and salad into the dining room. Mia was quiet while they ate, focusing her attention on her food while Jeff and Laura talked about Valle Rosa and about Laura's promotion to senior sportswear buyer at the large department store where she worked. It wasn't until they were halfway through the meal that Mia let herself study Jeff. She watched as he spoke to her sister. She watched his hands as he ate, thinking of the ways he had touched her with those hands, thinking about the taste of the skin on his neck, the scent of his hair. She remembered sitting with him on her porch the other night, after his nightmare. She remembered how he had clutched her arm, how he'd let her know he wanted her there. *Needed* her there.

He poured more wine for Laura, and he smiled at her

as he handed her the glass, but Mia could see there was
something missing in his smile. An emptiness. A shallow-
ness she hadn't seen in him before, and she realized all at
once that he didn't like Laura. It was a shock. A revelation.
A relief. He didn't like Laura at all.

After dinner he joined Mia in the kitchen, setting
mugs and teaspoons on a tray while she made coffee. She
dropped the paper filter, and he bent down to pick it up.
When he straightened again, he drew his hand under the
front of her skirt, slipping his fingers under the top of her
panties to rest his hand there, flat against her stomach.
She sucked in her breath, and he leaned close to her neck.
"I happen to be fond of this old skirt of yours and the easy
accessibility it provides."

She turned her head to muffle a laugh in his cheek.

"I'm going to miss you very much tonight," he continued. "And furthermore, your sister's a grade-A bitch.
My apologies for talking you into letting her stay." He
withdrew his hand then and left the room, carrying the
tray.

"So," Laura said, when each of them had a mug of
coffee in front of them, "did Mia tell you I've been given
the deep-six by my boyfriend?"

Jeff nodded, glancing at Mia. "Yes, she did," he said.
"Glen, right? He used to be Mia's old boyfriend?"

"Uh huh. He's an artist. He's made an art out of ditch-
ing Tanner women." Laura's eyes filled, and Mia knew
she'd reached her limit on being able to talk about
anything other than Glen. It was going to be a repeat
performance of the previous year, when she'd talked

obsessively about her break-up with Luke. Laura and her men. She couldn't exist apart from them.

Laura dabbed at her eyes with her napkin. "I'm sorry," she said. "I just don't understand him. Can you explain men to me, Jeff? I mean, he was totally in love with me and then wham, he's gone."

"I don't think unpredictability is a uniquely male trait," Jeff said.

"But to ditch me, out of the blue!"

"It's no different than what he did to me," Mia said quietly.

Laura lifted her mug to her lips. "At least in your case you can make some sort of sense out of it, with the mastectomy and all." She took a swallow of her coffee. "But with me . . . I just don't get what he had to complain about."

Jeff stood up suddenly. He pushed in his chair and rested his hands on its old wicker back. "Well, Laura," he said, "maybe it was your incredible lack of tact that drove him away."

Laura stopped her mug mid-air. "What do you mean?"

Jeff looked her squarely in the eye. "Or maybe you were as insensitive to him as you are to your sister."

Laura looked stunned. Her mouth was open in a little U-shape, her eyes disbelieving. Mia felt Jeff's hands on her shoulders as he bent down to kiss her on the neck.

"I love you," he said. "I'll see you tomorrow."

She watched him walk across the living room, and she kept her eyes on the door long after he had closed it behind him. She didn't dare look at her sister until Laura stood up and began clearing the table. There was a splotch of crimson low on her throat.

"He's got a mean streak," Laura said. "You'd better watch out for it."

In another minute, Mia heard the angry rattling of the dishes from the kitchen. She poured herself another cup of coffee and sat back with a smile, raising her feet to the chair Jeff had vacated. She would let Laura do the dishes.

38.

Tom Forrest and his New Jersey connection tracked down the first company Jeff had worked for after receiving his PhD and passed the information on to Carmen. The company was Environmental Classics in Passaic, New Jersey, and Carmen planned her phone interview carefully. She wasn't certain how much national media coverage had been given to Jeff and Valle Rosa, but she couldn't take the chance that someone she interviewed might be able to link Jeff Cabrio and Robert Blackwell. So when she reached Warren Guest, an old co-worker of Jeff's, she didn't even identify *News Nine*. She was calling from a station "out West," she said. Robert Blackwell was involved in a "small environmental issue," and she was interested in learning more about him.

"I just wanted to verify that he worked at Environmental Classics," she said.

"He worked here all right." Warren Guest laughed. "And we were glad when he left, because he made the rest of us look like slouches with a collective IQ of about 50. Seriously, it wasn't his fault his brain didn't work the same as everyone else's. When I see a problem, I see a problem. Rob would look at the exact same thing and see a solution." Warren paused, then added, "He was a pretty good guy, though."

Carmen now knew first-hand that Jeff was a "good guy." He had rescued her from covering that bus accident. He hadn't allowed her inside the warehouse as he and Rick moved the equipment to the roof, and there hadn't been much to see from the ground, but she'd managed to get a story out of the morning nevertheless.

"How long did he work at Environmental Classics?" she asked.

"Oh, let's see. Seven or eight years I'd say."

"Was he married or involved with anyone during that time?"

"Yeah, actually, he got married while he was here. I didn't go to the wedding. It was one of those small, quiet kind of deals. His wife's name was Leslie."

Leslie Blackwell. Where was she now? Could she and Jeff still be married?

"Do you happen to know Leslie's maiden name?" she asked.

"No, sorry. Don't have a clue."

"What was she like?"

"She seemed nice, though I didn't really know her. I just saw her at office picnics and that sort of thing. They had a baby a few years after they got married. A girl. I remember the pink ribbons on the cigars."

Carmen thought of the picture in Jeff's wallet of the two little blond girls on the elephant.

"Were Rob and Leslie still married when he left your company?"

"Yeah." Warren hesitated. "You mean he's not with her now, huh?"

"I'm not sure. I don't know too much about his personal life, but it appears they're no longer together."

"Well, that's too bad, but what is it these days—one out of every two marriages ends in divorce? Not the greatest odds, and he'd be a strange guy to be married to. He was strange enough to work with."

"In what way?"

"Well, he was different. The rest of us sometimes felt as though we'd been hired to clean up after him."

"What do you mean? Do you mean he was sloppy at the office, or—"

Warren Guest laughed again. "No. It was his *work* that could be sloppy. He would come up with ideas—brilliant ideas—and do what he wanted to with them, and the rest of us mopped up after him. At first I resented it. Then I realized that he wasn't merely a scientist; he was an artist."

Carmen frowned. "I'm afraid I'm not following you."

"Well, picture an artistic genius. Picture Picasso, right?"

"Right."

"You don't try to contain genius. You don't try to put limits on it. You watch him work, and he's frantically mixing colors, creating a work of art on the canvas, and if he happens to mix a color he doesn't like and tosses the brush on the floor as he starts to mix a new color, you don't say to him, 'pick up that brush before you continue.'"

Carmen laughed.

"You get it? So that's how it was with Rob. Once he was on a roll, you didn't stop him. You just stood out of his way and let him do his thing, and if he happened to screw up along the way, you cleaned up after him."

"Wow." Carmen was struck by Warren's creative analogy. She wondered how efficient Rick Smythe was at cleaning up. "When did Rob leave Environmental Classics?"

"Hmm. Five years ago, maybe? He started his own business as a consultant, he and a guy he knew from college, Kent Reed. Another whiz kid."

"Really. Do you know where I can find Kent Reed?"

Warren groaned. "He's the kind of person you try to figure out how to lose, not find."

"Why do you say that?" It seemed that, even as an adult, Kent Reed had won no popularity contests.

"Oh, he'd hang around here all the time, sticking to Rob like glue. The supervisor finally told him to get a life of his own, but Rob left shortly after that, and he and Kent started their business together."

"Do you remember the name of the business?"

"Probably have it in my Rolodex," he said. "I never get around to updating that thing. Hold on."

She heard him flipping through the cards.

"Blackwell and Reed Environmental Consultants," Warren said. He gave her an address in Morristown, New Jersey, along with a phone number. "This is old info, though. I know they're not still there. I'm not even sure they still work together. But you really should try to talk to Kent if you want to learn more about Rob. He knew Rob Blackwell better than anyone."

Carmen tried to find a number for a Leslie Blackwell with no success, and the phone number Warren had given her for Jeff and Kent's Morristown business now belonged to an elderly man who was overjoyed at hearing her voice, thinking she was his long-lost daughter. Carmen was nearly in tears by the time she managed to convince him that she wasn't.

Finally, she called Tom Forrest.

"Check old business licenses," he suggested. "No, never mind. I'll take care of it and get back to you."

"I can do it myself, Tom." She didn't like his paternal attitude.

"Come on, Carmen," he said. "You'll do all the work once I get the information. Let me do this much for you." After a moment's hesitation, he continued. "You're doing great, Carmen. That article in the *Union* was terrific."

An article in yesterday's *San Diego Union* had stated that getting a taste of Carmen Perez again "points up what has been missing from Channel Nine these past four years." Carmen had read the article three times.

Tom called her back in less than an hour. "Reed left the state a couple of years ago," he said. "I've got a forwarding address to Lamar, West Virginia, but it's a post office box. Tried to get a phone number for him there, but looks like it's unlisted."

Carmen wrote down the address. "All right," she said, "I'll take it from there."

She flew to Dulles International Airport in Virginia on a red-eye flight the following evening. Dennis Ketchum had given her the time off with some reluctance, and as she stood in line at the car-rental window, exhausted from the fitful sleep she'd had on the plane, she hoped this wouldn't be a wild goose chase.

The drive to West Virginia took her two hours, the last half hour seeming to go straight uphill. The countryside was beautiful and green. Even with the rise in altitude, though, the day was sticky hot, and she was grateful for the rental car's air conditioner.

She followed the map spread out on the passenger seat, and as she neared the town of Lamar, she realized that the jade-green crepe suit she was wearing wasn't the appropriate attire for this region. The terrain ranged from thick woods to open fields. Houses were spread far apart, and they were small and, for the most part, in need of paint and repair. Rusting metal furniture graced lopsided front porches, and statues of flamingos and baby ducks and upright, fully-clothed, kissing pigs adorned the yards.

She passed a small sign for Lamar, barely visible in the leafy overhang of a tree. This was it? Sighing heavily, she continued driving along the narrow wooded road, passing the occasional house, the occasional horse and cow. Lamar made Valle Rosa look like a metropolis.

Finally, she came to a cross street with a small store on one corner. She pulled into the parking lot, stopping near an old gas pump. The air bore down on her with its damp, sucking humidity as she stepped out of the car, and she pulled a clip from her purse to pin up her hair. Why would anyone choose to live here in this heat, she wondered, although she supposed the residents of Lamar might wonder why anyone would choose to live in a place where they could flush their toilets only once a day.

It took her eyes a minute to adjust to the dim light of the store after being out in the late morning sun. She appeared to be the only customer. A middle-aged man sat on a stool behind the counter, reading a newspaper and smoking a cigarette, while a woman arranged cans of soup on one of the shelves. They both turned to look at her as she walked in.

She approached the counter. "I'm looking for the post office," she said.

"You've found it." The man nodded to the row of post office boxes behind him.

"Oh," she said, surprised. "Well, I'm trying to find a man who has a P.O. box here. Kent Reed."

The woman and man exchanged looks.

"He lives up in the hills," the woman said.

"I thought this *was* the hills."

The woman smiled. She was in her mid-fifties and very pretty, her gray hair pulled back in a bun. "It gets hillier than this, honey." Then she cocked her head at Carmen. "You're not an old friend of his or something, are you?"

"No. I've never met him before."

The man chuckled, a puff of smoke escaping his lips.

"That explains it," he said. "Only someone who never met Kent Reed before would want to meet him in the first place."

The woman joined him in the laughter, and since their mirth didn't seem to be at her expense, Carmen smiled herself. She liked their accents and wondered what they made of hers.

The woman moved behind the counter to stand next to the man, and Carmen decided they must be husband and wife. Both wore gold wedding bands.

"Why on earth would you want to see Kent Reed?" the woman asked bluntly.

Carmen slipped off her suit jacket and folded it over her arm. Her back felt sticky with perspiration. "I'm a reporter," she said, "and I need to ask him a few questions for a story I'm doing about an old colleague of his."

"Well, good luck." The man stubbed out his cigarette in a metal ashtray.

"What do you mean?"

"He won't talk to you, honey," the woman answered. "He never talks to anybody."

"No one?"

The man folded his arms across his chest and leaned his back against the post office boxes. "He's lived here a couple of years, and he comes into the store once a month or so to pick up his mail and get groceries and—"

"He buys everything in cans," the woman interrupted him. "It's a wonder he doesn't have scurvy."

"He'll come in a little more often than that if he's

ordered parts from somewhere for one of his inventions," the man continued.

Carmen's mind suddenly kicked into high gear. Could Jeff and Kent be running from the same thing? They'd split up their partnership and taken off in opposite directions, trying to cover their trails.

"Do you think he's running away from something?" she asked.

"Civilization, I'd say." The man ran a hand over his chin. "He likes machines. He doesn't like people, and he'd be the first to tell you that. Kent Reed is your typical mad scientist, miss. That about sums him up."

She felt disconcerted by the word "mad."

"Am I in any danger going to see him?" she asked.

"Nah." The woman shook her head. "He's got a nasty bark, but I don't think there's much bite behind it."

"Well." Carmen swept a stray hair off her cheek, "I guess all that explains why his phone is unlisted."

"He doesn't have a phone," the woman said. "Or a television. Or a radio. He could be living in the year 2050 or 1962 for all he keeps up with things. I bet he doesn't even know who's president right now."

Carmen bought an ice-cold can of Diet Coke and drank it as the man and woman gave her a lengthy set of directions to Kent Reed's house. She was surprised when the shopkeepers suggested she borrow their four-wheel-drive truck. She declined the offer, but as her car chugged up the dirt road that cut through the wooded hillside, she began to regret that decision.

Nearly thirty minutes after leaving the store, she

rounded a bend to find herself at the end of the road. She stopped the car and studied the woods in front of her. There was a footpath, they had told her. Leaving the tape recorder in the car—she wouldn't risk asking Kent Reed if she might tape their conversation—she got out and located the overgrown path. After taking a few cautious steps into the thick woods, she was relieved to see a house come into view behind the trees.

The house was, as the general-store owners had described it, an old log cabin. It was fairly large, but as she neared it, she could see that the rear of the building was a recent addition, the logs there a warm brown in comparison to the age-darkened logs in the rest of the house.

She knocked on the door. Sounds came from inside the house. Metal sounds. Clanking sounds. But it wasn't until she'd knocked for the sixth time that the door flew open.

Carmen took an involuntary step backwards as Kent Reed appeared in the doorway. He was tall and extraordinarily thin, as though some disease had eaten away his flesh. His hair was dark and unwashed and hung limply around the crew neck of his graying white T-shirt. He wore loose-fitting jeans and brown moccasins, and his beard was long and streaked with gray. From inside the house drifted the unmistakable scent of tuna fish.

"Who are you?" he asked.

Carmen felt as if she'd stepped into a low-budget movie. "My name is Carmen Perez, Mr. Reed. I'm from television station KTVA." She held her identification card in front of her, but he didn't even glance at it.

"What do you want?"

"I'd like to talk with you about Robert Blackwell."

He jerked as if she'd struck him. "*Why?*"

Carmen had planned to be evasive, as usual, but there was nothing usual about this situation, and she made a quick decision to put caution aside. She had to find out how much this man knew.

"Do you know where he is and what he's doing?" She tested the question.

"No, I don't. Nor do I give a flying fuck." Kent Reed started to close the door, and Carmen surprised herself by reaching out to hold it open.

"Please," she said. "Just two more minutes of your time."

He sighed, looking down at her with a mixture of impatience and contempt. She tried to peer around him, curious to see the inside of his house. Against the wall to his left, chrome-colored shelves covered with equipment of one sort or another ran from floor to ceiling. The equipment looked exceptionally clean and orderly, which seemed almost bizarre given the disheveled state of the man in front of her. To his right, she could see a straight-back chair next to a TV tray. On top of the tray was a large can of tuna fish, a fork sticking upright from its contents.

"I thought you and Mr. Blackwell worked together," she said.

He sneered. "I don't work with people who are afraid of themselves."

"And Mr. Blackwell fell into that category?"

"Rob Blackwell had a gift," Kent snapped. "But what

did he want to do with that gift? He made toys for his asshole kids, that's what. And he remodeled the house for his precious wife." Kent waved his right hand around as he spoke, and for the first time, Carmen noticed the deformity he had lived with since junior high school. His index and middle finger were missing, the skin shiny over the remaining bony knuckles.

"He and I were a team." His voice frightened Carmen with its surly, simpering, caustic tone. This wasn't a sane man. "From the time we were kids, we had dozens of projects on the burner, and before he got . . . distracted, we would work on them twenty-four hours a day, seven days a week. Rob would even try to program his dreams so he could come up with solutions during the night. Not waste a minute of time." A faint smile crossed Kent's face, and his Adam's apple bobbed in his throat. "I thought he was God back in those days. Then he met the leech, and—"

"The leech?" Carmen asked.

"Leslie. His parasite of a wife. She ruined him. He started spending more and more time with her and less on our work. And once the kids were born, he was pathetic. 'Nights and weekends are reserved for my family,' he'd say, or he'd have to go see his old junkie stepfather in the joint."

"Is his father still living?" Carmen asked, sidetracked for a moment by the thought that Jefferson Watts might still be alive, but Kent didn't like the intrusion into his own train of thought.

"How the hell should I know?" he snapped at her, and

she felt a quickening in her chest. Despite what the woman in the store had said about Kent Reed having no bite to back up his bark, she was afraid. Yet she knew it was his anger that fueled his desire to talk with her. If anything, she would have to nurture it.

"Where was Jefferson Watts incarcerated?" she asked.

He glowered at her. "Why don't you go peddle your papers to the Jersey state prison, if you're so interested in old junkies? That's where they all go to die."

She thought he was going to try to slam the door on her again, so she hurried on, reminding herself he had no TV, no radio. He didn't keep up with the news in any way.

"Mr. Reed," she said, "Robert Blackwell has told some people who live in an area suffering from a long-standing drought that he can make it rain."

Kent stared at her, and for the first time she could read no anger, no emotion whatsoever in his face. Then he closed his eyes and ran a hand down his beard.

"Fucking bastard," he said, that weird smile on his lips again. "That fucking, shit-headed prick." He opened his eyes, shaking his head.

"What do you mean?"

"That was our pet project. We were working on it when we closed down the business." He seemed to be talking to himself, but then looked her in the eye. "So," he said, "did anyone get suckered into believing he could do it?"

"Well, actually, he did produce rain for a short period of time over a grove of trees."

"Sure," he scoffed. "That's not much harder than

making it happen in the laboratory. A nice, controlled environment. Forget it. If I were with him, he'd stand a chance. Knowing Blackwell, he might give you a few bolts of lightning, but he'll never be able to make it rain." He raised his hand toward her suddenly, and she took a step away from him. "See this hand?" he asked. "A bomb did this. It was supposed to be a precision device. That was my first lesson in Blackwell's need to be checked and double-checked. Once you've had a lesson like this"—he stabbed the air with his stubby knuckles—"you don't forget it. Rob can't do shit without me. He never could. He has no mind for details. All ideas. Ideas pop into his head as many times a day as you blink your eyes, but his work sucks."

Between her anxiety and the thick air and the smell of the tuna fish, Carmen could barely breathe. She forced herself to concentrate on keeping this man talking, feeding his narcissism. "You mean, Rob was the idea man and you were the one to put the idea into reality?" she asked.

"You could say that." He seemed to like the description. "Don't get me wrong. I had some ideas of my own, and he had the latent ability to give an idea life, but he lacked the discipline. He never wanted to put time into working out the details."

"Is that why you quit your partnership with him?"

Kent narrowed his dark eyes at her. "Did he tell you that? That *I* quit?"

"No," she said hurriedly. "I just assumed—"

"Our business was thriving," he said. "We knew how to work together. We'd done it since we were kids. Our reputation was good. People thought we were innovative. Then the bloodsucker—oh excuse me, Leslie to you—gets a job offer in Baltimore, and that's the end of that."

"You mean, Rob left the business to move to Baltimore?"

"Yes, because"—he raised his voice once more to that whiny, mocking pitch, obviously mimicking Jeff—"'Leslie comes first,'" he said. "'She's stuck with me through everything, and now it's her turn.' I finally said, all right, I'll relocate and we can start over down there, but the prick said he didn't want a partner any longer. He thought he could do it alone. Start his own business."

"And did he? In Baltimore?"

"How the hell do I know? I said, screw him, let him see how far he gets without me, and I came out here." A look of pure peace suddenly fell over his face. "This is real science here," he said. "No distractions. Cost of living's zip. I'm not working for anyone except myself. I can work any hours I want to, on any projects I damn well feel like working on. And," he craned his long neck toward her, "I can talk or not talk to whomever I choose. And right now, I'm through talking with you." He shut the door on her so suddenly that she had no chance to try to stop him.

She knocked again. "Mr. Reed? Have you been in touch with Rob since he left New Jersey?" She pressed her ear against the door but could hear nothing, not even the strange metal clanking she'd heard earlier, and after a few quiet minutes, she returned to the car. Maybe Jeff was simply running away from Kent Reed, she thought as she turned the car around on the dirt road. That would be completely understandable.

Back in Virginia, she checked into a hotel near the airport, then called Chris in his cottage at Sugarbush.

"I thought I should pass some information on to you," she said. It was the first time she had offered to share her discoveries about Jeff with him, and she sensed his surprise.

"What about?" he asked.

"Well, a few people I've spoken with have commented on the fact that Jeff was sloppy in his work. Sloppy about attending to details."

There was silence from Chris's end of the phone. "And?" he asked finally.

"And I thought you should know that. Maybe his work needs to be double-checked."

Chris laughed. "And who do you suggest I have double-check it?"

Carmen smiled. He was right. There was no one, with the possible exception of Kent Reed, who would be able to make any sense of what Jeff was doing. "Well," she said, feeling foolish, "I just thought you should know."

"Thanks." He hesitated a moment, and she wondered if he wanted to stay on the phone as much as she wanted him to. "You doing okay, Car?"

She pictured him sitting in his small living room with his windows open, the early evening sounds and smells of Sugarbush filling his cottage. She could see his blue eyes, amused and concerned as he held the phone, and the sudden longing she felt, for home, for *him*, took her by surprise.

"Yes," she said. "I'm doing fine."

39

The rain began on the last Friday in July. It started slowly at first, so slowly that Mia took no notice of the graying sky outside the office, or the few drops of water on the window next to her desk. She was immersed in her work at the typewriter when Chris walked into the room, and it wasn't until his shadow fell across the desk that she looked up at him. He pointed toward the window.

The rain was light, but steady. A faint wash of California sunlight still tinged the air, reflecting off the streaks of rain, making them shine like tinsel.

"My God." She stood up.

"Well, I don't know," Chris said. "Is it God, or is it Jeff?" Mia looked out the rear window to see that it was raining to the south as well. She remembered Jeff's restlessness the night before, his disinterest in making love, his preoccupation with his papers and his calculator. He had left the cottage very early this morning, long before sunrise.

"Jeff," she said. "It's definitely Jeff."

She and Chris stepped outside. The street was dotted with people; the real-estate agents from next door, patients from the dentist's office across the street, customers and waitresses from the Catfish House. They stood with incredulous faces tilted to the sky, holding their arms out at their sides, letting the rain wash over them. There was a lot of laughter, a few shrieks. Two young children chased each other around the mailbox on the corner.

In the distance, in all directions for as far as the buildings and eucalyptus trees would let them see, a line of clear yellow air—sunlight—clung to the horizon. It made Mia shiver. This rain was unnatural; the low gray clouds above them hung only over Valle Rosa.

Chris followed her gaze to the north. "Eerie," he said.

"Hey, Garrett!" One of the beer-bellied Catfish House customers called from across the street. "You did good, man! This is quite a show."

Mia combed the wet hair from her face with her fingers. She tipped her head back, opened her mouth. The rain was warm. She didn't mind it running off her chin, down her neck, beneath her blouse. She tried to laugh like the other people on the street. She tried to ignore the cold sorrow that was working its way into her heart. How much longer would he stay?

Chris touched her back. "Let's go see the magician," he said.

They drove to the warehouse in her car. She skidded once on the rain-slicked road as she turned a corner, and Chris grabbed the dashboard before breaking into a laugh.

"I haven't felt a car skid on wet pavement in years," he said. "What a rush!"

Jeff and Rick were on the warehouse roof. Mia could see them from a block away, but once she pulled close to the building, they were hidden from her view, just as they were hidden from the swarm of reporters and other people clamoring on the street.

"Christ, what a mob," Chris said, unbuckling his seat belt. Rick walked out of the warehouse as Chris and Mia were getting out of the car, and he was immediately surrounded by the crowd. At first, Mia was afraid for him. There were so many people, and everyone was so boisterous. She was relieved to see Rick lifted onto the shoulders of a couple of men, and she watched as he was paraded, laughing, into the street.

"Chris Garrett!" someone called, and the crowd seemed to turn all at once and move toward Chris. Before he could protest, he too was raised high above the throng. He was grinning broadly, his hair hanging straight and wet over his forehead.

Reporters shouted unintelligible questions at both Rick and Chris, while cameras rolled and people cheered. Suddenly, Carmen appeared near the men holding Chris aloft. She carried a green umbrella above her head, and she tipped it back as she reached up to shake Chris's hand. He grabbed her hand, but instead of shaking it, bent low to plant a kiss on her fingers.

Mia smiled, watching them. Then she leaned back against the car and looked up at the roof, but she could see nothing except the edge of one of the satellite-dish-like structures. Around her, the crowd began to chant, the sound soft at first, then growing, building:

Rainmaker, Rainmaker, Rainmaker.

A chill slipped over the skin on Mia's arms. People swarmed around the entrance to the warehouse, their heads raised toward the roof. Some of them carried umbrellas, but most of them let the rain pummel their heads and soak their clothes. They shouted to Jeff to come down, to talk with them, to let them shake his hand. Mia knew he would never come down, not as long as anyone remained on the street to ask him questions or snap his picture.

A few minutes later, as the chanting for Jeff's presence grew more demanding, Chris suddenly materialized at her side. He pressed something into her hand. She looked down at her palm. A key.

"It's to the rear door." He leaned close to her so that only she could hear him. "Move your car around back and get him out of here. Get him as far away as you can."

She drove two blocks in the wrong direction, then doubled back by a side route, nervous that someone might suspect what she was up to and follow her into the alley behind the warehouse. She had already decided where she would take him, someplace where no one would think to look.

There were a few people milling around the back of the warehouse, but they said nothing to her as she let herself in the door. She quickly locked it again behind her and started up the stairs to the roof.

He was studying one of the pieces of equipment from underneath a huge black umbrella, but he turned sharply when she stepped through the trap door onto the roof.

The fear in his face was quickly replaced by a smile as she walked toward him, and he reached out to pull her into a quick, wet hug.

"How'd I do?" he asked.

"I'd say you showed them." She had to raise her voice to be heard above the furious pounding of the rain. It sounded like fireworks exploding on the umbrella. "It's positively exhilarating." From the roof she could see the sunlit horizon in every direction, and she turned in a circle to take it all in. "But spooky."

Jeff looked at the horizon himself. "Right. It even gives me the creeps."

She stepped beneath his umbrella again. "I've come to spirit you away," she said. "You've got to get out of here." She looked at the equipment. "Can you leave? My car's in back. I'll take you up to the mountains for the weekend."

He shook his head. "I can't possibly leave with this going on." He waved an arm through the rain-filled air.

"Jeff, the vultures are not going to leave you alone."

He stared at her for a minute, and she knew he was listening to the chanting of the crowd down on the street. "All right," he said finally. "Give me a few more minutes here."

She watched as he adjusted some of the buttons and dials on the equipment. Then he followed her down into the building, where he wrote a long, long note to Rick. "He can handle this for a couple of days, I guess. I hope."

Only a few people saw him get into her car, and she drove out the back way to avoid the mob in front of the warehouse. They stopped at Sugarbush to change into dry clothes and throw a few things into suitcases. She didn't notice until they'd gotten into the car again that Jeff had his briefcase with him.

Mia frowned at him. "Any chance you can leave that here?" she asked. "Can you try to relax for a couple of days?"

He hesitated for a moment, then carried the briefcase back into his cottage. But they were not even out of Valle Rosa before he had taken a slip of paper from his shirt pocket and scratched a few figures on it with a pencil. She said nothing, and as she turned the car off the main road, toward Idyllwild, he put the paper back in his pocket.

"Stop here," he said when they'd reached the edge of Valle Rosa.

She pulled over to the shoulder of the narrow road. "What's wrong?"

He leaned forward to look up at the sky. "Pull up a little more. Just a few feet. Slowly."

She did as she was told, and sunlight suddenly poured through the windshield, making her duck back, squinting.

"Turn off the ignition," he said, turning in the seat to look behind them. "Whoa." He shook his head with an incredulous smile. "Check this out."

Suddenly, Mia realized why he had made her stop. The front of the car was in sunlight, the rear in rain.

"Even I didn't think it would be quite this abrupt a change between wet and dry," he said. "I'd better work on softening the edges or there'll be too distinct a line between brown and green."

Destruction and rebirth, Mia thought. "Yes," she said.

"You'd better work on that. And I hope it takes you a long time to get it right." She smiled at him to let him know that, at least in part, she was teasing, but he turned away from her to look back at the rain.

It was cooler in the mountains, the air hazy, the sunlight filtered through pines and oaks and more greenery than Mia had seen in a long time. They found a cabin about a mile from the little town of Idyllwild. It was old, more funky than rustic with its patched linoleum floors and rusting white refrigerator.

"At least the bed is good." Jeff sat down on the double bed tucked into the little alcove that served as a bedroom. He bounced a few times, testing the mattress, then held his hand toward her. "Okay, Mia," he said, "relax me."

She pushed his shoulders gently to the mattress and took off her shorts to straddle him in comfort, bending low to kiss him. He smiled, groaning, and seemed to beg for more with his lips and his tongue, but she drew her mouth away, teasing him.

"My rules," she whispered. She would make love to *him* this time. She would make love in such a way that he could never again entertain the thought of leaving her.

He clung to her when it was over, clung so hard that she guessed there would be bruises on her back in the morning. And although she couldn't have cared less, she made herself think about those bruises, about the shape they would take, and their color. She would think about anything to keep herself from crying. No tears. Not now. She wouldn't acknowledge in any way that there were limits on their lovemaking, limits on their time together.

"I love you, Mia," he whispered, when his breathing had quieted down. "I don't want this to end."

"Shh." She pressed her fingertips hard against his lips, and neither of them spoke again. His grip on her loosened as he fell into a deep sleep, and she rolled carefully onto her side, her hand resting on his chest. She envied him his sleep, doubting she would be able to sleep at all. The pillow beneath her head was cool and musty, and she knew that smell would forever be linked in her mind to both hope and fear.

In the morning, they walked into town for breakfast. They had blueberry muffins, which Jeff talked her into eating despite their fat content, and strawberry tea with lemon, and they talked about the fountain and the cat and where they might eat dinner that night. Mia relished every word, every simple, lazy, forgettable sentence. Toward the end of the meal, though, Jeff began to look preoccupied again.

"I should call Rick," he said, reaching into his pants pocket for some change and eying the pay phone in the back corner of the little restaurant. "He should be watching for any erosion."

Although she wanted to chastise him for worrying, she said nothing. She watched as he got up and walked toward the phone, knowing she had no right to stop him. His life was tied up in that equipment. That project. She should be glad she'd managed to get him away from it at all.

They walked most of the day, hiking on slender trails

cut through the woods. Jeff taught her how to use her
watch as a compass and how to determine direction by
studying ant hills, which he claimed were always built on
the south side of trees and rocks.

Her legs ached by the time they returned to the cabin.
"I need a long soak in the tub," she said, leaning against
the wall to stretch the muscles in her calves.

Jeff picked up his comb from the dresser and ran it
through his hair, studying his reflection in the mirror.
"Would you mind some company?" he asked.

She wrinkled her nose at the thought of facing him
across a tub of water in the stark light of the bathroom.

He met her eyes in the mirror. "We can leave the light
off," he said, reading her mind.

The tub in the cabin was old but deep, with a broad
yellow rust stain in the enamel near the drain. They filled
it with warm water, turned out the light and undressed in
the semi-darkness of the small, steamy bathroom. Mia
settled into the tub, her back against Jeff's chest, the water
nearly to her chin. She closed her eyes and sighed.

"I heard the satisfaction in that sigh," Jeff said.

"Mmm."

He bent his head to kiss her shoulder. They sat that
way for a few minutes, Mia feeling the tension melting
from her legs.

"I was hoping you'd bring the chemise I gave you,"
Jeff said. "Don't you like it? You never wear it."

She drew in a breath. She had hoped the subject of the
chemise would never come up. "It's beautiful," she said,

"but I'd feel funny in it now. I'll wear it after I have the reconstruction."

He was quiet a moment. She felt his chin against the top of her head; his thumb gently traced the skin where her left breast had been. "But then I'll never get to see you in it," he said.

Her tears were too quick for her to stop. She brushed his hand away. "You haven't talked about leaving since the first night we made love," she said. "I was hoping—"

"Mia." He wrapped both arms around her and held her tightly against him. "You know I can't stay."

"No!" She pulled away from him, splashing water onto the floor. "I don't know that. You don't tell me anything! *Carmen* knows more about you than I do." She twisted around to look at him, and even in the darkness she could see the deep crease between his eyebrows. "If you have to leave, at least tell me why. Don't I have the right to know? Or will I simply wake up one morning and you'll be gone. I'll never see you again, and I'll never even understand the reason you left me." She stood up and started to climb out of the tub, feeling awkward. Inelegant. She was glad the light was off.

"Careful." He tried to grab her hand, but she snapped it away from him and stepped, dripping, onto the floor. She groped in the darkness for a towel, wrapped it around herself, and walked into the living room.

The old wing chair by the window had the same musty, damp smell as her pillow. She sat down in it and let the scent surround her. It was dark in the room, even darker outside. Stars glittered from behind the trees, but they were small and cold-looking and blurred by her tears.

She heard him get out of the tub. In a moment he was in the living room, a towel secured around his waist. He picked up a hassock from the corner of the room and dropped it directly in front of her. When he sat down, he rested his damp hands on her bare knees, squeezed them gently.

"Yes, you have the right to know," he said softly. "You have the right to know everything about me, and Mia, I'm longing to tell you. I want to tell you about my childhood, and the crazy things I did when I was growing up and what my family was like—all those things that are so much fun to tell someone you're falling in love with. And I want you to know why I'm in Valle Rosa, and why I'll have to leave. You can't know how badly . . . God, it would be such a relief to tell you everything." He closed his eyes briefly, drawing in a breath, then locked his gaze with hers. "As unfair as it is that I can't tell you about myself, Mia, it would be far more unfair to you if I did."

She shook her head, still holding onto the anger. "Don't you know I would never tell anyone?"

"Of course I do, but someday you might be in a position of *having* to tell what you know. You'd have no choice. I don't want you in that predicament, for either of our sakes."

She leaned forward and put her hands on his shoulders. "Then take me with you when you leave," she said. "I'll run, too. I don't care."

He pulled her hands from his shoulders and held

them close to his lips. "I've learned a lot about myself over the last month or so," he said. "I guess I thought I could run forever, but I'm not cut out for it. I'm not a loner. I need other people too much. This last week . . ." He grimaced. "A few times lately I've let myself imagine staying in Valle Rosa, staying with you, making a new life for myself there. But when those news vans rolled up outside the warehouse today, with Carmen Perez as the ringleader, I knew I had to get back to reality. I can't stay in Valle Rosa. Yet I don't know how much longer I'll be able to tolerate running. One way or the other, I'm going to lose you. Now or later." He stroked his thumbs over the back of her hands. "You have a brilliant career ahead of you, Mia. But if you had no fixed address, no place to work, no way to let people know where you were— or even *who* you were—you'd come to resent me. And rightly so."

She felt hope slip away from her as if it were something tangible, something she had hung onto but never really possessed.

"When will you go?" She spoke very softly.

"I'll stay as long as I possibly can."

"Will you think of me at all after you leave?"

He looked stunned. "I love you, Mia. I'm never going to forget you. Wherever I am, I'll look at the stars at night and think, 'These are the same stars Mia's seeing in Valle Rosa.'"

"Except that Valle Rosa will be under a cover of rain clouds."

He laughed. "Yes. I forgot about that."

She didn't smile. "Jeff?" she asked. "Are you married? Can you tell me that much?"

His eyes registered another flash of surprise. Then he closed them, shaking his head. "No, Mia. I'm not married. I was . . . but not anymore."

She leaned forward then to kiss him. His hands slipped beneath her towel, tugging it away from her body. He parted her legs and lowered his head to her, and the last thing she saw before losing herself to him was the cool white blur of the stars.

40.

Carmen wasn't nervous, and that both surprised and pleased her. She sat in Dennis Ketchum's outer office, waiting to be called into the sacred inner chamber, not even bothering to rehearse what she would say when he made the offer. She would try not to jump at it—not right away. She would hold out for a little more money than he offered initially. When he'd called her last night to ask her to come in this morning, his voice had been lively and promising, and she'd thought to herself: *At last*. She was going to get *Sunrise* back.

Through the window, she could see the rain clouds far in the distance, hovering over Valle Rosa. This was the third day of rain. She had announced Jeff's plan on the news the night before: three days of rain, two of sun, repeating the pattern for as long as it took to fill the reservoir and bring life back to Valle Rosa. The sun was necessary, he told her, to keep spirits alive. Only a few people seemed disturbed by the unnaturalness of it all. Most were planning picnics and celebrations for the two days of sun, reveling in the predictability of the weather.

Dennis suddenly opened the door to his office. "Carmen?" He smiled. "Come in."

She followed him into the poshly decorated office and took the seat he offered next to his broad cherry desk.

"Well," he began, "every time I look in the direction of those rain clouds over Valle Rosa, I think of you. Our own Carmen Perez. I have to admit, I didn't think Cabrio was for real. I thought you were chasing a fantasy, but I didn't care, since everyone else in San Diego seemed delighted to tune in to *News Nine* and join you in the delusion. But this is something, Carmen." He looked out the window toward Valle Rosa, shaking his head. "This is really something."

It had been a long time since she'd heard such genuine words of praise from him. "There were moments when I had my own doubts." She sat back in the chair, crossing her right leg over her left. "What was it you wanted to see me about?"

He pulled a sheet of paper from the pile on his desk and rested it on the blotter in front of him. "Well, we don't have the numbers worked out yet, but I wanted to let you know that you're in for a big raise." He looked at her from under his bushy eyebrows. "A *very* big raise."

She tried to mask her confusion. Perhaps she was misunderstanding him or he was teasing her, prolonging her agony. "And what exactly will I be doing to merit this big raise?" She smiled, taking the bait she assumed he was offering.

"The *North County Report*," he said. "Not only the light stuff you've been doing, but the whole thing. All of it."

He was serious. She hid her shock, but an edgy tension ran through her body. "Dennis," she said, "I really think you should consider putting me back on *Sunrise*."

"On *Sunrise*?" He looked so astonished that she knew he hadn't given the idea even casual consideration.

"Well, yes." She attempted to smile. She wouldn't let him know how she was counting on it. "Did you read the article in the *Union* the other day?"

"Yes," he said slowly, frowning, "but . . ."

She leaned forward, resting one arm on his desk. "Oh, come on, Dennis." She spoke bravely, forcefully, as though they were equals. At one time, she would have spoken to him that way with absolutely no hint of the trepidation she felt now. "I want my show back. The *viewers* want me back. I created *Sunrise*."

"And you did an excell—"

"I have ideas for it. I—"

"Look, Carmen." He snapped a cigarette out of the pack on his desk and lit it, taking a long drag. "You did create *Sunrise*. You created the style and sass and bite that made it the top-rated morning show around. No one can ever take that away from you." He leaned forward, eyes narrowed. "But you're not that hard-driving woman anymore. I only have to look at you to see that you've lost your taste for the jugular. You're doing a great job with this Cabrio stuff, but it's work now—isn't it?—where raking people over the coals used to be your cup of tea."

"*No*, and—"

"And Craig told me you didn't want to cover the bus crash last week."

How did Craig know that? She thought she had concealed her panic about that assignment very well. "Jeff Cabrio was moving the equipment up to the—"

"The roof, yes. I know." He leaned back with a sigh, eying her skeptically, and she lowered her eyes. He saw through her. He saw her own doubts. When he spoke again, his voice was soft, and she tried to ignore the patronizing tone. "So, go ahead," he said, "tell me your ideas for *Sunrise*."

She cleared her throat and looked directly at him in an attempt to salvage some of her trumped-up bravado. "I would start off with a show no one would miss. I'd put on the people I've been interviewing about Jeff Cabrio. People from his past. People who know all the secrets he's so intent on keeping to himself."

Dennis's chair squeaked as he shifted his weight. He didn't look disinterested. "Go on."

"Dennis, Cabrio is hiding something. I still don't know what it is, but I'm not going to stop until I've uncovered it." She was surprised by how strong her voice sounded, as though she had no qualms whatsoever about continuing her intrusion into Jeff's personal life. This drive to reveal him at all costs sickened her, but if there was another tune she could sing, she didn't know it. The only certainty in her life right now was that she couldn't rebuild her career on the slim pickings of *North County Report*. Once Jeff's story had been milked dry, once the fires were out, she'd be reduced to covering Little League games and the avocado harvest.

"You still have tenacity, Carmen, I'll say that much for

you." Dennis stood up. "Listen. *Sunrise* is not up for grabs at the moment, but I will definitely think about something bigger for you with *News Nine*. That's all I can promise right now, all right? You keep up the good work. You show me your mettle, Carmen. I won't let it go unrewarded."

41.

Once again, Carmen was on a flight to the East Coast, this time to Philadelphia. Dennis Ketchum didn't balk over giving her a couple of days off. This would be her big interview, she'd told him. This one had to be done in person.

She changed to a smaller plane in Philadelphia and arrived in Trenton at three. After checking into a hotel, she immediately took a cab to the New Jersey State Prison, a chill-inducing collection of aging brick buildings and barbed wire.

It took her forty-five minutes to get through the red tape in the main office even though they were expecting her, and finally she was directed to a small brick building at the end of a long walkway.

There was surprisingly little security in the small building. She was told she could meet with Mr. Watts in the lounge, and she sat down on one of the blue vinyl sofas to wait for him. A few women walked past the open door, all of them in nurses' uniforms, and she realized this particular building must be the infirmary or whatever it was called in a place like this.

After a short while, a nurse appeared in the doorway with a man at her side. Carmen stood up. Jefferson Watts wasn't at all what she'd expected. The image of the strong, robust black man she'd held in her mind all these weeks suddenly faded. Jefferson Watts was old. Old, and very ill. At his side was an oxygen tank on wheels.

"I'm all right." He spoke to the nurse in a low, raspy voice. The woman nodded at Carmen and walked off down the hall.

Carmen approached him, reaching out to shake his hand.

"Mr. Watts?" she said. His hand was dry and cool, and there was no strength at all in his handshake.

"That's me." He gave a single nod of his graying head. "Take a seat, miss. Don't need to stand for an old man." He was dressed in a blue shirt and blue pants, and he walked into the room slowly, pushing the oxygen tank in front of him. A tube ran from the tank to his nose. He wheezed slightly as he sat down on a green vinyl chair. Carmen took her seat once again on the sofa.

Jefferson Watts pointed to the oxygen. "Emphysema," he said.

Carmen hadn't expected the rush of sympathy she felt. The old man's silver hair was cut close to his scalp, and he sported a neatly trimmed gray beard. He must have been very handsome at one time. There was still dignity in his presence.

"So," he said, "you with the police?"

"No, I'm not." She pulled her identification card from her purse and walked over to his chair to show it to him.

He took the card from her and studied it for a moment before handing it back to her with a nod.

"I work for a television station out West," she said. "One of your son Rob's inventions has been very valuable to a town there, so I'm talking to people who know him in order to put together a news story on him."

She looked questioningly at the old man. There was suspicion in his eyes. He wasn't stupid, not so old and senile that he could be easily taken in.

"Yes," he said, "Rob was always inventing somethin', and just about everything he made worked—or if it didn't he stuck with it till it did. So I believe you when you say he's come up with something valuable." He cocked his head to one side. "But I don't believe he sent you here to talk to me."

"No, he didn't," Carmen admitted. "I've come on my own."

He sighed, a sound like the creaking of an old door. "I never knew if I was hearing the truth or not from Robbie since I been here," he said, "and that's a hell of a long time. I don't mean he'd lie wanting to deceive me, only that he'd want to keep me from worrying, you understand?" He rubbed his bearded chin with one shaky, gnarled hand. "He moved, and I don't know where to get hold of him—if you know, don't tell me, though," he added hurriedly. "He obviously has some reason for wantin' it that way. Just tell me, does he need help? There somethin' I can do?"

She studied this sick, dapper old man, and felt like crying. When she spoke, her voice was thick. "I'm not sure he needs help, but even if he did, I doubt there's anything you could do from here."

"But is his health good? His family—they all right?"

Carmen hesitated. She simply didn't know what she could tell him, how *much* she could tell him, without causing him distress. "I'm sorry, I don't know them," she said. "I come from a small town in southern California, and Rob is there alone."

"California! Good for him. But Leslie's not with him?"

"No."

Jefferson shook his head slowly, letting out a wheezing sigh. "Like I thought, somethin's wrong. I haven't heard from him since before Christmas. That got me worried. Him and his wife always come up here on Christmas and bring the little girls with them. The cutest things. I still haven't seen the baby, not in person anyhow. I got a picture, though."

He stood up slowly and fumbled in the pocket of his blue pants. He pulled out a small, laminated photograph, and his hand shook so hard as he gave the picture to Carmen that she was tempted to take his hand in hers to still the tremor, to warm his cool fingers.

The photograph was a studio portrait of a man, a woman, and three children. She wasn't certain she would have recognized Jeff. His hair was dark blond, his face fuller. He wore a smile she had never seen before. Unguarded. Unworried. Trusting of the world. Leslie Blackwell's eyes were blue and enormous, almost round, bubbling with laughter and energy. The girls sat one on each of Jeff's knees, and they had their mother's eyes. The baby nestling in Leslie's arms was bald and sleepy-eyed and looked barely old enough to have come home from the hospital.

"They named him after me, you know," Jefferson pointed one finger in the direction of the photograph.

"No," she said, "I didn't know that. It's a very beautiful family." She handed the picture back to him, and he sat down again.

"They come at Christmas and bring me one of them dried fruit trays. You know the kind?"

"I think so."

"With the dates and apricots and such? I could go for one of them dates right now." He shifted a little in his chair, wincing. "Well, anyhow, I got a letter from Rob way back in November and he said he couldn't visit for a while. He didn't say why, but I know Robbie, and I know he's got some good reason. Still, I'm old and not in the best shape I ever been." He chuckled, and the sound turned into a cough. When he'd recovered, he added, "I don't like to think about not gettin' to see him before I check-out."

"I hope you get to see him again very soon." Carmen's eyes stung and she quickly shifted her attention to the oxygen tank, studying the long tubes connected to the apparatus on the metal top. When she was certain she was past the danger of crying, she looked at him again. "So," she said, "you haven't heard from him at all since November?"

"Well, I think I actually did. I'm ninety-nine percent

sure it was him, because it come on my birthday a coupla weeks ago."

"What did?"

"The tape. One of those little cassette things, you know?"

"What was on it?"

Jefferson Watts laughed. "Howling."

"What?"

"Animals howling. There was a note with it, but it was done on a typewriter, so I couldn't tell by the handwriting if it was Robbie or not. It said, 'Listen, and think of freedom.'"

Carmen frowned, perplexed. "Just howling? He doesn't say anything on the tape?"

"No, and I listened the whole way through to the end, though most of it was dead air. I was hoping to hear some of his voice." He looked down at the oxygen tank, ran a trembling finger over the top of it. "Haven't heard his voice in a while."

"I'm sorry, Mr. Watts." She wanted to complain to someone about the injustice of this man's continued incarceration. She wanted to pack him up and take him with her, take him back to Jeff.

"It's dogs. Or wolves, I guess," he said.

"Coyotes, probably. There are coyotes near where he's living."

"Ah! So he's out in the wilderness. That's probably why he couldn't take the little ones with him. Too dangerous, right?"

She forced a smile. "That's probably it."

"And the job he's doing is one of them hush-hush ones, I suppose." Jefferson nodded. He seemed pleased to have developed a theory for his son's silence and separation from his family. Suddenly, though, his eyes clouded over. "Kent ain't working with him, is he?"

"No, I don't think they've worked together for a couple of years."

The old man shook his head. "That's good. Kent and Robbie did a bunch of inventions together, but they didn't always see eye to eye on things. Kent used to give him no end of grief when Robbie wanted to spend time with his family instead of working. Robbie has more sense than Kent when it comes to knowing when to work and when to play. I think I taught him that."

Carmen smiled at the pride in his voice. "Tell me what it was like being his father."

The vinyl chair creaked as Jefferson leaned back into it. A pensive look came over his features, and he tilted his head to one side. "It was a joy, for the most part," he said. "Robbie was a good boy, but he had it rough coming up. I met Beth when she was just twenty-two and Robbie was seven. I was considerably older. Know where I met her?"

Carmen shook her head.

"Robbie don't know this, and I'd appreciate it if you don't tell him." He lifted a questioning eyebrow.

"I won't."

"Well, she was huntin' through the garbage back of an A & P, looking for food. I was parked a ways away, waiting for a connection—I was into the drug trade in those days—and she didn't know I was there. She was a beautiful girl, and my heart broke, watching her. My connection come, we did the deal and then I went up to her and gave her the profit I just made. She started to cry and told me she and her boy had no place to stay that night. She got kicked out of her boyfriend's, and she had a bruise on her leg to prove it. I took her home with me, and that's where she stayed."

He stared off into space for a moment and then suddenly started to cough. He couldn't seem to catch his breath, and Carmen jumped to her feet. She knelt next to him, her hand on his arm.

"Are you all right?" she asked. "Shall I call the nurse?"

He managed to shake his head, and in another moment the coughing stopped. His eyes were watering, though, and she handed him a tissue from her purse, her own hands shaking.

"Would you like to stop talking for awhile?" she asked.

"No, missy, this happens all the time. Listen, though. You don't tell Robbie how bad off I am, understand? Ain't no need to worry him." He cleared his throat once again. "Now you sit back down, and I'll go on."

She took her seat.

"My apartment was more than they were used to," he continued. "It was clean, for starters. Nice furniture. I gave them each a bedroom. Don't get me wrong, now"— again, he lifted a grizzled brow in Carmen's direction— "I wanted the girl, and she expected to have to sleep with me as payment. But I wanted her to sleep with me 'cause that's what she wanted. And after a while, that's what happened."

His expression changed, and a faraway look came into his eyes, as though he was remembering their lovemaking. Nothing lecherous—just a tenderness in his smile. He had truly loved Beth Cabrio.

He brought his attention back to the present. "The boy was so smart he scared me—I had a seven-year-old in my house who was ten times smarter'n me, and that can shake you up a bit." He laughed, and Carmen steeled herself for a fresh bout of coughing, which didn't occur. "He was doing shit work in school, though. We changed him over to the school in my neighborhood, and he started doing better right away. He had a glow on him when he come home in the afternoon."

Carmen was quiet as Jefferson appeared to lose himself in thought once again. When he next spoke, it was in a quiet, confidential tone.

"I never did drugs myself," he said. "I didn't even drink, and if I did, I woulda stopped 'cause of the boy. A few months after they moved in, I stopped dealing too, even though I sure coulda used the money with a family to support. I started working on people's cars, instead. I wanted Robbie to see me make a honest living." He grunted softly, waving a hand to take in the small, ugly room and what lay beyond. "But my past caught up with me. A coupla innocent people died 'cause of me, and so here I am."

Carmen swallowed. "I think Rob appreciated all you did for him," she said. "It seems as though the two of you were very close."

The old man smiled and looked toward the small

window at the far end of the room. "The first time he called me 'Dad,' I felt like some sorta hero, you know what I mean? He did it sorta shy-like to see how I'd take it, and when I acted like I expected it, he got this big smile on his face. I'd had other kids, a few of 'em scattered around, but none of 'em ever meant as much to me as Robbie. None ever needed me the way that boy did."

Jefferson Watts licked his papery lips. He no longer seemed aware of Carmen's presence. He leaned back in his chair and took a few labored breaths before speaking one more time.

"Robbie was the one thing I did right in my life."

42.

The following morning, Carmen stopped in a gourmet shop near her hotel and had them put together a tray of dried fruit, heavy on the dates and apricots. She wrote a note thanking Jefferson Watts for talking with her and arranged to have it and the fruit delivered to the prison.

She'd had a dream about the old man the night before. She'd dreamt that she and Chris had somehow freed him, not in any wild escape, but through legal channels, which seemed so plausible in her sleep that she was overwhelmed with disappointment when she woke up to realize they were only the optimistic work of her dreams.

On the plane from Philadelphia to San Diego, she sat next to an elderly San Diego woman who recognized her and who spent five hours telling her how pleased she was to see her back on the air and "prettier than ever." Perhaps, she thought with some amusement, Terrell Gates was right. Perhaps she *was* the darling of the geriatric set. The intrusion, at first flattering, quickly became an annoyance. She wanted time to think. How would she present her new information about Jeff on the news tonight? She had dug too deeply this time. Now that Jeff had made good on his promise to deliver rain, unearthing his secrets felt like even more of a betrayal. Whatever he was hiding no longer seemed important. Yet she knew she would have to dig even deeper.

It was late afternoon and the skies were clear when she arrived at the airport in San Diego. She retrieved her car from the long-term parking lot and drove toward Mira Mesa and the *News Nine* studio. In the distance, the dark rain clouds hung over Valle Rosa.

"I want it talky," she told Dennis before her broadcast that evening. "Folksy." So, they put her in the armchair, with the backdrop of one of Valle Rosa's avocado groves on the wall behind her.

There was an undercurrent of positive energy in the station. She'd felt it the moment she walked in that afternoon. They were whispering about her. Something was in the wind, something good, but no one looked her directly in the eye. No one was about to tell her what they had in store for her. She could wait though. She could be patient.

Watching the stage manager for her cue, she moved her script to the floor beneath her chair. It wouldn't be necessary tonight. She wouldn't be using names, and she would avoid dates and places, anything that might make Jefferson Watts—and his son—identifiable.

The red light flashed on the camera, and she looked into the lens. "I had the opportunity yesterday to meet with the man who raised Jeff Cabrio from the time he was seven years old until he was sixteen," she began, "and I found him to be a man of dignity and intelligence. Jeff and his young mother were homeless and penniless at the time this man found them and took them in. He provided not only financial support but love and stability as well, despite the fact that he was heavily involved in illegal activities at the time. He put aside his life of crime to become a father to the boy who had never had a father, and under his parenting, Jeff began to excel in school. But his father's past eventually caught up with him, and he was arrested on charges stemming from an incident years earlier. He is currently serving two back-to-back fifty-year prison sentences and is in failing health."

Dennis was grinning at her by the time she finished her report.

"You're leading up to something, aren't you?" he asked, walking with her toward the exit of the building.

She shrugged as though she knew the answer but planned to keep it to herself a while longer.

"What is it?" Dennis pressed her. "What's the old man in the slammer for? Organized crime? Murder? Rape? Drugs? And what's Cabrio's game? He's dealing, right? Probably the ringleader of a—"

"You know everything I know," Carmen interrupted him, loving her sudden power. If only she hadn't had to stoop so low to get it.

It was dark as she drove along the narrow road above the canyon on her way to Sugarbush after leaving *News Nine*. An occasional flash of lightning split the sky, and she remembered Kent Reed telling her that Jeff might give Valle Rosa a few bolts of lightning, but no rain.

"Well, Mr. Reed," she said out loud, turning up the speed on her windshield wipers, "you were wrong."

She was tired, but satisfied. As she drove past the reservoir, she tried to see how much it had filled in the last couple of days. But in the darkness it was nothing more than a black gaping hole in the earth, and she quickly returned her eyes to the road.

Pulling into the driveway at Sugarbush, she noticed lights burning in the second story of the adobe—in the bedroom and bathroom. Chris was there, working on the plumbing. Her first reaction was anger—he knew she'd be getting home around this time. He was supposed to be out of the house. But the anger faded as quickly as it had come. In its place, she felt a sense of comfort. She remembered the feeling from long ago, the small, simple joy at the knowledge that he was home, that in a few minutes she could talk to him.

Despite the occasional flashes of lightning, the rain wasn't heavy, and she didn't bother with her umbrella as she got out of the car. She took her suitcase from the trunk and walked through the darkness toward the adobe, so lost in her thoughts that she didn't see Jeff until he spoke.

"You stepped way out of bounds, Perez." He was standing in the shadow of the adobe, leaning against the wall, arms folded across his chest.

Carmen gasped and stopped walking, drawing her suitcase close to her side. There was something threatening in Jeff's stance.

"I don't know what you mean," she said, moving

toward the house again, but the muscles in her legs had turned rubbery, and her fingers shook as she reached for the door to the kitchen.

"Are you satisfied yet?" he asked. "Have they started kissing your feet at work?"

Chris had left the door unlocked. She stepped into the kitchen and tried to pull the door closed quickly behind her, but Jeff caught the knob in his hand and pushed his way past her into the room.

Carmen let go of her suitcase and drew back against the counter. "Chris?" she called. She wanted to turn on the overhead light, but the switch was on the wall behind Jeff. Still, the flashes of lightning provided enough illumination for her to see the fury in his face.

"Jefferson's an old man," he said. "They'll pump him for information about me, and they won't care if they kill him in the process."

"I didn't identify him," she said. "I was careful. I didn't even say where—"

He pounded a fist on the counter next to her and she jumped. She closed her eyes, wondering if she was in danger, if she should call once again for Chris.

"Just how stupid do you think they are?" Jeff asked. "Look what you've managed to find out. How long do you think it will take them to piece together the clues you've given them?"

She opened her eyes again. He loomed above her, tall and forbidding. The streaks of rain on the window were reflected in his cheeks and forehead, like gray, shifting scars. She forced herself to look at him squarely. "Who's 'they,' Jeff? The police? The Drug Enforcement Agency? The FBI? Who exactly are you running from?"

He shook his head, an incredulous look on his face. "You shove your way in wherever you want, don't you? Well, this time you went one goddamned step too far." He paced away from her, then back again. "You got me where I live. Is that what you want? How would you have liked it if, when you slit your wrists, some reporter stuck a microphone in your face and asked you how you were feeling?" He grabbed a juice glass from the counter and thrust it in front of her face. She tried to turn her head away, but he followed her with the glass. "How did you feel about your husband sleeping with a tramp and giving you VD, Ms. Perez?"

Carmen sucked in her breath. "Stop it!" She tried to push his hand away, but the imaginary microphone remained in front of her lips. The strength in his arm scared her.

"How does it feel to know your son lives in an institution, that no matter how old he gets, he'll never be more than an infant in any way that matters?"

Carmen covered her ears. She felt the rim of the juice glass against her chin and struggled once more in vain to brush it away.

"What's it like to turn your back on your own kid?" Jeff asked. "Your own little—"

"That's enough, Jeff." Chris appeared in the doorway between the kitchen and the hall, and Jeff was immediately silent. He stared at Chris for an instant, then slowly lowered the juice glass to his side.

Carmen dropped into one of the kitchen chairs, her hands shaking as she wiped the tears from her cheeks. She looked gratefully at Chris. He walked over to where she sat and put his hands on her shoulders. Still, Jeff wasn't quite finished.

Looking at Carmen, he spoke quietly this time, although the tremor in his voice still conveyed his rage. "You have one thing on your mind," he said. "And that's Carmen Perez. You don't care what happens to Chris or your son or anyone else who might be in the way of your rise to the top of the dung heap."

"That's not fair," she managed to whisper.

Jeff closed his eyes, and in the dim light she saw him trying to collect himself, control himself. For the first time since she'd known him, he looked weak. Defeated. She had crossed over into territory he'd felt was his, territory he could no longer protect. She felt thoroughly deserving of his wrath. Every ugly word he'd said was true. She had tried to escape from that truth by any means possible. She'd tried killing herself, drugging herself, withdrawing from the world, avoiding Chris, losing herself in her work. But suddenly it was all as unavoidable as his imaginary microphone in front of her face had been.

The pain welled up inside her, catching in her throat. Chris squeezed her shoulders. There was a strength in his touch she hadn't felt in years.

With a sigh, Jeff ran a hand through his dyed, dark hair. "You said Jefferson was sick." He looked down at her, the anger gone now from his features. "Is it the emphysema?"

"Yes," she said, her voice thick with tears. "He seems quite frail. He misses you. He misses his grandchildren. He . . . he loves all of you very much."

Jeff raised his hand to his eyes. "It's better he doesn't see me again. Better he doesn't know . . ." He looked at Carmen. "Are they taking decent care of him?"

"I think so. Yes."

Jeff walked toward the door, stopping only to touch Chris's arm. "Sorry," he said, and Carmen knew as he stepped out into the rain that the apology was for Chris and not for her.

As the door closed behind Jeff, Chris pulled Carmen to her feet and into his arms. She rested her head on his shoulder.

"Are you all right?" he asked.

"How could you have told him the truth about Dustin?"

"He's a friend, Carmen. He's the closest friend I've had in a long time."

A fresh wave of pain washed over her. "You used to think of me as your friend," she said.

"Yes."

She hesitated before speaking again. "When I was driving up to Sugarbush and saw the lights on, I realized you were here. I was annoyed at first, but then I felt happy. I wanted to see you."

He said nothing, but held her closer, tighter.

"Chris? Would you show me the pictures of him?"

"Of Dustin?"

"Yes."

For a moment he said nothing, and she buried her head more snugly into the crook of his neck.

"Maybe now isn't the best time," he said. "You're already upset. You're—"

"Now." She pulled back, lifting her face to look into the pale, shining eyes of the man who had never stopped being her friend. "I want to see them now."

Mia sat on the chair in front of the sculpture. Above her head, the rain beat its steady—*unnaturally* steady—rhythm, and outside her windows Sugarbush slept in darkness. If she leaned back far enough, though, she could see the lights on in the adobe. Jeff was there. She had seen him drive in an hour ago, but he hadn't come to his cottage—or to hers. Certainly he'd seen Carmen on the news tonight. Mia had felt the intrusion into his life as deeply as if it had been into her own. She knew him very well. If he cut his arm, she would feel the pain.

She had listened to Carmen's short, passionate recitation of her meeting with the old man in prison. This was the father Jeff hadn't felt able to talk to her about. This was the childhood he couldn't share with her. And his father was ill. Had Jeff known that?

She picked up the modeling knife she was using on the sculpture. She was working on the fine details now: the folds of Jeff's shirt; the veins in the backs of his hands; the delicate disks of his fingernails. And, of course, the details of his face. She had finally settled on an expression for him—or rather, it had settled on her. The day before, she had looked at the piece and there it was—

an overriding sense of fear, tempered by resignation. She saw it in the lined brow, the widened eyes, the tight jaw. What will come, will come, he seemed to be thinking. He would fight it, yes, but with a certain acceptance of his limitations, his humanness. He seemed God-like to the citizens of Valle Rosa. Yet in the final analysis, he was only a man, and he looked like nothing more than that in the sculpture.

The sound of his screen door slamming shut was faint behind the patter of the rain, but she had grown sensitive to any sound from his cottage. She covered the clay and left her own cottage, stopping only to pick up the umbrella from its place on the porch. She knocked on his door twice before he called to her to come in.

He was in the bedroom and he was packing. His suitcase was spread open on the bed, most of his clothes already in it, a few pieces still scattered in the open dresser drawers. Mia felt her heart stop, and she pulled in a breath to start it again.

"*No,*" she wailed.

He raised his eyes to hers. In his hand was the black ring box. "She's too close, Mia." He slipped the box deep into a back corner of the suitcase.

"Not tonight," she said. "Please, Jeff, not yet."

"I'm not leaving tonight." He folded a pair of jeans and placed them on top of a stack of T-shirts in the suitcase. "But I have to be ready. I need to have everything in order, because when I go, I'll have to go quickly. All right?" He was asking not for her approval but her understanding.

She folded her arms tightly across her chest. "All right." She felt herself pouting, child-like. "But after you're done packing, will you come over to my cottage? Will you spend the night there?"

He shook his head. "I won't be able to sit still tonight. I need to see Rick. I need to be absolutely certain he knows how to run the equipment."

"I'll go with you."

He paused in the middle of folding a shirt and looked at her. "I'll probably be up all night."

"I don't care."

He zipped the suitcase closed. "Okay, then," he said. "Let's go."

They spoke little on the drive to the house Rick shared with two other men and one of their girlfriends. It was the first time Mia had seen the small, stucco house, and as a bolt of lightning brightened the sky, she saw the array of surfboards littering the tiny front yard.

"His window's on the side," Jeff said as they got out of the car.

She followed him around the side of the house, jumping when something—Eureka, most likely—swept past her legs in the darkness. They skirted a gnarled old scrub oak, and the wet leaves brushed her cheek. Jeff walked to the open, screenless third window and rapped on the pane. His easy familiarity with the process told Mia this wasn't the first time he had awakened his young colleague in the middle of the night.

A moment later, a light flicked on in the room and

Rick appeared at the window. He pulled back the flimsy curtain, and Mia got a whiff of stale marijuana.

Rick was bare-chested, bleary-eyed. "Oh, no, dude," he said. "You're not leaving now, are you?"

"Not tonight, but soon," Jeff said. "We need to go to the warehouse. It's time for your final exam."

Rick groaned, but he was smiling. "Right. Be with you in a minute."

Shortly, they were headed to the warehouse, Rick and Jeff in the front of the car, Mia stretched out on the back seat, listening to them conversing softly above the swish of the windshield wipers.

"I saw the dragon lady mouthing off about your old man tonight," Rick said. "Quite a story. Did you know about his past when you were growing up?"

Mia reached up to touch Jeff's shoulder, and he took his hand from the steering wheel to briefly squeeze her fingers. She wasn't surprised when he completely ignored Rick's question.

"What if one of the trans-hydrators fails?" Jeff asked.

"Shift to the other two and increase the power and—"

"Increase the power to what?"

"Five hundred, at least. Keep an eye on the display. Maybe it would need a bit more, but I'd take it slow. Right?" He seemed unsure of his answer, but Jeff nodded.

"You know where the forms are to reorder parts?"

"In the black file."

The conversation continued, the questions and answers, and Mia dozed a little. When they reached the warehouse, Jeff turned to rest his hand on her arm.

"Why don't you stay here and sleep?" he asked.

She shook her head and sat up. "I'm coming in."

Inside the warehouse, Jeff spoke in Spanish to the two guards, telling them they could go home for the night. Then he and Mia and Rick climbed the stairs to the roof.

They had erected a sort of tent on the roof since the last time Mia had been up there. An enormous black tarpaulin was stretched above the equipment, attached in a few places to heavy, free-standing metal poles, and dotted with battery-operated lanterns. Mia curled up in a dry, dark spot between a couple of wooden crates, and Jeff took off his windbreaker for her to use as a pillow. She watched through half-closed eyes as they examined some of the machinery. The gentle slapping of the rain on the tarpaulin and the shafts of light slicing through the darkness gave her an eerie, dreamlike feeling.

She'd expected Jeff to spend the night engrossed in the equipment. She'd expected to be ignored and was resigned to that. But after an hour or so, he sat down on the roof next to her in her dark little burrow and held her hand with both of his as he continued questioning Rick. He stroked his fingers over her palm, up her wrist. One shaft of light played on his face, across his eyes one moment—lighting them so brilliantly she could see the reflection of his lashes in the dark-blue irises—and across his mouth the next, or his chin, or the lobe of his ear.

Rick sat down on a crate near the main piece of machinery, the console covered with knobs and dials and meters, and one of the lanterns caught him fully in its flare. His blond hair literally glittered.

The questions were coming faster than Rick could answer them.

"Where do you need to keep the most vigilant watch for erosion?"

"The south side of the canyon, especially near the reservoir, where the—"

"And where else?"

"The avocado grove east of the gully."

"And . . . ?"

"And over by that string of houses that runs along Jacaranda."

"Good. I don't think it will be a problem there, but if it did develop, it would be serious." Jeff slipped one hand to Mia's jeans where they covered her belly, surprising her, and she was glad she had picked this dark patch of roof in which to lie down. "What's the maximum distance you should ever have between the catalysts?" Jeff kneaded the denim slowly, and she arched her back to press against his hand.

"Two K."

"And the minimum?"

"Point-four K."

"Unless you feed them more juice." Jeff looked down at her, the light slipping over his eyes. There was love in them, mingled with desire. He curled the tips of his fingers under the waistband of her jeans.

"Right." Rick smiled patiently. "I know that."

Jeff suddenly removed his hand from her and leaned forward, out of the shaft of light. "Rick?" She heard the new tone in his voice, the genuine curiosity. "Do you understand why all of this works?"

Rick laughed. "No, man, I don't have the vaguest notion!"

Jeff leaned back into the light once more, smiling. "Good," he said. "That's just what I wanted to hear."

He took her hand again, and she shifted forward to nestle her head against his thigh. "And what do you do if Mia's not working right?" Jeff asked. "What do you do if she walks around moping all the time after I'm gone?"

"Hey." Rick grinned. "Sorry, but that's one thing I don't know how to fix."

"And I'd just as soon you wouldn't try." Jeff looked down at her again. She saw him swallow hard, and he squeezed her fingers, gently—so gently, it brought tears to her eyes.

43.

Carmen couldn't sleep. The rain fell softly onto the skylight above her bed, but it wasn't the drumming of the rain that kept her awake. She was accustomed to that sound now—it had become something of a lullaby this past week.

Resting next to her, on the blanket, were the photograph albums. She and Chris had sat in the living room for two hours after Jeff left, paging through the books and their evocative pictures. The one album was familiar to her, the one with their wedding pictures and the dozens of snapshots chronicling their early years—their happy years—together. But she had never seen the other pictures, save the one newborn shot of Dustin taken by the hospital. All wrinkled brow and dark hair. All promise and potential. She was astonished by the care Chris had taken in putting the album together, at how carefully he had organized the photographs, had dated and labeled each one. At how he was still, more than four years after Dustin's birth, adding to the collection.

At first, she had looked at the pictures objectively, with a certain clinical detachment: *My, Chris, what a good job you've done with this. Look at how beautifully you've arranged four photographs to a page, look at how neatly you've written the date below each one, when your handwriting is normally so indecipherable.*

It wasn't until they had looked at the last picture—a shot of a four-year-old boy in a beanbag chair—and Chris had turned back to the first page and said "Let's start over," that she realized how tightly she was hanging onto the slim thread of her composure.

"No," she'd responded, starting to get off the sofa. "Let's make some coffee."

But he'd held her down, one hand snug on her shoulder. "We're looking through it again, Carmen."

She studied Chris's face, and it was as though she hadn't seen him, hadn't really noticed him, in over four years. He had aged. When he didn't smile—and he wasn't smiling now—there was no boyishness left in his face at all.

"I can't," she said, her voice husky. "It was too hard the first time."

"You didn't even see these pictures the first time," he said, softly. "This time, I want you to look at them. Look at Dusty."

She lowered her eyes reluctantly to the picture of the baby she had carried with such hope, such terror, after losing his two siblings. Next to that picture was one of her sitting in their bed here at Sugarbush, Dustin on her lap. She could almost remember the moment Chris had snapped the shutter on that photograph. She had just nursed Dustin. Her robe was still open, one full breast partly exposed. Her gaze was focused entirely on the baby snuggled in her arms, her beautiful dark-haired son, and she felt again that aching in her breasts, that oddly pleasurable pulling in her belly.

She began to tremble. "I can't," she said to Chris. "It hurts too much."

"I know it does. Believe me, I know how much it hurts."

At first, she was frightened by her tears. She didn't want to lose control, afraid she might never find it again. But there was safety in Chris's arm around her shoulders, and the tears gradually began to feel welcome. Cleansing. She no longer struggled to hold them in. She no longer bothered to wipe at them with the back of her hand. They fell like raindrops on the plastic-covered photographs of the album as Chris turned the pages.

Her child's eyes were ruined. If he were ever to be out on the street, out in public, people would stare at him. Children would be frightened by him. They would ask their parents what had happened to that little boy. They would have nightmares that they themselves might wake up one morning with their own blue or green or brown eyes turned the sightless color of an overcast sky.

And yet there was such beauty in him. By the third or fourth page, she no longer noticed the milky eyes, but rather the thick dark lashes, the perfect, pouting mouth. "I've missed out on so much," she said.

"I'm sorry." The terrible wrenching tone of his voice told her that he misunderstood. He thought she was referring to what she'd missed out on by not having a healthy child.

"No," she said. "I've missed *him*. Dustin. I had him for just a few hours. A few days. They seemed so . . . magical. But then I turned my back on him. Jeff was right. I—"

"You were sick," Chris interrupted her.

She shook her head, a sense of conviction growing inside her. "I'm not sick anymore," she said. "Can we go see him?"

He didn't bother to mask his look of surprise. "Yes," he said. "Of course."

"Now?"

He smiled. "It's a little late. How about tomorrow?"

Carmen knew he wasn't quite convinced she was all right, because he said he would spend the night in her guest room rather than go back to his cottage. And that was where he was now. Two rooms away from her. Her husband. Ex-husband.

She got out of bed and left her room. The tiled floor was cool on her bare feet, and a breeze slipped past her as she walked down the hall. She opened the door to the guest room without knocking. Chris was lying on his side under the peach-colored blanket, facing the window. He turned when she walked into the room, and she knew he hadn't been sleeping either.

"Carmen," he said.

She raised her nightgown over her head and dropped it on the chair by the window. He drew back the covers for her, and she slipped into the bed next to him. And when he pulled her close to him, when he pressed his body against hers and buried his head deep in the crook of her neck, she knew she would cry again that night. But it would be a long, long time before she would cry again from unhappiness.

44.

They didn't talk much during the night, and Chris couldn't have said whether that was his doing or Carmen's. He knew there was a great deal that needed to be said, but nothing seemed as important as touching each other, as making love. He hadn't wanted to spoil the night with words—words that might be angry, or empty, or that might somehow ruin the spell that seemed to have wrapped itself around them.

They made love slowly, cautiously at first, as if neither of them could quite remember how, but their awkwardness soon gave way to a shared familiarity, an easy, loving intimacy. They held onto one another all night long, asleep or awake, while the rain pounded endlessly against the guest-room windows.

"What time can we go?" Carmen asked, as the black of night gave way to the gray sky of morning. Her head was on his shoulder, her hand on his chest, her leg twined between his. He hadn't even realized she was awake, although he'd been wide awake for a half hour himself, awake and enjoying the warmth of her next to him.

He'd been afraid she'd pull away from him once

daylight washed the night's enchantment from the room, but as she asked the question, she nestled even closer to him.

He smoothed his hand over her thick hair. "After breakfast?"

"Okay. I don't think I can eat anything, though."

She could never eat when she was excited or upset or anxious. He'd forgotten that about her.

Indeed, he found he had little appetite himself. He managed to eat half a bowl of granola while she sipped a cup of coffee, and he restrained himself from saying, *Remember all the mornings we started like this, sitting in this room together?*

The phone rang. Carmen picked it up, then covered the mouthpiece to tell Chris it was business, would he please excuse her? She carried the phone into the study, and she was gone a long time. He had washed the dishes and read the paper by the time she returned to the kitchen.

"What was it?" he asked.

"I'll tell you later." She was carrying two umbrellas, one black and one green, and she handed the black one to him. "I'm anxious to get on the road, all right?"

He couldn't read her face. He was curious about the call but wouldn't push her. She would tell him when she was ready.

"Let's go," he said.

They were still quiet with each other on the winding roads above Cinnamon Canyon. Chris turned on the radio, set to the station most likely to play a little folk music, and the windshield wipers tapped out their familiar background noise.

"The reservoir looks wonderful," Carmen said as they drove along the road high above the expanding pool of water. Chris couldn't see it from his side of the car, but he knew how it looked these days: in the rain, leaden and dull; in the sun, blue and bottomless. In either case, rising. Steadily rising.

Carmen didn't speak again until they reached the freeway. "The call was from Dennis Ketchum," she said then. "He held a meeting last night with the management staff."

Chris turned off the radio so he could concentrate on what she was saying. She'd spoken very quietly, not looking at him at all. She seemed engrossed in the bumper of the car in front of them.

"And . . . ?" he prompted.

"Well, I'm not supposed to talk about it, so keep this under your hat, but he said there's an excellent chance of my getting *Sunrise* back." Her hands were knotted together in her lap, and she twisted them, one over the other. "Apparently Terrell Gates doesn't have a clue that they're talking about this. But hell, she's young, she'll recover, right?"

He knew what this meant to her, and he wanted her to be back on *Sunrise* as badly as she wanted to be there. But he could tell by her subdued tone that she hadn't been made an offer—rather, they'd presented her with some sort of deal. "Go on," he said.

"He said that they love what I've been doing, that

they're very impressed. They're just about convinced I've still got whatever the hell it is I used to have." She pursed her lips in an expression of self-disgust that surprised him. "Want to know what he said exactly?" She glanced at him, and he returned the look.

"What?"

"He said, 'I can just about promise that if you unravel the Jeff Cabrio story, you've got the show.'" She was wringing her hands so forcefully now that her knuckles were white. "And they're all hot about my idea of kicking it off by bringing on the people I've interviewed who knew Jeff in the past. He said, 'You're doing a fantastic job, Carmen. You're dynamite.'"

Chris wasn't pleased by the tone or content of Dennis Ketchum's ultimatum, but he could see that Carmen was equally displeased, and that surprised him. He reached over to pry her fingers apart and wrap his hand around hers.

"So," he said, "what did you tell him?"

"Not much." She shrugged. "Nothing specific. I kept up the 'tough old Carmen Perez' facade." That self-deprecating twist of her lips again. "I said I was pleased they've regained their faith in me. I told him I'm feeling very strong and that I'm up to anything, any sort of challenge they want to throw my way."

He didn't envy her dilemma. "How do you plan to handle this?" he asked.

She sighed and looked away from him, out the window toward the string of new houses going up on the crest of a hill. "Well, I guess I keep looking for the dirt on Jeff," then added hurriedly, defensively, "He's a nice guy, Chris, I admit that. But he did something he had to run away from. Maybe it wasn't much. Maybe he stole a pack of gum from a convenience store. But whatever it is, he made his own bed and now he'll have to lie in it. That's not my fault."

Chris said nothing. If she wanted absolution, she was looking to the wrong person to get it.

She continued, ignoring his silence. "It's drugs, I think, although I admit he doesn't seem the type. But neither does his stepfather. He's a sweet old man." She shook her head. "Has Jeff told you anything about his father? Has he talked to you about his past at all?"

Chris sighed. "You know how I feel about this. Jeff is saving Valle Rosa. That's all I need to know about him. That's all anyone should need to know."

Carmen looked into her lap where Chris's hand was still locked around her own. "You disapprove of me pursuing his story," she said.

"Well . . . I think you're in a pretty tight bind, Car, but I trust you to come up with the best course of action."

She laughed. "And you're a diplomat, you know it? You're mayoral material if ever there was such a thing."

"Mmm." He smiled.

"Valle Rosa needs you."

"Uh huh."

She paused, then added quietly. "And I need you, too."

He glanced at her and tightened his grip on her hand.

"I always have. Even when I hated you . . . when I *thought* I hated you, I still needed you. You've been so good, Chris. I wouldn't let you near me these past few years, and yet I knew you were always there, looking out for me. I've never been a particularly . . . lovable woman, I guess, but—"

"That's not true," he interrupted her. It wasn't. He could give her a hundred examples of her soft and tender side. "That's not true at all."

"Well, these last few years I've been anything but, yet you've still loved me, haven't you?"

He nodded.

"Thank you."

"Don't thank me," he said with a smile. "It's not as if I could help myself."

"Last night was wonderful."

"Yes."

She rested her other hand on top of his. "Chris? I'd like you to move back into the house."

He was surprised, but he knew she was still captive to the mind-clouding effects of the night before. "Not yet," he said. "Let's wait a while, okay? I need to be certain that's what you really want before we live together again."

And you haven't seen Dustin, yet, he thought, returning his attention to the road. *You haven't seen first-hand the damage I've done.*

"Are you afraid?" He asked her as they walked up the steps of the Children's Home.

"A little," she said. "But only a little."

Chris had called Tina to let her know he would be visiting today and that Carmen would be coming with him.

"Really?" Tina had said. He could guess at the emotion behind the word. He knew what they all thought of Carmen. Probably they expected a camera crew to join them, to catch Carmen Perez in the act of being a good mother so she could show the footage on television. A bid to win back the sympathy of those who thought she was nothing of the kind.

It was immediately obvious that everyone knew she was coming. Tina greeted them by the front desk, but other members of the staff peered out of their office doors or slipped by them in the foyer, staring.

"I'm glad you've come," Tina said graciously to Carmen.

Carmen nodded, locking her hand tightly around Chris's arm.

"How's he doing?" Chris asked.

"Oh, he's having his usual ups and downs."

He knew by the look Tina gave him that Dustin's downs were more prevalent than his ups today.

Tina gestured toward the hall. "Let me know if you need anything."

Chris was glad she didn't plan to join them. He didn't want anyone else around on Carmen's first visit with her son.

They walked down the long hallway to Dustin's room.

"Smells kind of institutional," Carmen said disapprovingly.

"That's because it's an institution," he said. "But wait until you see his room. It's very homey."

Chris pushed open the door to Dustin's room. The

little boy was in bed. He lay on top of the covers in striped pajamas. His eyes were open, facing in their direction, and Carmen's hand flew to her mouth. Chris gripped her arm, fearing she might faint.

"Oh," she said, "he's precious."

Her reaction took him by surprise, and as she pulled free of him to walk over to Dustin's bed, he felt the threat of tears. She bent down to hug her son, and the little boy, startled, jerked away from her, sounds of distress coming from his lips.

"Unh! Unh! Unh!"

Carmen took a step back, her hands in the air. "What did I do?" There was an edge of panic to her voice.

Chris rested his hand on her back. "You startled him, that's all. Remember, he can't hear you or see you."

Dustin thrashed on the bed, grunting, still shaken by the intrusion into his small, silent world. Carmen pressed her fingertips to her lips. "I didn't mean to. I only wanted to hold him."

Chris wrapped his arms around her. She was trembling. He wished there was something he could do to make this easier for her. "I know," he said. "You'll get to hold him. You just need to learn how."

He bent down next to his son. "It's Daddy, Dustin." Slowly, he stroked the little boy's cheek, and slowly, Dustin screwed up his face and began to cry. Chris groaned. "Not today, Dusty," he said. "Come on. It's a special day."

"Is he hungry?" Carmen gingerly lifted the hem of Dustin's pajama top and grimaced at the sight of the feeding tube. "Or wet maybe? Could that be why he's crying?"

Chris stood again. "Nobody really knows why he cries. He just does."

Carmen reached for Dustin's hand, trying to touch it with the same tentative stroking motion Chris had used on the little boy's cheek, but the gesture was met with a fresh flood of tears.

Folding her arms in front of her, Carmen spoke dejectedly. "He's not going to let me near him."

"It's not you, Carmen. He's that way with everybody. Sometimes stroking his back helps. Sometimes holding him in the rocking chair. Sometimes nothing helps, so don't feel bad if that's what happens today. Let me try him in the rocker." He pulled the rocking chair close to the bed, then gently lifted Dustin, ignoring the little boy's wailing and thrashing.

"Don't hurt him." Carmen hovered over them. "The feeding tube. Maybe it's pinching him when you lift him up or—"

"Hey." He smiled at her, amused by her sudden parental concern. "I've been picking him up for years." He sat down in the rocker with his fidgeting, yelping son and began singing "All My Trials." By the time he started the second verse, Dustin had settled down. Chris felt him grow heavy in his arms.

"It worked." Carmen smiled. "You did it."

He looked up at her glowing face and saw the hunger there to touch her child. "Would you like to try holding him?"

"Yes."

He stood to let Carmen sit in the rocker. Then he carefully lowered Dustin into her arms. The little boy immediately began whimpering and squirming again, and Carmen struggled to contain him.

"He's so strong," she said, and Chris had to laugh at the maternal pride in her voice.

"Sing to him," he said. "That seems to have some sort of calming effect on him."

Carmen rolled her eyes. "You know what a great singer I am."

"Doesn't matter. He can't hear, remember? It's the vibrations he picks up on."

"Yeah, but I'll drive you out of the room."

"Talk to him, then." He pulled the beanbag chair next to the rocker and sat down, gently stroking Carmen's arm through the sleeve of her blouse.

"Dusty," Carmen said, wincing as he bashed his head into her chin. She held his head against her with the flat of her hand. "Your mama loves you, Dusty, even though she's had a pretty pathetic way of showing it. She's thought of you every day, though. Every single day."

Dustin began to settle down as she spoke, and Chris said a silent prayer of thanks to his son. Dustin rested against Carmen, his head on her breasts, his shoulders still heaving every few seconds in the aftermath of his tears. A small sliver of jealousy worked its way into Chris's chest. It seemed he wasn't the only one who could calm his child after all.

They sat that way for a quarter of an hour, with

Carmen speaking softly to Dustin. She seemed lost in her son, barely aware of Chris's existence as he listened and watched. But after a while she looked up at him.

"He's going to be like this forever, isn't he?" she asked.

Chris swallowed hard, but didn't take his eyes from hers. "Yes."

She pressed her lips to Dustin's brow, and Chris knew the scent she was breathing in the sweet, clean scent of the shampoo they used here. "Forever," she whispered into Dustin's hair. "I'll love you forever."

Tina knocked on the door and peered into the room. She smiled when she saw Dustin peacefully resting in Carmen's arms. "Just came to see how you three are making out," she said. "But I can see you're doing fine."

"He was crying before, though," Carmen said. "Nearly unstoppable. How often does he do that?"

Tina came into the room and let the door close behind her. "Kids like him cry a lot, I'm afraid." She shrugged. "It's just the way they are."

Carmen nodded down at her son. "But you can see that he calms down when he's cuddled."

"Not all the time," Chris said. He didn't want Carmen to think it was always this easy.

Carmen lifted her head, her eyes darting from Chris to Tina. "But couldn't it at least be tried? Is there enough staff to do that? If he starts crying could someone just spend a little time with him, cuddling him?"

Tina shook her head. "If we took the time to cuddle every crying child in this place, that's all we'd be doing."

"You need to talk to him at the same time," Carmen said. "He really responds to that."

Tina sighed. "Excuse me for being blunt, Ms. Perez, but I think I know more about what Dustin needs than you do. I've been here taking care of him every day for the past four years." *And in all that time, you haven't been in to see him even once.*

The unspoken words hung in the air between the two women, and Chris held his breath, stifling his desire to come to Carmen's rescue.

Carmen looked up at Tina, remarkably poised and unruffled. "Well," she said. "I'm here now."

Chris walked over to the window with its colorful curtains and view of Mission Valley. He didn't want Tina to see his smile, and he knew Carmen could hold her own with the nurse. Carmen didn't need his caretaking any more. If she needed him at all, now or in the future, it would be for something else. Something different. Something better.

45.

The suburban Baltimore neighborhood was quiet, the streets overhung with branches of summer-green oaks and maples. Solid-looking colonial homes were tucked away behind manicured lawns and meticulous landscaping.

Carmen drove slowly down the street in her rented car. She had found Jeff's address through a perusal of business licenses issued in Maryland during the past few years. He had started his own consulting business in Baltimore, maintaining an office in his home. She had even found him listed in last year's phone book at the library. Robert and Leslie Blackwell, 780 Meridian Drive, with a phone number that was now disconnected.

She had no idea what she would find at his old address. She doubted very much that Leslie Blackwell still lived there, but perhaps the current owners would know where she was. Carmen knew that her real motivation at this point was simply to see where Jeff had lived, what type of home he'd owned. She needed to satisfy her ever-mounting curiosity about the details of his life.

His home, however, wasn't there. She checked the

address on her notepad again. Seven-eighty. The lot flanked by numbers 778 and 782 was crowded with construction workers in the throes of raising a new house on the property.

Carmen got out of the car and watched the workers from the sidewalk for a few minutes. The shell of the house looked halfway completed, although it was still roofless. Several men, their arms glowing with perspiration, guided a crane operator as he lowered a roof truss into place in the rear of the structure. A few other men were beginning to set earth-colored brick along the front wall.

She thought of approaching them, of asking them whose house it was they were building, and she was about to start across the yard when she noticed a woman kneeling in the garden of the house next door.

The woman didn't look up from her work as Carmen started walking toward her. Her dark-blond hair was cropped short, and she was dressed in tan, many-pocketed gardening pants and a blue short-sleeved shirt. She dug vigorously in the earth around one of her many azalea bushes.

"Excuse me," Carmen said.

The woman raised her head. Her hair was streaked with gold and her skin was well-tanned, but despite her youthful appearance and energetic digging, Carmen guessed she was close to sixty.

"Could you tell me where the Blackwells have moved to?" Carmen asked.

The woman set down her shovel. "Were you a friend of theirs?" The distrust in the woman's face was impossible to miss, and Carmen knew she wouldn't be able to tell this woman the truth behind her interest in Jeff.

"I knew them in New Jersey." The lie didn't come easily to her lips, and she wondered if the woman sensed her discomfort. "This was the last address I had for them."

The woman sat back on her heels. She shaded her eyes, and Carmen was close enough to see sympathy in them. "You don't know what happened?" she asked.

The ominous sound of her words accelerated Carmen's heartbeat. She shook her head.

The woman didn't speak again right away, as though she was deciding whether or not to tell Carmen what she knew. "Come inside," she said finally, standing up and dusting off the knees of her pants. She reached toward Carmen, who allowed herself to be guided up the slate walkway to the front door of the house.

"I'm Delores Harvey," the woman said as they walked. "The Blackwells lived next door to me for a couple of years and I knew them quite well. They were the best sort of neighbors."

Carmen followed the older woman into a cool marble-tiled foyer, then into a spacious family room.

"Have a seat here." Delores indicated a beige love seat in front of an antique armoire. She looked hesitantly at Carmen. "I'd offer you something cool to drink," she said, "but I think perhaps you should see this before you do anything else."

"See what?" Carmen sat down on the edge of the love

seat. She was beginning to pick up Delores Harvey's anxiety.

Delores simply shook her head. She opened the doors of the armoire to reveal a television. Carmen watched as she rifled through a drawer of videotapes. There was a delicate pattern of perspiration on the back of the woman's shirt, a small triangular grass stain on the seat of her pants.

Jeff's former neighbor selected a tape and inserted it into the VCR below the TV. Then she sat down on the arm of the sofa, the remote control in her hand.

"I made this tape myself," she said, her eyes on the static-filled screen. "One of the TV stations bought it from me and used parts of it on their news, but I still don't know what possessed me to make it in the first place. I wish I hadn't, except that it's helped in a way." She pursed her lips. "It's helped make it real. I don't think I would ever have believed it really happened without the tape."

Carmen pressed her damp palms together in her lap. "I'm sorry, Mrs. Harvey," she said. "I'm not following you."

"Of course you're not." Delores nodded toward the TV, tapping the corner of the remote control against her chin. "It'll come on in a moment."

Suddenly, the television screen burst into orange light. A house was on fire. Tongues of flame licked out of the windows into the dark night. Carmen was immediately reminded of the houses in Valle Rosa that had burned before the rain, only this house was larger and made of brick. The fire glowed inside it like a candle in a jack-o'-lantern.

Carmen leaned forward, elbows on her knees. There was a great deal of noise accompanying the picture, and at first it was hard to separate one sound from another. Sirens. People—mostly men, it seemed—shouting. The too-familiar crackling, whistling sound of the flames. She knew how it would have smelled there. She could almost feel the searing, acrid scent burning her nostrils and surrounding her here in this peaceful, air-conditioned home. Behind all the other sounds, someone was screaming. A woman? A child? Carmen straightened abruptly on the love seat, locking her hands around her elbows.

A man suddenly appeared on the tape, running toward the house. "That's Frank, my husband," Delores said, as the man reached the front door and tugged at the handle. One of the fire fighters jumped between him and the door and literally shoved him away, both of his big, gloved hands on Frank Harvey's shoulders. A woman's voice, sounding very close to the camera, called "Frank! Frank!" and Carmen realized it was Delores, yelling at her husband while she taped the scene. Frank argued with the fire fighter for a few seconds before throwing up his arms and backing away from the house.

"Frank was beside himself that they wouldn't let him help," Delores said. "He wanted to get to Holly." The tape jerked to one of the glassless upstairs windows. At first, Carmen saw only the flame, but then there was movement, a dim blur. The camera zoomed in on the window, and Carmen gasped as she saw a child standing there, a dark silhouette against the fire burning in the room behind her. Suddenly all was chaos. The little girl's hands were on the windowsill. She raised one of her legs, trying to climb out. Her mouth was open in a scream that didn't stop. The fire fighters on the ground waved their arms at her, telling her to stay inside, that it was too far to jump, yelling something about a ladder.

"Holly! Stay there!" Delores's voice, close to the video-recorder's microphone, boomed above the others.

Carmen covered her mouth with her hand as Holly got one bare leg over the windowsill and sat straddling it. She could see the child's features now, could see the sharp terror in the little girl's face. Holly glanced one more time at the flames in the room. She called clearly, heart-wrenchingly, "Mama!" before swinging her other leg over the sill. She balanced herself there as the fire fighters lifted a ladder toward the window.

Then abruptly, unexpectedly, she fell, her small scream drowned out by the shouts of the fire fighters and the long, keening wail of Delores Harvey as she held the camera.

"Oh, God . . . oh, no." Carmen cringed, literally re-coiling from the horror on the screen. She wanted to ask Delores to stop the tape, but she was too numb to speak again, riveted by the real-life tragedy unfolding before her. It was hard to remember that it was over. Past. It seemed as if it was happening at that very instant.

The fire fighters and Frank Harvey raced to Holly's side, and the tape filled with anguished cries of des-pair that Carmen hadn't known men were capable of producing. They huddled over the little girl, big men in their bulky uniforms, shaking their heads at one another. One of them wiped a gloved hand across his eyes.

"She'd broken her neck." Delores pressed the remote control to her chin again. "They say she died instantly, which I suppose is some sort of blessing. But I keep thinking of how she suffered first, how terrified she must have been up in her room. She was so dear."

The picture suddenly jerked again, and the next thing Carmen saw was a news van out on the street. A camera crew leapt out of the doors of the van, while a woman with shiny black hair barked directions at them. Then the video camera was back on the house again, back on the hulking, defeated-looking fire fighters as they returned their attention to the task in front of them.

Carmen turned to look at Delores, whose face was scarlet. Tears flowed freely down the older woman's cheeks.

"What about Leslie?" Carmen asked.

"I'm sorry." Delores shook her head. "This probably was a poor idea, letting you find out this way. I just—"

"Leslie?"

Delores winced. "They lost her too," she said. "They said that when the explosion occurred—"

"Explosion?"

"Yes. It was in the basement, where Rob did his work. Right beneath the master bedroom. It killed Leslie and the baby instantly. Katie died of smoke inhalation, and Holly . . . well, you saw."

Carmen wanted to question her further, but her

attention was drawn back to the television by the sudden slamming of a car door and the sound of a familiar voice, off camera. Jeff.

"I can't watch this part," Delores said quickly. "They must have shown it fifty thousand times on the news." She stood up and walked into the next room.

Jeff, his hair dark blond, ran toward the house, calling for Leslie. Frank Harvey tried to grab his arm but failed, and Delores's calls for him to stay back went unheeded. One of the fire fighters caught up to him, catching him by the shoulder just as Jeff spotted the body of his daughter. He broke free of the fire fighter and ran to her, dropping to his knees and clutching her to his chest. Carmen could barely watch. How had he endured this? How did he endure it even now, months later? Surely he still carried this pain with him, every day. Where did he get the courage to go on? Where did he get the strength and the spirit and the faith he needed to help Valle Rosa, to give a town full of strangers back their lives?

The picture bounced a little, and Carmen could hear Delores Harvey's gasping sobs as she tried to hold the camera steady. Two of the fire fighters struggled to pull Jeff away from Holly, saying things to him that Carmen couldn't decipher. He fought them at first, then seemed to give in, to let them pull him away.

Suddenly the young, shiny-haired reporter was in the picture, her microphone held out in front of her, gold bracelets flashing on her wrist. She walked toward Jeff with a determined stride and an obvious sense of entitlement Carmen recognized all too well.

She'd had enough. Rising quickly, she turned off the TV, and the room was suddenly quiet again, the sirens and the screams and the orange light extinguished as if they had never existed. Standing in front of the armoire, Carmen covered her face with her hands and sobbed.

A few seconds later, Delores Harvey returned, blotting her own eyes. She pressed a tissue into Carmen's hand.

"What caused the explosion?" Carmen asked, when she could speak.

Delores seemed reluctant to answer. With a sigh, she sat down on the sofa. "You know about Rob's work?" she asked.

Carmen nodded, not quite certain what Delores was referring to.

"Well, they were getting ready to take a vacation, Rob and Leslie and the kids. They were going to the mountains to see the fall colors. They hadn't gotten away since they moved here, and they were really looking forward to it. As usual, though"— Delores shook her head, a small smile on her lips—"Rob had some work he wanted to finish up first—some project he was working on down in the basement. So Leslie was going to take the kids up to the cabin they'd rented, and then Rob would join them in a few days. But the day Leslie was to leave, Rob told her his work was going faster than he expected, why didn't she and the kids wait one more day and then they could all go together? So that's what they decided to do. Leslie came over here that afternoon with the baby." Delores suddenly pressed her hand to her lips, turning her head away. "That beautiful baby." She shook her head. "I'd sometimes sit for him. He had a smile that could light up the world." Drawing in a tremulous breath, she looked at Carmen once again. "Anyhow, Leslie was helping me design invitations for my oldest daughter's wedding—Leslie was an artist. Well, I'm sure you knew that."

Carmen nodded blankly. She hadn't known, of course, but what did it matter? What did anything matter any more?

"All her paintings were lost in the fire, too. Even the watercolor that won the award in New York. You know it?"

"I don't recall. Go on, please. What happened?"

"Well, Leslie was so happy, so glad she was getting Rob away for a few days. I think he was a good husband, and I know he was a terrific father, but she said that he'd been absolutely driven lately by whatever it was he was working on. He hardly ever slept, she said. He was always in that basement. I asked her how she stood it, but she said it was a really exciting project and she didn't blame him for being preoccupied with it. She couldn't tell me what he was doing—I guess Rob had sworn her to secrecy—but she said it was spectacular, something that had never been done before, something no one even thought was possible. You know how proud she always was of Rob." The woman dabbed at her eyes again.

Carmen's stomach was in knots. She remembered the allusions others had made to Jeff's recklessness. "The explosion," she said. "What caused the explosion?"

"Well, I guess Rob was working that night, rushing to finish up so they could take off the next day. Holly was sick. She'd come down with a cold, and Rob must have gone to the store to get her cough syrup, because they found the bag with the syrup in it on the sidewalk. Anyhow, the explosion occurred while he was out of the house, and it was related in some way to the work he'd been doing in the basement."

Carmen closed her eyes. "How horrible," she said.

It was a moment before Delores continued. "Rob was in shock after the fire. They took him to the hospital. Frank and I went with him—I didn't want him to feel as though he was completely alone in the world. He didn't cry or rant and rave, or anything along those lines. He was like a zombie, sitting there in the emergency room, saying over and over again, 'I killed my family, I killed my children.'"

"He blamed himself?"

"Yes." Delores nodded. "And he wasn't the only one. The police were suspicious to begin with because he was out of the house at the time of the explosion, and having him sit there saying he killed them wasn't helping his case very much."

"That's ridiculous." Carmen scowled. "He was in shock."

"Of course it's ridiculous. It still infuriates me that anyone could have thought it was anything but an acci-dent. All they'd have to do is talk to people who knew him to know what a good man he was."

"Yes." Carmen nodded. "Yes."

"The fire-investigation people said they couldn't figure out what he'd been working on down there, but they were certain it was something he shouldn't have been doing in a residential neighborhood. They were going to charge him with criminal negligence."

"And did they?"

"They didn't get the chance. We took Rob home with us that night. He had no place else to go, and I wasn't going to leave him alone. He simply wasn't himself. Who would be?"

Carmen shook her head.

"Well, he disappeared sometime during the night." Delores raised her chin and smiled. "God love him. Of course, that made him look even guiltier in the eyes of the police. They said he was afraid to face their questioning, but I know he was really afraid of facing the emptiness where his life had been."

Carmen looked out the window in the direction of 780 Meridian. "Do you have any idea where he went?" she asked.

"No, and I'm glad I don't. They found his car in Pennsylvania, and since he'd crossed state lines, the FBI got involved. Why they want to waste their time going after someone like Rob is beyond me. A man loses everything he cares about. Isn't that punishment enough?"

Again, Carmen nodded.

"They still haven't found him, and you know what I hope?" Delores asked. "I hope they never find him. I hope that somehow he's able to find happiness somewhere else."

Carmen managed to make the 4:30 flight back to San Diego. She had a copy of the videotape in her purse. She'd asked Delores if she could borrow the original to have a duplicate made, and although the woman looked a bit taken aback by the request, she produced a copy she already had. Carmen wasn't certain what she would do with the tape. Right now, she wasn't certain how she would handle any of the information she'd just learned. She only knew that, for the time being, she would tell no one, not even Chris, the truth about Jeff Cabrio.

They'd been in the air only a few minutes when she pulled out her notepad and began writing down everything she remembered of the information Delores Harvey had given her. She wrote for two hours, knowing that she now had the ability to put a lock on *Sunrise*. If she wanted it, the show was most certainly hers.

When she finished writing, she closed her notepad, covered herself with a blanket and tried to sleep. But each time she shut her eyes, all she could see was Rob Blackwell kneeling in front of his burning house, clutching the lifeless body of his daughter in his arms. She wondered if she would ever be able to safely close her eyes again.

It was ten o'clock when she pulled into the driveway at Sugarbush. After two rainless days, the air was dry and filled with the scent of eucalyptus, and the glow of an enormous round moon lit up the adobe. She had retrieved her suitcase from the trunk and was headed toward the door when Jeff's black Saab pulled up next to her car. She stopped and waited until he got out.

He closed the door to the driver's side and met her

gaze over the roof of the car. He looked tired. There was a question in his eyes, a question he didn't need to put into words.

And she needed to say nothing in return for him to know the answer.

46.

At first, Mia couldn't get her bearings. Was it the moonlight that awakened her? It poured through her bedroom window in a silver-white pool, so bright that she had to turn her head away when she opened her eyes.

It took her a moment to realize that Jeff was beside her. He'd still been at the warehouse when she went to bed, but he was here with her now. He had pushed her nightshirt up to her hips, and his thigh was planted firmly between hers.

"Jeff?"

"Shh." He quieted her with his lips and his tongue, his kiss so deep and long and breathless that she felt herself rising up, floating above the bed, still half in sleep. Was she dreaming? Or maybe it was actually morning. Maybe the moon was the sun.

She could see the clock on her dresser. Ten twenty-eight. He kissed her again, and when she closed her eyes, the green digits of the clock still floated in front of her. When he drew back, she ran her fingers over his face— over his chin, his cheekbones, his temples, as if he were clay—and there was the satisfaction that what she felt beneath her fingers was identical to what she had created in miniature.

His hands slipped under her nightshirt. There was an impatience in him; his usual gentleness was missing. If she hadn't known him, if she hadn't trusted him, she might have been afraid. The heat and the moonlight and his hunger made her restless herself. She threw the covers off, not even thinking of how her chest would look in the bright pool of light from the window. When he began nuzzling her breast, she arched her back, straining against his thigh where it pinned her to the bed, struggling to move, to bring him closer.

"Please," she said.

He shifted on the bed until he could slip inside her, thrusting into her with a groan. She moved with him, running her hands over his shoulders, the small of his back, his hips. She couldn't lose the ethereal feeling of this lovemaking, as though they were touching each other in their sleep, as though when she woke up she would be alone, with just a hazy, not-quite-real memory of his closeness.

Afterward, she shut her eyes and saw the white disc of the moon behind her eyelids. Jeff started to lift himself from her, but she closed her arms around him to keep him there. Against her ribs, she felt both their heartbeats; she couldn't separate his from hers, and she was nearly lulled back to sleep by their rhythm. It was only when the coyotes began to howl that she sprang fully awake, the world outside her bed suddenly real and intrusive. She felt the entire length of Jeff's body stiffen above her, and she knew then. She understood the reason for his rushed and wordless lovemaking, for the urgency in his kisses and the desperation in his touch.

"*No, Jeff.*" She'd planned to be strong for him. She had gone over and over in her mind how she would handle it when he told her he was leaving, and in her lucid, waking moments, she could see herself reacting bravely, supporting him wholly in what he needed to do. But she had expected him to tell her in words, not this way. Not in some dream-like rush that left her drained and defenseless. She swung her head from side to side on the pillow. "No, no, no."

He raised himself to his hands and slipped out of her, then sat next to her on the bed, stroking her cheek with one warm hand.

"She knows, Mia. I have to go."

She pressed his hand tightly to her cheek with her own fingers.

He gave her his old half-smile. "Have you finally figured out that you are a very desirable woman, and that there will be other men for you?"

"I don't want other men," she said, but she knew he was right. There could be others if she wanted them. For a moment she couldn't even remember why she thought there wouldn't be.

"And when you meet one you want, wear the damn chemise for him, okay? You're alive *now*, Mia. You'll look great in it."

"Shh." She pressed her fingertips to his lips.

"I brought the cat over." He nodded toward the

window where she could see the slender dark silhouette of his still nameless feline. "You'll take care of him for me?"

"If you'll stay till morning," she bargained.

He shook his head. "If I leave now, I can be a few hundred miles away by daybreak."

A few hundred miles! She clutched his arm, the reality of his leaving suddenly hitting her. "In which direction? Please, just give me an idea of where you're headed. At least give me the comfort of being able to picture you someplace."

He shook his head again. "No, Mia."

She sighed and bit her lip.

"Do you know how strong you are?" he asked.

She shrugged. She didn't feel strong at the moment.

"You're one of the strongest people I've ever met," he said.

"Then why do I feel like I'm five years old and I've gotten separated from my parents at the zoo and all the animals are about to be let out of their cages?"

"And they haven't been fed in weeks?"

"Right."

"It's temporary," he said. "A temporary setback. A normal reaction. In a day or two your resilience will take over, and you'll be fine." He lay down next to her. "I'll stay until you fall asleep, all right?"

"Then I won't sleep at all."

"Yes," he said. "You'll sleep."

And although she fought the lure of her dreams, when she next opened her eyes, the overcast light of a rainy day filled her room. She had wrapped her arms around Jeff in such a way that she thought he could never get free, but he was gone. She was alone. Only the cat keeping watch at the window let her know he had ever been there at all.

47.

The videotape rested on Carmen's lap as she drove through the early morning rain to the station. Dennis had called her late the night before to tell her he wanted to see her this morning. He wanted to find out what she'd learned, he'd said, to figure out the "best way to use it." He'd coughed toward the end of that sentence, and for a moment she thought he'd said "exploit it." *So*, she thought to herself, *what's the difference?*

In her still-numb state the night before, she'd told him she had a tape that would explain everything.

"What's on it?" he'd asked, clearly ecstatic.

"You'll see."

He'd laughed like a child enjoying a game she'd invented expressly for him. "Well, at least tell me if you have what you need to wrap up this story."

"Yes." At the very least. She could wrap up this story, solve an FBI case and ruin Jeff Cabrio's life, all in one fell swoop.

"That's what I like to hear," he said, and she could picture him rubbing his hands together. "Tired from your flight?"

"A bit."

"Get a good night's sleep, then, Carmen, and I'll see you early in the morning."

Sleep, of course, had been impossible. As she lay in bed, she could see the videotape on her dresser, propped up against the mirror. When she closed her eyes, scenes from the tape ran through her mind—the terrified child in the window, Jeff's panicky voice calling for Leslie, the hulking fire fighters huddled over the little girl. Three times she got out of bed and walked around the house, trying to free herself from the fiery, full-color images. She regretted ever having asked for the tape—it made it her responsibility. Worse, she regretted telling Dennis that she had it. That had been stupid, but she'd known how gleefully he'd respond to that news. She'd known how good it would make her look in his eyes, and she was easily—too easily—seduced by his professional respect for her these days, a respect that still felt new and fragile.

Chris had spent the night with her. Whether he decided to move into the house or not, she knew they would be sleeping together from now on. She didn't tell him what was disturbing her, although he tried to pull it from her. His fear for her was touching, and she had to reassure him several times that she was all right, that she wasn't about to harm herself in any way. At least not physically.

More than once during the night, she thought of showing him the tape. At least then she wouldn't be alone with the images that haunted her and the horror of what she'd learned. That would have been unfair, though. She let Chris hold her during the night, but that was all the comfort she allowed herself to take from him. "You've saved me from every other problem I've had in the past decade," she told him. "This one's mine alone."

Sometime very early in the morning, she heard a car pull out of the driveway, and she knew it was Jeff's. She knew, also, that he wouldn't be back. She cried then, quietly, not wanting Chris to wake up and ask her to explain her tears. She thought of Mia, left behind. She remembered Delores Harvey's hope that Jeff could find happiness somewhere after what he'd been through. Was it her fault that he hadn't found it here in Valle Rosa?

Perhaps. Undoubtedly she'd forced him to leave Valle Rosa sooner than he would have liked. But no matter how many names he assumed, no matter how many miles he traveled from his home, Robert Blackwell would never be able to keep a low profile. He would stand out wherever he went. Sooner or later, he was going to be found.

Dennis was waiting for her in his office. He stubbed out his cigarette when she walked in.

"Okay, Carmen." He gestured toward the chair next to his desk. "Tell me what you've got."

She sat down. "I can't talk about it," she said. "Not yet."

He leaned toward her, bushy eyebrows raised. "Uh," he said, with an annoying attempt at sarcasm, "you work for me, remember?"

"I haven't quite figured out how I'm going to present it."

"Well, how about you tell me what it is, and I'll tell you how to present it." He looked at her empty hands. "And where's the tape? Let's put it on so I can see—"

"I left it at home. I figured there wasn't much point in me bringing it over because I got it under slightly false pretenses. I won't use it until I get permission from the woman who made it."

"*Carmen.*" He was beginning to sound exasperated. "We'll get the okay. Whatever it takes, we'll get it."

She shook her head. "It would ruin my credibility with her to ask her right now. Then she'd never come on the *Sunrise* special and—"

"There won't *be* a *Sunrise* special unless you handle this right."

She moved her hands to the arms of the chair. "Look," she said, "you've trusted me so far to know what information to release and when to release it. And it's worked out pretty well, hasn't it?"

"I have to admit you're right there." He couldn't help a smile at the thought of *News Nine*'s inflated ratings. Then he sighed. "Well, you always were a controlling woman, Carmen. Always wanted a hand in everything, didn't you? I'd almost forgotten what a pain in the ass you could be."

He wasn't joking, and for a moment she felt afraid. She didn't want him to remember anything negative about her tenure on *Sunrise.*

She tried smiling at him. "I was a perfectionist, yes, but maybe that was why my ratings were always through the ceiling."

"You understand we can't firm up an agreement

on *Sunrise* until you come through with your end of the deal."

"I know. That's fine."

He stretched back in his chair. "Well, in case things move according to plan and we have that kick-off *Sunrise* special—which we should do the second we announce you're back on the show—I want to get the names of the people you interviewed. We'll get in touch with them and make them an offer. I want to try to get the old man on the show, too."

"Jeff's stepfather?" She pictured the wheezing, frail old man who knew nothing about the loss of his grandchildren or the trouble his son was in. She would never put him through this. "I don't think that would be possible," she said. "He's in for the rest of his life."

Dennis waved a hand through the air. "We'll persuade them to let him out for the show. Good behavior or compassion or whatever. If they won't agree, we can send you there with a crew for an interview and run that on the show."

"I don't want to disturb him again."

He narrowed his eyes at her. "Don't go soft on me, Carmen. Not now that I've just about got everyone sold on you doing *Sunrise*."

The phone rang on his desk and he picked it up. "Ketchum," he barked into the receiver. He looked at her, something like suspicion in his eyes. "Hold on a second, Frank." Then to Carmen, "Rumor has it Cabrio left town this morning."

She shrugged. "I didn't notice him at Sugarbush, but he's usually at the warehouse by the time I get up."

"Check it out," Dennis spoke into the phone again. "Make some phone calls. Call that Smythe guy, and get back to me right away."

He was growling when he hung up the phone. "Look, Carmen, at least give me enough of what you've got so we can run a teaser throughout the day. You know, 'Carmen Perez at last reveals the truth about Valle Rosa's mysterious rainmaker.'"

"Don't run teasers, okay?"

"No, *not* okay. How about, 'The drama of Jeff Cabrio's life climaxes tonight on—'"

Carmen groaned. "That's revolting. If you have to run a teaser, just say Carmen Perez concludes her story on Jeff Cabrio tonight at six."

"Hmm." His face reflected his disdain. "Real catchy, Carmen." He lit a cigarette.

"He's a human being," she said, "not some brand of toothpaste you're trying to sell."

He took a drag on his cigarette, eyes narrowed at her again. "What the hell did you find out?"

She was relieved when the phone rang, and he turned his scrutiny away from her. "Yeah?" he said. "Are you sure—shit." He hung up the phone, and she knew what he'd learned even before he told her.

"Your ticket back to the top just slipped out of town," he said. "You'd better pull out all the stops tonight, girl. We're counting on you."

48.

Chris was turning on the television when Mia appeared in the doorway of his cottage. Even through the screen door, he could see that her eyes were red.

"Can I watch Carmen with you?" she asked.

He opened the door, and she stepped into the hug he offered. He could feel her crying more than hear her.

Sometime that afternoon, he'd noticed the open door to Jeff's cottage. He'd walked inside to find all belongings cleared out, and the sadness he'd felt was so overpowering that he'd sunk onto Jeff's sofa and simply stared out the window for nearly an hour. He would have liked, at least, to have had the opportunity to say goodbye. And to thank him. There was so much to thank him for, though, that he wouldn't have known where to start.

He hugged Mia tightly, pressing his cheek to her hair. "What time did he leave?" he asked.

She let go of him, wiping her cheeks with her fingers. "Sometime during the night." She glanced at the television, then at her watch. "Do you know what she's going to say?"

He shook his head. "I have no idea. Whatever it is had

her upset most of the night. I don't think she slept at all."

Mia dropped onto his couch. "I couldn't watch it alone, you know?" she said. "I mean, I don't know what I'm going to see or hear or how I'm going to feel."

He turned up the volume on the TV and sat at the other end of the sofa. The anchors were beginning to roll with their news. Chris couldn't concentrate on what they were saying. Apparently Mia couldn't either.

"I'm so glad he's gone," she said. "I'm so glad he doesn't have to be here to listen to this." She bit her lip and gave Chris a worried look. "They'll go after him, though, won't they? Whoever it is he's running from? I should have let him take *my* car. He could have hidden his, and then they'd be looking for his car, but he'd actually be in—"

"He'd never do that, Mia, and you know it. He didn't want us involved any more than we were. It wasn't your place or my place to—"

"Shh!" She sat forward as Carmen appeared on the screen.

Chris was stunned by Carmen's pallor. "She looks sick," he said. "And she missed her cue." There was a second or two of dead air before Carmen began speaking.

"Rainmaker Jeff Cabrio left Valle Rosa today," she said. "The rain will continue on schedule, according to Mr. Cabrio's assistant, engineer Rick Smythe."

Carmen looked down at her notes, another second of silence filling the air. Chris felt a film of sweat break out across the back of his neck as she raised her eyes once again to the camera.

"Jeff Cabrio was a very private person," she said. "We've learned some things about him, some things perhaps he'd rather we had never learned. In many ways he remains a mystery to us still. All we in Valle Rosa really care to know is that we are richer for having known him, and we wish him Godspeed. Back to you, Bill."

The camera was once again on Bill Jackson with his patent-leather hair. His look of stunned surprise said it all—no one at the station had expected Carmen's report to be so brief and so thoroughly devoid of news.

"That's it?" Mia asked, the expression on her own face a reflection of Bill Jackson's confusion. "Jeff said she knew."

Chris smiled. He wished he was at the station so he could wrap his arms around Carmen. "She knew, all right."

"But she didn't tell." Mia broke into a grin, and an instant later, actually leapt up to stand on the couch, arms above her head. "Thank you, Carmen!" she yelled.

Chris laughed.

She looked down at him, her expression sobering. "They won't give her *San Diego Sunrise* back, now, will they?"

Chris folded his arms across his chest and leaned against the back of the couch, smiling up at Mia. "I guess she decided there are some things more important to her."

Mia flopped down again, and for a few minutes, neither of them spoke.

"Which way do you think he'll go?" she asked finally.

"I don't know." He had purposely not thought about this. He didn't want to know. "Let's just hope he goes far and fast."

She fell quiet again, one finger idly tracing a pattern on the sofa cushion. "Someone else will figure it out, won't they, someday?" she asked. "I mean, it's going to catch up with him sooner or later."

"Maybe not," Chris said. "Maybe he'll be lucky."

He knew Mia was right, though; Jeff couldn't run forever. But he wanted to hold onto the fantasy a while longer. It was fitting. With Jeff, the impossible had seemed possible. He'd nurtured the dreams of everyone he met. And when their lives had seemed irretrievably bleak and barren, he had given them hope. It would be his lasting gift to each of them. His lasting gift to Valle Rosa.

49.

OCTOBER

Mia hadn't realized how big a task it would be to clean out her desk. She shouldn't have left it until her last day at work. Between the phone interruptions and educating Chris's new office manager, Donna Caro, on the idiosyncrasies of the fax machine, she would never get it done.

It was nearly noon when she started sorting through her file drawer. Donna and Chris were at lunch, and Mia was alone in the office when the phone rang for the twentieth time that morning. She groaned and picked it up.

"Mayor's office," she said.

For a moment, there was silence on the line. Then, a male voice asked, "Is the wood sprite out of her jar today?"

She caught her breath, then burst into tears. "Are you all right?" she asked.

"I'm okay. I'm fine. Better than I have been in a long time."

She wasn't certain how to tell him that the phone might be tapped. She couldn't bear the thought of him hanging up on her, abruptly, in fear. But she had to say something. "They might try to trace this call," she said.

"Doesn't matter," he answered. "We'll make it short. I can't say too much, anyway. I've made a decision about what I have to do, and I feel good about it, but first I wanted to thank you for all you did for me."

"All *I* did for you?" He had it completely reversed.

"Oh, yeah," he said. "You gave me back something I'd lost, Mia. Valle Rosa gave me something back. I felt worthwhile again. I helped a few people out of a mess."

"You helped a lot of people who were on the brink of disaster," she corrected him.

"Mmm," he said, and she could hear his smile. "It's still raining there, right?"

Mia glanced out the window at the chaparral flourishing on a distant hillside. "One day a week," she said. "It's perfect."

He hesitated a moment, then said, "I'm not a total screw-up after all, I guess. I'm not totally inept."

"Jeff . . ." She frowned. "Of course you're not."

"And I'm capable of loving someone. I didn't think I'd ever be able to do that again."

She suddenly understood why he felt grateful to her. To Valle Rosa. She knew his past now. The time for hiding the truth—any and all truths—was over.

"Carmen had a videotape of the fire," she said. "She showed it to Chris and me before she destroyed it. She destroyed all her tapes and notes about you." All three of them had cried, watching the tape, Carmen most of all. That very evening, despite her refusal to share the rest of

Jeff's story with her audience, she had been asked to host *Sunrise* again. Not only did she turn down the offer, but she quit *News Nine* altogether. Having no idea what lay ahead, she'd been frightened that night. But new offers came pouring in the instant word was out that she was a free agent. She now had her own morning show—a very different sort of show—on a competing station.

"I'm sorry you had to see that," Jeff said.

"I'm sorry, Jeff. I'm so sorry. Your children. I can't imagine how—"

"Shh," he said. "Don't try."

She chewed on her lower lip, wondering how much she should say over the phone. "At first I was hoping you'd come back," she said, "that somehow you'd learn Carmen hadn't revealed anything more about you on the news. Did you know that?"

"Yes. And I realize what a sacrifice she made for me."

"Well, I was hoping you'd think it was safe. I wanted you to come back so badly, but I'm glad you didn't. The FBI was here."

"I'm not surprised. I knew they couldn't be too far behind me." He sighed. "Did they hound you?"

"I was glad I didn't know where you were." They had questioned her for two full days, and she'd been grateful to Jeff for telling her so little. She understood then why he hadn't wanted Rick to know exactly what made the rain machine work. The agents were quick to realize that Rick genuinely had no idea what he was doing, and they left him alone.

"Today's my last day as Chris's office manager," she said. "I sold a few pieces of my work after the Lesser Gallery show, and I can afford to sculpt full-time for a while."

"Fantastic, Mia! Just don't become more of a hermit than you already are," he said. "And how's the cat?"

"Fine. I named him Blackwell."

He laughed. "That's a pretty weird name for a cat."

"Better than no name at all." She ran her fingers over the files in her drawer. "Where are you, Jeff?" she asked. "I mean, where have you been? Can you say?"

"Wandering." He sighed again. "Trying to savor my freedom, but freedom is not much fun by yourself." A second or two of silence filled the line. "I miss you, Mia," he said. "I love you. I wish—"

He suddenly fell quiet, and when he began speaking again, he sounded rushed. "I've got to get off now," he said. "I'll try to get in touch again, but I'm not sure what's going to happen next."

"Jeff, I—"

He was gone. She heard the click of the phone being hung up. After a few minutes of staring at the overcast sky out her window, she resumed sifting through her files, the emptiness building inside her once again.

50.

NOVEMBER

Chris's desk was covered with papers. It was one week to the day since the mayoral election, and if life were predictable, he would be cleaning his office out for the arrival of Joyce DeLuis or John Burrows. Instead, he was working on legislation that would turn one of Valle Rosa's old abandoned warehouses into a hiring hall for the workers who lived in the canyons. It was his top priority.

Sometime in October, he'd found himself waking up in the middle of the night with ideas—ideas that would solve some of Valle Rosa's more pressing problems. *Good* ideas. He'd pull the notepad and pen from under his pillow and scribble his thoughts down in the dark. Always a light sleeper, Carmen would wake up, smiling from her side of the bed.

"What are you going to do with all these ideas, Chris?" she'd ask him. "No one's going to pay much attention to your thoughts about how Valle Rosa should be run when you're teaching high school again."

He finally admitted to himself that he wasn't ready to

turn the reins of Valle Rosa over to someone else. By that time, however, it was too late for him to get on the ballot. It didn't matter. Even as a write-in candidate, he won the election by a landslide.

Donna Caro, Chris's new office manager, suddenly appeared at his door. "Turn on the radio!" she said. "Hurry!"

He hit the power switch on his desk radio, breaking in on the middle of a news report. ". . . and when Mr. Blackwell surrendered," the newscaster was saying, "he stated that the first thing he wanted to do was get in touch with his stepfather, who is suffering from emphysema in a state prison in New Jersey."

The newscaster moved on to another story, and Chris raised his eyes to Donna's.

"He turned himself in?" he asked. But before she could answer, he was already reaching for the phone.

There was a fax machine next to Carmen's desk in her office. The machine was so ceaselessly productive that, in her month and a half at KBBA, she had learned to ignore it. It was clicking away as she slipped a script for to-morrow's show into her briefcase, clicking away as she stood to put on her coat. She slipped the paper from the machine and was adding it to the mounting pile on her desk when her eyes were caught by the words at the top of the paragraph: JEFF CABRIO SURRENDERS.

Setting down her briefcase, she held the paper closer to the light. The words blurred on the page as she read them. She fumbled on the desk for her phone, but it was already ringing.

Mia's television was on. She knelt on her plastic-covered living-room floor, about to tear a slab of clay from the mass in the bucket, when she heard his name. Leaning forward, she turned up the volume, not even bothering to wipe off her hands, and the black button glistened with the smear of clay from her fingertips. She sat back and listened, her hands slipping slowly over the slick, wet clay in the bucket, her eyes held in trance by Bill Jackson and his patent-leather hair.

"Jeff Cabrio surrendered this morning to the Maryland police," he said. "Cabrio—whose real name is Robert Blackwell—hadn't been seen since leaving Valle Rosa in August, after having developed the rainmaking technology that saved that small town from a devastating drought."

There was footage accompanying Bill Jackson's report. Mia gasped when she saw Jeff, her hand flying to her throat. Two men led him to a car. His hands were cuffed. Her glimpse of his face was brief—just long enough to break her heart. He was gaunt. She glanced toward the bronze sculpture on her coffee table. Yes. He was much thinner now. Although Jeff wasn't fighting, not resisting in any way, one of the men lowered his head rudely, roughly, to force him into the back seat of the car.

So this was what he had meant in his phone call, she thought, when he'd told her he'd made a decision.

Bill Jackson had long since finished discussing Jeff's

surrender by the time Mia turned off the television. For the first time, she wished she had a phone so she could call Chris or Carmen. It was nearly 5:30; Chris would be at his office for another hour or so. She could see him there. Putting on her jacket, she left the cottage.

Outside, the early dark of winter was already falling over Sugarbush. The cottage that had been Jeff's stood empty on the rim of the canyon. Carmen seemed in no hurry to rent it, but lights burned in the third cottage, the one Chris had lived in before moving to the adobe. A Guatemalan couple and their baby lived there now, in exchange for working around Sugarbush. The rain had brought plenty of work with it. Wild mustard and other unwanted scrubby weeds had cropped up all over the property.

Mia reached the driveway and was opening her car door when Chris's Oldsmobile pulled in, immediately followed by Carmen's Volvo.

"Do you know about Jeff?" Chris asked as he got out of his car.

She nodded. "I was on my way to your office to tell you."

"I'm glad we caught you, then," Carmen said as she circled Mia's car to stand next to her. "We were coming home to make sure you knew. You've got to get a phone, Mia." Carmen suddenly frowned at her. Holding Mia by the shoulders, she turned her so that the patio light shone on her face. "Are you okay?" Carmen asked, and only then did Mia realize she was crying.

She nodded, wiping her hand across her wet cheek.

Carmen wrapped her arms around her, easily, gently. It wasn't the first time she'd hugged Mia—that had occurred after her appearance on Carmen's morning show, when she and several other young women openly discussed their experiences with breast cancer. Carmen's guests sometimes cried on this new show, but it was never because they'd been belittled or berated. Carmen's bite had been tempered, her abrasiveness replaced by an empathy that seemed to come naturally to her. Her hug had comforted Mia then; it was even more of a comfort now.

"He looked so thin," Mia said.

Carmen let go of her. "He's going to be all right."

"Come on, Mia, let's go inside." Chris walked toward the kitchen door. "Carmen and I will tell you our plan."

Inside the adobe, she and Carmen sat at the kitchen table while Chris brewed a pot of coffee.

"So, Mia." He smiled as he got the mugs from the cupboard. "Are you up for a trip to Baltimore?"

She met his smile with a grin. "Yes!"

"Good. Because I took the liberty of booking the three of us on a flight tomorrow morning."

"And . . ." Carmen leaned across the table toward Mia, "I spoke with Daniel Grace. He was the guy who was Jeff's good friend when they were kids, remember?"

Mia nodded. "The attorney, right?"

"The criminal *defense* attorney," Chris said, setting the full mugs on the table. He sat down next to Carmen.

"I told him the whole story," Carmen continued. "He lives just outside of Baltimore, and he's on his way to see

Jeff tonight. He sounded very optimistic. And he'll do what he can to get him out on bond."

Mia pressed her fist to her mouth. She was going to get to see him, and not through a piece of glass in a cold prison visiting room. "He needs to see his father," she said.

Chris nodded. "We'll make sure he does."

They sat for a while longer, talking, planning. Finally Chris looked at his watch. "We'd better start packing," he said. "Flight's at eight in the morning."

Mia wished she could take the sculpture of Jeff with her. She had a photograph of it, but it didn't capture the true-to-life expression present in the bronze sculpture itself. She hoped that pensive, hunted, resigned look was one he would never have to wear again.

Spreading her empty suitcase open on her bed, she began filling it, slowly, not certain how much to take, how long she would be gone. She packed two pairs of jeans, two sweaters, a dress. Two bras with their pockets for the prosthesis. Dr. Bella had told her she could have her reconstructive surgery any time she liked, but she no longer felt the rush. *You're alive now*, Jeff had told her, and she knew he'd been right.

Where had he been these past few months? Wandering, he'd said on the phone. Had he stayed in one place long enough to develop any friendships—any ties with other people, other women? She hoped he hadn't been alone, but she stopped short of hoping that he'd loved anyone as deeply as she knew he loved her. Or that some other woman was packing to be with him right now—packing and planning to bring him comfort and strength.

She studied the pictures on her bulletin board, then began plucking some of them from the cork to take with her. First, the fountain, which stood now in the park—newly named Cabrio Park—next to Chris's office. Chris had installed the plumbing system necessary to turn her design into a functioning fountain, and the dedication ceremony last week had drawn a spectacularly huge, spectacularly happy crowd.

She slipped a few recent pictures of Blackwell into the suitcase, but she didn't pack the pictures she'd taken of the federal agents as they snooped around the warehouse, as they studied the rain machine. They hadn't dared to touch the equipment, however, as if they knew that despite its solid look and flawless operation, an inexperienced, incautious touch could destroy it all too easily.

Jeff had been no different from the rest of them, she thought, as she closed the flap on the suitcase. No different from Chris or Carmen or herself. She had come to think of herself as something of a freak, much the same way that Chris had seen himself as useless without a ball and glove, and Carmen had perceived the softness in herself as a failing. All of their self-images had been based on a twisted reality conjured up out of hurt and insecurity, out of the damage they'd suffered. And Jeff had been no different. But he knew better now, as they all did. His phone call had told her that. Whatever lessons they'd learned from him, he'd taught himself as well.

She imagined seeing him, holding him, sleeping with him. She should not allow her optimism such free reign. Maybe they wouldn't be able to help him at all.

We'll do our best, Chris had said as she'd left the adobe. *We'll pay him back in whatever way we can.*

She was ready to zip the suitcase closed when she remembered one last thing she needed to pack. Opening her top dresser drawer, she dug to the bottom of the stack of underwear and nightshirts and pulled out the green satin chemise. Folding it carefully, she rested it on the other clothes in the suitcase, hoping she would have the chance to show Jeff that she was, indeed, very much alive.

The story behind the story

I grew up on the east coast of the United States—which is where I still live—but for a twelve-year period, I was a Californian through and through. I lived in San Diego, where I received my bachelor's and master's degrees, worked as a clinical social worker, and started my writing career. I adored California, but the east coast was always calling me home. The wonderful thing about writing is that you can live in one place and *almost* live in another by setting a book there. The setting for *Fire and Rain* was borne of a bout of California homesickness.

You can't live in the southern part of California for long without experiencing drought and fire. I recall waking up some mornings with my house surrounded by red air and ash falling from the sky like snow. Remembering those mornings, I decided that drought and fire would form the backdrop for my story. Research for *Fire and Rain* began with a trip to San Diego County, of course! I stayed with my best friend, Cher, and we walked her property while I took notes about the flora she described and drank in the dry heat I'd nearly forgotten about during my years in Virginia, where I was living at the time.

I decided to focus the story on a man who had the ability to save the town, but who also had secrets to protect. To heighten the conflict, I brought in Carmen, a woman who was losing a career that could only be saved if she uncovered those secrets. Mia and Chris, with the difficult turns their lives had taken, added complications of their own.

Every writer finds herself visiting the same themes over and over again, whether she means to or not. I'm no exception. My stories tend to deal with forgiveness and sacrifice, often among people I've thrown together in tight quarters. *Fire and Rain* certainly covers all those bases. By creating Carmen's house and her three small rental cottages, I forced four people, all of whom had their own reasons for wanting to be alone, to interact with one another. They hid their secrets, nursed their wounds, and fell in love. They forgave and they sacrificed. Carmen, for example, learned to forgive Chris and ultimately sacrificed her own career goals for the sake of Jeff's welfare. There are other examples where these themes played out in the story, but I won't go into them here. Instead, I'll tell you more about the research that went into the story.

How was I going to make it rain? I had a long conversation with a guy at the National Center for Atmospheric Research in Colorado as I tried to figure out how Jeff could pull off his miracle. The guy I spoke with gave me enough information to make my brain hurt, but the bottom line was that I was looking for the impossible. So I had to invent the "trans-hydrators" myself, and the machinery and the way it works is as much a mystery to me as it is to the townspeople of Valle Rosa.

I knew I wanted Jeff to be a larger-than-life character, someone whose light was hard to hide even though he tried his best not to draw attention to himself. I decided to make him a real problem solver, a man who couldn't help but be noticed. I found a Readers' Digest book titled *Practical Problem Solver*. In the pages of that book, I learned 'how to catch a mouse in an umbrella', 'how to pick up broken glass with a slice of bread' and a few other Jeff-isms. Remember all this research was done without the Internet! I'm not sure I'd know how to begin today.

Mia was a challenging character to create. Having worked as a medical social worker, I knew all too well that breast cancer doesn't care whether you're young or old and the toll it can take on a woman as she's just beginning her life adds an extra dose of cruelty to an already cruel disease. I interviewed a couple of women who were kind enough to talk with me about the emotional devastation they endured as they fought their cancer. I wanted Mia to have a gift, though, something she could lose herself in as she healed, so that is why I made her an artist. To complete my research on her, I visited a local sculptor who helped me understand not only how Mia would make her creations but how her art could feed and sustain her as well.

To understand Carmen's world a bit better, I wrangled an invitation to sit in the newsroom of a Washington, DC television station both before and during a broadcast to observe what went on behind the scenes. It never fails to amaze me how generous people can be when I ask for help with my research.

Finally, a word about the dedication in the beginning of this book. While I was writing the story, my twenty-year marriage fell apart in one of those sudden, shocking, soul-searing ways you hear about but can barely believe. The man I'd considered my best friend was gone, but my women friends—wow. They rallied around me, each offering her own brand of support. They taught me so many lessons about friendship and I am forever grateful to all of them. Without them, I never would have been able to finish this book.

Thanks for reading this peek into the creation of *Fire and Rain*. I hope you've enjoyed it.

—Diane Chamberlain, 2011

Acknowledgements

I am indebted to the following people for generously sharing themselves and their expertise with me:

Sharon Brooks, Jeff Doranz, Elizabeth Falk, Virginia Herrmann, Mo Javins, Julia Mitchell, Jed Nitzberg, Rhonda Roberts, Craig Ross, and Pam Saunders;

To my former agent, Adele Leone, and my former editor, Karen Solem, for their unflagging confidence;

And, as always, to Cher Johnson, Mary Kirk, Peter Porosky, and Suzanne Schmidt, as well as to the Mount Vernon Writer's Group. Thank you all.